No Witness, No Case

To my very good friend
        Trevor
with my best wishes
and very fond memories
of our High School days.

        Bill
            31·12·13

Published by Brolga Publishing Pty Ltd
ABN 46 063 962 443
PO Box 12544
A'Beckett St
Melbourne, VIC, 8006
Australia

email: markzocchi@brolgapublishing.com.au

National Library of Australia
Cataloguing-in-Publication data
     Author: Robertson, Bill
     Title: No witness, no case / Bill Robertson.
     ISBN: 9781922175243 (paperback)
     Subjects: Organized crime--Fiction.
             Refuse and refuse disposal--Fiction.
Dewey Number: A823.4

Printed in China
Cover design by Chameleon Print Design
Typeset by Wanissa Somsuphangsri

BE PUBLISHED

Publish Through a Successful Publisher. National Distribution, Macmillan & International
Distribution to the United Kingdom, North America. Sales Representation to South East Asia
Email: markzocchi@brolgapublishing.com.au

No Witness,
No Case

Bill Robertson

For Molly
my mother-in-law.

A great lady who proudly listened and always encouraged
as each chapter unfolded.

And Graham

whose honest and humourous input kept me grounded.

" … human courage and dignity are always the most potent weapons against corruption."

- Robert Payne
1975

PROLOGUE
Autumn, 2012

Powerscourt Gardens, laid out by Daniel Robertson in 1831, had become a favourite retreat for Sinaid and Finn O'Donnell. Fingers entwined, they strolled through shafts of sunlight slanting between moss covered elms and oaks. In autumn, the gardens were magical. Ahead, five-year-old son Patrick happily pointed out swans to his younger brother, Thomas. The elegantly sculpted landscape was mellow and harmonious – markedly different from Australia's blue green eucalypts, azure skies and strident red, brown and yellow soils.

The O'Donnells had moved from Australia to Ireland in 2007, and after five years in County Wicklow, marvelled at the rich and blessed lives they had created.

On this mild afternoon, traces of wood smoke brought a wistful, yet deep solace to the grounds. Tomorrow, the O'Donnells would meet Australian friends they had not seen for six years. They looked forward to their reunion and to showing off their two boys.

Finn gave Sinaid's hand a squeeze as little Thomas came trotting back, his chubby hand clutching the silvery grey pinion feather of a red-footed falcon.

'Look, look,' he squealed, 'I've got a lucky fevver. Look Mummy, a lucky fevver.'

'Ah little man,' murmured Finn, 'that is indeed lucky because for us it means freedom and safety and one day, when you are old enough, we'll tell you why.'

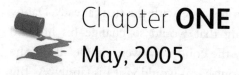

Chapter **ONE**
May, 2005

Danny Browne was worried. For weeks he had secretly visited the doctor about his rapid weight loss, night sweats and sleeplessness. He told Alice, his wife, that a big activity spike at work was responsible, but he now knew it was a virulent form of cancer.

At 3:00 a.m. he was pushing the huge Kenworth tanker at a steady ninety-five clicks along the Northern Highway towards Heathcote, Central Victoria. In the padded cabin, instruments glinted from the bird's eye maple bulkhead and Chris de Burgh's *Lady in Red* caressed the rich sound system. Here it was warm and relatively quiet above the big motor. Twin halogen beams lanced a brilliant white tunnel through the blackness, hunting the road-edge for kangaroos.

Yet the cancer and distress it would cause his family was not all that worried Danny; it was also the highly toxic chemicals he was about to dump near Knowsley. He had been doing this work for nigh on twenty years yet only recently had connected the poisonous concoctions with his cancer. And it was this, that for the first time, made him think seriously about his past activities.

Danny had worked at Aldrittson's waste business for twenty-five years. At the beginning, after five years of reliable effort, the boss, Big Jack Aldrittson, had asked him whether he would like to double his income. With a young family and new mortgage he had jumped at the chance. Now he winced recalling that long gone discussion.

'What's the catch?' he had asked, intrigued.

Big Jack had smilingly replied, 'No catches Danny, but if I tell you how things work, your life will never be the same. How you deal with that is your problem. Take some time before you answer. Whether you accept or reject my offer, once you know what it is you're mine forever.' Given his time with the firm already, Danny could not imagine anything that would so change his life and accepted. Sworn to secrecy, the conditions were simple: if ever he revealed what he knew, serious harm would visit his family. As Big Jack explained this, his quiet voice was laced with menace. It was impossible for Danny to misunderstand his new situation.

And so began a secret life – covertly dumping toxic waste across the Australian countryside in return for lucrative underhand cash. The more noxious the load, the bigger the bonus. He had marvelled at this but well understood that Big Jack believed totally in nurturing his business.

He had not worried about what he did back then. The family prospered, enjoyed a cosy well-appointed home and two cars, and soon his children would enter university. Alice loved him and his kids were a joy. None suspected the true source of their wealth. But declining health forced him to consider the possibility of a link to his unlawful activities. Quietly, at home, he surfed the net looking for information about the various chemicals he hauled. To his horror, there were clear connections between different types of cancer and some of the chemicals he had been dumping.

A month ago, his general nausea changed to regular vomiting and diarrhoea. He had deflected Alice's pestering to see their doctor by saying he had caught a touch of dysentery from a workmate who had holidayed in Thailand. He exaggerated his workload and blamed his tiredness on a new waste contract. Finally, he gently diverted Alice's attention by talking of their forthcoming Canadian holiday.

Secretly, he had taken medical tests and learned of his invasive blood cancer known as *hairy cell leukaemia*. The link between this disease and benzene was clear, and benzene was regularly on his black inventory. Even tiny amounts of the stuff on skin could induce harmful results but if ingested, a mere drop in forty-four gallons of water was enough to kill. Over the years, he had been splashed by benzene more times than he could remember.

His spirits lifted as he thought of the Canadian break. Tapping to the beat of *Don't Pay the Ferryman,* he carefully nosed into Schoolhouse Lane, a gravel road leading to the dump site. As quickly as his mood soared it plummeted, anchored in worry. He knew only too well this scam was concealed inside an old and highly respected waste disposal business. Of the sixty or so employees he thought maybe only ten undertook black work. Yet he wasn't even sure about that. Jack had implied he was the only one involved. Nevertheless he suspected there were others, just like him, who had been hand-picked.

He wondered if any of them had cancer. Last week the media was screaming about poisons dumped on public land and demanding answers. And, not long ago, the Environment Protection Authority (EPA) had reported noxious chemicals in the water supply of the small town of Walwa. He was thankful this site was not on his dump list but wondered who had released the stuff.

With these sombre concerns in mind he went to his foreman, Bernardo Santini. Santini scheduled disposals for all forms of waste. The normally easy-going Santini had been unusually caustic and probing over Danny's questions about the press and EPA. He had not mentioned his illness yet mulling over their encounter, he felt Santini's abruptness barely stopped short of an accusation. Something malicious and unknown to him. Now, reflecting on that conversation he made a sudden decision: *Well fuck you Santini, and double fuck you Aldrittson. I've got nothing to lose now. I'm takin' this lot to the EPA.*

A sense of peace swept through him. After crossing Derrinal-Crosbie Road and feeling a new sense of purpose, he pitched violently forward as the tanker erupted into a giant ball of flame, smoke and blistering heat. It was Danny Browne's last thought as air whooshed from the cabin and his body was engulfed in searing white flames. It was 3:20 a.m., Thursday, May 20, 2005.

Chapter
TWO

Andy Drummond woke instantly to the whump of Browne's exploding truck. Years as a military policeman had honed his reflexes to the sharpness of a Ghurkha's kukri.

What the hell was that? Alert, he lay still … listening. The silence of his thick-walled, straw-bale house was dense and comforting. He was accustomed to the muffled thump of artillery from the army base at Puckapunyal, but that was north east of his farm. This noise was from the west.

Sliding out of bed Drummond, a thirty-nine year old tall, sinewy, ex-soldier often ribbed about his "Robert Redford" looks, padded along the hall and out to the north verandah. To his left, a red glow pulsed in Schoolhouse Lane. Another explosion rippled through the crisp night air, more subdued, he thought, than the first noise. Running inside, he pulled on a track suit and work boots and dashed to his ute. He flew down the curving driveway to Schoolhouse Lane, chattered over the cattle grid then speared left.

At Derrinal-Crosbie Road Drummond was greeted by a roaring, leaping inferno — the rapidly emerging skeleton of a blazing truck. Branches from overhanging gums burned fiercely. He jumped from his ute and peered into the flames looking for the driver. Shielding his eyes from the heat and glare, he walked forward. At thirty metres it was impossible to get closer. Wild, malevolent, fiery tongues crackled and spat from a gaudy palette of colours.

Christ, he thought, *if the poor bastard driving this didn't get out he's buggered*. Bobbing and ducking from the debris of constant small explosions, he circled searching for the driver. Finding nothing, he phoned his friend and local police sergeant, Tony Maud.

'Tony, sorry to wake you, it's Andy. I'm at Schoolhouse and

Derrinal. A bloody great truck fire.'

'Anyone hurt?' Tony yawned.

'Not sure. I can't find anyone and I've been around the truck. I don't know who's involved or what happened. Can't get close enough to find out. I can't even tell you what kind of truck it is apart from a tanker of some kind. I'm actually watching the metal frame burn as we speak. The flames are all multi- coloured. I reckon it's a load of chemicals.'

'Okay. Thanks cobber. Keep an eye on it, I'll raise the cavalry and be there ASAP.'

At 4:00 a.m., Tony Maud and Senior Constable Ian Patching arrived in the police four-by-four. Hot on their heels a local Country Fire Authority truck pulled up with a half dozen volunteers.

Maud was a big man, better than two metres tall and carrying a large gut. His moon-like face sported a healthy moustache and at this early hour, a robust stubble. Now fifty-two, he had arrived in Heathcote ten years earlier. He and his wife Mary had fallen in love with the clean fresh Heathcote air, hot summers and cold, starlit winter nights. He circled the blaze and made his way to Drummond. 'What's the go Andy?'

'I was asleep and got woken by what sounded like an explosion. At first I thought it was night-firing at Pucka, but when I went outside, I could see a funny kind of light down Schoolhouse. That's when I heard another explosion. I belted up here and found this. I've been around the truck a couple of times but haven't found anyone.'

'I don't like the feel of this.' Maud frowned. 'Like you said, looks like chemicals. Jesus! Cop that!' He pointed to three fire fighters thwarted from getting foam onto the fire and retreating under the protection of a misting spray. 'Those sprays are bloody good cover. If they can't ...'

A crashing detonation sent an enormous column of ink-black smoke spiralling skywards. It was accompanied by a spectacular shower of glimmering sparks and a fusillade of hissing, whistling missiles. At the same time, one of the heavier burning branches crashed to the road in flames.

Patching ran up saying, 'Boss, I've just had word from Tommy Harrigan. We've gotta go, fumes are poisoning the air. He's instructed his men to wear breathing apparatus and he hasn't got enough for us.'

Maud turned to his friend. 'I reckon now's a good time for you to nick off mate. I'll get some troops from Bendigo. I might even call on forensics too. Depends what we find. I'll come by in a day or two for a statement.'

Andy drove home thoughtfully. *What had caused the fire? Where was the poor bastard who had driven the rig?* Nothing suggested a loss of control or crash with another vehicle. As he drove he recalled hearing large vehicles on Schoolhouse Lane several times over the past twelve to eighteen months, usually between 2:00 and 3:00 a.m. He had never seen them, only heard them. There had been no consistent pattern to their presence and nothing recently until the explosion tonight. He wondered if this was the truck he had heard in the past. *Where in the hell was it going? And what on earth was it carrying?* When the police activity died down, he would sniff around for himself.

Chapter
THREE

Bernardo Santini was pleased. He was, as usual, at the Aldrittson Waste Depot early. On his way he had listened expectantly to the 5:30 a.m. ABC news bulletin and heard brief reference to a truck fire near Bendigo. There was no mention of the driver or truck identification. He was satisfied with that. It wouldn't be long before those issues were raised and he was well prepared for when that happened.

Opening up his computer Santini hummed tunelessly as he checked the daily manifests. As foreman, this was one of his tasks. To many of Aldrittson's workers he was the cheerful roster clerk who worked out the hours, days, drivers and job lots. He enjoyed the computer because it made life easy. At sixty years of age, he had glided into the cyber world like an eagle on a summer thermal. He could plan work for the forty drivers comfortably, cover for illness, breakdowns, maintenance schedules, high and low demand, country and metropolitan jobs and, after all that, meet his manifests with ease. As with most aspects of his life, Santini was adaptable and meticulous.

Born in Sicily during the sunset of German power in 1944, he had arrived in Australia with his parents in August 1954 on the *S.S. Neptunia:* a wiry, energetic, inquisitive ten-year-old. Today, he recalled little of Enna, his mountain top birthplace. To the contrary, he professed small interest in its rich and turbulent history; a city said to have been continuously settled since 1200 BC. He was grateful his parents had chosen Australia as their new home. While settling in had been a challenge, language came easily to him and he had garnered authority over his parents as their translator. Thus, at an early age, he tasted and revelled in the exhilaration of power and decision making.

In the Snowy Mountains where his father worked, the young Santini blended in. As one of many children from a host of countries who had arrived in similar circumstances he mastered the art of becoming unseen among people, a skill he could seemingly invoke at will.

And so it was at Aldrittson's. When Santini joined the firm he had quietly blended in and none suspected his real power. Old Thomas Aldrittson, founder of the company, was still running the show then. At the end of World War 1, the Old Man had seen opportunity in scrap metals, repatriated war equipment, glass and, much later, worn-out car batteries. He had been careful and selective in business, loyal to his men and scrupulously honest. Like most, he was hit hard by the Great Depression of the thirties but took little from the company, managed to retain his tiny workforce, paid them frugally and nurtured them all through it.

By the 1950s, Aldrittson Waste Disposals was renowned across Victoria. Their hallmark was fair trade, fair prices and excellent service. As the firm continued to grow, so too did Old Tom's acts of generosity. He was commonly rumoured to support a variety of organisations among which his favourites were the Salvation Army, Trade Union Movement and Queen Victoria Hospital. Above all else however, he cherished his diamond-like reputation for honesty and integrity. The wags said that even his wife and son, both of whom he adored, ran second to maintaining his reputation.

Santini mused briefly upon the Aldrittson story as he coordinated the day's activity and waited for Jack, Tom's son, now head of the family business. Old Tom had died unexpectedly from a heart attack in 1972 never knowing that his beloved Jack, for at least three years prior to his death, had been secretly diversifying their business.

Like his father before him, Jack Aldrittson was tall, imposing, silver-haired and charming – the resemblance ended there. Jack's life interest was money. Amassing it. He was shrewd, professional and business-like, yet sly, dishonest and ruthless. In 1963 at Melbourne University he had chanced upon Rachel Carson's book, *Silent Spring*. Impressed by her warnings about protecting the environment and reducing the many forms of toxic and other pollution, he perversely saw her plea as an opportunity for plunder. Convinced that many manufacturers were lazy or venal in treating their waste, Jack saw lucrative prospects in toxic waste removal at competitive prices. And so, concealed by a highly respectable disposal trade, Jack, through patience, stealth and cunning created a burgeoning illegal enterprise beneath his father's nose.

He quickly realised he had a competitor far tougher and more ruthless than himself. The Mafia. While he was *discovering* Rachel Carson, *they* were already active. By the time he finished university and perfected his clandestine plans, the Mafia had well and truly claimed the business of toxic waste disposal.

Believing that "fortune favours the bold", Jack eventually arranged a meeting between himself and Mafia Don, Giuseppe Antonio Pescaro. The occasion was significant for Aldrittson who was fixated with a daring and creative vision for waste disposal and endowed with an asset of value to Pescaro: superb camouflage for an illegal business and the capability of removing most of Victoria's toxic waste through a respectable cover. His imaginative dream, legitimising the illegitimate, lay well into the future. Instinctively, he knew that Pescaro's grunt could generate action far beyond that which his own resources could accomplish. Aldrittson foresaw a time when their illicit monopoly would, with appropriate technology and the right political conditions, slide into the open as a government approved toxic waste treatment plant for the whole state. Although the *when, where* and *how* of his dream was uncertain, the Don had agreed to a partnership.

Aldrittson had no need to remind Pescaro of Capone's folly but he did argue for adherence to sound business principles. All aspects of the law regarding their *legitimate* business were to be scrupulously observed. To minimise conflict and safeguard loyalty, Aldrittson insisted on good pay and regular bonuses to maximise efficiency. The underlying principle was simple – draw no unnecessary or adverse attention to the firm. The Mafia role, naturally, remained invisible.

For those who worked the covert enterprise, only one rule applied: keep your mouth shut. Business boomed and the workers were richly rewarded.

Painstakingly researched dump sites, carefully planned drops, generous pay and fear of exposure among the clients, not to mention the occasional use of Mafia muscle had delivered impregnable protection. Aldrittson's good fortune had been further bolstered by a generally negative attitude towards environmentalists whom the wider community tended to regard as fringe lunatics. The EPA too was perceived as a toothless tiger. But, as time went by, the green crusaders began making an impact and global warming became a household conversation piece. At the same time, accelerating consumerism fuelled endless demand for the disposal of all kinds of waste. These competing tensions demanded that Aldrittson be constantly and increasingly vigilant with both his workers and disposal sites.

Thus it was a total surprise to Aldrittson when Santini said Danny Browne had become a business risk. Browne was a good bloke who had been with the firm a long time – hard working and never trouble. But, if Santini said Browne was a risk, a risk he was.

At seven-thirty that morning, Aldrittson parked his black BMW in the yard and strode into the administrative building. He greeted Santini briefly on the way to his office knowing that in five minutes, he would appear with the daily briefing and fresh coffee. Shortly afterwards, the aroma of coffee preceded Santini's presence before he had even reached the door. It was a familiar routine.

'Take a seat Bern. What's happening today?'

Santini placed the coffees on the desk and removed a small note book from his shirt pocket.

'I assume you heard the ABC news this morning Mr Aldrittson?' he said, referring to the notebook, his tone low and respectful. Notwithstanding his years at the company, Santini's formality was genuine and intrinsic to his camouflage.

Curiosity flashed across Aldrittson's face. 'Yes,' he replied, 'I listened to it on the way in. Was there something in particular?' Aldrittson sat upright in his chair, his full attention upon Santini.

'Yes, Mr Aldrittson,' said Santini in his soft, husky voice. 'The truck fire. I believe it could have been one of ours. I've taken the liberty of preparing all the paperwork for insurance, the manifest is okay, but I fear Danny Browne may have met with an accident.'

'Have the police called yet?'

'No sir. It could be some time before they identify the truck but, in due course, we should alert them to the fact that Danny Browne is overdue.'

Aldrittson steepled his fingers. 'Do you think we should check with Alice Browne, just in case Danny is at home?'

'Yes sir. Although, not yet – he's not due back until six tomorrow night. But I will visit Alice at the appropriate time. A phone call is rather impersonal don't you think? Naturally we'll wait until after we have contacted the police. I've already prepared a note for the pay office to release Danny's pension quickly and to pay a good bonus. He's given good service over a long time.' The dishonesty of this charade caused Santini's brown eyes to glint with suppressed amusement.

'I agree. Just make sure it's set up for the right time. By the way, what was Browne's destination?'

Santini smiled inwardly. Jack Aldrittson never missed a comma on the manifests. 'The manifest,' he said, 'shows Browne travelling to Mildura for a load of asbestos sludge. He should have been going up the Calder Highway to Bendigo, or perhaps through Marong.'

Throughout this theatre, both men remained impassive.

'And what time was he due back?' queried Aldrittson.

'About six o'clock tomorrow night,' repeated Santini watching his boss keenly for reaction.

Aldrittson's pale blue eyes narrowed, his face was stony. 'Bernardo, this incident is not to be taken lightly. We've been running this scam for nearly thirty years. In anyone's terms, that's a bloody long time for something so risky and dangerous. I don't want any snafu's now, especially as our bigger goal is within reach.' He continued in flinty tones, 'This is the first time we've been exposed to serious threat. If it all goes tits-up, Pescaro's wrath will obliterate anything the courts could think up as punishment.'

Santini nodded, his face placid. 'You asked me to deal with a problem Mr Aldrittson, I assure you, it *has* been dealt with.' He withdrew quietly knowing their key business for the day had concluded.

Chapter
FOUR

When Santini returned to his desk the office staff had arrived and were hard at work. He tucked Browne's pension memo into his day book two days in advance and finished checking the outstanding pickups and deliveries for the next day. His last task was to ensure that interstate and country jobs were spread evenly between drivers, a simple act to keep pay cheques and feelings balanced.

Satisfied, he summoned Martin Judd. Judd was Santini's understudy but knew only of the legitimate business and had been with Aldrittson's for three years having joined as a driver. Eighteen months earlier a serious collision had cost him his right leg just above the knee. Rather than sack him, Judd had been brought into the office to learn the ropes. Although paid less than a driver he was happy because he still had a job and Aldrittson's had been generous with his medical bills. He enjoyed his new endeavour and was a good learner.

'Martin, I'm going out to a client, keep an eye on things will you. If you get stuck with something you can't handle, ring the mobile. I should be through by about midday, half past at the latest. Okay?'

Judd nodded.

Santini left the office. He was a compact man, only 170 centimetres tall with wavy, receding light brown hair, a man whose dress sense suggested he might have invented the word "neat." Almost sixty-one, his longish, unlined face and pleasant mouth belied his years. He looked barely fifty. Dressed in sharp, understated clothes and well-polished shoes, Santini, with his soft clear speech conveyed a mild, low-key image of respect, attention and efficiency. He had worked hard developing this persona as it enabled him to be inconspicuous. Now, it was like an old coat –

familiar, comfortable and natural.

In reality, Santini exercised great authority as Pescaro's trusted *Consigliere*. No one at Aldrittson's, including Jack, suspected his double life or his influence inside the firm. Indeed, by the age of eighteen, Santini was already a tough and feared standover man who had cut his teeth on the Queen Victoria Market murders. Over time and inside Aldrittson's, he had risen in Mafia ranks to his current status.

The market deaths of 1962 had caused the Victorian Government to bring in John Cusack, a highly skilled investigator from the USA. Cusack was thoroughly familiar with the ways of the Honoured Society and well placed to advise police about Mafia violence. His final report was informed and insightful. Anticipating Cusack's advice, Pescaro had counselled patience, reduced activity and cessation of hostilities. He predicted that Cusack would either be ignored or forgotten. Ultimately, he was proven correct: Cusack was forgotten. In time, Mafia business was as strong as ever.

During this lull Pescaro laid his plans for control of the infant toxic waste racket and thoughtfully placed the young Santini before Old Tom Aldrittson. Santini's intrinsic efficiency, strong work ethic and respectful nature would, he knew, appeal to the old man. In no time, Santini was part of Tom's staff. His new role sheltered him from the fall-out of the bloody market murders and covertly granted Pescaro influence inside the company. When Jack finally met with Pescaro to discuss a partnership, he had no idea the event had been stage-managed by Santini.

As Pescaro saw it, owning a treatment plant for toxic waste was akin to owning a mint. And he *wanted* that mint. It was only the impeccable reputation of Old Tom's business combined with Jack's scrupulous care of their scam that allowed the partnership to remain as Pescaro had, on many occasions, contemplated removing his partner. Permanently. Ultimately, however, he had contrived an ingenious situation where, under certain conditions, Jack's business would transfer to one of his legitimate blind companies.

From the beginning, Aldrittson and Pescaro discussed various means of legalising their black waste activities. They were, however, constantly frustrated by governments of both persuasions. Now, their long wait seemed almost over. In the current political climate, Jack scented the possibility of victory. Environmental issues had become prominent in public and political consciousness and an all encompassing toxic waste treatment centre would be of enormous public value.

Through adroit management and the occasional accident involving potential competitors, Pescaro and Aldrittson achieved a situation where most producers of toxic waste took advantage of their services. Even the hospitals, substantial producers of contagious bio-waste and, in their own world, advocates for strict accountability, were more interested in getting stuff off their premises than knowing how it was dealt with.

Over time, and with Santini's malign influence, both the legitimate and illegitimate arms of Aldrittson's business expanded. Pescaro virtually controlled both a money making and money laundering facility of almost endless capacity. Privately, he sometimes sentimentalised to Santini that Capone would proudly have included him in the *Outfit*. This seemed especially true since it was Capone who first devised the tactic of "legitimising the illegitimate" through labour unions.

Santini stopped his car outside a set of imposing, black, wrought iron gates in South Yarra's prestigious Glover Court. The Court hugged a generous sweep of recreational space on both sides of Alexandra Avenue along the River Yarra where Como Park and Herring Island enhanced the parkland vista at this corner of the waterway. Here, on a bluff above Williams Road, Pescaro enjoyed spectacular city and river views.

Entering the gates, Santini drove through manicured gardens

and stopped before the modest, but gleaming, two storeyed *Villa del Rosa*. Although not lavish in size, everything about the place bespoke class and style; from sparkling French windows and tasteful drapes to the discreet but generous balconies and beautiful hand crafted slate roof.

The care and love lavished on the house and grounds was the work of Pescaro's long time, and now ageing, husband and wife domestic team: Concetta and Carlo Di Ponti. Concetta tended to the household chores and meals while Carlo maintained the house and grounds.

As Santini mounted the steps, the panelled mahogany door was opened by a young woman wearing a smartly tailored black suit. Teresa Marchese was Pescaro's private secretary. In her early thirties, she was an attractive woman with a pale clear complexion, steady grey-green eyes and an expressive cupid-bow mouth which perfectly complemented her fine oval face. Her dark hair was softly bobbed and although she stood only 163 centimetres, her trim appearance concealed a well toned, strong and athletic body. Marchese was far from being merely a waifish and perfectly tailored personal assistant; she was also a woman of intellect and outstanding business and financial acumen.

She lead Santini along the wide, tessellated hallway, her slim heels tapping sharply. 'Giuseppe is taking coffee right now, would you care for some?' she said, glancing over her shoulder. She was polite but cool towards Santini. When she stopped outside the library Santini nodded, acknowledging her invitation and walked inside.

The library was exquisitely furnished and hung with a variety of expensive paintings in oil and watercolours. Ceiling height windows opened onto a spacious garden, pool and the Melbourne skyline. Facing the door, a crammed book case filled the entire wall. Before the books stood an elegant French desk which, curiously, brought a touch of femininity into this otherwise masculine room.

Pescaro sat comfortably in a leather chair, *The Age* newspaper across his knees, a cigar smouldering in a tray nearby. At seventy-four, Pescaro was trim, tanned and alert. Lined and hawklike, his avian appearance was accentuated by a sharp, beaky nose. Thick white brows seemed to bring a permanent glower to his face. Beneath the rampant brows, deep set brown eyes hinted intelligence, shrewdness and power. Pescaro was a man used to being obeyed.

'Sit, Nardo,' said Pescaro without rising. The deep resonant voice never failed to surprise Santini: it was so unexpected from a man of both his years and slightness. Santini sat opposite.

'What outcome from Browne's death?' Pescaro cut to the chase.

'None yet Don Pescaro, but I think the police will struggle to find the fire was deliberate. The load was prone to combustion and the explosive was located on one of the bogies. It will look as if a spark from the brakes ignited some leakage. On top of that, the chemical mix was blended to produce an intensely hot, destructive fire.'

'Nardo, there are big risks with this death, especially as we near the end of our project. Refresh my memory: why was it necessary to *kill* Browne?' The question, as Santini knew, was not an idle one. Having risen from soldier to lieutenant – and now *Consigliere* – in a violent and bloody career, Santini was ever-mindful of Family supremacy. Members who broke *Omerta*, or whose violence was excessive, had a limited future. Although long time friends, Santini neither presumed upon that friendship nor underestimated the Don's ruthlessness. For Pescaro, there was *only* Family business.

'Don Pescaro, you have known me a long time. You know how well I scent danger, even when none is apparent. As Aldrittson's foreman, I keep a close eye on the staff and can truly say I am good with them. About six months ago I noticed small changes in Browne. He looked tired, he began arriving late for work, occasionally he complained of a crook guts and his sense of humour vanished. All this was uncharacteristic of the man. I watched him.

About three months ago his colour looked bad, ashen. He had become thin and sometimes I heard him vomiting in the toilets. He never said a word. I overheard him arranging tests he didn't want his wife to know about. Later I acquired copies of the results. Cancer. Not just cancer, but a type I discovered could be triggered by some of the liquids he dumps. Last week, he spoke to me about the Walwa business, freaked out by the thought of the EPA catching him. He went on and on about how the stuff we dumped caused cancer. Knowing he was a strong and decent family man, I sensed real danger that with his condition he might dob us in. He had nothing to lose. In truth, there *was* nothing tangible, but my radar was screaming. There was no choice, I had to remove the threat.'

'Okay,' said Pescaro, 'how is Aldrittson taking it?'

'His only concern is *you* and what you might do if the shit hits the fan.' Santini smiled wryly, 'he had no qualms about dispensing with Browne and will soften the family's pain with a good cash payout. I think he'll be okay.'

'Are the coppers on it yet?' Pescaro spoke thoughtfully as he chewed an almond biscotto.

'Before coming here I put out some feelers. So far, only the local bloke is involved. While I won't be complacent, in my experience most country coppers are slack. I don't think this guy Maud from Heathcote will be any different but, we'll watch him.' Santini smiled again.

There was a soft knock at the door. Teresa Marchese entered and deposited a cappuccino on Santini's side table. 'Anything more Giuseppe?' she enquired.

'No Teresa, but keep on with that property analysis, I'd like to know by 4:00 p.m. if we have to pressure Blanchard's family.' She nodded and left the room, her perfume lingering in the cigar smoke.

'Nardo, Teresa's finalising the last property acquisition for our waste treatment scheme. I believe it's time to lean on our politician … get him softened up.' He paused before continuing. 'I am hearing certain things which disturb me, things that suggest it's time to accelerate our scheme. I'll be speaking to Jack but he doesn't need to know just yet that you're talking to Ben. Get it happening will you.'

'Don Pescaro, I have been buried in this firm a long time. Neither of the Aldrittsons actually know I work for you. If I lean on Ben that will compromise my role there.' The oblique query was polite but valid.

'I doubt that is a risk of much substance Nardo. I have been investigating Ben recently and he is a very corrupt man. Indeed, it surprises me that those around him don't suspect him of wrong-doing. I want this waste scheme in place and I want him to understand that what he does, he now does for me. I want him to feel my power. Your talk with him will make that clear. He works for me.'

'I understand. He *will* be clear about how things stand.'

'Nardo, this Browne thing could be trouble. I want our scheme legitimised as soon as possible. The capacity of this project will not only manage Victoria's crap, but can handle the other states too. No one really wants to deal with toxic shit. Who knows, with the technology we've got lined up, we might even get a licence to destroy overseas stuff – maybe even nuclear waste. That would bring mega dollars. And there you have the difference between me and the Genovese mob. They were too impatient, thought too small and had no vision for the future. We can learn from that. So, be clear. I want things on the rails and smooth.'

Chapter
FIVE

Three days after the truck fire, Drummond was hauling logs to a growing pile in the paddock. The fresh autumn morning was crisp and clear and the low sun pale. When a police car turned into the drive from Schoolhouse Lane he stopped the tractor, released the haul-chain and burbled uphill to the house. Tony Maud was leaning against a veranda post when he got there.

'G'day Tony, how are you?'

'Good cobber. What are you playing at down there? You rich bloody retirees. Why couldn't you do something useful!' Drummond grinned. Banter between them was constant since they forged their friendship at a tree planting project several years earlier. Maud was older than Drummond who had quit the army a year after he and his wife Susan won the lottery.

'Quit ya bitchin' and come inside. You can give me the drum on the truck fire.'

They entered the house and walked through the lounge-dining room, the hub of Drummond's home. He called it "the big room" since it was the size of a decent shed. At its western end was a three seater divan and several cavernous club chairs around a low messmate coffee table. Behind the table, a fieldstone fire place. With its abundant space, soft buttery coloured walls, paintings, family artefacts and thick straw-bale outer walls, the room possessed a charming cosiness. Drummond loved it. Especially during winter when the fire blazed.

They went into the kitchen, a compact space backing onto the dining area. There, an ancient slow combustion Aga found at a clearing sale filled the room with gentle warmth. On its firebox sat an ancient, blackened, cast iron boiler with a bright brass tap. Boiling water was ever ready.

'Grab a stool mate, tea'll be ready in a jiff. Do you want something to eat? I've got some of Gaffney's wholemeal fruit and honey loaf.'

'Dish her up cobber,' said Maud smiling, 'I was in Tooborac at sparrow fart this morning. Some silly bastard tried to rumba with a 'roo. Trouble was, the 'roo was sober and he was pissed and now his car's a write-off. Breakfast was a century ago.'

Propping at the counter, Maud continued, 'I guess you've seen all the guff on telly about the fire. Well, I'll need your statement for an inquest. When we finally got the bloody fire out we found the driver's remains in the cabin. Poor bastard. He was just a charred, black twist. At the time I didn't understand why the fire was so bloody intense. The engine block was a fused heap of crap, nothing left of the tyres and most of the truck frame had disintegrated. Anyway, our forensic guys spent two full days at the scene and their findings indicate the truck was full to the bloody brim with chemicals. It became its own bloody furnace. I'm still waiting on them to find out what chemicals were involved and maybe, what caused the fire.'

'What about the driver?' enquired Drummond, 'do you know who he was?'

'No, nothing. No information about where the truck came from either. Although, coincidentally, a firm in Brooklyn called Aldrittson Waste Disposals reported a driver overdue. Supposedly, he was on his way to Mildura for a load of asbestos sludge. Trouble is, we can't yet say if this body was their man. All the usual identification markers, number plates, chassis and engine numbers, don't exist anymore. And, if he was their man, he was in the wrong place. In other words, nowhere near here. But, *if* he is their man, there's another inconsistency, the truck should have been empty. So … bit of a mystery at the minute. *Anything* you can help with will be good.'

As Drummond listened he considered telling his friend of

the early morning trucks in Schoolhouse Lane. For the moment though, he decided against it. He had nothing of substance to give him. As a military policeman trained by the Victoria Police Detective Training school, reputedly the toughest in Australia (the bastards even set the *pass* mark at seventy-five per cent) he was confident he knew enough not to blur the boundaries for Tony.

They finished their tea and Maud took Drummond's statement on his laptop. It was little more than he had already said the night of the fire. After packing up, the two men went out to look at Drummond's latest project, a terraced area he was paving between the house and dam. As he explained, with such great views and later, a pergola covered in wisteria, it would be the perfect spot for a cold beer on a hot night.

'Righto mate,' said Maud, 'I'll leave a copy in your post box in town. I'm off to the scene again. The lane'll be closed a couple more days while we continue scouting for evidence.'

Back on his tractor Drummond dissected the new information; *waste disposal company, dead driver, chemical fire, how did all this fit together?* Naturally, the police would be thorough in their examination of the scene and if local stickybeaks had tromped around there too, precious little was likely to be left to learn from it. Nevertheless, he was keener than ever to look at things for himself. He would have to be patient a few more days.

Chapter
SIX

The Speaker's gavel thumped the bench resoundingly, underlining the terseness of his bellow. 'Would the Honourable Member for Melbourne Ports resume his seat and stop interjecting. The Minister for Business and Trade has the floor!'

Suave, urbane Ben Aldrittson, Minister for Business and Trade, was answering a back bencher's question about payments to the giant American multi-national computer company, Phoenix. 'Mr Speaker,' resumed Aldrittson smoothly, 'Phoenix's presence in Victoria will increase our competition with Japan's miniaturised computer components, consolidate our rising position as a quality software manufacturer and enable us to aggressively pursue trade in competition with the growing Chinese computer market. Above all, Phoenix will create job opportunities for Victorians.'

Simon Candy, Member for Melbourne Ports, had been trying, unsuccessfully, to emphasise his point that Phoenix was internationally renowned for its hardline management and exploitative work practices, a style that would cause workers to suffer. He was arguing that companies like Phoenix were unwelcome in Victoria. 'Local industry returns might be slower, but the benefits to Victorians will be greater, especially if those industries receive the same kinds of generous grants and tax perks being offered to Phoenix.' Frustrated, he smacked his fist into his palm and yelled, 'Furthermore, there will be no need to seize public parkland and profits will stay here.'

Aldrittson had sneeringly replied that Candy would be better off examining his backside for enlightenment rather than denigrate international friends and allies, a remark that had caused the Chamber to dissolve into uproar.

Opposition jeering was directed not only at Aldrittson's

insensitive remark but also to his consistent refusal to acknowledge the small, expanding local company, Scintilla. Three months earlier, Scintilla had won a major international science prize for its unique application of nano-technology to computers. Labor had been pressing hard arguing that, as usual, the Americans were being fattened by huge taxpayer dollars to the detriment of local enterprise. It was furious too that the government had re-zoned public land to enable Phoenix to build its factory.

Amid the hullabaloo, the Speaker hammered the bench furiously. When finally he secured order, Aldrittson was instructed to withdraw his offensive remarks. Smirking, he rose calmly, acknowledged the instruction then swiftly moved that land identified for use by the software manufacturer Phoenix be excised from Northern Memorial Park. He further moved that tax breaks, financial and other venture capital incentives be granted to secure the company's presence in Victoria. Amid continuing catcalls, Aldrittson's motion predictably passed on Party lines.

Later that evening Aldrittson knocked discreetly at the door of an exquisitely appointed villa unit at Crown Casino. When the door opened, Chuck J. Taylor, Managing Director of Phoenix welcomed him with a lazy drawl.

'Well, how are you Ben.' After taking a quick look up and down the corridor, the thin, bronzed, two metre Texan beamed down and ushered him inside. They shook hands.

'I take it nobody saw you coming here?' Taylor nodded towards the corridor. Without waiting for a response he went on. 'I'm having a mineral water. What can I get you Ben?'

'A whisky and ice will be fine thanks Chuck. And no, I was bloody careful as usual,' a trace of annoyance in his tone.

Taylor shrugged and fixed the drink. They sat. Taylor studied Aldrittson a few moments before speaking, a shrewd and calculating look in in his eye. 'So … How did the vote go today? Did we get what we wanted?'

'Yeah, no problems Chuck. As I told you at the beginning, the tricky part was convincing my side. The Opposition didn't have the numbers and the Independents don't know which way is up. A bit noisy, but it got through without real difficulty. The Foreign Investment Review Board has almost become a paper tiger since the Free Trade Agreement with your country so I reckon that within three months, you'll be turning soil at your new site.'

'Well done Ben, a darn fine site it is too, out there on the cusp of the Northern Ring Road and Hume Highway. You've done well. Now, let's conclude business before we get down to some serious eating. At six o'clock tomorrow morning, your time, 1.5 million will go to your account in Banque Suisse, Switzerland. Okay? I know it's a tad more than we agreed, but you've done better than we hoped. And just to make it clear, you do understand we intend crushing Scintilla don't you?'

'Sure Chuck, that's business.'

At 1:00 p.m. the following day, Santini sipped his coffee beneath the Nova Cinema in Carlton. He was waiting for Ben Aldrittson. People were flowing in and out of Border's, meeting and greeting for lunch, browsing for books or queuing for film tickets. Still others were spread around the plaza dining. It was a wet, cold day and a damp muskiness permeated the air. Outside, in Lygon Street, cars and buses churned past, tyres fizzing in the wet.

Santini had chosen this spot because it was unassuming in its bustle and clutter of people, a prosaic place suited to his low key style. It was also familiar territory.

At 1:10 p.m. Aldrittson arrived draped inconspicuously in a long, dark, woollen coat, a black beanie covering his thick blond hair. He walked towards Santini who marked his presence by a slight incline of his head. Sitting at the table he enquired, 'How goes it Bernardo?'

'Well Ben. Thanks for coming. I've already ordered a long black for you.' Santini turned and, catching the eye of the Asian girl behind the counter, raised a finger, nodded and pointed to Aldrittson. She smiled and nodded back.

'Read about Phoenix in *The Age* this morning Ben. You're still kicking goals then?'

'Yep. In the long run it will be good for Victoria. A few whingeing bastards will get their noses out of joint but … hey. So what's up?'

As usual, Aldrittson came bluntly to the point. He was something of a chameleon and, in some ways, resembled Santini whom he had known all his life. A handsome man, he was the charming politician when it suited, a tough and canny deal broker, a narcissistic man contemptuous of fools. Like his father, he loved money. But, he idolised power and influence more and had found these qualities enabled money making to take care of itself.

Santini, intimately familiar with Aldrittson's character, believed that while he had numerous strengths, he also possessed a streak of weakness. In his opinion, Aldrittson had never been properly tested and now he was about to do just that.

At school Aldrittson had been very bright and, with effort, an accomplished sportsman. He had cruised through his final year at St. Andrews as school captain, enjoyed a punishing year in athletics, the school musical and inter-school debating team. After final exam honours he had entered Melbourne University for a double degree in law and commerce, joined the Young Liberals and graduated with distinction. At the young age of thirty-two, he had beome Secretary of the State Liberal Party. From this position he began his run for a parliamentary career. He quickly established a prodigious work ethic, was a clever mediator and not afraid to step on toes when pursuing his goals. Easing into politics, he found his father's enormous wealth an excellent salve for sore spots in need of some occasional "healing."

He developed his bribery skills to an art form by identifying, exploiting, manipulating, compromising and corrupting individuals and public officials across many fields common to his interests and was able to reach into a multitude of government departments, local government areas, large corporations and the media. To his continuing annoyance he had been unable to infiltrate the Australian Broadcasting Commission. Ben Aldrittson was a consummate and dangerous politician driven by power and wealth, a man who took pleasure watching others squirm from his manipulation.

'Ben,' murmured Santini, 'your father has suggested we ramp up activities on the black waste project. As you are probably aware, I've known about it for years and he now wants me to take a proactive interest. I thought we should compare notes to ensure we are in sync.'

Aldrittson was curious. His own role in this scheme was important and he believed it was presently on hold. He was immediately suspicious of Santini's motives. Instead, he said neutrally, 'Okay, tell me how it looks from your side.'

Santini hunched forward, speaking succinctly and softly. 'As you know, we've quietly been buying land for the last ten years. Our last property came on stream today. We own about twenty square kilometres around Nanneella and Timmering between Rochester and Kyabram. It's shitty farming land, but okay for our needs. We've secretly had the world's best environmental and waste management experts develop eco-friendly methods for handling toxic and other waste, including the mining of toxic waste. That is, recovering and refining stuff to distil original chemicals, minerals and fluids. Our plans for buildings, equipment and earthworks are all done. This whole scheme is a world first. Now it's time for the next phase: legitimising the illegitimate. It's time to create the legislation to make it all happen. And that's your job.'

Aldrittson listened impassively, his eyes never leaving Santini's face. He was intimately aware of these events as much of the progress had been down to him: calling in favours, leaning on officials, bribing others and slicing red tape with his Ministerial razor.

'I grant you it's an excellent start,' he said 'but there's a hell of a long way to go. Unfortunately, the political scene is still not right. For instance, the National Party will scream when they find out what's proposed and plenty of my own lot won't like it either. Politically, waste disposal schemes are dynamite. The Greens punch well above their weight and they've had a hell of an impact on this issue. A bloody lot of people take this climate change crap seriously. They keep banging on about insufficient pressure on the Feds to sign up to Kyoto and not doing enough for the countryside about water conservation, especially after this bloody drought. People see climate change and waste management as all part of one problem: stuffing up the environment. We're not ready for this scheme yet. While you might have the land and the plan, the politics of waste is still too controversial.'

Santini sat back and skewered Aldrittson with a bleak stare.

'Ben,' he almost whispered, 'understand me.' Aldrittson registered a prick of fear. 'This discussion is not about raising obstacles, it is about compliance. We are ready to move and it is your turn to do what you have to. You are the right man in the right place with the right contacts and the right capabilities. Now, *make it happen.*' The menace was unmistakable.

Unused to being threatened, Aldrittson challenged. 'What the hell do you mean, *We are ready*? *You* work for *my* father, *you* do as *he* says. When *he* asks me to move on it I will, but last time we spoke about this he said we were about twelve to eighteen months away from action. Don't tell me what to do, I won't have it.' Although

Aldrittson had not raised his voice, his tone was dismissive, his lip curled to a sneer.

Slowly, Santini leaned across the table, his mouth wore a smile but his eyes were chilling. 'I do work for your father,' he said, 'but I also work for others and those others feel you are slacking. They want to see some action.'

His hand snaked out catching Aldrittson's wrist, fingers clamping with surprising strength, middle finger, stiff as a bridge spike, lancing the nerve at the base of the wrist. Aldrittson paled from the searing pain and gagged, his arm immobilised. 'Ben, I shall not speak of this again. This is an exercise of compliance, *your* compliance. We'll meet ten days from now and you *will* bring a plan outlining your argument to the Premier and your method for convincing the Greens and Nationals of the benefits of this project. You will also have an outline of the media strategy. And you will explain to me how *you* will make everything happen. And don't crap me off about it being impossible. I've watched you for years and know exactly what you can do. Remember this, in the next six months there has to be an election. You *will* have every necessary thing in place before then. Now, get on with it.' He paused before continuing. 'One more thing – I *know* how corrupt you are and I am happy to share that information with your Premier if necessary.' Santini's voice, barely above a whisper was frightening.

He released Aldrittson. The exchange had lasted barely ten seconds and to any casual observer, Santini's grasp may have appeared a simple act of friendship. But it was far from that. Aldrittson was stunned by Santini's change of mood and character. He had scared the shit out of him. Uncertain of his next move, Aldrittson remained mute.

Santini rose, pushed his chair under the table and smiled. 'I look forward to seeing you in ten days Ben.' With that, he slipped into the lunchtime crowd and out onto rainy Lygon Street.

Chapter
SEVEN

Aldrittson sat in pain, rubbing his wrist and thinking furiously. *What the fuck had come over Santini?* Christ, he had been with the company since his grandfather's days and Aldrittson had known him since he was a toddler. He had never seen Santini change so quickly, become so ominous. And what was that frogshit about his father wanting to crank up the waste disposal concept? It was ridiculous to even think his father would have Santini asking *him* for plans. His father only had to phone him. *Who was Santini working for? Who were these 'others?'* Something didn't add up. And just what did he mean when he said he was happy to share his 'corruption' with the Premier? *What did the bastard know?*

He rose abruptly and went to order a second coffee. As he massaged his wrist he perceived depths to Santini he had never suspected. Santini had to be considered a threat, a man who was dangerous and evidently fearless. Before today he had always known him as a mild, hard working, loyal, trustworthy friend of his father's. Never as volcanic, maverick or violent.

Should he tell his father? No, or … at least, not yet. Aldrittson had been in politics long enough to suspect that what, or whoever motivated Santini would be subterranean and the matter was unlikely to be resolved through his father. Besides, he guessed his father would be ignorant of Santini's demand. What he had to do was find out who was pushing Santini's buttons.

The prick had made three things clear. He wanted a plan to overcome political opposition to their waste scheme, he wanted to view the underpinning legislative framework and, most difficult of all, he wanted that legislation in place *before* Parliament prorogued for the election. Unfortunately, Aldrittson was like everybody else, he didn't know the election date. That was the Premier's secret.

Santini was making a huge and ridiculous ask. Aldrittson knew he could produce a strategy plan, that was simple. Christ, he had talked about it with his father for years. Getting the scheme accepted by Premier Meadows at short notice would be difficult enough, but having underpinning legislation in place *before* the election was impossible. He had to find out what was behind Santini's demand. When he knew that, then he would decide whether Santini should be taught a lesson.

Aldrittson had the power to deal with Santini his own way. Make him disappear for instance. Given his threat to leak to the Premier, that was not a bad idea. A scary thought suddenly nagged. *What if Santini was connected to the Mafia?* His father had been dealing with Don Pescaro for years and crossing the Don would arouse a viper's nest. In all the years he had known Santini, he had never seen or heard anything personally linking him to the Mafia. He knew Santini carried out the odd job for his father which involved Pescaro, but being a member of *the Mob?* That was something else. Grappling with Pescaro would create risks for his father's firm, particularly the black waste scheme.

Santini controlled daily activities and, as far as he knew, no one else, apart from his father was involved in that. The volume of toxic waste disposal had become so large he couldn't afford to create hiccups that would bring the system to a standstill. Moreover, the customer base continued to grow. Danny Browne's death was already causing pressure and if Santini went, Jack would have to resume daily management. Logistically and strategically, that could cause a whole bunch of new problems.

With a score of issues on his mind, Aldrittson drove from the underground car park into belting rain and joined the slow drifting river of cars. Arriving at the Sunset Fitness Club at Toorak and Darling Roads he drove under the building to his reserved space, parked and went upstairs.

Tanya Taylor, a trim, attractive marathon runner was at reception. 'Hello Tanya, is Spencer in today?'

'Yes Mr Aldrittson, down the back office. Can I get him for you?' She rose in readiness to leave her desk.

'No, no.' Aldrittson switched on a dazzling smile. 'I'll go surprise him.'

Spencer Johnson was Aldrittson's most useful asset. An ex-federal policeman, he knew people who could get things done, organising others so they never knew who he was organising for.

Aldrittson knocked briefly on a door at the end of the corridor and entered. The small office was a veritable museum to Spencer's history as a young body builder. These days he belonged to the Grand Master category and was not quite so successful. Pictures, plaques, certificates and trophies adorned the shelves and every other available flat space. The exception was the immediate work area on the desk in front of him where he was developing a program for a client. At fifty-five, Johnson preferred to run his gym, occasionally enter some of the Natural Body Building Association's competitions overseas, devise his programs and "organise" a few things for special friends like Ben Aldrittson. The last activity earned him big dollars.

'Yo Benny, good to see you. Pull up a chair. Come for a work-out today?' The huge, brawny man with a marine buzz-cut grinned and waved a thick arm at the chair opposite his desk. 'Can I get you a drink – juice, mineral water?'

'No thanks Spence.' Aldrittson hung his coat on a hook behind the door. 'Mind if I shut this? I need you to do something for me.'

'Sure thing Benny. Just a minute.' He flicked the intercom on his desk: 'Tanya, are you there pet?'

'Yes Spencer, what can I do for you?'

'Hold all calls and visitors till I say will you pet? I'll let you know when we're through.' Without waiting for a response, he flicked the switch off. 'Okay, let her rip Benny.'

'I need information about a man called Bernardo Santini. I may have mentioned him from time to time, he works for my father. He was born in Sicily and started working at the firm under my grandfather. My Old Man kept him on and I reckon he's been there about twenty years; that should tell you something about his ability. He lives at 205A Nicholson Street, Collingwood and drives a white '99 Magna – I can't remember the number. Santini has just given me a ten day ultimatum on something – I don't bloody like it. The prick also paralysed my arm in some weird kind of hold I didn't even see coming. And, he did it all in front of scores of people. Jesus Spence, I've known him since I was a kid but I've *never* known him like this! I want to know what he does when he's not at work, where he goes, who he sees, who he sleeps with. Anything and everything. Someone has wound him up and I want to know who and why. He said he was there on behalf of my Old Man, but that's bullshit. He's got to be working for somebody else.'

The ex-federal policeman regarded Aldrittson quizzically. 'And then what? After you have the information?'

'I'll tell you when I get it Spence. Just remember, insulate me from the drones. Santini is sharp. I know what he's accomplished at the Depot over the years. Don't underestimate him.'

'Righto Benny, anything else?'

'For the moment, no.'

'Okay. Usual fee – $25,000 in used notes. Ten for me, fifteen for the workers. I'll be in touch in a few days, well before your deadline. If you have to follow up with anything, there will be plenty of time.'

Taking his coat, Aldrittson nodded and retraced his steps. He was mildly disappointed to find Tanya missing, he enjoyed perving on her small tight tits.

True to his word, Spencer Johnson got straight to work. He rang Sergeant Brendan Little at the Victoria Police Bureau of Criminal

Intelligence. After giving him details it was agreed that he and a colleague, Penny Jamieson, would build a three day, "out of hours" surveillance program around Santini and check out Victorian and interstate police data-bases. Aldrittson's warning about Santini was passed on.

In half an hour, Little rang Johnson. They had an unconfirmed and obscure link between Mafia boss Giuseppe Pescaro and Bernardo Santini which meant they would plan their task carefully. Johnson told Little to set aside a day during the following week when he would meet them both for "lunch".

Settling back into his chair, Johnson closed his eyes. It was none of his business, he just organised things. *Why the hell was Aldrittson wanting to apply grief to a possible Mafia type? Did he know Santini might be Mafia? Perhaps he didn't. Maybe that was why he was so cagey about what he would or would not do. Aldrittson was a shifty bastard.* In any event, Johnson inferred that whatever Aldrittson decided to do would fall to him anyway. In which case, that meant mobilising a particular set of skills. He had better check out Fox's availability and have answers for Aldrittson next time they spoke.

Chapter
EIGHT

Drummond warmed himself before the log fire and gazed across the farm to the south west. It was three o'clock Thursday afternoon. Heavy rain had fallen for an hour, hammering on the iron roof. Roiling black clouds bludgeoned the sky, further darkening the gloomy light. The choppy wind had intensified and small branches were snapping through the air. About to walk to a window seat, Drummond heard a tremendous crash at the southern end of the house. He scooted to the laundry. A huge branch had splintered from one of the towering ironbarks in the back garden and smashed to the ground. *Bugger*, he thought, *nothing worse than the old trees losing shape – a chainsaw job for tomorrow.*

Returning to the big room he snugged into a window seat with his newest Henning Mankell novel. It was the perfect afternoon for a break and even better for reading. But he couldn't get started, Tony Maud's lunch time phone call nagged at him. Maud had received a positive ID on the corpse from the truck fire. Dental comparisons confirmed it was a Danny Browne, a driver from Aldrittson Waste Disposals or AWD as Tony referred to them. Additionally, traces of benzene, paint stripper, used engine oil and other noxious compounds had been found on the truck which suggested a load of toxic waste. Enquiries with AWD had drawn a blank. Browne was supposed to have been driving an empty truck to Mildura. AWD could not explain the toxic load or Browne's route: both were contrary to their manifest. Since the journey was scheduled a week in advance, they could only suggest Browne was moonlighting. Additionally, they had already reported him missing to police.

Aldrittson's explanation was convincing and there was nothing to contradict it. Drummond had scoured the fire scene after the officials and in spite of his best efforts, found nothing. The cause of the fire was unknown and Browne's presence in Schoolhouse Lane remained a mystery. Maud was now arranging for one of his detective mates in Melbourne to poke around AWD to try to scrounge a look at their books and natter to staff. Although this wasn't absolutely kosher, he had done it before with good effect.

Drummond still had not mentioned the late night trucks to Maud because he thought their link to the fire too tenuous. But, *if* these trucks and the fire were connected, then it was plausible for AWD to somehow be involved, and that implied someone was lying about Browne. Yet given their Brooklyn base, it made little sense for one of their trucks, supposedly travelling to Mildura, to be here in Knowsley.

He checked the Aldrittson company on the internet and found they had a long history in waste management, returned high profits, were leaders in workplace safety, and, according to the *Financial Review* and *Business Review Weekly*, had a blue chip record for effective management and integrity. With such a fine reputation, they would be crazy to be messing with toxic stuff. Yet his gut instinct suggested otherwise.

By 3:45 p.m. the wind was slumbering and the rain had eased to a mist. Gradually, the sky began to lighten and Drummond decided to inspect Schoolhouse Lane for fallen branches. Fierce winds would often bring farmers out to check for tree falls. Walking into the cold damp air Drummond savoured the fresh smell of rain on earth mixed with the unmistakable tang of wet, summer-dried grasses. Overhead, from north to south, the sky was a lumpy purple–black canopy. To the west, crouched barely above the horizon as though the huge stormy dome had been prized open, a sliver of clear sky allowed a flush of red–gold light to gild the world in mellow coppery tones. As he looked about, Drummond felt his heart swell at the power of such unbridled beauty.

In the carport, he slung his chainsaw and parts box into the ute and drove to the Lane. After a clear run to Derrinal-Crosbie Road he was stopped by a heavy branch across the road at the site of the earlier truck fire. Severely burned, the limb had snapped in the strong wind. He cut it into pieces and threw the bits into the verge. Finishing, he picked up a leafy branch and broomed the last of the debris from the road.

As he pitched the branch towards the freshly cut billets, a brief ruby-like glint flashed near the bottom of a tree a few metres off the road. Drummond stood still and moved his head until the gleam re-appeared. Stepping into the rough to investigate, he found embedded in the tree about seventy centimetres above the ground, a small, bright piece of metal. Squatting, he peered at the tiny piece which had sliced through the bark and flattened against the wood of the trunk. Past experience told him he was looking at a detonator remnant. Knowing the site had been almost vacuumed by the forensics team he understood why this tiny morsel had been missed by them. Were it not for one of the logs he had thrown gouging a chunk from the tree, it would have escaped detection probably forever.

He found the bark chip and carefully fitted it to the tree. The metal fragment vanished. He rose and studied the tree from several locations. The fragment and cut-scar were concealed completely beneath the rough shaggy bark. Sheer fluke had revealed this prize. He smiled to himself. *Sometimes luck just happens*, he thought.

'Tony? Andy here mate. I'm out at the fire scene. I've found something you need to see in situ. If it is what I think it is, your fire might just have become a crime scene. Bring a camera and a couple of strong torches, it's getting dark out here. I'll hang about to show you.'

'Thanks, see you in twenty. Want to tell me what it is?'

'No old son, I'd rather keep you in suspense.'

Maud arrived twenty-five minutes later. Alighting from his

four wheel drive he threw a torch to Drummond. 'Righto show me what you've got. Are we going far? I need to keep an ear on the radio.'

'No Tony. It's just here. First though, I want you to look at that tree by the fence.' Drummond pointed to the one he meant. 'Look near the base and tell me what you see.'

Tony peered into the rapidly dimming light. 'Can't see anything unusual. Should I be able to?'

'I wouldn't think so. Come up here.'

They stopped about two paces from the tree.

'Shine your torch on the trunk, about a half metre from the ground. What about now?'

Maud played the beam over the base of the tree. 'I can only see a bit of a dent where one of those cut logs hit the tree. I assume you did that, right? Otherwise, nothing.'

'Good,' said Drummond, 'that's exactly why the forensic blokes didn't find anything either, nothing looks out of place. Let me show you.'

They went to the tree where Drummond carefully peeled away the bark chip he had replaced.

'Tony, I am 99.9 per cent certain this little scrap of metal is from a detonator. If you look at this bark chip which, incidentally, I did knock off, you will see a small clean cut across the bottom of it. Because it's still green and unhealed, I'd say this cut is recent. I reckon this piece of det. flew into the tree not long ago. If you look back to the road you'll see we are to the east and some metres behind the fire site.'

'So, what are you thinking,' queried Maud, 'that the truck was blown up?'

'I am. So far, you don't have a cause for the fire. This detonator cap could be the explanation. A botanist or someone might be able to determine how old the bark cut is. I don't know. But if they could say, for instance, the cut is between seven and nine days old, you've got a timeframe consistent with the fire.'

'You're right. I'll get a few pics and remove it. Tell you what, why don't you shoot off home and boil the billy? I'll finish off here and call in for a quick cuppa. I'll come back for some daylight shots tomorrow but now we've got this little treasure, I want it safe and sound.'

Thirty minutes later, Maud rapped on Drummond's kitchen window and walked into the warm house. Drummond filled a teapot from the boiler on the stove.

'I cut a wedge from the tree with the fragment in place after I photographed the scene. Who knows … we might learn something from the depth of penetration about velocity and size of charge. I'll leave that to the experts. The wedge is the next best thing to sending them the whole tree.' He grinned at the image he had just conjured.

They walked into the big room. Drummond switched on a couple of lamps, gave the fire a boost and threw on another log. They sat comfortably either side of the fire.

'How exactly did you find this little piece of metal?' enquired Maud.

Drummond recounted his actions explaining how the fragment remained unseen until he was about to leave. 'It was a strange thing Tony. The storm had just passed and was followed by a short period of coppery gold sunlight. I was cleaning up a fallen branch and chucked the last piece in towards the fence when this flash of ruby coloured light appeared. It was tiny but brilliant so I went to look. When I saw what it was and put the bark chip back in place, the metal disappeared. What do you make of it?' he asked his friend.

'To be honest, I don't know. I accept that *you* think it's a fragment of detonator, but … I'm not sure. If it was the cause of the fire, why blow up such an expensive vehicle? Could there have been detonators in the load? Was the fire deliberate? Why? Could it simply have been accidental? Could someone have been after the driver because of a grudge? Was someone gunning for AWD for some reason, industrial sabotage perhaps? Could it be Aldrittsons themselves? Is this some kind of insurance scam? But perhaps the most basic question of all is: does this tiny piece of metal have anything at all to do with the truck fire? It might be entirely coincidental. I can't rule anything in or out just yet and I'm not exactly sure which way to jump. What do you think?'

'I reckon there are just *too* many questions right now,' said Drummond thoughtfully, 'and now I'm going to add to them. I've held back telling you this Tony because I couldn't see any relevance, but this piece of detonator changes things, at least for me. Over the past twelve months or so, I've occasionally heard a large truck going up Schoolhouse Lane towards McIvor Highway, roughly between 2-3:00 a.m. Never seen it, just heard it. I know we've got quarries and large trucks over at Axedale but, at that hour, it's generally too early for them. I have nothing to connect them to AWD but … I am suspicious.' His statement hung in the air. 'I've checked the company on the net and it has a pristine reputation. But I am almost bloody certain the trucks I heard sounded consistent with that one in the fire.'

Maud gazed into the fire digesting this new information. 'You're right, I don't know whether what you've said is a help or a hindrance. Nevertheless, I'll check the all-night servo's between here and Kilmore and Romsey. It's possible our dead truckie stopped for coffee or something to eat. When you put it all together, it stinks: a truck fire, a truck off route, a truck full when it should be empty, a truck owned by a respectable waste firm carrying toxic stuff, detonators and mystery trucks in the night. This whole friggin' thing reeks.'

'What say, my good friend,' said Drummond with a grin, 'that I help a little. I've got my place in Melbourne and could spend a few days having a decko at Aldrittson's. I'll report back if anything looks suss and call in every couple of days to keep you up to speed.'

Maud's eyes twinkled. 'I couldn't sanction that, you might get hurt.' He smiled,. 'I'd be bloody shot if my boss found out. Still, we do seem to have a blue chip company involved in something shady. As you know, I can't clobber them without evidence. A sneaky look around might be helpful. And, if that piece of detonator is relevant, the matter will be out of my hands. Homicide will deal with it. In the meantime, I don't want AWD thinking they're under my spotlight so I'll cancel that semi-official poke around I've organised with my mate Gerry Riley. If you do happen to go to Melbourne, keep a lid on things. Okay?'

Chapter
NINE

That Friday evening, Don Pescaro and Jack Aldrittson were enjoying the good food and fine wine of *J'taime*, a French provincial restaurant in Toorak Village. In reality, it was an excuse for business.

'Jack, I want to move on legalising our black waste program. There's an election soon and we need legislation in place before then. I know Meadows is cautious but, as a Liberal, he's prepared to crack heads. If we present him with the full package, I think he'll roll over quicker than a dog with fleas. It's time Ben made things happen at his end.'

'I hear you Giuseppe, and I have spoken to him about it. We feel another twelve to eighteen months would be more appropriate. The election is possibly only six months off and we don't think we could have things in place before then. I know we have …'

'Jack,' Pescaro's soft voice was biting. 'We have waited a long time and worked bloody hard to pull this off. Whether you realise it or not, I have been incredibly patient. It is time to *act*. There are new pressures I am dealing with and I can't afford to be hamstrung by a change of government. If those soft bellied lefties take over they'll clog everything with reviews, committees and consult the bloody world. In the end they'll do just as they please and screw you in a fog of confusion. New governments are all the same, especially Labor ones and punters are backing a Labor victory. We know Meadows – how he thinks and acts. I will *not* wait any longer. Nardo has just told Ben to pull his finger out and bring me a plan in a few days. I don't want you mistaking the source of that request.'

Jack's thoughts somersaulted. *Why is Pescaro asking Santini to prod Ben? I employ Santini. What am I missing?* Trying to stay calm he said, 'Ben hasn't said anything to me. What's happened?' He resented the intrusion. It was, after all, his business and his skill that had made their duplicitous activities seem lily white. He didn't want Pescaro fucking up a major opportunity for serious wealth. 'What have you asked Bernardo to do?' His question was guarded.

Pescaro's eyes glinted in the soft light of the restaurant. 'Nothing, other than talk to Ben.'

'Well, I'm not sure we have enough time …'

'Jack, please, no obstacles.' Pescaro frowned. 'If you become part of the problem, I'll suffer indigestion; indigestion requires medication. You understand me? Let's just enjoy our dinner and let matters take care of themselves. You know how efficient Nardo is. For him, everything is business. Never personal, just business. You need to think that way too Jack, it causes less ulcers.'

Alarm bells clamoured. Pescaro was disclosing an intimacy with Santini that was entirely new to him. Santini had always been the go-between for the two of them and there had never been a hint of anything more. He was a bloody 'go-fer' for Christ's sake. Now Pescaro was implying other efficiencies which he understood only too well. His stomach contracted. He had to find out what the hell was going on. Why hadn't the little shit spoken to him anyway? He decided to play along with Pescaro, finish his meal then plead another appointment. That way he could save *some* face. He had been anticipating a long and leisurely evening with Pescaro, maybe even a turn at the casino. Not now. He needed to talk to Ben.

But Pescaro had other ideas. He watched Aldrittson's inner turmoil and pressed his advantage. 'Jack, forgive me,' he said in his courtly, old fashioned style, 'how long do *you* think you have employed Nardo?'

'Jesus Giuseppe, what kind of question is that? You know he started under my Old Man, he's been with us for bloody years.'

'No Jack, Nardo works for me, he's always worked for me. You are his paymaster. *You* actually came to *me* through him, even though you thought you cleverly set it up. Everything happening in your firm, everything between you and Ben – I know about. I have thought of removing you both many times. Ben in particular has expectations beyond his ability, but you really don't cause me trouble. Now it's time for Ben to learn who he really works for and to demonstrate the balls he *thinks* he has. Nardo will help him understand his new truth.'

Aldrittson's belly stopped convulsing, it had become glacier-like with fear. Occasionally he had puzzled over Santini's relationship with Pescaro but had found nothing tying them together. Sure, there was contact through the firm, but nothing he knew of outside work. Perhaps he had not looked hard enough. With Browne's death fresh in his mind, he dreaded what Santini had in store for Ben. All interest in his meal disappeared. He wanted to leave. Now.

Pescaro continued, quietly, patiently, remorselessly. 'Santini is often called the *Wraith* in our circles. He moves softly, smoothly and at times, invisibly. People overlook him because he is so ordinary, because he is small, because he seems meek and because he is humble. But let me assure you, he can be as tough and callous as the worst. He is all of those things and none of those things. He is what he wants to be for any particular purpose. He was my efficient destroyer for the Market Murders in the sixties, he blew up my opposition's amphetamine lab at Wantirna during the seventies and he has removed several troublesome painters and dockers. Most recently, some of the less savoury drug dealers in this town have been whacked by Nardo. All these things were done for me while you thought Nardo just prepared rosters and paid your staff. Like most people, he has a different life away from your firm. I'm telling you this as a friend Jack. Impress upon your beloved son not to do anything foolish, he only has to do what he's been asked. For the moment, Ben is very healthy, but things could change. You both need to be aware of that. Loyalty is mutual only so long as *you* continue to give it.'

Charles Trenet's dulcet rendition of *La Mer* suddenly became sickening. To Aldrittson, the very air he breathed felt like treacle. Even sitting, he felt unbalanced. He could only stare numbly at Pescaro. He had been exposed to a perversion of Santini he could never have imagined. He was seized by a compulsion to speak with Ben, to tell him to be very careful, to just ride along because, in the end, they could all still benefit.

'Jack,' continued Pescaro smiling kindly. 'I know you understand what I am saying. Ben is young and impulsive, he's a politician and believes himself invincible, untouchable. I know too that your wife Nancy does not enjoy the best of health and Ben should be mindful of the effects of bad news on her. *Comprende*? Now,would you like to order desert and coffee?' The mild enquiry was, to Jack, incongruous after the frightful insight he had just received about an employee he had trusted for years.

Aldrittson rose. His limbs were shaking with fear, rage and impotence. His tongue felt too large for his mouth as he mumbled, 'No Giuseppe, I will have a word to Ben.'

Pescaro smiled benignly. 'I'm sure you will Jack, I'm sure you will.'

Big Jack leaned against his car shaking. He had worked hard at staying on Pescaro's good side because he truly feared the alternative. Now he had learned, as casually as one might swat a fly, that Pescaro had considered removing him and Ben from the business. *His* business. He shuddered. Aldrittson considered himself a mean bastard but he had never *personally* harmed anyone. Poisoning the land, creeks, rivers and lakes for thirty years with deadly compounds was business, and business was about money. That the loads he ordered carried by Browne and others might be poisoning them was not his concern

He climbed into his BMW and punched Ben's number into his phone.

After three rings Ben answered, 'Hello Dad, what's up?'

'Can't talk about it on the phone Son, where are you? I'll come and see you.'

There was silence. 'I'm up in Sydney Dad, I won't be home till Sunday afternoon – late. You sound stressed, is Mum okay?'

'Yes, your mother is fine. But we have to talk. I'll come Sunday evening. What time do you get in?'

'I should be home about seven o'clock. Why the mystery? What's going on?'

'Santini and Pescaro. That's what's going on. You be bloody careful up there.'

'Righto Dad. See you Sunday evening.'

At 9:30 that evening, Little and Jamieson parked their nondescript rent-a-wreck fifty metres from Santini's home, comfortably blending into the streetscape. They had followed him from Brooklyn, watched him park in front of his house and go inside. Having reconnoitred during his absence, they knew there was no rear exit. They were confident Santini had settled in to watch Friday night football. After a quiet night, they packed it in at 5:00 a.m.

Colin Fox watched them come and go. He knew they were covering Santini and would report to Spencer Johnson. Anything important would be relayed to him by Johnson. At fifty-two, Fox, an ex-Special Air Services warrior was superbly fit. Slim, hard, tough and poised, he regularly worked out at Johnson's gym. He and Johnson were good mates going back years to a period when they both were in the UK and occasionally, when Johnson was overseas competing in veteran body-sculpting contests, Fox managed the gym.

Fox had trawled past Santini's home early Friday morning after being rung by Johnson. He had noticed the house opposite was for sale and vacant. He arranged an inspection at midday and at four o'clock that afternoon, quietly, illegally, let himself inside. He carried a sizeable airline bag with the things he needed, including food and water. The inspection revealed the partially furnished house had been on the market for eight months. Its wonky floors and cracked walls were such a disincentive that even inspections had dried up. It was a perfect base.

He too had watched Santini enter his home and saw Little and Jamieson drive by. Fox thought Santini had chosen well, it was a good secure location. A workman's cottage from the 1890s, it extended from one side of the narrow block to the other. In studying the house, Fox perceived his target to be a fussy bastard. Three steps led to a bull-nosed veranda mounted on shapely poles with elegant fretwork between them; ancient wisteria crawled through the fretwork. A doorway on the right suggested a main hall with all rooms off to one side while a common brick wall divided the house from its twin on the right.

Fox could see no evidence of telephone lines to the house and wondered if, like many people today, Santini used only a mobile.

That could be problematic. At 11:00 p.m. the lights went off and stillness descended. Fox settled into his chair, set his wrist alarm for 4:45, and relaxed. At 5:00 a.m., he saw Little and Jamieson quietly leave. He breakfasted on dried rations and water and waited. At 10:30 a.m. Santini emerged, got into his car and drove to Johnston Street where he turned towards the city.

Unhurried, Fox walked to his motor bike a few doors north of Santini's and rode after him. Santini was about a block ahead. Traffic was light, the day cool and sunny, a typical Melbourne autumn morning. Fox closed on Santini while keeping cars between them. Their destination appeared to be Carlton. Presently, Santini drove into the Wilson Car Park west of Lygon in Elgin Street. Fox followed, parking a level higher to watch him.

Santini made his way into Lygon Street. Drifting like a tourist, Fox followed, watching him pass in and out of Italian shops and restaurants where he openly received envelopes. In a few locations short, animated conversations occurred before an envelope was given. Fox understood the pattern and calculated that as Santini made his way along first one side of Lygon Street, then the other, he had relieved around eighteen shop keepers of an unknown sum of money. At DiMattina's, Santini stopped for coffee, cake and conversation. After about twenty-five minutes, he left and made his way back to the carpark.

Fox gave Santini two minutes then followed. He came out of the carpark, drove to Swanston Street and then down to the Queen Victoria Market. Fox didn't like this; too easy to lose Santini in the bustle and throng of the vibrant Saturday market. He moved to within one car of Santini as they drove through the barrier into the car park. There, his concerns were immediately allayed. The park was sluggish with long delays caused by people searching for spaces. Santini couldn't go anywhere fast. Fox peeled right and parked in a reserve for motor cycles. He could see Santini's car trapped in a squash of immovable vehicles. He removed his helmet, donned wrap around sunglasses and a peaked cap, took a shoulder bag from his pannier and slowly sauntered after Santini. From now on, surveillance would be easy. Suddenly, a glut of cars moved, and, like jig saw pieces, slotted into empty spaces around the market buildings. At a leisurely pace, Fox followed.

The little man was not difficult to shadow. He was dressed snappily in a tweedy-looking soft brown cap, light tan leather jacket and sharply creased brown woollen trousers, his crisp shirt was the deepest of browns. All around the market buzzed. People moved, vendors called, buskers played, children laughed and chattered while the aroma of sizzling sausages and onions, incense, soaps, coffee, cheese and fresh vegetables pervaded all. Making the odd purchase here and there, Fox watched Santini visit stalls, speak to owners and receive envelopes, until he arrived at the fish market. There, a terse exchange occurred with the vendor. Fox watched Santini pat the young man on the arm to calm him but instantly, the man turned ashen and leaned in towards Santini nodding vigorously. He reached beneath the counter and gave Santini an envelope. What intrigued Fox was Santini's disregard for the surrounding crowd.

Fox turned and almost collided with Penny Jamieson. *Shit! Where had she come from?* He hadn't noticed her before ... *Not good enough.* Jamieson barely gave him a glance, her focus was Santini. *Well, well,* thought Fox to himself, *full marks to you girl. You've obviously been on him all morning. And I thought you'd gone home!* He moved past her and looked over his shoulder. Recalling his movements, he realised that she *had* been there all morning, he had just not recognised her in DiMattina's.

He decided to call it quits. Walking back to his bike, he wondered how much and how often Santini milked the shop owners and stall holders. He figured Santini was taking hundreds, if not thousands, of dollars.

Chapter
ELEVEN

At 6:00 p.m. Ben Aldrittson landed at Tullamarine. He had been in Sydney to steal business from the New South Wales Government and enjoy a raunchy weekend. Jakob Kindler, Managing Director of Hart Lite, a sophisticated and fast growing solar energy company had seen to that. Aldrittson had, for some time, been trying to convince Kindler that moving to Melbourne would be more lucrative and less frustrating than endlessly skirmishing with the New South Wales Government. He told Kindler that because of federal reforms, taking his technology south would benefit Hart Lite. Aldrittson also boasted that since the Victorian and Federal Governments were Liberal, there was delicious irony in taking a prize from the New South Wales Labor state.

Aldrittson offered Kindler land, tax incentives, transport points and significant relocation benefits in return for continuous employment and steady growth. He believed Hart Lite would crack not only the Australian market, but the international scene too. State government trade support almost guaranteed that. Hart Lite had pioneered, and perfected, a radical new method for converting solar energy to electricity using a technique almost 150 per cent more efficient than any other comparable product. Kindler had pioneered a radically different conversion method which, like many things in nature, was simple. Moreover, his new methodology was inexpensive.

Given mounting public pressure to reduce fossil fuel emissions, hostility towards nuclear energy and rising ambivalence towards wind turbines, the efficiency, effectiveness and cost of the new, green, solar technology was appealing.

Aldrittson's true motivation for enticing Kindler to Victoria was quite different – he wanted a share of a potentially enormous global market. The two men agreed to stay in touch and when

Aldrittson obtained the go-ahead, Kindler would relocate.

Grant, the New South Wales Premier, needed only to provide tax relief to Kindler to forestall the hijacking of Hart Lite. Aldrittson thought Grant short sighted. But Grant was driven by voters bitter about huge tax benefits to the wind industry. Pointed questions flew thick and fast inside and outside Parliament about the amount of power the turbines could generate, their reliability, disruption to rural peace and their siting. Frequently these giant structures were established on the most picturesque areas of coastline or inland hills. Grant wanted no further backlash.

So Kindler had laid on wine, women and song in a debauched cruise along Sydney harbour commencing early Saturday evening and concluding around three o'clock Sunday afternoon. Kindler had agreed upon a one per cent sales royalty to Aldrittson one year after the company's establishment in Melbourne, an outcome that thrilled Aldrittson. He was equally pleased for having bedded five different women during the cruise and the last thing he wanted tonight was to talk about Santini. He had made his decision about that gent and didn't intend confiding in his father. All he wanted now was sleep.

Aldrittson parked beneath his units at the corner of Alexandra Avenue and Chapel Street, Prahran. Perched more or less on the edge of the Yarra, the complex provided magnificent views across the city, was central to Aldrittson's work place, gym and favourite night life. It was also in the middle of his electorate. As always, he got a buzz from the expansive views of the twelfth floor. He went straight to his phone and checked his messages. Spencer Johnson's hearty voice bellowed, 'Benny my boy, this is Spencer. I have positive news on your current project. I don't know what you've got in mind but be careful. I can help with resources if you need them. The fees will be the usual.' The import of Johnson's cryptic message was clear.

Aldrittson took his bags to the bedroom, unpacked and threw his washing in the laundry basket. His cleaner would deal with it tomorrow. He jumped into the shower and felt fatigue slide away as energy trickled back through his veins. He had scarcely dressed when the doorbell rang.

Jack Aldrittson stood at the door looking drawn and pallid.

'G'day Dad, come in. Are you okay? You don't look so flash.'

'Yeah … yeah, I'm good son, good.' He sounded distracted. 'What was your weekend in Sydney like?'

'Fine. Got laid, got paid and got made. You know what it's like. Had a bloody good time actually. Now, would you like beer, scotch or brandy?'

'Beer's fine, Son.'

Ben waved vaguely towards a large, comfortable armchair.

'Sit down while I get organised then we'll talk.' After handing his father a cold Heinekin, he settled himself with a Jameson's on ice. 'Your timing's impeccable Dad. I've only been home about twenty minutes. So … Santini and Pescaro have been cooking up a storm have they?'

Jack looked quizzically at his son. 'Yeah, that's about right. I had dinner with Pescaro last night and he frightened the living shit out of me. He as much as told me he had seriously considered removing you and me to take our business for himself. And, I've got to tell you, he has very little time for you – thinks you don't show enough respect He told me your aspirations outweigh your abilitiy. He wants Santini to teach you a lesson … well, he didn't quite go that far, but, I'm bloody certain that's what he meant. And that's another thing – that fucking Santini has always been *his* man from day-fucking-one. Bottom line is, he wants our scam legitimised before the election. I'm buggered if I know what's eating him, but I know, he's not kidding. He mentioned something about new pressures. Vague as shit. But, I don't much like the alternative. The little bastard even threatened to harm you and pointed out the effect that would have on your mother's health.'

Ben examined his father intently. He was a tough old bugger, not easily frightened, not known for giving up, ruthless when he wanted to be. They had had their differences, often volatile, particularly over politics but, by and large, they were mates. Like most men, they did not talk about their relationship, just got on with it. Ben now saw fear in his father's eyes and realised, for the first time, he was stronger than him. Until today, he had seen himself as his father's equal, now he believed he was better. He placed no weight on Pescaro's opinion of him.

Not that he under-rated Pescaro; one did not become a Mafia Don without considerable talent, albeit, malevolent talent. With his father directly connecting Santini to Pescaro he inferred that Santini was the latter's "Rottweiler". After his recent meeting with the man, he saw Santini as a cunning, ruthless, thug, a man to be watched.

In a harried tone, Jack continued. 'He told me things about Santini I would never have believed possible. He's killed people. Lotsa people. He's blown up places, extorted and heavied people most of his life, *including while working for me.* I never had a bloody clue. And I sure as hell didn't know Pescaro and Santini were an item. Sneaky bastards. I'm worried about Pescaro's threat that Santini will teach you a lesson. What do you think we should do?'

With a calm he did not quite possess, Ben Aldrittson attempted to soothe his father's fears.

'Dad, I think it's pretty straight forward. Last week Santini asked me to get a briefing proposal for our waste strategy ready for Meadows. I told him the scheme was unlikely to be passed this close to an election, but he wasn't interested. He wants the briefing I am to give Meadows by next Thursday.'

'Did he tell you it's for Pescaro?'

'No, although I wondered what the urgency was. And, like you, I didn't know those two bastards were on the same team. But look, it's nearly ready and by Thursday it will be. Don't worry. My difficulty will be getting Meadows to hear me on the bloody thing any time in the next six months. You know what election campaigns are like. Sometimes I think the "clever people" driving the party machine haven't got a fucking clue about what John and Betty Citizen want. Until election day, until a result, a lot of water passes beneath the campaign bridge that counts for very little. I know, I'm part of the process.'

'Your attitude astonishes me Ben. I've just told you Pescaro's considered bumping us off and you're as cool as ice. And what about Santini? You never even told me the little shit spoke to you, how come?' Jack's rapid fire questions betrayed his anxiety.

'Dad,' said Ben in a calm voice, 'when Santini met me last week he said *you* asked for the plan, not Pescaro. I did think it was odd at the time because you and I had already agreed not to proceed for another twelve to eighteen months. But,' he lied, 'with my election activity beginning and government work in Sydney, I saw no reason to ring you. He made your request sound very plausible. As for Pescaro, I don't know what he'll do. You've both been developing this plan for years, you know him better than I do. What I don't understand is this sudden rush for action. I can only do as I was asked. Everything will be ready on the due date and I'll do my best to get it before Meadows. However, as I told Santini, the timing is up to shit. Maybe if they'd asked for this twelve months ago things could be different, but, with the election soon, he's got Buckley's. I think Pescaro's pissing in the wind ... posturing. Unless there's an agenda we don't know about. If Pescaro wanted to do something to us, he would just do it, there wouldn't be any warning. The important thing is, we've learned Santini's not to be trusted. If I were you, I'd be going through his work. Check what he's been up to, get on top of it; see if he hasn't concealed things from you; re-familiarise yourself with what he does. Do it soon because now we know he's Pescaro's plant and he could have been doing anything.'

'You are so bloody right about that. The cunning little shit set me up with Pescaro and all these years let me think I'd done it. The prick must have been laughing his head off.' Although still unhappy, Jack was more settled and had regained some colour. 'You obviously have things under control. Maybe when Pescaro gets the plan he won't have too much to complain about. We'll have to wait and see what happens next. My impression the other night was we were both dead meat but it mightn't be so bad. In the meantime, I'm gunna have a bloody hard look at what that shit-wit Santini has been doing.'

'Good,' replied Ben, 'let's leave it at that. The bastards have put us on notice and we can play that game too. I've got no bloody intention of being fucked over by them.'

Chapter
TWELVE

Santini relaxed in front of TV. It was eight o'clock Sunday evening. He sipped the Jacob's Creek Cabernet Sauvignon opened for his meal earlier. Turning down the volume, he reflected on his day with Giuseppe Pescaro.

The old Don was charming company. They'd enjoyed a great tussle over a game of bocce on the rolling back lawn, an exquisite alfresco lunch, fine wine and even finer thick coffee. In truth, they had both enjoyed a day off together. Pescaro had raised business only once – Ben Aldrittson. Santini told him he had no reason to think his message to Ben had gone unheeded.

He settled deeper into his chair. There was no Mrs Santini. Sometimes he regretted that but he had chosen his course and there was no place in his cold, dark and often violent world for a wife and family. As he mused upon the notion of family, his mind wandered to Ben Aldrittson. In a strange way, he was family; he had known him since birth, seen him grow up, develop and harden into quite a tough nut.

He pondered his warning to Aldrittson a few days earlier and smiled at the reaction. It wasn't personal, just business. He had to be certain Aldrittson understood the plan must be provided when Pescaro wanted it. Santini thought of Ben as a pompous prick. He did however, acknowledge and respect Aldrittson's network of contacts. To be fair, it was primarily due to his extensive reach and manipulation that much of their black waste concept had come so far.

His own actions were meant to show Aldrittson promise without actual harm, and without, he hoped, generating too much fear. Pescaro would be taking a similar line with Aldrittson senior.

He relaxed, sipped more wine and idly wondered. What if he

had pissed Ben off? Would he retaliate or just meekly comply? He recalled an incident ten years earlier. Pescaro had become enmeshed in a short but vicious struggle for control of a protection racket in the Sunraysia District of northwest Victoria.

Leonardo Falcone, a Griffith *capo* working for the Sydney Mob, considered Pescaro's interest intrusive. To the contrary, Pescaro had strictly confined his activity to Victoria, an arrangement agreed at a Mafia "sit down" in the 1940s. Then, the bosses thought Australia's population too small and the country too large to operate on anything other than state boundaries. It was agreed there would be only one Don per state and no cross-border encroachment. For this reason, there was no *capo di tutti capi*, or boss of bosses. Occasionally, at border towns, as people moved around, lines blurred, practices shifted and matters sometimes became a little tense. Overall, the original agreement held well. That sit down had also decreed that anyone flouting the arrangement would taste traditional justice.

Falcone commenced expanding the territory of his Don, Lindoro Riina. At the same time, he was skimming off the top by quietly entering Sunraysia and breaching the long standing agreement on borders. Santini investigated and after talking to several growers, decided Falcone should be told to quit while he was ahead. That was a mistake of underestimation on his part.

On his way to Griffith, Santini was run off the road by a truck. His car had barely stopped rolling when bullets whacked into the upturned body. He had crawled from the back window and hidden behind a tree. Seconds later the petrol tank exploded. His attackers had been slack and failed to check whether he was dead or alive, they merely assumed he had been incinerated.

After hitching a lift to Hay, Santini spent a week under the radar nursing his scrapes. He had reviewed his options and considered potential actions that could be taken by Falcone. Falcone's most likely choice would be to go to Mildura and eliminate Pescaro's snitch.

Santini took a bus to Mildura, hired a car in Falcone's name and drove to Nichol's Point. Nothing seemed amiss at the grower's home. He decided to return each nightfall for the next week.

At nine o'clock on the fourth evening, a black Celica pulled up at the house; Falcone and one of his men stepped from the car. Santini was concealed by a thick Oleander bush at the corner of the front veranda. Falcone strode to the front door while his thug snuck around the back. Santini followed him. While Falcone talked to the grower, Vincenzo Rizzi, his thug entered the house.

Santini drew his knife and silently crept after him. A wide, darkened veranda stretched across the back of the house providing access to a central passage inside. Santini heard angry voices at the front of the house. The fearful cries of a woman joined in. Falcone's man was in the passageway moving quietly through the gloom to the front. As Santini eased the flywire door open and stepped inside, the latch snapped audibly. Tense with concentration, the man whirled, gun in hand then fell to the floor with a grunt as Santini's heavy knife ploughed into his chest. Blood sprayed the polished floor. His hand twitched and the gun fired aimlessly into the wall. In the following silence, Santini moved quickly. He grabbed the gun from the quivering hand and bounded into the lounge room. Falcone held Rizzi's wife in front of him, an arm tightly around her throat, a revolver pointed steadily at Rizzi's head – all of them frozen near the front door. Santini used the oldest trick of all. Standing stock still, arms by his side, the gun concealed behind his leg he said in a low voice, 'Cut it out Falcone, you're finished.'

Falcone snarled, 'Not yet Santini, I've got a little surprise in store for you.'

Santini nodded and said, 'Me too. Shoot him Ludo.' Rizzi's wife fainted. Hampered by the woman's dead weight, Falcone spun in the direction of Santini's nod. Smoothly, Santini raised his arm and shot Falcone in the side of his head. Rizzi too collapsed to the floor.

Constructive experience mused Santini – never underestimate an adversary. He considered Aldrittson weak but recognised his gutsy performances in Parliament. Perhaps weak was not quite the term for Aldrittson, Santini reflected, the stakes were high and Aldrittson had much to lose. He reconsidered his opinion and concluded that familiarity and, yes, even a touch of arrogance may have caused him to underestimate Ben Aldrittson. *Okay. What could Aldrittson do? He liked power, had contacts, unlimited wealth and influence, and,* thought Santini, *while he does confront people, he's bloody sneaky about it. Aldrittson had only two choices: comply or retaliate.* The more he thought about Aldrittson, the more he leaned towards his own underestimation of the man. He took a large gulp of wine and reached for the phone.

'*Pronto?*' The deep voice spoke softly.

'Don Pescaro, I've been thinking about my recent meeting with Ben Aldrittson. I've no grounds for alarm, but you know I am careful. I think we should take precautions.'

Santini listened to Pescaro's thoughtful silence.

'Anything else Nardo?'

'No Giuseppe, that's all.'

'I'll deal with it Nardo, *ciao.*'

In the empty house across the road, Fox listened to the cryptic conversation through a pair of tiny speech activated microphones hidden at Santini's front window. Having established that Santini and Pescaro were together for the day, he had taken a closer look at Santini's house. In a cap and Red Cross vest, Fox doorknocked both sides of the street canvassing for donations. He grinned and felt good at the thought of someone in the Melbourne Red Cross office opening an envelope with $132 and a "good luck" card inside.

Knowing Santini was not at home, Fox had planted his bugs under the ploy of creating sufficient noise to wake the dead or, in this case, bring Santini to the door. Santini's neighbour emerged to check out the fuss. Fox explained who he was then left after receiving a $5 donation from the man. His success was marked by this captured conversation.

Fox dialled Spencer Johnson's hotline.

'Yes.'

'Fox. Santini's radar just kicked in. Far as I can tell there is nothing either we, or Aldrittson, have done to trigger his warning bells. He just asked Pescaro to take precautions in regard to Ben Aldrittson.' Fox spoke succinctly.

'Thanks mate. I might get Little and Jamieson back on the job. Perhaps split them and have one watch your back. I'm not yet sure just what Aldrittson has planned, but he must be untouchable. And, we can't afford to underestimate Pescaro, he's got big resources. Anything else?'

'No, but listen, I don't need those two. Last time they were here they stood out like country dunnies. If Santini is tuned in, he won't miss them.'

'Righto ate, I'll leave it to you.'

Fox settled back in his camp chair. His bug revealed that Santini was now watching the Sunday night movie. At 10:45 p.m., Santini's light went out. Fox settled himself for sleep and set his watch for 4:30 a.m.; he wouldn't need it, just a precaution. He didn't want to miss Santini leaving for work.

Chapter
THIRTEEN

At 9:45 a.m. Monday, June 1, Andy Drummond parked at AWD in Brooklyn. A bright yellow sign pointed the way from the car park to the Reception Office. Carrying a copy of the employment section from *The Age* on Saturday, he walked to reception. Entering, he found himself in a foyer with several comfortable seats and a large counter running across its width. A sign on the counter declared: *Ring for Assistance*. Drummond pressed the buzzer and waited.

A door behind the counter opened and a woman in her fifties appeared.

'Good morning. Can I help you?' She was neatly dressed, hair in a bun and bespectacled, her face was motherly, her manner friendly.

'Yes,' Drummond smiled. 'I've come about the ad. for a tanker driver.' He brandished the paper.

'Do you have an appointment?'

'Well no, I assumed from the way the ad. reads it was just a case of coming in.'

'That should be alright dear. Mr Santini's put mornings aside all week and has just finished with someone. He shouldn't be long. Help yourself to coffee or tea. What's your name?'

'Thanks,' Drummond smiled. 'Andy Drummond.'

She nodded and disappeared through the door.

Drummond had given a lot of thought to this meeting and while he didn't know Santini, or his role in the company, he had decided to trust no one. Intuitively he also felt it would not be helpful to mention the location of his farm or the truck fire but remained uncertain about that. He was still mulling this over when the receptionist reappeared and beckoned him.

'Mr Santini will see you now dear.'

'Right thanks. Anything I should know about Mr Santini that will help present my best side?'

She smiled gently. 'You'll find him very quiet and pleasant. He's a good listener and very fair. Just tell him why you want the job and what your qualifications are. I'm sure you'll be alright.'

She led him down a corridor. To the right, behind a glass half-wall, lay an open office in which twenty or so people worked. The place looked professional, well organised and superbly equipped.

The woman paused before a door near the end of the corridor, knocked briefly then ushered Drummond into the office. 'Mr Santini, this is Andy Drummond, he has come for a job interview in response to Saturday's advertisement.'

Drummond saw a smallish man in his mid to late fifties rise from behind a well polished wooden desk. He was neatly and fashionably dressed and peered at Drummond with shrewd, unwavering, deep brown eyes. Drummond's impression was that Santini appeared coiled, like a spring – full of latent energy.

Stepping away from the desk Santini offered his hand. Drummond noted it was hard and dry and the grip strong.

'Take a seat please Andy.' He spoke quietly in measured tones and gestured to the chair in front of his desk. 'What made you apply for this job with Aldrittson's?'

'I've got a few shares in the firm, so I know that financially it's a good company. And recently, I read an article in the *Financial Review* that was pretty positive about the management here, you know, caring, good pay, bonuses and all that. Apart from that, I've met some of your drivers over time and they spoke well of the place. Lastly, I made some enquiries and found that jobs for drivers here are few and far between. That says a lot about the joint.'

Santini had not taken his eyes from Drummond's face. He listened impassively. 'So you've done your homework then. What qualifications do you have?'

'Four wheel driving, light commercial trucks, heavy vehicles and articulated vehicles. I can handle bull dozers and I'm a qualified fork lift driver. I spent a long time in the army and got my qualifications there. I brought copies if you want to see them.'

Santini waved his hand dismissively. 'Not yet. I'm interested in why you want to come and work for Aldrittson's. You haven't told me that yet. Where do you work now? Why do you want to leave that for here?'

Santini was no one's fool – he had gone for the jugular. Behind the impassive face Drummond saw watchfulness and caution. Santini and bullshit were mutually exclusive. He decided to tell part of the truth. 'My wife Sue died of ovarian cancer three years ago. Since then I've been lost.' Santini's caution prompted Andy to test the waters. He continued. 'I've got a small property at Heathcote which we started together about eight years ago but, since her death, I can't seem to settle or stop thinking about her. Being a driver would take me all over the place, put me in touch with lots of different people, keep me busy and help reduce some of my thinking time.'

With the exception of wanting to be a driver, all of what he had said was true. He didn't add that he and Sue had received a bumper start from winning a half share in a seven million dollar lottery first prize six years earlier. Back then, he still had a year of his term to serve in the army and Sue was teaching. They were happy and satisfied with what they did and saw no reason for Drummond to finish his career prematurely. They invested wisely and began planning for life outside the army.

At the mention of Heathcote, Santini's eyes hooded slightly. Drummond knew then exactly how to proceed. He continued, 'As a matter of fact, I went to a truck fire near my place recently. I don't know whose truck it was and the local coppers don't know much either. It provided a bit of excitement for a couple of days. Yeah, strange it was. Seemed to be no reason for the fire. Driver got incinerated … charred to a twist. Horrible! As far as I know, the coppers still haven't identified the truck owner or the driver. Hell of a way to die.'

'Yes, it sounds terrible,' said Santini smoothly. 'I suppose it's one of the hazards of long distance driving. Now, perhaps I could see your driving authorities.'

Drummond passed his certificates to Santini and watched as he checked them carefully.

Santini looked up, a mild expression on his face. 'Mr Drummond, I'm sorry, we may have wasted your time. You have very good credentials but I'd like to see a few more people yet. Thank you for coming in. I'll be in touch.' Although obviously lying, Santini was courteous yet cool. He remained seated and didn't offer to shake hands again. 'I'll have Mary show you out.' Hardly had he finished speaking when she reappeared, a look of surprise on her face.

'Yes Mr Santini?'

'Mary, show Mr Drummond the way out please.'

Her eyebrows rose slightly as she said, 'Of course, come this way Andy.' She closed the door and escorted Drummond back to the foyer. 'Well, that was quick. He's been taking thirty to forty minutes. Did you say something wrong?'

He grinned at the suggestion. 'I don't think so Mary. Perhaps I didn't have the qualifications he was looking for. By the way, has the job been filled yet?'

'No, not yet. Two drivers have been interviewed this morning and there's another scheduled for 11 a.m.' She was silent for a moment then continued, 'the reason I asked if you'd said something wrong is that you were in and out so fast. That was unusual. He's a hard man to upset.'

'No, I can't think of a thing I said wrong. I'll just have to look elsewhere. Thanks Mary, nice meeting you.'

At 5:00 p.m. Drummond rang Maud and told him of his meeting with Santini. The response was immediate and fiery.

'Andy, you are pissing me off! I told you not to get up to mischief and you go on the bloody offensive. If the shit hits the fan it's my neck on the friggin' chopping block.' He sounded truly offended.

'Don't worry, it's okay. I promise you Tony – no damage done. Santini wanted me out of there quick smart and I am keeping you informed. It's just that there are all these bloody questions about this fire and no answers. I simply wanted to see if I could push a couple of buttons to provoke a response. I got one. He didn't want to know me.'

Tony calmed down. 'Alright, alright. Do you think Santini is involved in what ever's going on?' He sounded doubtful.

'I am. Well, I think so Tony.' He almost sounded confident. 'As soon as I said I was from Heathcote the shutters fell. He remained polite and courteous but the room temperature dropped ten degrees. He just seemed to withdraw and suddenly, the interview was over. Then, ever so nicely, he threw me out. I won't be hearing from him again.'

Maud accepted that. 'Okay mate. But so far, Aldrittson's have been nothing but helpful. Once they established it was their truck and their man, they bent over backwards to help. I'd say they want this cleared up as much as we do. I was told they arranged the funeral and have already handsomely compensated the driver's widow and family.'

'Sorry to be cynical Tony, but that sounds like a pay-off to me. I think their actions are designed to throw us off the scent.' Drummond sounded thoughtful. 'I mean, usually, people hiding things are obstructive or defensive and want to make life difficult. If Aldrittson's are using distraction as reverse psychology they're probably hoping you'll quickly disappear without looking too deeply.'

Maud pondered the idea. 'I've mainly been dealing with the boss, Jack Aldrittson. I may have spoken to this Santini bloke a couple of times, can't be sure. He was quiet and polite. He certainly didn't cause any trouble or create the impression of being anxious. But I have to say, when Aldrittson told me about the payout to Browne's wife, $300,000 and he's not even cold yet, I did wonder.'

'You just reminded me,' said Drummond, 'I told Santini the police didn't know who the driver was or where the truck came from. He never said a word to correct me. If they have nothing to hide you'd think he would have said something. Look, I've got no real reason for saying this but my impression is that Santini knows something. I could be wrong, but gut instinct tells me differently. Where does he live?'

'Why? Have you got rocks in your bloody head or something?' Maud was annoyed again. 'Why do you want to know?'

'Calm down, I'm not stupid. I just thought I could drive by to see what sort of place he has and how he's set up. Call it intelligence. I won't go snooping around his house or anything like that and I *will* keep you posted.'

'Okay, I've got a couple of favours to call in. I'll see what I can find out. I can't say when I'll get back to you I'm on call tonight; one of the lads here is sick and I'm covering the late shift.'

Drummond smiled to himself as he hung up, confident he would be checking on Santini later. Tony Maud was a good copper and would come up with the address.

Chapter
FOURTEEN

As soon as Mary Edwards closed the door, Santini lifted the phone.

'*Pronto*,' said Pescaro.

'Don Pescaro, I've just had a man here wanting Browne's job as driver. Said he was Andy Drummond from Heathcote. He seems to know all about the truck fire. Said he was ex-army but he gives me a bad feeling. He looks and smells like a copper. Oh, and on that, how's the dossier on the local copper going?'

'Slowly Nardo, but building.' Pescaro's tone was thoughtful.

'I think it would be a good idea to have our man check out this Drummond,' suggested Santini.

'I agree,' Pescaro responded, 'Leave it to me.'

Pescaro was not unduly worried by this turn of events, it was to be expected, but he was annoyed. He had pushed Jack Aldrittson and through him, Ben. Jack's reaction at their recent dinner had surprised him.

Over the years he had seen plenty of Jack's meanness and toughness. By his standard they were not the high tensile qualities born of personal combat or loss. He had thought Aldrittson was tougher. He was a bully who paid others to do his dirty work and all his life he had been insulated by money. First Old Tom's and then his own. *Yes, he was a spoilt bully with no real guts.*

Ben Aldrittson though was different. After observing him in public and private life, Pescaro concluded he was resilient, engaged his enemies directly and didn't mind occasional losses for the strategic advantage of some grander plan. He was highly intelligent and rat cunning. Despite attributes which, in most crooks would be regarded as assets, Pescaro had little respect for the younger Aldrittson. He grudgingly conceded however that Ben was probably more formidable than his father. With Santini's intuition about Ben on high alert, it was important to keep pressure on Jack to bring the younger man to heel. Timing was everything and what Pescaro wanted now was compliance without bloodshed.

He wondered if Drummond and Ben Aldrittson were somehow connected. After his conversation with Nardo, it wouldn't surprise him to find that Drummond's visit was arranged by the politician. Ben would *want* to retaliate that was a given. It may well have been this mood in Ben that Nardo had tuned into.

He rang a number at Tooborac. A voice answered faintly, barely audible over the noise of machinery.

'Mario, this is Don Pescaro. I want to talk to you.' Pescaro heard the machinery begin to fade.

'Sorry Don Pescaro. I'm in the yard cutting wood. Go ahead.' Mario Embone was attentive. He was one of Pescaro's legion. Arriving in Australia thirty-five years before, he had established himself as a wood cutter at Tooborac in Central Victoria. He collected from the Heathcote State Forest and farmers who wanted fallen trees removed. Known throughout the district, he was a reliable and industrious man with a tight mouth. People in the area liked him.

'Mario, what's that copper Maud up to?' Embone's task had been to provide reports on local activity since the truck fire.

'Nothing new Don Pescaro. I've talked to 'im a few times at Gaffney's Bakery. 'E likes nattering with da counter ladies. 'E's not let anything slip about da fire we don't know already.'

'Do you know a man called Andy Drummond?' queried Pescaro.

'Sure, 'e's gotta small farm near da truck fire. I wouldda like his big, fat ironbarks.'

'Does he know Maud?'

'Don Pescaro, everybody knows Maud. Apart from being da local copper, 'e does stuff with kids – you know, cricket, football, tennis and bike safety – 'e sees da schools regular. 'E's on da

Progress Association and pushed for the Bendigo Bank 'ere. 'E's as big as a house and good with trouble – thinks before 'e acts. A betta question is: who doesn't know Tony Maud around 'ere?'

Pescaro's lip curled at Embone's description of the country cop. He didn't sound much of a threat. Nevertheless ... better to take nothing for granted.

'Is he particularly friendly with Drummond, Mario? Do you know that?'

'No Don Pescaro, I don't. Is important?'

'Mario, if I ask a question the answer is always important.' His tone cut like a cleaver. 'Ring me when you have something concrete.'

Monday afternoon the Lower House was noisy and fractious. Ben Aldrittson was presenting Jakob Kindler's Hart Lite concept. The Member for Melbourne Ports, Simon Candy, was giving Aldrittson a hard time. Candy, still fuming over the government's refusal to use the Victorian firm, Scintilla, for a major project constantly interjected.

'Mr Speaker,' roared Aldrittson, straining above the din. 'The Honourable Member is obviously deaf. I *agree* with the need to monitor the environment. I *agree* with the urgency to tackle green house effects and reduce carbon emissions. That is *why* we must take a serious look at this solar energy scheme. My colleague Mr Baker, Minister for Environment, shares my view. We have a golden opportunity to lead the nation *and* develop a huge global export market using Australian know how and Victorian labour. Furthermore, we could use this opportunity to establish a carbon trading scheme.'

'Who will you shaft this time Aldrittson?' interjected Candy. 'You've always got an angle. You're as slippery as the Premier's election date.' The Opposition howled with derision and the speaker thumped his gavel.

Unflustered, Aldrittson resumed. 'I seek your indulgence Mr Speaker because I would like to touch on the fossil fuel industry a moment. The Australian Greenhouse Office reported recently that climate change in Australia is unequivocal. Predictions are for a hotter climate, more droughts, more frequent and violent storms, agricultural losses and serious agricultural damage. We all know, on both sides of this House, of the cosy and long standing relationship between the Federal Government and the fossil fuel and mining industries. Recently, through the media, we've also learned of secret meetings between representatives of those industries and members of various federal governments. These "arrangements" have substantially shaped the power industry and its practices today. And we, at state level, *on both sides* of this House, are no less blameless. For the greater good, we *all* must change. We must continue reducing green house emissions by all means available. To that extent, the Victorian Government is firstly going to limit, then phase out over the next three years, all State benefits to the coal industry.'

Sounds of disbelief arose from the Opposition benches.

'We will then transfer those benefits to a range of projects like the Hart Lite program and show leadership in an arena the Federal Government continues to walk away from. We will reduce reliance on fossil fuel in this State by encouraging new forms of power generation, sun, wind, sea and geo-thermal, all non-nuclear. Additionally, we will work harder to find an effective method of cleaning fossil fuel emissions because we have to minimise the damage caused by residual coal fired power plants. We have to encourage the major coal fired energy producers to invest, to innovate, to explore and to develop in these new directions as well. As you perceive Mr Speaker, I am presenting two key strategies here; a new generation of solar engineering unique to this country and a new energy philosophy and policy for Victoria. The new solar technology can be retrofitted to any building, is about 150 per cent more effective than any other form of solar power now available and is a quarter the price of solar units currently on sale. Once the new factory is underway in Victoria, unit costs will reduce even further. I therefore give notice, Mr Speaker, of the Government's intention to acquire the Camp Road Reserve, 800 metres west of the Hume Freeway to build a new industrial complex devoted to the manufacture of these solar energy units.'

With cries of 'hear hear' ringing in his ears, Aldrittson sat down smiling. He had run his speech by the Premier before delivery and had his blessing. They had all had a gutful of the various federal/state conflicts, energy and climate change being just one of them. Moreover, from the subdued Opposition, Aldrittson knew he had them thinking.

Only Candy shouted, 'You don't fool me Aldrittson! You've got as much depth as a pane of glass. This is merely teflon politics and a pathetic attempt at electioneering.'

Unerringly, but unknowingly, Simon Candy was right on the money. Aldrittson's environmental commitment *was* phoney. Although willing to be a conduit for environmental matters, his real target was the sales potential of Kindler's product, a target he believed would deliver him millions of dollars. It was this possibility that cloaked his speech with a veneer of sincerity.

Chapter
FIFTEEN

At 9:15 p.m., Tony Maud rang Drummond, he was brisk and business-like. 'I've got that address Andy but I can't talk. I've got a prang to get to – bloody kangaroos! 205A Nicholson Street, Collingwood is the one you want. Call me in the morning and tell me what you found.' He hung up.

Drummond didn't write the address down, it was engraved in his mind. He showered and was in bed by 9:30, his mental alarm set for 1:00 a.m.

At 9:45 p.m., Colin Fox entered the house opposite Santini. Hopefully, it would be his last visit – Santini's elimination had been requested. He stood inside the front door listening – all quiet. He retrieved the recorder which kept him abreast of Santini's doings. Tonight he was interested in the previous hour.

Commencing the playback he heard the last minutes of a phone call between Pescaro and Santini. He rewound the reel. Santini was saying, 'Have you got anything yet on Drummond?'

'No, but Mario is working on it.' Conversation from Pescaro's end petered out. Santini often moved around when using his mobile and sometimes that caused signal problems.

'Okay,' Santini had said, 'but I tell you, this Drummond bastard feels like a copper to me. I know he said he was ex-army and his driving quals. seemed to be from the army, but I'm not convinced.'

Although this was news to Fox, the information was irrelevant. He had decided Santini's fate. The event would be spectacular and although he would do his best to minimise collateral damage, he couldn't guarantee it. The insurance companies would be shitty, but hell, their business was risk. Scrupulously, he began checking and cleaning the house he had made his base. By 11:30 p.m. he was satisfied that all traces of his presence were gone, including, after a swift dash across the street, the bugs at Santini's house.

At 1:00 a.m. heavy rain began to flail the front window. Fox smiled grimly. *That'll keep the bastards inside*, he thought. Half an hour later, dressed in black from head to foot, he stood on the step of the vacant house, eyes adjusting to the night. It was still raining and the wind gusted boisterously. A small pouch was strapped to his waist and his black airline bag carried the items he had brought to the house. He surveyed the street once more – empty.

Santini's home was dark. Apart from the wind and rain, the neighbourhood was silent. He locked the door and moved to the gate – a shadow. He hooked the airline bag on the gatepost – inside the fence, out of sight but accessible.

Fluidly he crossed the road and lay prone beneath Santini's car – invisible. From his belt pouch he took a small powerful magnet and remote controlled explosive device. It would simply and elegantly remove the wheel from the car. He placed the magnet on the backing plate of the right front disk brake. The exercise had taken less than ten seconds. He was about to leave when a set of headlights glistened on the wet road. He closed his eyes and waited for the car to pass.

Taking in as much detail as possible, Drummond slowed the hired van as he passed Santini's home just after 1:30 a.m. He couldn't stop and didn't want to be seen moving too slowly. About sixty metres south of Santini's, he parked at the eastern kerb. Even though the street was deserted, he opened and closed the driver's door for effect then scrambled into the back of the van without stepping outside.

From the rear window, he surveyed the street and Santini's home. A white Magna was parked out front and he wondered if it was Santini's. He lifted his night vision glasses. There was nothing outstanding about the house or the car both looked well cared for. He noted the registration number for Tony, just in case. Rain began to bucket down. Inside the van, Drummond had the feeling of being trapped inside a kettle drum. He cursed as the cold window misted from his breath and lowered his glasses to clean it.

Fox watched the van pass and the driver's fancy little manoeuvre with the door. *Ah huh,* he thought, *someone else has joined the picnic.* He lay quietly. Rain coursed off the road crown and streamed into the gutters. Although saturated, Fox was unmoved by it. Patiently he waited. The rain continued, whipped by the unruly wind into misty spectres. Time to go. Ignoring the van, he slid from beneath the car, ran across the road, collected his bag and loped off towards Johnston Street.

To his surprise, Drummond saw a black shadow slip from under Santini's car, stand, then glide to the opposite side of the street. He threw his glasses up in time to see a man in black carrying a shoulder bag jog towards Johnston Street. He swore loudly. The rain and parked cars obscured his vision. It had all happened so quickly and at just the wrong moment!

He sensed that what he had seen was sinister. He decided to follow the man but ring Maud first. He punched the number into his mobile and got the message bank. Leaving a brief message he drove after the man.

At Stafford Street, Fox turned right as the road curved north to meet Johnston Street. He headed towards a gated factory lane to his parked motor bike. He jogged into the lane, pulled his leathers from a pannier bag and slipped them over his wet body suit. Zipped up tight he would achieve a wet suit effect and regain some body warmth.

Fox waited under an awning for fifteen minutes. He didn't know who had been watching Santini but he would tell Spencer about it later. As he anticipated, the Hertz van drove slowly past the lane entrance. He decided to stay, reasoning that if the driver had seen the lane, he would probably return to investigate. He moved into the rain behind a large industrial waste bin opposite his bike and hung his bag on its hinge. Five minutes later, the small van crept into the alley, illuminating the end of the *cul de sac* created by a large, spiked factory gate. Fox stepped onto the ridge seam between the bottom and side of the bin and gripped the hinge firmly. Anyone looking under the bin would not see his feet.

Drummond was wary of his location, a closed factory lane. He thought the big black bike could be a get-away vehicle. On the other hand, parked under the awning with a helmet strapped to the seat, it might simply belong to some factory hand out for the night. He wanted its number and to know if it had been recently used. He got out of the van and checked. Rain pinged off the cowling and petrol tank; the motor was stone cold. Obviously it had been there for some time. He had no idea where the man on foot had gone or even if he was connected to the bike – he had simply vanished near Johnston Street. He flicked his torch beam over the bin on the other side of the lane then ducked down to look under its wheeled base. Nothing. He returned to his van with the number QR 742 fixed in his mind. Slowly, he reversed down the lane and drove home.

Fox waited another fifteen minutes, confident his tracker would not return but careful anyway. He thought about Santini's earlier comment to Pescaro: 'Looked like a copper but said he was ex-army.' Whoever he was had been prepared, all blacked up and armed with a collapsible baton. Fox thought he moved well and looked fit. He grinned broadly in the dark. He had seen how tough the MPs could be in his early days in Queensland. He didn't feel threatened by his pursuer, he had always had the upper hand – surprise. If nothing else, Fox never doubted his ability in combat

– ever! He was resourceful, skilled and deadly.

It was 2:30 a.m. and Fox was not yet done. He rode into Lygon Street, Carlton and found himself an all night café. Ravenous, he ordered spaghetti bolognese and super hot coffee. His wet leathers were uncomfortable but he could put up with it. As he ate his meal, he thought about the task ahead. In watching Santini he had discovered he was a man of habit and today, those habits would cost him his life.

Santini would leave home shortly before 5:30 a.m. and travel the same route to arrive at work around 6:00 a.m. Fox planned to pick him up in Flinders Street. After his meal and another coffee, Fox left the café at 5:30.a.m. At Flinders Street he waited at the kerb between Elizabeth and Queen Streets. The rain had diminished to light showers, roads were still slippery and the wind had strengthened. These conditions would reduce speed limits on the Westgate Bridge, an irritation to Fox. Nevertheless, he had a day to spare so if today did not work, tomorrow had to.

Santini's Magna cruised past on the way to Westgate Bridge. Fox eased into the traffic. As usual, it was medium to heavy with a lot of trucks on the go.

Entering the bridge approach, Fox positioned himself in the lane closest to its western edge. The bridge's advisory speed sign warned that travel was limited to sixty kilometres per hour. But, as often happened, many transports ignored the warning and hurtled along ten to fifteen kilometres above the limit, their tyres spinning dancing ropes of mist. Ever cautious, Santini took the middle lane, doggedly sitting on sixty while others passed. Fox was three vehicles behind Santini – about thirty metres away – in the lane immediately on his left. Watching his rear view mirror closely, Fox saw what he wanted: a heavily laden 'B' double transport speeding along the lane to Santini's right. As Santini neared the crest of the bridge, the 'B' double began to overtake him. Fox allowed the truck cabin to pass the front of Santini's car then hit the detonating switch taped to his handle bar.

The Magna dropped heavily on its right front side as the wheel blew off, spearing the stub axle and wishbone into the bridge deck. The forward motion of the car continued, causing it to veer right, then pivot in a lazy clockwise circle on the glassy surface. The rear of Santini's car slewed under the second trailer of the 'B' double between the fore and aft bogies. The Magna was dragged forward under the trailer amid a shower of sparks and rending metal. The rear bogey of the truck rode up and over the car, crushing the cabin flat, the windscreen exploding like diamonds flung into the sky. Parts of the car disintegrated and flew across the road.

Having pulverized the Magna, the driver of the rig was fighting to regain control and slowly, began to brake and resume command. Unfortunately for Santini, the 'B' double was followed by an empty cement truck whose driver had also ignored the speed limit. Its broad, deep, bull-bar pushed the Magna straight ahead and into the rear end of the rapidly slowing 'B' double. Sparks, squealing metal and rubber rent the air as pieces of Santini's car were chewed up by the second impact. Then, with an awesome crunch, the Magna was crushed into the rear end of the 'B' double as surely as if it had been placed in a vice.

Fox's mind recorded the action in slow motion while, in real time, he fought to maintain equilibrium on his motor bike. Cars and trucks all around him had begun braking and skidding as soon as the Magna lost control. The wet conditions and speed caused many vehicles to skate across the road and collide with one another while Santini's car ruptured into chunks and peppered the carriageway. Sound from sliding, slewing, slamming vehicles tortured the air. And through the crunches and crashes, Fox gunned his bike and shot down the bridge and away.

Back up on the bridge deck, the growing peak hour traffic convulsed as cars and trucks began to slow, then stop, trapped by the enormous spaghetti-like entanglement at the top of the bridge.

Fox got home tired after his night's work. He gave Johnson a brief account of the previous twelve hours and went to bed. At 7:00 a.m., Johnson rang Ben Aldrittson and told him to watch the morning news program. At 8:00 a.m., Jack Aldrittson rang Ben to say that, most unusually, Santini had not arrived for work and was not answering his mobile. He was aware that the mother of all pile-ups had occurred on the Westgate Bridge and could Ben use his connections to find out whether Santini had been involved in the bridge collision?

Chapter
SIXTEEN

The day after his address to the House about Hart Lite, Ben Aldrittson was in the office of Lance Baker, Minister for Environment. They were discussing Kindler's Project. Baker, although supportive, was not interested in helping to fund it. A short, nuggetty, pugnacious man of abundant energy with an inflated opinion of himself, he was a hardworking, earnest politician. Married to a shy but wealthy woman from an old Melbourne family, he had two small daughters and lived among the "smart set" of Brighton. Proudly, Baker claimed a direct lineal connection to Major George Druitt, Chief Engineer of the Colonial Establishment of New South Wales during Governor Macquarie's time. As a Government Minister he saw himself as an extension of Druitt and his good works. And right now, Baker was feisty. Aldrittson, contrary to what he had told Kindler, wanted Baker to supply *all* the infrastructure budget for Hart Lite. The two men were in conflict over the impasse.

'Listen Ben,' Baker growled, 'I've got a lot of things on the go right now and I haven't got extra funds for your schemes. Get used to it!' Aldrittson remained placid.

'You don't think you're being short sighted do you Lance? I mean, with the election coming up, your support for this will be seen as extremely positive. It is, after all, as much a project for the environment as it is for business and trade.'

'For Christ's sake, I don't need a bloody lecture from you on my own portfolio, I *know* it's a good project. It's because of the bloody election there aren't spare funds,' he barked. Baker paced his office. 'I've got investigators working under the radar with a New South Wales Environment Services team looking at that shocking toxic dump near Walwa. We believe Walwa, and other places, have been used for this kind of dumping before. New South Wales have identified at least six locations. Piece by piece we're building a shadowy pattern of toxic dumping along the east coast. Not much to go on, whispers here and there, the odd sighting or two. I want to announce something positive about it during the election. If you want more money, go screw it out of the Treasurer!'

Aldrittson, only recently aware of Baker's covert enquiry, wanted it stopped. To achieve this he had decided to use information that would, if brought to public notice, permanently disable Baker.

'Before you make a final decision Lance, you should know I talked to a reporter friend of mine the other day about matters of interest to you. Seems she's been working on an undercover story too – about paedophiles. She's got solid information that a prominent Victorian politician is involved in a nasty little paedophile ring, right here in Melbourne.'

Baker stopped pacing, straightened and turned to glare at Aldrittson. 'What are you implying, you slimy little shit?' He was bristling with hostility, a biting edge to his voice.

Aldrittson continued, unruffled. 'Yes, it seems this politician uses a non-de-plume which is not very original, or careful. Calls himself "The Major". Can you imagine it? Seems he's the main procurer of boys and girls used by this sick group.'

If Baker was intimidated, he didn't show it. 'Is there a point to this? If not, get out of my office!' He scowled savagely.

'Well the point is this. I made enquiries of my own and confirmed the politician's involvement, along with a Judge, a couple of lawyers, some doctors, police and one or two others. All of them occupy positions of influence and some have real power. I imagine exposure would be immensely damaging.'

Baker advanced on Aldrittson, he was pale and trembling. Aldrittson was uncertain if Baker's reaction was one of fear or rage.

'Listen Aldrittson, I don't know what you are raving about and I resent your insinuation. Get out of my office arsehole.'

'Language Lance, language! I'm not sure that's such a good

idea. You see, I know the real identity of The Major. I have the number for what he believes is a secure mobile phone. I've also acquired the phone records of that number for the last six months and they do make for interesting reading. Would you like me to ring the number to see what happens?'

Aldrittson stopped talking. Baker had come face to face with him. He was ashen but unbowed by the implied threat. 'Listen prick,' he hissed, 'put up or shut up. Either way, know that I am going to have the living shit beaten out of you. How dare you threaten me!'

Aldrittson laughed scornfully. 'I think not you grubby little pretender. You can delude yourself all you like by poncing around in public. I might even keep your odious little secret but, it will cost, so *you* listen up, *prick,'* Aldrittson snarled. 'I have all the documentary and film evidence I need to bury you and your band of cockroaches forever. So think about it.'

In their parliamentary lives, Baker and Aldrittson had clashed many times; the score was roughly even. This time, whether he admitted Aldrittson's accusation or not, Baker was vanquished. Aldrittson intended keeping it that way. It had taken considerable effort and a lot of money for Spencer Johnson's network to find this information. Aldrittson wanted Baker to squirm with shame, drop the waste investigation and pay the start-up costs for Kindler's Project.

Baker was breathing raggedly but admitting nothing. Shaking, he pointed to the door. 'Get out you piece of scum, you'll get nothing from me,' he ground in a low voice.

Ben laughed. Sauntering to the door he said, 'Your choice, but do think about it Lance. I'll call you tomorrow when you've had time to consider *all* the implications.' He paused, casually withdrew his mobile and punched the hot key. Closing the door he heard his call ring in Baker's office.

That same morning, Andy Drummond was in the kitchen of his small Balwyn unit. Idly, he had half an ear to the radio as he pottered about. The ABC announcer was saying: *Westgate Bridge remains closed and police have confirmed that one man has died in an extraordinary multiple collision on the bridge at 5:55 this morning. Police sources have confirmed a total of thirty-five vehicles were involved in the spectacular smash. It appears to have occurred after a north bound car veered beneath the wheels of a 'B' double transport travelling beside it. The car was dragged forward by the truck for some distance. Eyewitnesses have said that the car appeared to experience a blow out then spin under the truck. An unladen cement truck travelling behind the transport ploughed into the wreckage of the car crushing it into the rear of the 'B' double. Miraculously, only three other people received minor injuries. Police have not yet released the name of the deceased person and the cause of the collision has not been confirmed. Anyone who may have witnessed the collision is asked to contact police through Crime Stoppers. The bridge is expected to be open by three o'clock this afternoon.*

Although the item registered, Drummond was more interested in trying to work out the meaning of someone getting under Santini's car. As he sat down to lunch, the phone rang.

'Jesus!' he growled aloud, 'a man can't even eat lunch in peace.' When he answered, Tony Maud said quietly, 'Did you say yesterday that Santini's car number was HGF 001?'

'Yeah, why?'

'Did you also say you saw someone crawl from under Santini's car?'

'You know I bloody did. What's going on?'

'Did you hear about the pile up on the Westgate this morning?'

'As a matter of fact it was on the news a couple of minutes ago. I think someone was killed. Why?'

'Andy, that someone looks a lot like Bernardo Santini and you have just become a witness again. Santini's death changes the complexion of the truck fire up here altogether. I've got a really bad feeling about this. Stay there and John Oliver from Major Collisions will come and talk to you. Tell him everything you can remember. Christ, how could a job interview lead to this?'

'I don't know whether my interview has any bearing on things, but okay, I'll jot down some notes for this Oliver bloke. How do you want me to play this? Your involvement I mean?'

Maud was brusque and unhesitating. 'Straight down the middle cobber, no other way. This investigation has just bumped up a couple of levels and we don't need any funny business mucking it up.'

After Maud hung up, Drummond contemplated this new twist. He was in no doubt that the man he had seen in the rain last night was connected to Santini's death. But how did that tie in with the truck fire? Clearly, the Aldrittson company was common to both events. Maybe the truck fire had more riding on it than appeared on the surface, especially since toxic waste was somehow involved. Aldrittson's owned a waste disposal firm, perhaps waste was the key.

Chapter
SEVENTEEN

At midday, Teresa Marchese brought Pescaro a simple lunch of cheese, pesto, olives, ham, crisp bread and coffee. He took it in his study.

'Thank you Teresa. Sit with me a while.' Pescaro was sombre, the invitation to stay unusual. Generally he ate alone. 'I've had some bad news this morning,' he said softly. 'Nardo Santini is dead. I'm still waiting for details but a police source has confirmed that Nardo died on the Westgate Bridge this morning.' Teresa sat very still, watching Pescaro whose focus was far away.

'I'm told Nardo's tyre blew out causing him to veer into a truck beside him.' He sighed and slowly shook his head. 'Such a fate is unexpected. Nardo was so careful on the road … and with his car. But, I'll know more later.'

Teresa was amazed by Pescaro's announcement. She had been too busy for news bulletins today. Personally, she disliked Santini – found him unnerving and cold. Given his position however, she had always shown respect and attempted to keep her feelings hidden.

She spoke gently. 'I am sorry to hear this Giuseppe. I know Bernardo has been a lifelong friend and confidante to you. Can I do anything?' Teresa knew others would fill Santini's shoes and expected a request to arrange their attendance.

Instead, Pescaro astonished her. 'For the moment, I want you to take his place as my *Consigliere*. I know this is unusual and some will disagree, however, most of the *capos* will support you, especially when they see what you're made of. Whether you realise it or not, you have prepared all your life for this and fate now delivers opportunity. Your role will be different from others. Yes there will be mediations and negotiations still, but your most important role will be caring for our legitimate businesses, expanding, diversifying and laundering money through them. This is the way of the future.' Pescaro spoke thoughtfully. This decision, Teresa could see, was not lightly made. Her feelings were tumultuous; never had she anticipated being a *Consigliere*. Indeed, she knew immediately she had no peer among her kind.

Pescaro observed her as the gravity of his decision sank in. Then, briskly, he said, 'There are things to be done, starting now. First, you need to know that Nardo recently warned me about Ben Aldrittson. Nothing more than intuition but he believed Aldrittson is more dangerous than we think. You know all about the waste project and the Aldrittsons responsibilities in that. On Thursday he was to give Nardo copies of documents prepared for the Premier, explanatory and strategy papers for easing our project into parliament. You will meet Aldrittson and get those documents. However, be careful. The timing of Nardo's death after his meeting with Aldrittson causes me to think his death is not accidental.'

Pescaro handed Teresa some keys. 'Take these, I want you to get into Ben Aldrittson's unit and look around.' Teresa's eyes widened as she took the keys. *How did he come by these?* He continued on, seeming not to notice her surpise. 'If you find anything that links him to Nardo's death bring it to me. Getting in shouldn't be difficult, any day now he'll be on the campaign trail for this election. Next, I want you to dig up everything you can on a man called Andy Drummond. He comes from Heathcote, near Bendigo. Yesterday he applied for a driver's job at Aldrittson's firm. Nardo said he looked and smelt like a cop even though Drummond said he was ex-army. He mentioned Browne's truck fire and I'm not sure whether that was very clever or just coincidence. Find out if there is any link between Aldrittson and Drummond. Lastly, I want you to organise Nardo's funeral at St. Patrick's Cathedral in East Melbourne. Spare no expense and invite the other Families. *Comprendé?*'

Teresa nodded. 'Yes Giuseppe. I'll start with that first.'

'Thank you Teresa. You will make a good replacement for Nardo, in fact, he and I discussed it some time ago. Expect to be overwhelmed at times but talk to me when you need. Now, bring me the cigar box please.' Pescaro had ignored his lunch.

Teresa rose, walked to the book shelves and removed an ornately carved rosewood box sitting in its own space. It was of great age and beauty. She took it to Pescaro.

'There is something pressing you must attend to right away.' He opened the box and removed three keys on a ring and passed them to her. 'These belong to Nardo's house. You know where it is. The large key opens the front and back doors. In his yard there is a barbecue, it is Nardo's secret place. Remove the firewood and you'll find a door which the small brass key will open. Bring me the security box. Make sure you put things back. And, look around. If there's anything the cops shouldn't find, bring it here. We talked of this day – he will be prepared. Go now because the cops will already be sniffing about.'

Driving to Santini's Teresa grappled with all Pescaro had said, especially her 'promotion'. It was hard to imagine Santini talking of her as his replacement. She suspected he knew she didn't like him. In fact, she could scarcely bring herself to use his name, mostly she had called him *Mister*, or nothing at all.

She listened to the midday news drone on about Iraqi insurgents, world crude oil price rises and slow progress at the International Whaling Commission conference. The bulletin concluded with an update of the Westgate Bridge crash. The deceased driver's name was still not available. That was good, Santini's neighbours wouldn't be unduly inquisitive. Still, no room for complacency. She had brought a large shoulder bag for Santini's security box and fervently hoped there was nothing else to carry.

She parked in Johnston Street and walked down Nicholson

Street towards 205A, pulling her coat closer and turning up the collar as she went. A beanie hid most of her hair and plain spectacles altered her looks. The wind was strong and the sky a heavy, slate grey. Being so cold, her woollen gloves were not out of place.

Teresa knocked on Santini's front door and waited. No one seemed interested in her. She entered and closed the door. The old house had undergone substantial renovation. It was tasteful in a masculine way and clean. Nothing looked at all out of the ordinary. A large leather recliner was close to the front window, the prime TV spot. An empty mobile phone cradle, charger and answering machine sat on glass coffee table beneath the window. Teresa hit the play button and heard Jack Aldrittson calling at 7:10 a.m. asking why Santini was not at work; he sounded annoyed. At 7:50 a.m. he had left a similar message. She left both on the tape.

She went out back to retrieve the security box. Stepping into Santini's yard was a surprise. She had only ever heard him disavow his Sicilian origins yet this small, neat, backyard could have been transplanted from the Old Country. Terra cotta paving, neatly pruned vines, a small fountain and a healthy garden overflowing with vegetables. What an enigma he was.

She went to the barbecue – a brick and marble affair – unpacked the sawn logs and found the metal door. Unlocking the door she removed the security box and after re-stacking the wood and sweeping up some bark she took it to the kitchen.

Following Pescaro's instructions, she began her search. Opening the spacious pantry she poked and pried but found nothing unusual. She moved on to the well stocked fridge. It contained a variety of frozen meats and vegetables which she lifted and checked. The tub of ice cream was too heavy for its size. She took it to the sink and searched until she found a skewer: something was concealed in the tub.

Taking a bowl from the pantry she removed the ice cream to reveal a firearm wrapped in plastic. After rinsing the package in warm water she wrapped it in another plastic bag. She tipped the icecream back into its tub and returned it to the freezer.

Quickly, but thoroughly, she searched the rest of the house. Finding a battered, leather bound photo album in a wardrobe, she took it to the kitchen for examination. It was full of small sepia and black and white photographs, many from overseas. Not knowing their importance, she decided to take it with her. As she closed the album, a loose black and white photograph fell from the back pages. Three people she recognised smiled at her from a beach; her parents and a young Giuseppe Pescaro. She didn't know the fourth person, a woman. Turning the photograph over she read: *Sorrento, 1973, Bon Voyage! Giuseppe, Angelina, Alfredo and Adriana.* She looked at the photograph again. She hadn't known of any friendship between her parents, Pescaro and … his wife? It was the first time she had even considered that Pescaro might have been married. Why would Santini have this photograph? A cold finger of dread lanced her stomach. She slipped it into her coat pocket and packed the album, security box and firearm into her shoulder bag.

After a last look around, she rinsed and dried the bowl and sink of ice cream. Out in the street, drizzly rain was falling. She stepped through the front gate and looked casually right and left, noting the 'For Sale' sign on the house opposite and its drawn curtains. She turned left and walked back to her car. The whole operation at Santini's had taken fifty minutes. She had been thorough but was more tense than she realised.

She sat in her car as cold misty rain fell quietly in Johnston Street. After a few moments, she started the motor and turned the heater up to high. Waiting for the warmth, she opened the photo album. On the fly leaf, in beautiful handwriting, a simple inscription in Italian read: *Our journey through life, 1942. Bernardo and Simonetta Santini.*

The initial pages contained many small photos of the young

Bernardo Santini – Nardo's father. He was photographed at various ages from childhood to manhood in different parts of the Sicilian countryside. Next came a similar series of Simonetta Rossini and her family. All the snaps reflected a time before, during and after World War Two. Following Simonetta's early life were photographs of a simple country wedding in 1942. From the past, the young Bernardo and Simonetta beamed their love for each other.

Teresa thumbed the pages noting the appearance of baby Nardo, the ravages of war around Rome, *S.S. Neptunia*, life at sea, various ports and images of the scowling, smiling or laughing ten year old Nardo. Then came Princes Pier, Bonegilla, the wild, wide Snowy Mountains, work camps at the Snowy scheme, picnics, school and the growing boy. All the pictures spoke eloquently of the young Santini family and their unfolding lives.

She removed the picture from her pocket and peered again at the group of happy people on holiday. Teresa's insatiable curiosity was piqued. There was nothing at Pescaro's home to suggest a wife or children. She re-examined the photograph: Pescaro and Angelina were wearing matching wedding rings. She had never seen any ring on his hand. Inexplicably, her mouth was dry, fear wormed into her belly. Thoughts of the harsh Mafia culture blossomed in her mind.

With mounting apprehension, she opened Santini's box. It was filled with money: neatly ordered bundles of used $50 and $100 notes secured by rubber bands. She didn't know how much was there but it had to be thousands. She lifted the bundles aside, burrowing to the bottom. Nestling between two packets of notes were about a dozen letters bound in a slim white ribbon. Keepsakes from Santini's parents? She opened the first envelope to find a beautiful letter that quivered with passion and tenderness. Written by Angelina Pescaro, she was shocked to see it addressed to her father. Dazed, she rushed through the bundle: some were from her father, others from Angelina. All were ardent testaments to a deep and powerful love between them.

Immediately, her mind conjured the inevitable outcome of this relationship. Infidelity between mafia husbands and wives or unmarried mafia couples was not tolerated. A bullet to the back of the head was preceded by torture, the hacked off penis stuffed into the man's mouth, and finally, a graceless discovery of two naked bodies in a car boot somewhere. It was degrading, humiliating and ruthless. Teresa's belly somersaulted. She felt sick and wound the window down. Rain spattered softly on her face as a gush of cold air blew in.

She had always believed she was orphaned by a boating accident. Nobody had even whispered of a relationship between Angelina Pescaro and her father. Her heart contracted. And what of her mother? What pain had she endured? What was the truth of her death? In seconds, a life she had believed and was comfortable with, had shattered. Suddenly she was gasping for air, tears coursed down her cheeks. Her pain was crushing. She glimpsed her grey waxy face in the rear view mirror. What sense could she make of this? Why did Santini have the photograph and letters? Was he the assassin? Her dislike of Santini convinced her she was right.

Her world had suddenly fragmented and the new life offered by Pescaro would have to be seriously re-considered. She lay back, breathing slowly and deeply. Gradually, she regained control. Whatever *might* have been was finished. Now, there could only be a search for truth, and possibly, revenge.

Driving back to the Villa, she looked for a service station offering photocopying. Stopping in Bridge Road she copied the thirteen letters, re-ordered the originals in their ribbon girdle and returned them to Santini's box. The copies lay like lead in her coat pocket alongside the Sorrento photograph, a dreadful and malevolent secret.

Starting with her parents, she reviewed her life as she drove. Her feelings for them were always warm and tender. She could remember little other than a happy home. The drama of their deaths was only vaguely recalled and she had always believed they died water skiing when their boat hit a rock. What she had been told was that the impact killed her father and a piece of the boat's timber struck her mother causing her to drown. She had understood all this as the lore of her life and would now have to prove whether it was fact or fable.

Alfredo and Adriana Marchese had migrated from Rome to Melbourne in 1970 after which Teresa was born. With her parents dead, at the age five Teresa went to live at Sylvan with the Benedetti family. Life with Benedetti's had been as loving as any family could be and Teresa had never felt alone or unwanted. Her addition to the five Benedetti children was seamless and unconditional. She loved the family and their market garden and found school a place of mystery and satisfaction. She proved to be quick, intelligent, energetic and enthusiastic. In her final year at primary school it was suggested she sit for a scholarship at Genazzano College, in Kew. To no one's surprise, she won easily.

In 1982, aged twelve, she went to Deepdene and lived with the Bellini family, friends of Benedettis. Genazzano was short tram ride away. At fourteen, in Year 9, she became a term boarder and returned to Sylvan during holidays. Later still, she spent less holiday time at Sylvan and more with different school friends. Possessing an unquenchable thirst for knowledge, her outstanding scholastic results were matched only by her driving curiosity. She was a natural at rowing and swimming, but in her more senior years, slipped easily into the martial arts.

In Year 11 her life changed after a six month exchange visit to Italy. There, she discovered her Italian roots, polished her language skills and enjoyed the Italian lifestyle. Back at Genazzano, she felt that another facet had been grafted to her personality. She continued to study hard and entered Monash University. She was just under eighteen.

Her application to a double degree in law and commerce seemed effortless. In her second year, at a family celebration, the Benedettis introduced her to one of their oldest friends. For Teresa, Giuseppe Pescaro's appearance was timely. He took an immediate interest in her and offered her work at one of his restaurants. Needing money for her course, rent and a small car, she worked hard and progressed quickly from waitress to weekend manager. Slowly, Giuseppe encouraged her into bigger and better restaurants where her responsibilities and pay increased. At the time, she had accepted these opportunities gratefully but now wondered if there had been an ulterior motive.

In her third year, yearning for deeper knowledge and experience of her parent's birthplace, she undertook a semester in law at the Prato Centre in Italy. It was a journey substantially cushioned by Pescaro whose generosity was unlimited and whose influential 'contacts' seemed endless.

On completion of her degree, Teresa became a full time manager at Pescaro's largest restaurant in St. Kilda where she earned a good livelihood. Wanting her to maximise her education Pescaro first suggested, then arranged for Teresa to work in a bank. Natural aptitude took her into the field of shares, investment, financing and overseas trade. Three years later, he organised a series of powerful and significant jobs for her overseas. The first in London, with an international investment firm, the next in Germany with one of that nation's largest stockbrokers to concentrate on international trade and global politics. The final move was to Switzerland with one of the world's oldest, largest and most discreet financial institutions. There she would obtain a detailed understanding of global financial systems but, more importantly, learn how their discreet and confidential services functioned. Four busy and exciting years vanished in a flash.

Friendship with Pescaro was always interesting and constantly fruitful. Teresa applied intellectual rigour, skill and energy to her work and Pescaro – without her knowledge – used his network to ease her into job and personal growth opportunities. In late 2002, whilst at home on holidays from Europe, Pescaro suggested she stay and work for him.

Her workplace would be the Villa at Glover Court. Pescaro explained the nature of his interests without revealing it was Mafia. Astonished by the size and diversity of his empire: building, finance, shipping, gambling, waste management, food and agriculture, among others, Teresa had little trouble agreeing.

Her skill and overseas experience ensured that Pescaro's already sound "business" became even more so. Over a period of months she learned the truth about Pescaro but, by then, was enjoying the excitement of her work and excellent pay. Somehow, she was not surprised he was Mafia but initially was uncertain of her own feelings. Teresa didn't want to be engaged in violent crime and had doubts about her future, but in the end, she succumbed to being a team player. Randomly, over time, Pescaro gave her small operational jobs to perform. Her forthcoming visit to Ben Aldrittson's unit was one of these. Pescaro respected her and, within the confines of their personal and business interaction, bestowed freedom and trust. In short, she seemed to have become both family and friend to him even though her role officially remained that of private secretary. Now, approaching thirty-five, Teresa had worked for Pescaro for almost three years.

Although informed and well connected, Teresa didn't know the detail of the dirty business of crime: the drugs, prostitution, torture, murder, extortion, robberies, insurance scams and other forms of serious bastardry. For his own reasons, Pescaro had shielded her from this dark side of business. For her part, Teresa revelled in taking money generated by crime, laundering it and making it grow through valid business ventures. While it was a lifestyle that enabled her to turn a blind eye to the source of her personal income, there remained always, a chip of restless conscience.

It was a unique situation. Indeed, one day after some particularly hefty gains on the futures market, Pescaro surprised her by revealing details of his long running and lucrative insider trading scam at the stock exchange. 'Crime,' he had explained, 'is merely one set of cogs in a big money making machine. Parts of the machine are legal, other parts are not. What both parts have in common is profit. It is through profit where the clarity of what is legal and what is illegal becomes opaque, and it is here especially where we strive to optimise our returns.'

Today, she had come full circle. Her life, it seemed, had always been shadowed by Pescaro and her discovery of the letters and photograph confirmed that. At 1:40 p.m. she drove into the Villa. She was calm, controlled and implacably committed to two things: learning the whole truth about the death of her parents and discovering as much as she could about Angelina Pescaro.

Chapter
EIGHTEEN

'Spencer,' said the familiar voice in Johnson's ear, 'care for a bite to eat tonight? I'll see you at *The Squid's Legs*, 7:30.' Ben Aldrittson hung up without announcing himself or waiting for a reply.

Johnson could tell from the tone of voice that Aldrittson was pissed off about something. *Well, it wouldn't be the first time.* He figured it had to be Santini's death.

Johnson had already met Fox for a debriefing and knew about the "watcher" in the Hertz van. He had ticked Fox off for not dealing with the watcher. Fox had rejected the smack. 'Listen Spence,' he had said, an edge to his voice, 'I don't have a problem killing people, just certain kinds of people. Rapists, drug dealers, murderers, paedophiles and Mafia villains are *all* on my "A" list. People like the bloke who tagged me last night are not. Get used to it. I know nothing about him. If you think I'm being hypocritical, remember this, all that damage on the bridge – minimal impact on others. I *designed* it that way. Don't lecture me on principle; it shits me.'

Fox was right. Even so, his attitude had rankled.

'Listen Foxy, your failure to deal with this bloke could bring a blow torch to all our arses. You should have thought of that.'

Fox had laughed it off. 'Cut it out Spence. He got nothing. Not me, not my bike, nothing. You ought to be more concerned about Aldrittson; he's a loose bloody cannon. And, I've got to tell you, he's only a tick off full membership to my "A" list.' Fox had seen Aldrittson many times at Johnson's gym and assiduously avoided him. He detested the man's double standards and smug self-importance.

Privately, Johnson thought Aldrittson should rate AA+ on Fox's list, but he paid exceptionally well and without quibbling.

Instead, he rumbled, 'We'll have to watch it.'

Fox had smiled lazily. 'Listen up mate. It will be neither your nor my doing that brings Aldrittson down ... he'll manage that by himself. Mark my words.'

At 7:30 p.m. Johnson walked into *The Squid's Legs* in Stokes Street, Port Melbourne. Not far from the beach, it was a quiet restaurant with a reputation for fine ocean cuisine. Nautical themes decorated the alcoves circling the main room and in the dim light of marine lanterns, Johnson saw Aldrittson furthest from the entrance. Reaching the table he boomed, 'Benny my boy, good to see you.'

Aldrittson didn't bother rising, merely nodded and pointed to the chair opposite. Johnson turned and signalled the waitress. Aldrittson *was* pissed off! He ignored the pointing finger and remained standing. The girl arrived swiftly and he ordered freshly squeezed orange juice. She melted towards the kitchen.

Johnson sat having subtly made his point. 'What's on your mind Benny?' His voice was low and neutral.

'Let me tell you Spence.' Aldrittson's eyes flashed, his voice was husky with anger. 'You fucked up. The coppers think Santini was murdered. They know someone got to his car last night and they're going through the wreck with sieves. And they'll already be turning his house over ... with a microscope and tweezers. I don't need this.' He was furious.

'You're jumping at shadows Benny. The coppers have nothing. It was raining, it was dark and my man was not discovered. They've got nothing. Okay, so maybe they're talking to someone who *saw* my man, but all they will have is a vague description of someone acting strangely in the rain. Nothing else.'

Aldrittson was not assuaged. He continued at a slow burn. 'My police sources tell me they've got enough to make them regard Santini's death as murder rather than a car crash. That's where you fucked up! Santini's death was supposed to look accidental. Now it's been compromised and Pescaro's going to be on the hunt too.'

Johnson liked Aldrittson's money but not his attitude. 'Listen up sport. This whole bloody thing is down to you, no one else. Remember that. Bloody unfortunate this bloke turned up, but have you asked yourself why? Who is he? Where's he from? What was he doing there? None of that's coincidental, so any compromise occurred well before Santini's death. Have you thought of that? Don't feed me bullshit about my man compromising your little plan. He didn't.'

Aldrittson drew back mollified, reflective. Finally, he said, 'I can tell you who he is and where he's from; the coppers told me that much. He's from Heathcote and his name is Andy Drummond. Why he was there I don't know.'

Johnson settled back into his chair. Aldrittson could see things ticking over in his mind.

'My man heard a conversation between Santini and Pescaro where Drummond's name came up. Seems he applied for a job at your old man's firm yesterday. Santini knocked him back; thought he was a copper. Drummond claimed he was ex-army. Anyway, Santini was concerned about him. Given Drummond's from Heathcote, that your truck burned there and suddenly he's knocking at your door for a job I'd say is more than coincidence. Seems to me Benny, your old man's firm is under some kind of scrutiny. You'd better be careful old son.'

Aldrittson was dismissive. 'I don't know about that but what I do know is, I *don't* want the coppers sniffing around. Some of the bastards are honest and if they get their hooks into this, they could be hard to stop, even with my contacts.'

Johnson sat passively, thinking. 'You need a diversion, something to take their attention away from the firm. Some new garden path to lead them down.'

Aldrittson reached for his wine, face shadowed, eyes glinting. 'What about creating some friction, or the appearance of friction between Asian gangs, or the Lebanese Tigers or someone? We could make Santini's death seem connected to that rather than our firm. Could you fix that Spence?' As he voiced the question, he was struck by a different thought – political advantage, difficulties for the cops. The concept appealed to him, especially with the election coming up.

Johnson watched Aldrittson's anger dissipate and smelt more big money, yet the idea was fraught. Manufacturing false hostilities could lead to his own demise.

'Benny my boy, that *is* risky business. Let me think about it and make a few enquiries. Right now I'm not saying yes and I'm not saying no, but your idea is very bloody dicey. I'll get back in a day or two. One more thing though – we might be able to funnel Pescaro in the direction of this Drummond character. That should at least keep his eyes off you. In the meantime, let's have some good food.'

'Bloody good idea Spence.' Aldrittson was in better humour, 'but in the meantime, give that prick Drummond a lesson anyway. Smart arse! He needs to know it's unwise to stick his nose where it's not wanted.'

'No problem,' grinned Johnson.

Chapter
NINETEEN

After being interviewed by John Oliver, Drummond decided to return to the farm. He rang Tony Maud to fill him in and immediately was invited for dinner.

At 6:30 the following morning, Drummond walked downstairs to his ute. Nearing his truck, he stopped abruptly. His tyres were slashed, the tonneau cut to ribbons and a thick, foul smelling oil poured over the cabin, windows, bonnet and tray.

He was furious. Not only because of the damage but because he prided himself on sleeping with one ear on full alert. He had heard nothing. The audacity and scale of the attack lit his rage to white hot fury. Bounding upstairs, he rang the local police then took his camera down to record the damage.

Half an hour later, two uniformed police arrived in a Divisional van to take his complaint. They were sympathetic but unhelpful. They had had no similar calls and nothing suspicious had been reported during the night. They said they would pass it on to local detectives before their shift finished. Drummond believed they were disinterested and would palm it off as soon as they could. After twenty minutes of questions and form filling, they left.

By then, he had calmed and begun to think. Although nothing connected the two events, he wondered if his experience outside Santini's was linked to this attack. Instinct said yes, logic said presumptuous.

After a time wasting and expensive morning of restoration and repair, he left for Heathcote. Driving home Drummond considered events of the last forty eight hours. The person under Santini's car, the damage to this ute, Aldrittson Waste Disposals and the truck fire. Somehow, they all seemed related. He wondered too about the rapid compensation for Browne's widow. It was too neat and too quick. He was suspicious of AWD and after Maud had told him about toxic residues on the burnt-out truck, he suspected them of dumping illegal waste. But, therein lay a contradiction. Every scrap of information he had heard or read about this firm extolled propriety and excellence. Nothing suggested the Aldrittson company was in any way shonky.

Arriving at Heathcote, he pulled up for fresh bread and milk at Gaffney's Bakery and was followed in by Mario Embone. Behind the counter, Jacqueline Thibault greeted Drummond as though he had been away for a month.

'Welcome home stranger. Where have you been?'

Drummond grinned, the red haired Jacquie was always trying a line. An unmarried mother of thirty something, she was cheerful, talkative and generously proportioned.

'Just in Melbourne a couple of days Jac. How have you been?'

'Yeah, goodoh. Did you bring me back something nice?' She smiled wickedly as she asked the question.

'Not this time Jacquie love. As a matter of fact, some bloody ratbag trashed my ute. I wasted the whole bloody morning getting things fixed. Bloody bastards, if I could get my hands on 'em I'd kill 'em.' He told her about the damage, she sympathised and moved to another customer.

Embone, patiently waiting his turn, listened to the exchange with interest. He wondered if Pescaro was trying to provoke something. He would check later to find out.

In Melbourne, Ben Aldrittson was climbing the stairs to Spencer Johnson's gym. With electioneering about to start he needed to tone up. After fifteen minutes or so, Johnson wandered across to check his progress.

'Yo, Benny. How's the program? Let me see.' He checked Aldrittson's chart and said, 'you could manage another ten kilos on that bar, you're doing it too easy. Speaking of easy, a friend of mine had some bad luck last night. His ute was pretty badly trashed. It's going to cost him quite a few bob to fix it up. Jeez there's some bastards in this world.' He slipped Aldrittson a sly wink and moved on. Aldrittson kept pumping iron but allowed himself a wry grin. *Good*, he thought, *maybe this prick Drummond will disappear back to his farm and stay there.*

At her own small home in Rose Street, Burnley, Teresa selected clothes for her visit to Ben Aldrittson's unit. Since the shock of finding the letters and photograph at Santini's she had steadied. Even so, unanswered questions kept pummelling her mind and causing distress. If her parents had died in a boating accident, why keep their friendship with Pescaro secret? Had Pescaro known of the affair between Angelina and her father? Why did Santini have the letters and photograph anyway?

Pescaro had said nothing about the security box or its contents and received the firearm in silence. She noticed, however, that Santini's old album now lay on his desk in a place reserved for things of importance.

Teresa felt a coolness towards Pescaro that was difficult to conceal yet she was acutely aware of the honour he had bestowed in making her his *Consigliere*. She felt torn between a duty to parents she didn't really know and desire to experience her unique new role. If she chose to pursue the truth about her parents it might be impossible to stay with Pescaro, yet leaving him would almost certainly result in her death. She felt trapped. In the end, despite the risk, and driven by boundless curiosity, she decided to seek the truth.

To her great sadness she realised she could no longer rely on the Benedettis, they were part of the deception. She had to continue with Pescaro as before, quietly searching for answers, slowly building the layers. What she discovered would ultimately determine her final action.

She settled on a shoulder length blonde wig, plain silk blouse, bright red and white Argyle patterned top, jeans and red and white sneakers. From her knowledge of Aldrittson, her image would fit the kind of girl he was often seen with and wouldn't arouse too many suspicions at his apartment block.

At home, Giuseppe Pescaro quietly enjoyed an aromatic rum and honey cured cigar while listening to Django Reinhardt's *Jazz in Paris*, a collection of 1935 classics. The westering sun suffused his study with a coppery glow. He was thinking deeply. He knew exactly what Santini's box contained, he had always known. What he couldn't be sure of was whether Teresa had inspected its contents. She had said nothing and he had not detected any noticeable change in her behaviour. She appeared just as industrious, just as balanced and as ever respectful. She had arranged Santini's funeral to his complete satisfaction and learned that a chain of legislation was to be rammed through Parliament before it prorogued. Tomorrow she would use that legislative wagon-train to minimise risk when she visited Aldrittson's unit.

He was, however, intrigued by her silence over the box. Sending her to collect it had partly been a test for her new position. No matter what his personal feelings might be, business came first, last and always. If she did not pass this test, then, ultimately, she was expendable. That was why her silence gnawed at him. He had expected her to raise the contents of Santini's box and discuss them with him. He even thought she might have raged at him, that *would* have been natural The story behind what lay in the box was unpleasant, yet, to this point it seemed to lie unchallenged.

The telephone intruded upon his reverie. '*Pronto*?'

'I do not yet 'ave the answer to your question Don Pescaro,' Mario Embone said, 'but I thought you might be interested in two things. First, Drummond is back, second, someone trashed 'is ute last night. I 'eard 'im talkin' to one of the girls at Gaffney's.'

'Did he know who was responsible?'

'No. 'E said if 'e did 'e wouldda like to kill 'em. Idle talk Giuseppe, butta shows 'is annoyance.'

'Good work Mario. An interesting piece of information, nothing to do with me though. Ring me when you find out about Drummond and Maud.' He wondered what might shake loose.

Chapter

TWENTY

At 6:00 p.m. Mario Embone's phone rang. About to step into the shower, he answered with a curt, 'Embone.'

Pescaro's deep voice rumbled down the line. 'I have another job for you. One of my police sources says Drummond was interviewed yesterday. Seems he had something to do with Nardo's "accident". As I suspected, Nardo's death is suspicious. I want you to give this Drummond a terminal headache. Call me tomorrow morning.'

'*Pronto* Giuseppe.' Embone's plans had just been ruined but he was not unhappy. It had been a long time since he had had a job like this one. He didn't mind the new shape of his evening at all.

Also on the dot of 6:00 p.m., Drummond pulled up outside the police residence. With roses and a beautiful bottle of *Syrah* from Vinea Marson, one of Heathcote's newest wineries, he sauntered to the front door and rang the bell.

A beaming Mary Maud stepped forward and embraced Andy to her ample bosom, kissing him on both cheeks. 'Andy love, how nice to see you, come on in. Got the ute fixed? Tony told me about it.'

'All fixed … bastards,' he growled. Then he grinned at her. Their relationship was as close as brother and sister. Mary had been a staunch supporter during Sue's illness and following her death. Not only had the two women become close friends through the bond between their husbands but they also shared a common interest in teaching. Auburn haired Mary was a steady, cheerful woman with limitless compassion, a perfect foil to Tony and a wonderful back stop. Locally, she was renowned for her intense interest in current affairs and blunt views on politics.

As they moved to the kitchen, Drummond savoured the mouth watering aroma of roast lamb.

'Where's Tony?' he asked.

'Next door in the "shop". Jerry Riddell needed a trade plate for a van early tomorrow morning. He said it would only take five minutes. Now, what have you got there?'

Andy presented her with the roses. 'For Mary, our Goddess Rhea, Queen of Comfort,' he laughed. 'I got these at Kilmore and they assured me their colour is surpassed only by their fragrance.'

'Oh Andy, I'm not even going to say "you shouldn't have", how wonderful.' She smiled again and gave him another hug.

'Cut that out you two or I'll be suing for divorce tomorrow.' Tony Maud bustled through the back door, filling the room with his presence and grinning like a fool. He pumped Andy's hand vigorously.

'How about I trade you Mary for this bottle of *Syrah*?' responded Drummond.

'You're on,' laughed Tony.

Mary giggled. 'I didn't know you had that much money, it must have been priceless.' They all laughed.

'Sit down boys. Do you want a beer before dinner? Tony, be a love and get me a sherry will you, while I finish the gravy.'

The men sat at the table with their beers.

'So, tell me what happened this morning?'

Andy took a long, slow pull at his beer and sighed. 'I went outside at half six because I had a few things to do at the farm and wanted to leave early. And, there it was – a bloody mess! Cost me nearly nine hundred bucks for four new tyres. The new tonneau will be close to five hundred. It took nearly an hour to get all the crap off the truck and out of the tray. I'm certain the bloke at the car wash wanted to shoot me. Should have seen the look on his face when I drove in! He was not a happy camper.'

'Do you think this was a random attack or somehow connected

to your recent nocturnal activities?'

'Hard to say Tony. I think probably the latter, although I've got nothing to base that on, just gut feeling.'

'Did you call the cops?'

'Of course, but they weren't all that interested. I think I interrupted their breakfast. City coppers aren't the same as you country blokes.' He grinned at his friend.

'Did you call John Oliver and tell him?'

'No mate. To tell you the truth I was so angry about the whole bloody thing it didn't enter my mind. And then, when I calmed down, I just went at it to get everything fixed so I could get home.'

'Fair enough. I'll call him tomorrow. He might organise a flea in the ear for those local blokes you saw. Now, what about Santini. Tell me again what happened.'

Andy described in detail the events of that night. He had just finished explaining about the motor bike when an imperious signal from Mary's clattering plates interrupted. The fragrant smell of roast lamb, baked potatoes and vegetables mixed with rich gravy drifted across the kitchen.

'Righto, suspend hostilities you blokes. Come and get this tucker. I'm not waiting on you, I gave up slavery twenty years ago when I married him.' In her usual style, Mary had dished up a huge roast dinner causing Andy to almost drool with anticipation.

The wine, a deep red, was the perfect accompaniment to the dinner and dessert of baked apples, cinnamon syrup and double cream. For Drummond, this was the essence of a home life lost to him since Sue's death, a loss still as painful as the day it occurred.

After dinner, Mary shooed them into the lounge room.

'Finish nattering. I want to clean up and make a couple of phone calls. I'll bring tea in later.' It was her way of giving them space.

Settling into arm chairs, Maud turned on the gas fire to take the edge off the early winter chill. They sat in comfortable silence while the heater warmed the room.

'Got any info back yet on that bit of metal?' Drummond queried. 'Was it a detonator?'

'Yep it was. Just today I learned forensics can prove the detonator was responsible for the fire. They found minute traces of the same chemical cocktail on it as on the truck. That now makes this a homicide investigation and officially takes it out of my hands.'

'What are your thoughts about Santini's death Tony?'

'At this stage, none. He was a key man at AWD responsible for organising pickups, dispatches, rosters and so on. So far, the blokes in town have found nothing to link Santini's death to the truck fire.'

'Maybe it's not linked. Maybe it's unrelated, some kind of private dispute, or something like that,' said Drummond thoughtfully.

'Well, who knows? At present nothing can be ruled in or out, but I'll tell you this, if you hadn't been in Nicholson Street the other morning, we would never have known about that bloke under Santini's car. That changed everything. John Oliver's already told me Santini's death looked as though it happened as the result of an unfortunate blow out. What you saw changed all that. Now forensics is looking at Santini's car with very different eyes. As for your ute – hard to say. Could be vandals, could be related to Santini's death. I can't see any connection between it and Browne's death in Schoolhouse Lane.'

'I agree,' Drummond responded, 'and I didn't want to sound as though I was jumping to conclusions. But, driving back today, I had a good think. I'm inclined to the view that my ute was either a warning or payback for being in the wrong place at the wrong time.'

'Yeah, that sounds plausible. We could have two strands here: Santini's death and Browne's death. Both are connected through AWD but that doesn't mean they actually relate to one another. Somehow though, I can't believe they're coincidental. We've decided to quietly put Aldrittson's under the microscope. And that won't be easy. Apart from being a reputable company, Jack Aldrittson's son is the Minister for Trade and Business. He's a mover and shaker with a reputation for being a prickly bastard with lots of clout. We can't afford to cock up.'

Drummond took notice of Tony's view of the Minister. Because of Mary's firebrand opinions about politicians, he tended to be more than usually circumspect about them. Drummond had not made the connection to the waste firm.

'Is it possible that Aldrittson's have some kind of illegal waste racket going Tony?'

'Don't know,' responded Maud. 'Anything is possible – until we begin investigating no one knows. One of our problems will be Jack Aldrittson's reputation. It's rock solid. And, as I said, his son rides shotgun. They could create quite a fuss if they get pissed off.'

'Any joy from the motor bike rego I gave you?' Andy asked.

'Nah, it's a bodgie. Did you look at it closely?'

'Sorry mate, the plate looked fair dinkum but I didn't scrutinise it. It was pissing with rain and I just took the number,' Andy replied.

'Righto, that's enough.' Mary appeared with a large tray of steaming tea and thick fingers of boiled fruit cake. She smiled at them both. 'You know that old saying: *Too much work ...*'

'Okay Mair. I give up.' Tony rose to take the tray and smiled affectionately at his wife.

'Andy,' said Mary, settling herself on the lounge near him him, 'have you met any nice girls recently?' Her voice was soft and gentle, the enquiry of an interested and concerned friend.

He looked sheepish – it was a regular probe by Mary. 'No Mary, I just can't get used to life without Sue and can't bring myself to even think about anyone else.' His voice trailed off huskily.

'Well, you need to think about it sooner or later. You're only thirty-nine – far too young to spend the rest of your life alone. And too good looking! I know of at least three eligible and attractive women in this village who would love to park their shoes under your bed.'

'Only three,' laughed Tony.

Mary grinned at her husband, she well knew the depth of love between Andy and Sue. And, from her many conversations with Sue also knew she had not wanted Andy to live alone after her death. Often she had said that what counted most was their time together, not fidelity to a memory. That, Sue maintained, was just plain silly.

'I could invite one of these women to dinner if you like.' She leaned across and patted his arm, delivering her warning with an engaging, warm-hearted smile.

'I'm flattered Mary. Maybe we'll talk about it some other time,' was all he could manage. His discomfort provided a perfect opportunity to leave. 'Well folks, nine o'clock,' he said, 'I must be getting home. It's been an eventful day and I need an early start tomorrow. Mary, thank you so much for the wonderful dinner, it was just super.' He stood, then bent to kiss her cheek.

'Tony, on the way out, give Andy that container on the bench. I cut him some fruit cake.'

'Thanks again Mary,' said Andy, 'see you soon.'

The two men walked to the front door. 'Don't think unkindly of Mair,' said Tony, 'she worries about you. I know she promised Sue to keep an eye on you.'

'That's okay.' Andy nodded, touched by the concern of his friends.

They shook hands and Drummond walked to his ute, relieved that the rotten start to his day had ended so pleasantly.

Mario Embone watched Drummond carefully. Rugged up against the cold, he had chosen a vantage point east of the crest of the drive where a half dozen oaks planted last century provided good cover and an excellent view of Drummond's lounge and kitchen. He had brought his Winchester .270 mounted with telescope. He raised the rifle to check the view. Drummond was fixing the fire: it was like watching a silent movie, perfectly clear actions but no sound.

Within a few minutes, the stove was blazing cheerfully. Drummond took a jug from his pantry and topped up his boiler. Embone's view of Drummond was good. He slipped a shell into the breach, cocked the rifle and waited, watching through the 'scope.

The bright, clear, round image revealed a man intent on the simple task of boosting the fire in preparation for a cup of tea. He moved about the kitchen, organising his tea and putting things away in his pantry. Drummond walked outside and returned with an armful of wood and placed it on the hearth. Embone waited patiently.

Drummond moved and stood directly in front of the firebox. The small door between his legs was open and Embone could see the flames behind him. It appeared that Drummond was warming his backside while he waited for the urn to boil. Embone checked his scope again and put Drummond's chest dead centre of the cross hairs. He slowed his breathing until the image stilled then … gently … gently … squeezed the trigger.

In the kitchen, Drummond, who had been warming his bum, bent to retrieve a large ember that dropped into the wood stack on the hearth. In that same instant, he heard a loud, sharp crack, followed by the sound of splintering glass and a small explosion above the stove top. He knew instantly he had been shot at. He dived to the floor, grabbed the poker, and slithered across the door and turned the light off. Under the protection of darkness he dashed to the laundry. There, he grabbed a small torch and his snake gun – a Savage .22 magnum/410 under and over. Quietly, he let himself out the back door.

There were no more shots, just the night quiet and a filigree of icy starlight. Drummond moved silently to the western side of his house, slid beneath his car and quietly elbowed himself toward the rear end. From this vantage point he could take in a 180 degree arc from east to the west. Nothing moved, there was only the stillness of endless silence.

He waited ten minutes. Nothing happened. He figured his assailant had fled after the one shot. He worked his way from beneath the car and headed west. He would make a wide looping circle to the oak trees east of the house: locus of the shot. Automatically back in full military mode, he worked methodically, silently and carefully towards the oaks. He lay on the ground twenty metres from the trees scanning the scene. Nothing.

Embone was long gone. He had used a gully in the neighbouring farm that took him to Schoolhouse Lane, 500 metres north east of the oaks. His vehicle was about two kilometres away and he was in no hurry. He had certainly delivered the headache as requested – just unfortunate it was not permanent. He would report to the Don and bide his time.

Drummond moved towards the oaks then looked at his house. The centre of the grove best suited the line of sight taken by the shooter. He played his torch on the ground and saw fresh scuff marks in the soil; no shell casing. He would tell Tony tomorrow. Tonight, he didn't have the energy to deal with it. For Drummond, the rule book was now in the bin; he would be working for himself in his own way to find out what the hell was going on.

The slim, attractive woman stood in the foyer of the modern south suburban police complex. At 9:00 a.m. Friday, the reception counter was unattended. She saw a sign and rang the bell. No one came. She felt as though she had been standing for hours in this barren place. She noticed a grubbiness and lack of pride already appearing in the new building and felt unwelcome.

Behind her, glass doors banged opened. Two young policemen dripping with weapons, handcuffs, radios and mobile phones bustled out. One carried a large black brief case, the other, a street directory. She turned, thinking they had come to her aid. Laughing and talking, they barely glanced at her and continued on through the foyer. She felt like running from the place but rang the bell again and waited.

Senior Constable Aleisha Campbell pushed through the glass security doors on her way home. She was tired. It had been a long night dealing with a fatal accident. The stupidity of drivers depressed her. Already two hours past knock off, she was looking forward to a hot shower and bed. Entering the foyer she saw the solitary woman at reception. Her bearing bespoke despair, anxiety and grief. The woman looked at her pleadingly.

'Are you being attended?' asked Campbell.

'No,' said the woman, in a strained and husky voice.

'Can I help you?'

'It's my husband, he's missing.' Tears trickled slowly down her cheeks.

Aleisha introduced herself. 'Come in,' she said kindly and thinking, *Lazy sods inside don't give a shit. They must have heard the counter bell!* She held the door and ushered the woman into a passage and along to a large room with rows of desks and computers.

Several uniformed police chattering to each other, drinking from mugs and working on computers were oblivious to their presence.

'Sit down here,' said Aleisha. 'Now, tell me, what's happened?'

Still weeping silently, the woman made an effort to compose herself. 'My name is Marnie Baker,' she said. 'My husband is Lance Baker, Minister for the Environment. He hasn't been home since Wednesday. I can't reach him at his office, he's not answering his mobile and his secretary hasn't seen him since late Wednesday afternoon. I've contacted a few of his friends and they haven't seen him either. He's vanished. I know he's been under pressure getting ready for the election and so forth. We had a row about that on Wednesday morning. I thought, when he didn't come home Wednesday night, he was punishing me and the girls. Sometimes he gets into moods … But when I heard nothing Thursday, and he still wasn't home Thursday night, I started to worry that something had happened. And now, I know it has. I am sick with fear.' Fresh tears ran down her face.

Campbell listened. Her radar screamed at the words "missing" and "Minister." She drew close to Marnie Baker and put a comforting arm around her shoulders. 'Let's have a cuppa eh, while I get the details. But could I ask, why on earth didn't you call us to your home? I mean, your husband is a Government Minister.'

Marnie's eyes welled with tears again. 'I know. I just didn't want to make a fuss if I was wrong. You know, police cars at the house and so on. Lance can get so upset, especially about mistakes.'

Privately, Aleisha read 'bully' into the comment and assessed Marnie as a somewhat timorous woman. 'Okay. Stay here Mrs Baker, I won't be long.'

Marnie looked grateful. She dabbed fresh tissues to her eyes but couldn't stem the tears.

Campbell left the office to find Tom Daley, the Duty Sergeant.

He was in the mess room and as she made the tea, she briefly filled him in on the missing Lance Baker. 'Sarge, we'd better pull our finger out on this. No one bothered to attend this poor woman at the counter and if her politician husband *is* missing and we muck around, the shit's gunna hit the fan.'

Daley agreed. 'I'll deal with it. But, and I know this is an imposition, would you mind staying on while I get the ball rolling. I'll see you right for overtime. Bring her up to the Sergeant's Office, it's more private.'

Campbell returned to the general office with the tea. As she entered, a loud hoot of laughter came from the police at the computers. Marnie Baker seemed to shrink even further and slump in her chair, tears streaming.

'Here you are then Mrs Baker.' Campbell passed a mug of tea and spoke encouragingly. 'I've briefed Sergeant Daley; he will take over right away.' Marnie Baker looked apprehensive at the prospect of being passed on to someone else.

Sensing her concern Campbell said, 'It's okay, I'll stay with you while we get things underway.' Gesturing towards the passage she led Baker to the Sergeant's office.

Tom Daley was gentle, reassuring and patient. Aleisha Campbell sat quietly as he explored and recorded the details of Baker's absence. At the end of his information gathering Daley concluded that not only was Baker missing, but that his shy, sensitive wife was verging on shock. He arranged more tea and took Campbell aside. 'Would you mind staying with her a little longer? I know you're on night shift, but you've got a rapport with her and she needs support right now. I'm going to have her driven home. We need to make sure she's got someone with her and that she can cope with the kids. I'll pass this straight up to the Super. The last politician I recall going missing was Harold Holt, and we know how *that* finished up.'

Campbell nodded and returned to Baker. It was 10:00 a.m.

and she was very weary. She tipped out her tea and made herself a strong black coffee.

At that time, a spunky blonde in a red and white top and designer jeans parked her sports car in Alexandra Avenue, Prahran. She walked to the tall apartment building at the corner of Chapel Street. The front entrance of the block, normally locked, was propped open as removalists struggled to take a large couch through the door. Frustration with the size of the couch and the narrowness of the opening was obvious from their spicy profanities blistering the air.

Teresa stood silently watching the Herculean pantomime, amused by the language. Unabashed by her presence, the two sweating, straining men continued their colourful invective. At last it was through and Teresa followed them inside, showily fishing keys from her shoulder bag. Waiting for the lift she scanned the resident directory and memorized some names on floors nine to twelve. Stepping into the lift she hit the button for the twelfth floor, relieved the removalists were continuing their battle via the stairs. As she ascended, she pulled on some clear surgical gloves.

In the foyer on twelve, Teresa saw doors to four units. All but Aldrittson's bore the owner's name in a slot beneath the door bell. She inserted the key and held her breath, praying it was not alarmed. When the door opened quietly she entered and closed it behind her.

Standing just inside, she took in the size, shape, texture and atmosphere of the unit. The city view was expansive, breathtakingly close and clear. The unit itself was rectangular. To her immediate right was a small and tasteful kitchen. Ahead, a broad and generous open space divided into dining and lounge areas. Aldrittson's taste was elegant and expensive; nothing, it seemed, was wanting.

At the entrance beside her were four long blackwood doors. She opened one and found a neat work space with a computer, stationery shelves, dictionaries and other texts. She fired-up the computer, found it needed no password and quickly scanned the contents. The files were innocuous: letters to constituents, parliamentary speeches, family details, business matters and accounts. Innocuous or not, a copy was going with her. She plugged in her memory stick and commenced downloading. Silently, she moved forward and looked into a doorway on her left: Aldrittson's bedroom.

The big western windows allowed city views to flood the bedroom. These views were bounced around the room by floor to ceiling mirrors on the southern wall. A king-sized bed with side cabinets and lamps stood in front of the mirrored wall. To the left, a sliding door led to a walk-in wardrobe and small stylish bathroom. Like the rest of the apartment, everything was tasteful and well designed. Yet, something about the bedroom bothered her. Compared with the rest of the unit, it was Spartan and didn't fit the prevailing style.

She commenced her search in earnest. First the bathroom, next the walk-in robe and then the two bedside cabinets. The left cabinet contained several books, the right one was empty. She checked the bed, the mattress and under the bed: all clean. She found nothing, not even in the pockets of his clothes.

Quietly, methodically and carefully, she worked her way around the lounge, dining and kitchen areas and back to the cupboards at the entrance. In effect, she had nothing to show for her visit apart from the contents of Aldrittson's computer on her memory stick. Knowing his reputation and some of his antics, she refused to believe he was without records of some kind. She wondered where he kept his most private information – at his parliamentary office or some other location? If it was another place, Giuseppe's soldiers could find it. In the meantime, she would think about it.

It was almost midday. She had turned the place over meticulously and was satisfied she had neither missed nor left anything out of place. Before leaving she checked Aldrittson's answering machine.

It contained a call from someone named "Spence" who wanted to discuss Ben's gym program. She didn't know Spence and was not surprised that Aldrittson worked out. She surveyed the foyer through the front door spy glass: all clear. She left as quietly as she had arrived and found the removalists still working on the ground floor. Nonchalantly, she walked to the car.

She now had another task. Today marked the beginning of her search for information about her parents. Driving towards the city, she felt a growing apprehension.

Chapter
TWENTY-TWO

Parking in Collins Street, Teresa fed the meter and walked a block to the Registry of Births Deaths and Marriages. This was her first opportunity to delve into the deaths of her parents since finding the letters in Santini's box. She thought the easiest way to start was by lodging a request for death certificates. She could have done it on the internet but preferred a personal approach. Her drive to discover the truth was not entirely rational; she knew that. Dealing directly with the record keepers she thought might bring her a little closer to her parents. And that was illogical too. Her strange feelings were further complicated by a fear of what she would find.

With legs feeling like lead, Teresa walked slowly into the request area, selected a leaflet on how to obtain certificates and sat, quietly reading. The respite calmed her apprehension.

Normally, she was not hesitant, but having copied the letters and deciding to follow her heart, she believed she had crossed an invisible line that now put her constantly on tenterhooks. At times when she least expected, the letters and photo catapulted thoughts about her parents into her mind reinforcing the realisation she knew so little of them. In the absence of truth, and uncertain about the future she knew only that when she found that truth, action *would* follow.

She submitted the forms, paid the fee and left knowing that in ten to fifteen days she would have some answers. Maybe not all, but some.

Stepping into thin winter sunshine, Teresa felt a sense of buoyancy she had not experienced since first visiting Santini's. The quest had begun. She drove to Swanston Street and found a car park near the State Library.

The Grande Old Dame had been commissioned in 1854, her north wing completed in 1864 and the imposing Doric columns and front portico added in 1870. Teresa hadn't been there since university days when, like many before her, she had inhaled the rich historical atmosphere of the octagonal reading room beneath the huge glassed dome. In her mind's eye she pictured the green shaded lamps and oblong reading tables radiating from the centre of the room like spokes in a wagon wheel. She could even recall that unforgettable essence seeping from thousands of books lining the shelves – a unique aroma distilled from leather, linen, paper, ink and gum.

Today her destination was the papers and periodicals section, a functional place not nearly as elegant as the old reading room. Obtaining the 1975 microfiche records for the *Sun News Pictorial* she concentrated on the months June to December. It was during this period she had gone to live with the Benedettis. She had only a hazy idea of what she was searching for but felt she would recognise it when she saw it.

Like most years, 1975 carried its share of triumphs and tragedies. The bulk shipping carrier, *Lake Illawarra*, had collided with the Tasman Bridge, knocked out two pylons, destroyed the road and killed at least ten people; Saigon unconditionally surrendered to the Viet Cong; Australian identity, Dame Mabel Brookes, renowned for her energetic charity work and long term presidency of the Queen Victoria Hospital died; wage indexation was adopted by the Australian Arbitration Commission; North Melbourne won its historic football grand final over Hawthorn and *Think Big* won the Melbourne Cup. The climax of the year was the sacking of Prime Minister Gough Whitlam by Governor-General Sir John Kerr.

Hoping against hope to find an account of a ski boat accident, Teresa ploughed through a morass of stories and almost missed it. Several seconds passed before it registered, but there it was – September 15, 1975: **Brutal Double Murder At Sorrento.** Her stomach knotted, her mouth dried, her throat constricted painfully. The naked bodies of a man and woman were found jammed into the boot of a 1969 Holden on the Sorrento foreshore. Joggers were alerted by a terrible smell from the car. Bare details disclosed the bodies were missing heads, hands and feet; they bore no other wounds apart from genital mutilation of the male.

Teresa put her head in her hands, she felt ill and was pierced with dismay. She had no doubt it was her father Alfredo with Angelina Pescaro. She steeled herself and followed reports of the police investigation over the next few months. The bodies remained unidentified. No one claimed them and no one reported them missing. Enquiries had been made interstate and overseas and, by December, the bodies were still unidentified. Teresa scrolled back to the original story and slowly moved forward in case she had missed something. A small article on September 20 momentarily caught her eye. An unidentified female body, fully clothed, had washed up on the beach at Greenwich Bay, Williamstown. She continued to the end of 1975, satisfied she had missed nothing important.

Returning to the desk, Teresa arranged for print outs and asked for the 1976 microfiche. Her head pounded and her stomach felt like barbed wire, but the nausea was gone. She wanted to cry but somehow, held back. It was grim work. She began scrolling carefully through 1976 and found a small article which unleashed a lightning bolt that literally made her tremble:

Open Finding on Drowning

Blinded by tears, Teresa read that an inquest into the drowning death of Adriana Marchese, whose body was found on a Williamstown beach on September 20, 1975, had returned an open finding. The police investigation revealed that Mrs Marchese had taken a night boat trip around Port Phillip Bay on September 15, 1975. She had come alone and from the evidence of passengers, had made no attempt to join on-board festivities. Nobody had noticed her failure to disembark. Coroner, Peter Miller, noted that nothing suggested foul play and there was nothing to indicate whether Mrs Marchese had fallen or jumped overboard. No suicide note had been found. The cause of death was drowning but the reason was unknown. The article concluded by stating that Mr Marchese's whereabouts was unknown and their five year old daughter was being cared for by family friends.

Frozen with grief and shock, Teresa sat at the desk silently weeping, tears streaming down her cheeks. It seemed as if a lifetime passed before she could mentally and physically centre herself. She didn't know what had happened but suspected that after discovery of the bodies at Sorrento, Adriana had either been told or inferred their identities and taken her life. At five years of age, Teresa knew nothing about the relationship between her parents, a gap compounded by the time she had been without them. Santini's letters revealed that her mother's love for her husband stretched beyond infinity.

So often had she read the letters between her father and Angelina Pescaro she could almost recite them – the passion between them was palpable. Yet their relationship was complex. Several times Alfredo mentioned his despair over Adriana who, in her innocence, cherished him unconditionally. Torn by guilt, he had finally suggested to Angelina that because of Adriana's love and their beautiful little Teresa, they should end their affair before it destroyed them.

After what she had read in the microfiche today, Teresa believed they had been found out. How she would confirm her frightening suspicion was, right now, too difficult to imagine. She rose, managed to get herself to the counter and waited for her documents. No matter how bad she felt, she still had one more call to make before returning to Pescaro's.

By the time she reached her car, Teresa's resolve had returned. She sat motionless for some time then dialled Aldrittson's parliamentary office.

Chapter
TWENTY-THREE

Jack Aldrittson rubbed his forehead. Santini's death had caused nothing but trouble. His personal workload had doubled and with Danny Browne's position unfilled, the black jobs were mounting. Clients were complaining about the slow disposal rate and, worst of all, he had just learned of an arsenic leak into the headwaters of Port Phillip Bay. Right now he didn't know if he was responsible or whether it was the idiocy of some other bastard. Either way, the implications were unpleasant and the timing diabolical.

Recently, his only satisfaction had come from taking Ben's advice: he had started looking over Santini's shoulder. Give him his due, the little shit had been smart. Santini's system for concealing black disposals was now very sophisticated. He wondered if Santini had secretly changed things to suit Pescaro. Ben's suggestion to check Santini's activities troubled him. What had prompted him to make it? His timing, so close to Santini's death was, if not suspicious, worrying. He didn't want to dwell on that – sometimes it was better not to know things.

He turned his mind to Martin Judd. Santini had considered Judd competent in all but the administration of black waste. Jack was uncertain whether Judd's ignorance of their scam was a ploy by Santini to ensure that he, Santini, remained indispensable, or whether Santini feared Judd too honest to possess the knowledge. Judd would have to be properly vetted. Jack had helped Judd after his accident and knew money was important to him. But was that enough? It occurred to him that if Judd passed muster, Santini's death provided the perfect opportunity for placing greater control back into his own hands – an opening for easing Pescaro out of the loop. *That would be a bloody good thing!*

Pescaro was a worry. Although he had been quiet since Santini's death, he remained fixed in his drive to legalise their waste racket – now! What drove that demand was perplexing Aldrittson. So too was the pressure Pescaro was applying to himself and Ben. Of all the things that had occurred in their long relationship, this was most uncharacteristic.

Aldrittson mentally reviewed their discussions over the past eighteen months. They were unanimous about how to get their scheme in place; there had never been any dispute about timeframes; they had recently acquired their last parcel of land and had generously accommodated influential local government opinion makers. Finally, and with great stealth, they had completed an exhaustive environmental impact study of their proposed site. It had taken three years and cost a bomb, but it had been a brilliant investment.

The clean, green strategy included reafforestation, wetlands, chemical, mineral and substance reclamation and recycling. The entire project would use sustainable energy sources: solar, thermal and wind and, with Blanchard's farm completing their fifteen square kilometre buffer zone, the project could proceed. They intended commencing with waste destruction standards equalling world's best practice and planned on setting new standards over time. Continuous improvement, or *Kaizen* as it was referred to in the business world, was integral to their plans. Only the media strategy remained to be completed and that too was almost ready.

Aldrittson believed everything was beautifully positioned to commence lobbying a new parliament. Pushing for approval *before* the election was madness. Whatever demons were driving Pescaro, they were unknown to him. In the meantime, Martin Judd would be checked out as a potential replacement for Santini.

Ruffles, on Southbank, was a tasteful and chic restaurant where Melbourne's smart-set loved to be seen. Nestling on the edge of the Yarra river, the view west took in the re-sculptured landscape making this part of the city appealing. Teresa had arrived a little before 8:30 p.m., a good half hour before her meeting with Ben Aldrittson. She had showered, popped a couple of Panadol and relaxed in a long meditation to remove the shock and sadness of her day. Nothing would prevent this meeting. She wanted to be there first and was certain Aldrittson would come despite the brevity of her message. Her plan was simple: to look as feminine and vulnerable as possible. Tonight was not only about obtaining a copy of the Premier's briefing package for Pescaro, but to also hook Aldrittson, to lower his defences and to begin initiating his downfall.

Teresa's hatred of Aldrittson began in her final two years at Genazzano. The parents of her two best friends, Abbie Nathan and Emma Dunlop, were financially, physically, emotionally and spiritually ruined by the ruthless destruction of their company, *Generunner*. For more than a decade the small Victorian company had painstakingly developed a technique for analysing dog blood. Specific to greyhounds, it could highlight defects, markers of superiority (size, speed, muscle tone and stamina) and indicators of good health. The dog-racing industry stood to gain significantly from breeding super-dogs through a process that eventually could eliminate flawed genes.

The two scientists, Graeme Nathan and Evan Dunlop, had been lifelong friends whose interest in greyhounds stemmed from their fathers. Aldrittson, not then in Parliament but working for the Liberal Party, had engineered a range of agreements for *Generunner's* developers which promised to take them to the next growth phase. Without explanation, Aldrittson suddenly switched support to a huge French conglomerate. Publicly, he argued their size and experience would benefit Victorians through jobs growth and scientific achievement. *Generunner* was then systematically strangled by the French until, as their last hope for survival, Dunlop and Nathan sold their firm and patent rights for a pittance. Much later, it was discovered the conglomerate had been developing similar, though not as effective, technology. *Generunner* and its innovative technology disappeared. Everything the two scientists had worked for was gone. In its place was the debris of two fractured families; among them, Abbie and Emma. Teresa believed Aldrittson had orchestrated the Nathan-Dunlop collapse and despised him with a passion. Since working for Pescaro, her sources had returned persistent rumours that, covertly, Aldrittson had financially benefited by supporting the French. Nothing less than his complete exposure and destruction was acceptable to her for the damage he had inflicted upon her friends and their families.

Teresa's soft, black frock clung to her trim figure, the discreet neckline revealing only a hint of cleavage. Around her throat she wore a fine silver chain and pear shaped diamond which, beneath the dazzling, pencil-thin halogen lights, blazed with white fire. Her dark hair gently framed her face accentuating the high cheekbones and luminescent, smoky green eyes. She knew she looked alluring and sensual, yet she also wanted to carry an indefinable air of vulnerability.

She ordered a macchiato and waited, absorbing her surroundings.

Aldrittson arrived a few minutes after her coffee order. She watched him enquire at the register where she had booked under Santini's name. He looked every inch the politician – a tall man in a deep blue suit, pale blue shirt and crimson tie.

Approaching her, his eyes widened in pleasure and surprise as he realised whom he was meeting. Over the years he had seen her several times but only ever at a distance. He had meant to find out about her but with everything else going on in his life, had not found the time. He strode the last few metres, commanding, gallant, dripping with charm.

For her part, Teresa sat demurely – waiting and watching. She remained seated when he arrived at the table, extended her hand

and said, 'Good evening Mr Aldrittson.'

'Good evening … Miss Santini?'

'Please, call me Teresa.' She didn't bother correcting him.

'Bernardo's death – a very sad thing. Please accept my condolences for your loss.' Aldrittson, appearing suitably concerned was reluctant to show his ignorance about what, if any relationship existed between Santini and Teresa.

'Thank you,' said Teresa gently, understanding his dilemma immediately and unwilling to change his perception.

He sat. 'Would you like something more substantial to accompany the macchiato? Cognac, benedictine, or champagne, perhaps?'

She smiled, 'a cognac would be very nice.'

Aldrittson summoned a waiter and ordered a long black coffee for himself and cognac for them both. Before the waiter could leave, Aldrittson turned to Teresa. 'I've eaten, have you?'

'I have,' she replied, 'the coffee and cognac will be fine.' Her smile induced near meltdown in Aldrittson.

He was intrigued by her voice: It was warm and earthy, slightly husky. As he took in the trim shapely figure, rounded in all the right places, he thought – *this is my kind of a woman*. He noted her necklace and guessed it was worth a small fortune. Though she was dressed simply in black, she looked both elegant and sexy. And yet … he discerned a hint of melancholy. He was already thinking of conquest.

Teresa looked at him directly. 'Let's get the business over with first, shall we?'

He eyed her approvingly. 'Of course.' He withdrew a long and thickish envelope from inside his coat. 'I believe this is what you need.'

'Explain it to me, briefly,' she said, a smile playing on her lips, her gaze unwavering.

He hesitated. *Why should he reveal anything to this woman? She was a stranger for Christ's sake.* A cold shiver ran down his spine at the memory of his last meeting with Santini.

'In very simple terms,' he commenced, 'it's a proposal to build a waste disposal and treatment plant in Central Victoria. It will handle the most toxic of wastes except for radioactive stuff. In point form, this paper sets out site and plant benefits in political, economic, strategic and technological terms. It also summarises our environmental impact study and provides a comparison between current legal disposal standards and those set by our environmental study. These, I might add, are higher than any waste disposal standards in Australia. There is also a media campaign framework and indicators for future development. The latter are significant because capacity could easily be expanded to accept toxic waste for the whole country. Everything is costed but the project's best features are these: first, none of it will cost the government a cent, everything will be paid for by private industry, so, no taxpayer dollars; second, the proposal seeks an independent, government owned, quality control process to monitor every aspect of treatment. These two elements should make the scheme a winner. That's it in a nutshell.'

Teresa remained silent but nodded for him to continue.

He studied her momentarily before resuming. 'At this stage, a broad concept is all that's needed to win approval for the next step. That will be progression of the feasibility study and advice to the public about the plan. All background scientific work has been done in preparation for that. Although there are the bones of a media campaign, it still needs a bit of thought. For instance, in 1986, the Government announced plans to create a toxic dump in the Darghile Forest near Heathcote but furious opposition defeated them and it never happened. Factors like that have to be carefully considered. Apart from that, I'd say eighty per cent of the detailed project work is complete. We were not expecting a request to move so quickly so the remaining twenty per cent is still a bit underdone.' Aldrittson had skirted the truth: the present *demand* for action had leapt from the blue and Teresa knew it.

She smiled broadly. 'Quite the political briefing there, Mr Aldrittson. You have been busy over the past ten days.' She was gently telling him that she knew exactly when Santini's request had been made.

He shrugged and sipped his cognac. 'I still don't understand Pescaro's rush to bring this on. Surely he knows that politically this is the worst time? A scheme like this is immensely contentious and politically fraught. The likelihood of cabinet giving this a green light so close to an election is almost zero. To them it'll be a sea anchor. Doesn't he understand that?'

Teresa listened in silence, nodded and said, enigmatically, 'He has his reasons. He never does anything without purpose. He will be pleased you have completed the proposal. Now, I have to ask, when are you presenting it to the Premier and cabinet? Or have you already done so?'

Aldrittson studied her keenly. Vulnerable or not, the woman was sharp. He decided to play it straight. 'No. I haven't presented it to cabinet. I am hoping to get an opportunity sometime in the next two weeks.'

'Good,' said Teresa smiling warmly, 'but try *no later* than Friday week. We'll meet here at the same time next Friday. You can tell me how it went. And of course, you realise this 'request' does not come from me.'

Aldrittson was silent for some moments before he said, 'Something's going on here, something I don't understand. It isn't appropriate to push this plan so hard without me knowing the reason for it, especially if that reason is likely to prevent the Premier and cabinet endorsing it.'

Teresa said sharply, 'You're in no position to bargain Mr Aldrittson. I'm delivering a message.' She softened her voice and continued. 'If you have any doubt about the consequences, talk to your father.'

Aldrittson suddenly felt as though he had poked a cobra. Her rapid change of manner certainly underscored the message. He decided, for the present, to go along with her. 'Okay then, if we're meeting next Friday, why don't we do dinner? There's no need for you and me to be at odds with one another.'

'Of course Mr Aldrittson, I'd be delighted.' Teresa smoothly switched to temptress mode. The game had begun.

'Why don't you call me Ben, Teresa. I feel it's time to be a little less formal, don't you?' He was all polish and poise and, as Teresa gazed upon the handsome face, cobalt eyes and thick blond hair, she smiled warmly at his invitation while thinking, *Boy, am I going to enjoy your demise you black-hearted bastard. And so too will Abbie and Emma.*

'Ben, that is one of the most positive things you've said all night,' she purred, fluttering her eyes. 'Merely because we have different masters doesn't mean we can't become friends.' Although her words were an invitation, her manner remained coy.

Now, even more interested in this beautiful woman, Aldrittson decided on full-scale pursuit. 'What about a nightcap back at my place?' he enquired, his deeper meaning transparent.

Again, she laughed softly and nodded. 'Thanks, but not tonight. I've had a very long day and this is a pleasant way to finish. Maybe next Friday?'

Aldrittson was pleased. This was far from a rebuff and he could wait. This woman was different from most others he had bedded and although he wasn't sure why, he felt a sense of danger and excitement around her. It was not just her Mafia connection, it was something more subtle, indefinable. On this first meeting she had definitely beguiled him and he desperately wanted to explore the trim, firm body beneath that clinging black dress.

'How do I get in touch with you, Teresa?'

She paused before answering, dipped her face then looked directly into his eyes as though she had reached an important decision. 'I'll ring you during the week. I have your parliamentary number and I can leave a message with your secretary.'

'No, no, that's too convoluted. Here, this is my private mobile number, use it. I'll be happy to hear from you any time.' Aldrittson passed across a business card which Teresa took and tucked into her purse.

'I'll be looking forward to next Friday. Thank you for this,' she raised the envelope he'd given her. 'Now, I must go.' She rose gracefully and extended her hand. Aldrittson took it and squeezed gently. *Funny*, he thought, *I didn't notice that grip before, or its suggestiveness.* He stood watching her as she left. *What an interesting package. Finding out about her will be a job to Spencer's liking.*

Chapter
TWENTY-FOUR

Saturday afternoon was cool and sunny and the breeze, although gentle, carried a bite. Hardly surprising, it was straight off the bay in early June. Spencer Johnson sat on the promenade near St. Kilda Baths drinking coffee with Colin Fox, Johnny Holmes and Eric Stanley. Holmes and Stanley were at the pointy end of crime and knew what was going on. They had form for violence, burglary, robbery, drugs and extortion. Only in their early thirties, they'd spent more than half their lives inside institutions. To Fox, that was good reason to be cautious – they didn't belong to Mensa *and* they were careless. Johnson, on the other hand, wanted to pick their brains without them realising it. He was hoping they could confirm a rumour about the Russian Mafiya. So he had spent nearly half an hour with them drinking coffee, perving on young female joggers and talking crap about crime and stupid cops. A saving grace was the venue – it was as pleasant as their conversation was mundane.

'So Eric,' Johnson said, concluding his fishing expedition, 'you've heard some whispers about the Russians eh? Do I need to be careful?'

'Shit no Spence,' Stanley snorted. 'You wouldn't even stir their fuckin' tea. Nah, they want some real action – big bucks. Problem is, the fuckin' Mafia's got things locked down tight, and the Russkies ain't strong enough to start pushin'.'

Holmes broke in. 'Don't be fuckin' stupid. They got balls as big as emu eggs, they don't worry about numbers, they're the meanest bastards on earth. I tell ya Spence, ya wouldn't wanna cross these pricks. They don't give a flyin' fuck when it comes to vengeance – anywhere, anytime, anyhow is their motto.'

Johnson wanted a little more. 'Yeah, I heard they're vicious.

But seriously, I heard rumours about the pricks wanting to move into the fitness industry. I don't fancy being heavied by some ex-KGB bastard.'

'Nope, heard nuthin' like that mate. What I heard is they wanna get right into drugs, prostitution and people movin'. Couple of bods mentioned garbage too. But, I reckon you're safe for now Spence.' Holmes laughed. 'An' mate, if they come after you, don't fuckin' call us.'

Fox finished his coffee and sat, stone-like. Johnson had only hinted at the purpose of this meeting but he could see where it was headed. He decided that if Aldrittson was behind what he *thought* was coming, then he could pay more – a lot more. In Fox's opinion, Aldrittson was entering a world that was dangerous, nasty and way beyond his comprehension. But, because he was such a ruthless little shit, he supposed Aldrittson didn't care.

Johnson had what he needed. After slipping Holmes and Stanley some cash, he left with Fox.

Walking back to the underground carpark Johnson asked, 'Got a plan? A germ of an idea?'

'I have,' said Fox laconically, 'want to know about it or read about it?'

'Think I better know about it,' said Johnson. 'It could get messy and we have to think it through.'

Fox peered at Johnson. 'Do you reckon that idiot Aldrittson has any concept of what he might be unleashing if we go ahead with this Spence? You know as well as I do, the Russians are serious grief.'

Johnson looked uncomfortable. 'Yeah, I know, but he doesn't give a rat's. As long as he gets what he wants.'

'Well, do *we have* to give it to him? You could tell the prick to piss off – use another team.'

'Jesus Foxy, you know better than that – we'll be sidelined. He's bloody good with the readies and, for something like this, he'll pay plenty. At least if we take it on we might be able to guide it a little bit.'

Fox nodded. Although neither had voiced their thoughts, both were on the same wave length – warfare between the Italian and Russian mafiosi. They walked in silence to the car.

'Do you reckon a stoush between these two groups would work?' asked Spencer as he leaned on the roof over the driver's door.

'It could,' was the quick response, 'the Reds are hungry. They might be low on numbers but they're accomplished and they're ambitious. They want to make a name for themselves, assert their authority and presently, they're in a very limited market. They want territory and income. Sooner or later they'll take both. In effect, we'll be starting the inevitable only maybe it'll be earlier than they wanted.'

'What do you think Pescaro will do?'

Fox thought a moment. 'He'll fire straight back because he's stronger, but he could negotiate space. I say that on the basis of events in the US. The Russkies have no honour and no rules; they play for keeps and thrive on violence and bastardry. If it gets out of hand, I reckon Pescaro will negotiate. It depends on what the Reds have in mind. If they're after something Pescaro cherishes it'll be mayhem till there's a winner. Probably Pescaro. But, there'll be an awful lot of pain in between. I suspect his mob have gone a bit soft and won't have the stomach for serious warfare. Not on the Russkies' terms anyway.'

Johnson nodded slowly. 'Well, if you're going to start this, what do you need?'

Fox grinned. 'Neat bit of footwork Spence – I thought it was *we*.' He laughed. 'First off I need really sound intelligence. I can't rely on what those two cretins had to say. And probably we haven't got time to scout for ourselves. I want to know the watering holes of at least three Italians and three Russians. They should be at different levels in the food chain. So, a pair of soldiers, a mid-level boss and a senior, but not top boss. Find out what the Russians want. We should try and match our pairs to the goal they're after. Bumping off a couple of the pricks in their area of special interest ought to generate action bloody quick time. We then withdraw and watch what happens. Make no mistake Spence, this is going to be bloody tricky business and we don't want to be caught in the middle. It goes without saying that neither side must suspect the whole catastrophe was engineered. What really bothers me is that the Russkies are no respecters of life or dignity – they won't care if innocents are hurt. You know me Spence, I don't like that. So let me make this crystal: I am *not* in agreement with this operation and reserve the right to withdraw. *I'll* determine the quality of the intel and let you know where *I* stand.'

Johnson nodded. 'Yeah, well I'm inclined to agree with you.' Colin Fox was particular about many things – especially killing people. Johnson thought of Fox in contradictory terms as a cold but principled killer. 'I'll find out what's needed, speak with Aldrittson and get back to you next week. Where do you want to be dropped?'

'St. Kilda junction is fine with me. Got to see someone near there. Come on, let's piss off. It's bloody freezing.'

Drummond parked the car half a kilometre from the end of Export Lane and walked quietly towards Aldrittson's Depot. It was 12:10 a.m., June 5, a cold night with a new moon. Dressed in black, he carried a back-pack with various accessories. The five acre site was enclosed by a 2.5 metre cyclone fence topped with strands of barbed wire. Seeing this, he decided to walk the perimeter and probe for weak spots, camouflage, vantage points, guard dogs and security.

His reconnaissance confirmed two free ranging German Shepherds, security cameras, tall poled security lamps and evidence of mobile security patrols. From the wad of cards stuffed in the front gate he reasoned the guards called hourly.

Overall, the site was almost a square with long truck shelters and work shops hugging the north and eastern boundaries. The southern side held a large bitumen car park with access through double gates on the west. Lawns, shrubs and trees were planted around the western and southern fences. The administration block squatted in the centre of the site, its entrance facing the carpark.

Drummond considered his best route to the offices was over the north fence and through the shadows of the truck sheds. Negotiating the security beacons would be difficult, their overlap with cameras meant anyone in the yard after dark would be caught on film. There was also the possibility of either sensor or silent alarms to the security firm. But he wanted information – he had to take the risk. Trees outside the fence would shield his entry and he had found one with a limb above the fence.

Crouching under the tree he took a rope and folding grappling hook from his backpack. He buckled on an equipment belt and added pepper spray, a slender Maglite, some memory sticks and a collapsible baton. Swinging the hook into the tree he checked that it held his weight and ascended. In the tree, he dropped his rope onto Aldrittson's side then removed a white paper parcel from his pack. He sat listening for anything unusual. Apart from frogs and the faint drone of traffic on Westgate Freeway, the night was quiet. He emitted a shrill, urgent whistle. Somewhere within the compound the dogs started barking. He waited and whistled again. Soon, two German Shepherds were snarling beneath him.

He unwrapped the package and began dispensing chunky squares of meat liberally laced with valium. The barking rapidly turned to contented snuffles. When the meat was eaten the dogs sat looking up expectantly. After twenty minutes they were prostrate and powerless. The dose would last about four hours and carried few consequences for the animals. He had to be gone no later than 4:00 a.m.

He moved along the overhanging limb, lowered himself full length and dropped to the ground. At the same time he heard a vehicle travelling down Export Lane towards Aldrittson's. He lay flat with the dogs. A small van stopped, lights illuminating the gates. He watched a man in uniform alight, walk to the gates, rattle them and stuff another card in the lock. Drummond shook his head in disgust – the check was sloppy and futile. The security man returned to the van, reversed and drove away. The transaction had taken less than a minute. Drummond was certain that if Aldrittson knew the quality of the security he paid for he would be ropable. On the other hand, perhaps he *was* getting what he paid for.

The dogs had not stirred. Keeping low, he moved to the nearest shed and worked his way around the edge of a sulphur-hued pond of light. There would be little on the camera that could identify him. His target was a dark spot where two lights just failed to fully overlap near the Administration Centre. Moving quickly, he cut across to the building and worked his way around it, testing for open windows. He knew he would be on film so kept his face to the wall. The one window he least expected to find unlocked turned out to be Jack Aldrittson's. Certain now there were no audible alarms, he still hurried in case of silent alarms wired directly to the security centre.

Inside the building Drummond found the external security lights bright enough to do without the torch. He closed the window and went straight to Aldrittson's desk, systematically searching and isolating papers he felt might be important. Aldrittson's computer was locked by a security code so he moved on quickly. There was little in the room or desk of value.

In the general office he identified Mary Edwards' desk from a photograph of her and, presumably, her husband, on a snow trip. He activated her computer and got straight into the office programs.

He plugged in a memory stick and began downloading. He had given a lot of thought to the type of information that might reveal wrongdoing and looked for employee details, customer information, waste disposal schedules by type, collection and disposal point. He was pursuing an idea that had arisen in discussion with Tony Maud on the Friday night – the possibility of Aldrittson's running another activity inside their main business.

He turned the copier on and moved from desk to desk for insight about the work performed by the occupants. After twenty desks he was satisfied he had located the main personnel and customer service areas and could retrieve some useful information. But again, he was stymied by computer security codes. He returned to Mary's computer and searched several folders and concluded he could probably get most of what he wanted from her computer if it was networked.

With senses honed, Drummond began systematically searching for anything that would link Aldrittson to the truck fire and two deaths. He moved to Santini's office. Switching on the computer he was again denied access. After several failed attempts to break security, he had an idea. He went back to Mary Edwards' desk and searched her folders. Santini's folder was empty but she had made an unprotected short-cut for Jack Aldrittson titled: "S-Code." He memorised the single alpha-numeric line, returned to Santini's computer and entered it – in like Flynn. He opened *My Documents* then a folder marked *Jobs*. Clicking on it, he saw items arranged in years. Opening the current year and month, he found blocks of entries in long alpha-numeric strings. He inserted another memory stick and started downloading. As best he could tell, these files were concealed from the general office system. He started to search Santini's desk although he didn't expect much – Santini had been dead nearly four days and the contents had probably been cleared.

The top right drawer was unlocked. It contained a plastic

insert for pens and pencils but otherwise was empty, as were the other drawers. It was obvious from the waste bin however, that someone was using the desk. He checked the contents and found it contained a few crumpled pages with long sets of handwritten numbers; he took two. Looking at Santini's book case, he saw volumes of four post binders going back years. He opened 1978 and found it full of customer invoices, trucking manifests, waste disposal schedules and pay records. He opened folders for 1981, 1987, 1993, 1996, 2002 and 2005: all records seemed similar.

Back in the main office he copied several days of entries from each of the years he had selected. Halfway through 2002, he heard the security patrol return. He nipped into the entry foyer and saw the watchman rattle the gates and put another card in the lock. As he made no attempt to enter the grounds, Drummond was confident there was no silent alarm back to the security centre. He finished copying and stashed the pages in his backpack. He returned the folders to Santini's shelves then removed and stowed his memory stick from Santini's computer. In the main office he found the download from Mary's computer had also finished – he removed the USB and stuck it in his belt. He switched the computer and photocopier off and took a last look around. It was now 3:15 a.m. and he felt as though he had been there only five minutes.

Returning to Aldrittson's office he heard a chilling sound – the window being quietly raised. *Somebody else was coming in.* Drummond moved to the desk nearest Aldrittson's office and knelt beside it facing the door. He waited. Whoever had come in had not closed the window. Soft steps rapidly swished past the desk – the intruder was clearly on a mission. He peered into the gloom: the newcomer was small and trim and in dark clothing. A waft of perfume invaded his nostrils – *a woman!* He looked again. Carefully, but purposefully, she made her way towards Santini's office. *Shit,* he thought, *if she doesn't already know I'm here from the dogs, she'll know it the minute she touches Santini's computer — it'll be warm.*

As soon as she was in the passage, Drummond crawled to Aldrittson's office and slipped out the window. He moved quickly along his previous route to the fence where his rope hung. He tested his weight again and cursed when the hook speared down on top of him. He swung it up again; it held firm. Bidding silent farewell to the still sleeping dogs, he shinnied into the tree, stashed the hook and rope in his pack, moved to another limb and dropped to the ground. He stayed a few moments before raising his head – no sign of the woman. He jogged quietly to his car. The absence of other vehicles in Export Lane suggested the new intruder had entered the grounds in a spot different from his. Right now however, he wasn't concerned with that. He had what he wanted and needed to be gone.

Chapter
TWENTY-FIVE

Teresa woke slowly on Sunday morning, exhausted from the previous forty-eight hours. She lay still, recapping. The turned off but warm computer and copier at AWD had alarmed her. Certain she had company, she searched the premises without result. Later, there had been that odd thing with the dogs. She had neither seen nor heard them when she entered the depot, yet as she left, they had barked and bounded out of the night. She smiled remembering – they had seemed drunk as they staggered and fell trying to leap at her in the window. Pepper spray had quickly dispatched them. It seemed obvious they had been drugged. Someone definitely had preceded her.

She had learned about the toxic waste racket soon after becoming Pescaro's office administrator. While he had openly referred to Aldrittson's role in finessing their scheme through Parliament, she had never actually heard him implicate Ben in its operation. But she inferred from his slick presentation to her on Friday night that he was deeply involved. She believed that if she could directly tie him to the unlawful dumping she had the perfect tool for exposing him. However, he *was* teflon-coated and she had seen him cruise his way out of too many seemingly impossible situations before. She wanted proof, hence the unorthodox visit to the depot.

There was, however, a serious flaw in her idea: exposing Aldrittson meant exposing Pescaro. Her feelings about Pescaro were ambivalent. As *Consigliere*, her position was unique and life in this role would be exciting. She was genuinely fond of Pescaro, yet looking ahead, she believed the future was threatening. Perhaps when she knew more about the demise of her parents she might feel differently, but right now she was in torment. The only thing she was certain about was that the Don's wife could never have been killed without his sanction.

Her visit to the depot was disappointing – she had not found what she wanted. From her book-keeping and the overheard discussions between Pescaro and Santini, her knowledge of the waste scam was intimate. She had known what to look for and where, and was familiar with Santini's coding system. She had even copied some of the damning information. But she had nothing cementing Ben Aldrittson's complicity in the fraud.

She contemplated the value of Santini's records and the letters she had found in his home. They would be ripe pickings for anybody interested in *her* activities, particularly if she went public. She decided to make copies and keep them somewhere safe – not at home. She also gave herself a mental prompt to be more careful and observant about what was going on around her. That someone else might have been inside AWD that night was truly unsettling.

Mulling all this over brought new insight. Pescaro would be *waiting* for her to comment on the Santini letters, to raise issues and ask difficult questions. He knew her curiosity was insatiable and he had given her a key to the box. He was *expecting* her to examine its contents. He could have withheld that key, but had not. He would be intensely curious about her silence. By straying from her normal behaviour and remaining quiet she had probably engineered the very opposite of what she had intended. Pescaro would be alert to that.

She thought about it some more. *Why would Pescaro want her to know about Alfredo's and Angelina's infidelity?* Especially given the shocking outcome. It had to be a test of some kind. She burrowed further under her doona and considered the possibilities. She had become Santini's replacement without the accompanying ritual for such an elevation. Being a female in this position was unique – it also carried the onerous responsibility of Mob mediator. She had never been a true *Picciotto*, flunkey to a fully fledged member.

Being a *Picciotto* meant fetching, carrying, collecting, punishing, heavying and betting. Nor had she undertaken the final phase of this type of apprenticeship – running her own criminal activities, showing she could profit and expand while exercising control and building respect. Instead, she had assumed Santini's mantle because of exceptional business, financial and entrepreneurial skills; essential attributes for today's Mafia. The Mob was as much interested in legitimate business and clever entrepreneurial acumen as it was in murder, violence, drugs and brutal law breaking. Teresa was the face of the modern Mafia.

Membership no longer depended on being Sicilian or of Sicilian extraction; these days any individual with particular and needed skills was recruited. But one thing would never change: undying allegiance to the Family. That was absolute. She had never been exposed to any test. The secrets of Santini's box had to be some form of initiation. Well, she was ready for it. After Santini's funeral, she would tackle Pescaro head on.

At 7:00 that Sunday evening, Senior Constable Aleisha Campbell was cursing her common decency for assisting Marnie Baker the previous Friday. She had finished nightshift at 7:00 a.m., slept, and rushed back to work for the quick changeover at three o'clock. At 6:35 p.m., the police Communications Centre, D.24, contacted her station: Lance Baker's body had been found near Lades Hill, close to Strath Creek, about twenty kilometres east of Broadford. It looked like suicide. Because she had helped with Baker's missing person report, she felt compelled to take the task. The Duty Commissioner, D.24 warned, had been notified. He would contact the Chief Commissioner who would inform the Minister for Police. This was not an everyday suicide.

Campbell had rung Sergeant Connor O'Dowd at Broadford and obtained details, including a faxed copy of the suicide note. She hated death messages and knew from Friday's meeting that both Marnie's and Baker's parents were together in Europe. Lack of family support would only make things more difficult.

Campbell parked the police car in Glyndon Avenue, Brighton, opposite the Baker home. She informed D.24 she would be off-air attending their last dispatch and walked down the pathway. *I am a harbinger of gloom. The minute I give this woman the news about her husband, her life, and those of her daughters will collapse and fill with pain. God I hate these jobs.*

Taking a deep breath, Aleisha knocked at the door. It was opened in a trice by Marnie Baker. Not a word was spoken. Marnie Baker's eyes filled with tears, her face blanched and her hands covered her mouth. In a strangled voice she said, 'You've found him. He's dead isn't he?'

Numb and feeling the transfer of Marnie's emotion, Aleisha simply opened her arms. There, on the door step, Marnie fell into them and wept, noisy, huge racking sobs, breath hard to find. Aleisha held her tightly, gently crooning and stroking her head, comforting as best she could, her folder making spontaneous compassion awkward. Slowly, she moved Marnie into the house.

She found the kitchen and detached herself from Marnie who was clinging, limpet like, and sat her at the table. Aleisha began to heat the kettle for tea. Gradually, the sobs subsided. Marnie asked chokingly, 'Where did you find Lance?'

'Just outside Strath Creek, near Broadford at about 5:30 this evening. We had to be sure it was him before we came to you. Unfortunately, you or someone else, will still have to formally identify him.'

'How? How did he die?' Marnie whispered.

'It's too early to be certain but it looks like suicide, I'm sorry. I have a copy of a note that was on the front seat of his car. It seems as though he drank some whiskey, took some pills and then turned the motor on and gassed himself from the exhaust. I'm so sorry to bring you this news. There is no easy way to say what I know must be devastating.' Aleisha went to Marnie and hugged her again.

Sitting opposite, Aleisha said gently, 'Marnie, I deeply feel your loss and I could see how distressed you were last Friday, but there are things I need to tell you and it would be good if someone was here to help you. Can I contact anyone for you? Would you like any of your neighbours here?'

Baker quivered as she pulled herself together. 'My sister Michelle lives at Korrumburra. We've been in close touch since Lance went missing. She'll come but I don't think I can speak to her just yet' Her eyes filled with tears again.

'Give me the number, I'll give her a call. By the way, where are the girls?'

'I've been so worried about Lance I asked friends to help out. Sarah is with a school friend and Jessica is with a friend from Kinder.'

'Good. Now, before I call Michelle, I need to tell you that your circumstances are different from most people in these situations. I'm sure you already appreciate that but I just want to run through a couple of things. There will be press and TV reporters once this story breaks. They will be intrusive and disruptive and possibly hurtful. We've not passed the story on yet, but these things have a way of getting out whether we like it or not. It's also possible the Premier and other Ministers will want to come and see you – that will mean more press. In the note your husband left …' Aleisha paused and withdrew the fax from her folder and passed it to Marnie, 'he mentions a solicitor's firm. I think it would be good if you contacted them as soon as you can. In a month or two there will be an inquest where the Coroner will enquire into the cause of your husband's death. That's likely to generate more media interest. I guess what I am trying to say is, you will need to prepare yourself for very close scrutiny of your husband's life and probably, your own.' She paused again, Baker's face had become stricken as she read the note.

*

Thursday
June 3, 2005

My Dearest Marnie,

I know that by the time you receive this note, you will be terribly distressed. I deeply regret leaving you and Jessica and Sarah in the way I have, and, though it will be meaningless to you now, I am truly, truly sorry. I feel however, that I have no choice.

I have always worked hard at maintaining our relationship and I have loved and respected you as powerfully as I could. I deeply love our daughters and would always protect them against harm; certainly I would never do anything to hurt them in anyway.

As you know, I have worked hard for the Government and for my constituents. Work was the most effective means I had of suppressing a dark secret in my life, a secret which has always made me feel ashamed but sadly, could not change. I do not want my sins rebounding on either you or the girls; this is the only way I can think of to prevent that from happening.

Some horrible people have discovered my secret and I greatly fear the consequences. Certainly, I do not trust my persecutor. I suppose, working in public life, I have always known that truth would catch up with me. Well, that day has come.

As best I can, I have protected your wellbeing against this day. All legal matters are in order and there should be no obstacles in your way. John Rattree of Devlin, Dunne and

Devine has seen to everything and will help you through this period.

I am so sorry. I love you all, but do please get on with your lives. Marnie Darling, I hope that one day you can find it in your heart to forgive me.

Lance

*

'What does this mean for God's sake? What's going on?' Marnie was anguished and again, wept uncontrollably. Campbell sat, quietly waiting, feeling the strain.

After a time she said, 'I don't know what this note means. But I did want to ask if you were aware of anything adverse going on in your husband's life?'

Feeling weighed down, Marnie shook her head. Brokenly she said, 'The only thing I can think of is the election. He never discussed anything with me that sounded like trouble. He certainly didn't hint at any secrets, or a persecutor. I don't know anything about that. This is really scary. I told you we had a row that last morning he went to work. I said he was putting in too much effort and I didn't think Meadows appreciated his work. I told him so in plain terms and he was really cranky about it. Other than that, I don't know of anything that worried him. Now, I have this awful feeling of dread. How could he be so cruel to us?'

Aleisha detected a shift in mood. 'I really don't know but I'll ring your sister now. As it's going to be a while before she gets here, is there anyone else you'd like to have with you while you wait?'

'Yes, please. The Jennings next door at 48 are dear friends. They'll come and stay until Michelle gets here. I would like that. Thank you.'

Campbell went to the lounge room and rang Michelle Brown at Korumburra. After a ten minute conversation she returned to the kitchen. Marnie stood, walked to Aleisha and embraced her. She spoke quietly, more composed. 'I have a thousand questions but I don't know where to start. You have been so kind and so understanding I cannot thank you enough. I realise now that when I met you last Friday you were on your way home after nightshift. Yet you stayed with me – all that time. If all the police were like you, we'd have the best force in the world. Thank you is inadequate I know, but I mean it sincerely.'

Aleisha nodded and smiled, her eyes moist. 'I'll go next door and talk to the Jennings and briefly explain the situation. Are you okay with that?'

Marnie nodded.

Enveloped in the fug of his favourite Cusano cigar and the syrupy tones of the *Ink Spots*, Pescaro sat in his study. Comfortably settled in a deep leather arm chair and sipping aged brandy, at 9:00 p.m. he was hard at work.

Pescaro adored luxury and found the solace of his study conducive to clear thinking. For him, success was measured as much by the degree of thought devoted to a task as the final outcome.

He was thinking about Teresa. Her silence on Santini's security box interested him, he was even beginning to think she might not have inspected the contents. Yet here was a small mystery – a locked strong box for which she had the key. Not inspecting the contents would contradict everything he knew about her. If nothing happened soon, he would have to prod her.

But enough – Teresa was the least of his worries. It was his black waste business that required serious thought. Of itself, this was a major irritation. His empire and interests were extensive, yet this one issue was beginning to seem like his *only* interest. To an extent, he blamed himself; he might have been too hasty pressuring the Aldrittsons.

He had received Ben's briefing paper for the Premier, a slick and practical document he had to admit, and understood he couldn't control the timing for his scheme. He even conceded that trying to win government support for the concept right now was probably close to impossible. It *was* too close to the election and other 'vote catchers' would be occupying the minds of the Premier and his Ministers. His timing was totally awry. But that was only part of the problem. The driver creating his nightmare was the Russian Mafiya.

Russian criminals were arriving in Australia any way they could and were quietly planting themselves in the community. Just like the USA, law enforcement authorities here seemed largely ignorant of their presence. But unlike America, two elements impeded Russian establishment: Australia's relatively small population overall and, within it, a tiny Russian community. The minuscule Russian populace severely curtailed opportunities for exploitation and extortion and compelled the Mafiya to look elsewhere. And it was this that had become the focus of Pescaro's concern: intense Russian scrutiny and jealousy of *his* long held preserves.

The Russians were trouble. Even though they likened themselves to the Mafia, there were many differences. For instance, they had no firm family structure, a matter of significance to the Mafia. The only sense of family Pescaro could see was their predilection for inflicting unfettered violence on other Russians. There was little to suggest a heritage of close familial support and evolution. Their clans were loosely structured and bosses frequently came and went. Even their roots were a matter of conjecture. Some believed they stemmed from Communist Russia's black market economy while others argued they sprang from the horrific prison camps of Peter the Great. Those barbarous places had spawned violent criminals whose tight, vicious gangs followed an unbreakable creed which demanded they never work legitimately, pay taxes, fight for the army, or, under any circumstance help police unless to trick or harm them. As a fraternity, they called themselves the *Vor V Zakononye* or just Vors, meaning "thieves in law" or "thieves within the code".

Pescaro's North American experience had certainly not endeared the Russian Mafiya to him. To the contrary, after his visit in 2002 he began to study them fearing they would see Australia as a submissive frontier ripe for plunder. Such an assault would diminish his own empire – a most unpalatable prospect. He found that four dominant Vor groups had spread from Moscow across Europe and beyond: the Georgians, Chechens, Dolgoprudanskaya and the Ukrainians. In the wings, like wolves sniffing for carcasses, were scores of powerful, but lesser brigades. To make matters worse, one of their intimidating features was that many of their leaders were highly educated – PhDs in maths, engineering, physics and computer technology. Many were also thoroughly schooled in the Russian political system. These strengths were consolidated by an abundance of followers whose military backgrounds bristled with weapons training and other deadly abilities.

This unwholesome blend of skill, violence and brains had resulted in what Boris Yeltsin once termed 'a super power of crime.' No more powerful an example could be found than in the Vors' flagrant co-option of private Russian banking to a level where they controlled eighty per cent of the central banking system. Such immense influence provided unlimited access to sources of western aid and financial support. The benefits had been enormous. Pescaro's Sicilian colleagues had expressed their envy and apprehension at this extraordinary power. Vors had bled millions of dollars from these sources and entrenched their global criminal economy to a position of virtual impregnability. Indeed, some believed that Vor control of Russian funds exacerbated the 1998 Wall Street crash. Pescaro had no doubt the Mafiya was financially stronger than the Mafia and its collective ambition was to become the undisputed Czars of world crime.

Looking ever more deeply into their practices, Pescaro discovered that Perestroika had enabled thousands of Russian Jews to move into Israel, among them, huge numbers of Mafiya. Their consolidation and asset building was so voracious that some Israeli leaders considered them a serious threat to the country's political and economic stability.

From experience, Pescaro knew that Vors established links with other criminal groups, like his own, including the Serbian Ravna Gora, Colombians, Triads and, when it suited, savage individual criminals. He also knew they could not be trusted. He had heard one of John Gotti's associates grumble that the Russians were crazy and would wipe out any man who offended them, including his entire family. On his same visit to the USA, Pescaro read of a Los Angeles cop saying that 'murder was a blood sport for the Mafiya and they would shoot you just to see if their guns worked.'

These were the factors that fuelled his concern. Reports had been trickling in from various quarters that pressure from Russian criminals was mounting. Pescaro sensed a restlessness and growing impatience among them. They wanted a piece of *his* action. So far however, no Vor had requested a "sit down" to discuss boundary realignments or any restructuring of criminal activity. Even if they had, he would have pissed them off, he had been Don for too long to give anything away. While he was confident his Mob could match anything the Russians had to offer he was reluctant to become involved in a blood bath, the Vors were clever and cruel adversaries. What was particularly pissing him off now was their increasing forays into waste disposal – *his* waste disposal business.

Additionally, they were slack-arsed and arrogant about local custom and culture. Out to make a quick buck, they employed standover tactics and disposal practices that were certain to attract attention, attention that could so easily rebound on his and Aldrittson's long nurtured and well planned activities. *I've invested too much money, time and effort on our project to have it ruined by a bunch of fuckwits from Russia,* he thought. But, at seventy-four, he was feeling too old for heavy conflict and thus far had not taken retaliatory action. Furthermore, no one was certain about how many Vors were in the country which meant that assessing their resources and capability was difficult.

To make matters worse, his successor was awaiting burial. Pescaro had intended for Santini to become the new Don once their waste scheme won government acceptance. But Santini's death and the growing Russian pressure had wrecked his plans. He worried too as to whether Teresa was strong enough to withstand a Russian onslaught if it all broke loose.

Teaching the Russians a lesson would be hard; they were formidable foes. He had even heard the FBI say the same thing. He smiled inwardly as he thought about that. Coppers were inevitably in a "no win" situation fighting with one hand tied behind them. They were compelled to follow all the rules with few resources while his, and other criminal groups, had unlimited resources and none of the rules. The cops would present little barrier to Russian plans.

Pescaro had no intention of playing second fiddle on a stage he considered his own. Yet, Mafiya boldness was breathtaking. They had taken prostitution to a new level by kidnapping scores of women, girls and boys from Croatia, Bosnia, Poland, Russia and the Ukraine. Then, sold as sex slaves with no regard for their wellbeing, they were slipped into different countries, made into sexual or pornographic objects, subjected to appalling depravities, discarded or killed. Heroin and global weapons trade, including atomic bomb ingredients such as Caesium-137, Strontium-90 and uranium, were all part of Vor activity. And, for light relief, they had raped the diamond mines of Sierra Leone to build lavish casinos in Costa Rica. These were hallmark signatures of the Vor code: wealth accretion and social disruption.

Pescaro grinned wryly to himself. He could hardly complain, many of their activities were similar to his own. However, the breadth and scale of their ventures in other countries heralded conflict for his own empire and the more he pondered that dynamic, the less he liked it. Although the Vors and Mafia often teamed up, particularly for fraud and tax scams, such a partnership was unlikely here. Keeping them at bay would be difficult.

It was the sum total of these pressures which had caused him to lean on the Aldrittsons. Their secret waste disposal plan just *had* to be ready for the election. The advantage of progressing the scheme was relief from an accelerating demand for disposal of black waste. This had grown slowly over time as a consequence of 'encouragement' by Santini. It was now approaching boilover as a result of some sneaky enquiries into illegal dumping by the New South Wales Government. If their scheme gained approval their clients would at least be able to store their waste knowing a legitimate solution was underway. This decision, Pescaro believed, would diminish the Russian's opportunity for exploiting his plans. Yet nothing could be taken for granted – especially when it came to politicians.

Chapter
TWENTY-SEVEN

An extraordinary and unscheduled Cabinet meeting was about to commence in the premier's office. It was eight o'clock Monday morning and the agenda was Lance Baker's death.

'Alright ladies and gents.' Meadows rapped the table top with his knuckles. 'A bit of shush please. I have called you here because, as you all know, sadly, Lance Baker our Minister for Environment, took his own life. I have asked John Plattern to address you.'

Plattern was the sixty year old Minister for Police and Emergency Services. A grizzled, crew-cut, ex-navy captain, he was dour, practical and didn't waste words. His background had helped facilitate a first class rapport with the police, prisons, fire and emergency services people.

'Thanks Mr Premier. Colleagues, a bit after six last night the Chief Commissioner of Police informed me that Lance Baker, formally reported as a missing person on Friday last, was found dead near Strath Creek. He was discovered in his car about 5:30 p.m. at Lades Hill. A hose was attached to the exhaust pipe. The post mortem is today. On the front seat was a half bottle of whiskey, an empty bottle of Temazapam tablets and a note which I'll read. Needless to say, Chatham House Rules apply – the contents of this note stay in this room, and'…he looked around balefully, 'there will be no copies.'

Plattern read the note Aleisha Campbell had earlier given Marnie Baker. When he finished he examined their faces. Most were troubled and the two women ministers were dabbing their eyes. He caught Ben Aldrittson's expression – completely unmoved. That irritated him. He sat as Meadows rose again.

'People, this note is a concern. We don't know Baker's secret and we don't know the identity of his "persecutor". I only hope to God no one here is involved. The police will be examining his life through a microscope: taxes, mistresses, bad habits – everything. The Chief Commissioner has indicated the force will be conducting a "no-holds barred" investigation – as they should – but collectively, we have a problem. I intend announcing the election date very soon. We all know it has to be before November 26 and I want a short, sharp, hard hitting campaign. The strategists believe mid to late September would be best. That will be enough time for our media program, funding, policy proposals and costings to coalesce into what I believe will be the tightest and most focussed campaign we've ever run. We are going for a third term and cannot afford complacency. Traditionally, voters get rid of governments in their third term, especially if there are signs of waste, dysfunction, friction, lethargy or cover-up. Baker poses a threat. Christ knows what skeletons are in his cupboard. Irrespective of what you thought of him before, his action now is not good news. Our task is to get re-elected. So I'm reading the riot act. From here on, I want absolute cohesion and strict discipline. Anyone foot faulting in any way, shape or form, anyone not toeing the party line goes straight to the back bench after re-election. Lance Baker was an earnest and hard worker. He was a loyal party man. As far as we know, he was devoted to his family. His death is a shock to all of us and we can be sympathetic. We can't discuss any aspect of his private life apart from what I just mentioned. Later I'll distribute a list of Lance's achievements as Minister for Environment, and before that, as Minister for Education. Use these to illustrate his work ethic and interest in the people of his electorate and Victoria. The media are going to hound us so we have to be singing from the same hymn sheet. Before going on, does anyone have any idea why Baker took his life? Who the persecutor is? What the secret might be? Anyone?'

Silent faces stared back at him.

'Ben. I'm told you had a run-in with Baker last Wednesday.

What was that about?'

Aldrittson was unfazed by the question. 'I saw him after my address on the alternative power and land acquisition proposal. I suggested he might like to contribute to the infrastructure costs. Although I'm proposing this plan, it's as much about the environment as business. He basically suggested I go screw myself and hit the Treasurer for more money. He was quite obnoxious about it, as I'm sure some of you will have found he could be. That's all it was.'

Plattern scrutinised Aldrittson hard. He wondered about his lack of compassion for Baker and intuitively knew he was lying. Why, or about what he didn't know but mentally, he took a big step back from his parliamentary colleague and resolved to treat him with caution. He had, from time to time, heard some oblique and unsettling whispers about Aldrittson – about his wealth and the way he made it and about favours traded. Nebulous and vague, there was nothing of substance. Yet muted undertones of sly dealings remained persistent. Was the Premier aware of them too?

'Is that it?' Meadows asked, his voice tinged with faint surprise.

'Yes, nothing else,' was the flat response. Aldrittson had never intended using Baker's paedophilia publicly, that was his private leverage. Public knowledge of *that* vice was a surefire guarantee for an election loss and he didn't want that. Obviously, *he* was Baker's persecutor. *Well, tough shit. Anyone who messed with kids that way deserved to die.* Aldrittson had nothing but contempt for Baker. Still, he had paid the price.

'Alright, listen up everyone,' Meadows continued, 'this morning I'm contacting the PR firm, Centaur and Chimera – they'll put the best spin on this situation. We need to be ready for the midday news and thoroughly prepared for the evening news and *7:30 Report*. So far, the newshounds haven't caught the scent but it won't be long. I'll take the running on this: pay my respects to Marnie Baker and organise flowers. Has anyone got a press conference today?'

Paul Newbegin, Minister for Transport raised his hand. 'Yes Premier. I'm cutting ribbons on our new trams to celebrate completion of the super stops on Route 109. It's scheduled for 3:00 p.m.'

'Okay Paul, see me before you go. The spin doctors will have an angle by then. Remember, play up his hard work, emphasise his achievements in Environment and Education and endorse his loyalty to the party. Don't go near his family life except to say he was devoted, we don't know what the police will find. And, finally, heed John's advice: Chatham House Rules. Okay, thanks everyone.'

As a body, they rose and filed across the office.

'Oh, one more thing,' called Meadows, 'it's possible – although I don't expect it – that Opposition members could play hard ball on this. I'll speak to Clive Crystal at the first opportunity. I don't want a shit fight with the Opposition about Baker. Remember, if you demean someone, you diminish yourself. If they want to play that game, they will suffer. Don't get snared in that trap. Thanks.'

Muttering and murmuring, singly and in pairs, they left Meadow's office. It had been a long time since a Member of Parliament committed suicide. No one liked it.

Aldrittson returned to his office. Helen Jones, his secretary, handed him four phone messages and a sealed envelope.

'Thanks Helen. Any chance of a coffee? It's going to be a long day. Baker's death has already soured things and the bloody agenda is jammed with new and amending legislation. I'd kill for a coffee.' He looked pleadingly at her.

She smiled. Ben Aldrittson was a good boss: little gifts from overseas trips, post cards, trinkets for her kids when they were younger. Coffee was no problem.

Aldrittson scanned the phone messages and smiled to see one from Teresa. His father had called and the others were from business associations. He looked at the sealed envelope. Plain white, posted, typed address and marked: *Absolutely Personal*. He slit it open and withdrew another envelope – it was parliamentary stationery and the handwriting was unfamiliar. He opened it as Helen returned with fresh coffee.

'Here,' she said, 'stoke the inner man for battle.' She set it down on his desk, made a couple of rapier thrusts through the air, laughed and walked out. *I'm lucky*, he thought, *Helen's a bloody good workhorse and she keeps secrets.* He sipped his coffee and withdrew the note, also on parliamentary stationery. He glanced at the signature, Lance – bloody – Baker!

*

Wednesday
June 2, 2005.

Aldrittson,

You always were, and will remain forever, a piece of shit. I meant what I said – you'll get nothing from me. Nothing! Feel free to blow the whistle on whomever you like, including me. Just know that you won't be hurting me – only Marnie and the girls. If you can do that, you are an even bigger turd than I thought you were.

Although, I'd expect you to hurt Marnie, just to get even.

But your day is coming Sunshine. I found out quite a few things about your family company and believe me, that investigation will not stop.

I will pay for my sins and I'll meet you in hell arsehole because you sure won't be going elsewhere!

Lance Baker

*

Aldrittson drank his coffee distractedly tapping Baker's envelope on the desk. At their last meeting Baker hinted at a shadowy pattern of illegal dumping in Victoria. He had also mentioned a partnership with New South Wales to find the culprits. His father's sites were up and down the eastern seaboard and he wondered if some of their drivers had been seen discharging waste. He hoped stuff couldn't be traced back to the firm but one could never be sure. Maybe a truck had been noticed looking out of place. He could kill off enquiries by the Victorian Department of Environment – that's *why* you needed leverage – but his influence didn't extend to New South Wales. He would have to see what he could flush out.

Options? Apart from opposition to the federal government's desire to build a radioactive waste site in their state, nothing about toxic dumping had been heard from South Australia. *Perhaps Jack could increase volume there and decrease dumps in Victoria?* In any event, he had better let Jack know about the New South Wales problem which would also rule out Queensland. Far too risky to travel through New South under these circumstances. Better to just keep out.

Threats? Not dumping in other states raised exposure risk in Victoria – more trucks, more dumps, greater visibility. Apart from that, Danny Browne's replacement remained an issue. More journeys by fewer drivers heightened the possibility of mistakes. The Old Man was also under increasing pressure because of Santini's death. Perhaps he had been too hasty there? No. Santini had pushed his luck and deserved what he got.

Time was getting on. He buzzed the intercom. 'Helen, the calls this morning from the Sporting Footwear Association and Association of Drillers, Hydrologists and Petroleum Explorers, would you ring them and find out what they want? If it's a dinner speech, slot them in to my schedule. Tell them I apologise for not calling personally, pressure of work and all that. Hold all calls for now, I've got three to make and then have to dash.'

'Yes Boss. I'll let the Associations know you can't do anything in the month before to the election. Anything else?'

'No … Yes. When did that letter arrive? The one marked personal.'

'This morning. It came in the mail with others for the office. I didn't open it because it was confidential.'

'Good morning Teresa, Ben here. What a pleasant surprise to receive your message. What can I do for you?'

'Hello Ben. I thought I'd ring to say how positive our discussion was the other night. I was tempted to ring Friday but I didn't want you getting big headed.' She chuckled softly.

'Teresa, that certainly would have been a possibility," he laughed, picking up on the innuendo. 'But yes, I enjoyed our meeting too. How about dinner tomorrow night? I know a really good, discreet place at Port Melbourne.'

'Thanks Ben.' Teresa laughed down the phone. 'I'm really tempted but I have a heavy week and, much as I'd like to, I can't. I'll look forward to Friday. Maybe we could go to the Port Melbourne place on Friday instead of Ruffles?'

'Sounds good. It's called *The Squid's Legs*. Why don't I pick you up at your place around 7:00 p.m. I'll book dinner for seven forty-five.'

'The meal time is good but I'm sorry, I'll be working until seven. I'll just meet you there at seven forty-five. Okay?'

Aldrittson was disappointed. He wanted to see her home, inspect her private domain, learn more about her. He said instead, 'Well that's probably better for me too. I'm pretty busy myself. There's a heavy legislative agenda on in the House right now, you know, election and all that. If things get bogged down Friday afternoon I could well be in trouble myself. However, I've enjoyed talking with you and I'm looking forward to Friday night.'

'Thanks for calling back,' she added before hanging up.

Aldrittson got off the phone feeling upbeat and spent a few moments recalling the sensual vision he had met last Friday. He rang Spencer Johnson.

'Yo, Benny. How are you my boy?' said Johnson.

'Good Spence. I need a work-out and some alterations to my program. Can you fit me in at say, seven tonight?'

'Sure thing, I'll see you then.'

Finally, he rang his father. They exchanged pleasantries before Ben asked, 'What's on your mind Dad? You don't ring here very often.'

'Well, I'm a bit pushed Son and it's becoming a real bloody

headache for me. Do you remember Martin Judd? The driver who lost his leg?'

'Yes, you put him in the office didn't you?'

'That's right. He was Santini's understudy – a bloody good one too. But there was one aspect he didn't get to work on. I'm thinking of putting him to work on *all* of Santini's responsibilities, but I need to make sure he's good for it. Could your helpers check him out for me?'

'Sure. I'm glad you called about it. I'll stop by tonight'

Chapter
TWENTY-EIGHT

'Hi Mary, how are you doing?'

'Fine thanks Andy.' She smiled into the telephone. 'Tony's outside planting those roses you gave me. Want me to get him?'

'No Mary, I'm in a bit of a hurry actually. I rang to let you know I'm back in Melbourne. The Foundation has a few things they want me to take care of. If Tony or his crew are out my way, would you ask them to check on the house for me? '

'Sure Andy, I'll tell his Lordship. How long will you be away?'

'Not certain, a week, maybe two. But I'll call later. See you Mary.'

Drummond didn't like lying, but sometimes it was necessary. His partnership with the Royal Women's Hospital had started when Sue contracted ovarian cancer. After her death, he had donated $500,000 to their Foundation to help exploration of the causes and treatment of ovarian cancer. He and Sue had discussed the idea before her death and agreed it was a practical way of helping women in the future. As a result, he had won a minor role with the Foundation and attended meetings several times a year. He liked the contact because it maintained connection with Sue. In this case, he was simply using the Foundation as his foil for being in Melbourne.

Drummond had transferred Aldrittson's material from the memory stick to his computer and spent Sunday organising and examining the stolen records. He now had a fair understanding of who worked at AWD, employee numbers, where they lived, pay ranges, job functions and the overall scope of the firm's activities. He knew who worked at Brooklyn and who worked at Bayswater. He had boned up on Bayswater for the interview with Santini. It was a substantial and highly mechanised plant boasting a powerful computer-controlled destructor and several recycling functions.

Even though large, comparatively few people worked there – a salute to modern technology.

In sorting people by job function he had discovered three broad employee categories: clerical and administrative, maintenance and engineering, and transport. Each of these groups contained sub-groups, the smallest of which was drivers: trucks, cranes and forklifts. With few exceptions, most drivers were qualified in all three fields.

The generosity of the AWD pay system caused him to whistle aloud. Two things stood out: waste was a big money maker and Aldrittson believed in sharing that money around. Driver pay, by anybody's measure, was generous and overtime allowances liberal. It would indeed be a rare employee who complained of being underpaid.

He wondered about pay for non-drivers. Again, he was surprised. Not only did clerical and maintenance receive good money, but they regularly received bonuses. The arrangement kept them in touch with the more highly paid drivers. Even more surprising was that these pay arrangements seemed to have no adverse effect upon profit margins. He was beginning to understand why *The Financial Review* had written so positively about this firm.

When he opened his file from Santini's computer he experienced intense dismay. It was completely different from everything he had been working on – all of it was coded. The upside was it had to be significant.

According to the personnel files, Santini was foreman and office administrator. Probably that meant he was responsible for pickups and driver scheduling. He re-examined the codes in Santini's system. A typical entry read:

D.000123.32.0600.010305.4.C.1800

He checked the personnel records again. There were several

possibilities: D could be a simple indicator for driver while the number following might be a personnel or payroll number. He scrolled through a series of numbers and found a name against each one. He then searched for the dead driver, Danny Browne, and found him recorded as 000123. From experience he suspected that 010305 was a date. That seemed right, the truck fire in which Browne died was May 20, 2005. The date he was now checking implied Browne had worked on March 1, 2005. Time in the army suggested to him the numbers 0600 and 1800 could be start and finish times – 6:00 a.m. to 6:00 p.m. *What about the other numbers? No idea, but if Santini was in charge of rostering and scheduling, they could relate to clients and waste.* A lot of "coulds" and "maybes" ...

He looked for patterns. Eventually, he saw two strings, or sets of numbers. The first set typically contained between twenty-three to twenty-eight digits while the second had twenty-nine to thirty-six digits. The second set was also recorded differently. He wrote down two of Browne's number sets:

> D.000123.32.0600.010305.4.C.1800
> D.000123.169.3.37.B.d.0600.070305.6.2100.H

There were similarities: employee code, start/finish times and date, but apart from that, he was stumped. He scrolled endlessly and eventually saw another pattern: the longer number was limited to the same twelve employees.

Personnel records showed forty drivers, yet only twelve undertook whatever the longer number stood for. After examining the short set again he saw that all forty drivers were engaged equally across this activity. Nothing obvious differentiated the special twelve from the other twenty-eight drivers.

His broad understanding now was that all drivers shared the same kind of work but twelve were singled out for something different. He puzzled over how he might learn what that "something" was. Danny Browne was one of the special twelve. His journey for the day of the fire was listed in a short number set. That should be right, it accorded with what Maud had been told: Browne, supposedly, was on a rostered trip to Mildura.

It was all too hard. Drummond rose and walked onto the balcony to clear his head. It was cool and sunny and a light breeze was blowing through almost bare trees. Clouds were banking in the west and the sun would soon be gone. He looked at his watch: *Good God, 4:15 p.m.* He had been so deeply engrossed in his puzzle he hadn't noticed the day slip away.

Back inside he made fresh coffee. If he could think of some personal event that coincided with a journey by one of the unknown Schoolhouse Lane trucks, he might find a starting point for unravelling this mystery. He wracked his memory and recalled a Foundation meeting in Melbourne on February 18, 2005. He had come home late and was restless because of the endless bloody heat. Around 1:30 a.m. he got up for a drink, heard a truck and watched the headlights pass along the lane.

He trawled the February records and found a long number set for Browne on that date. There were no entries for other drivers so he felt comfortable assuming it was Browne in Schoolhouse Lane. According to his interpretation of the numbers, Browne left the depot at eight o'clock Thursday evening, February 18, 2005 and returned at 7:30 the following morning. Allowing for say, two hours to get from the depot to Schoolhouse Lane, there was a gap of three and a half hours. Similarly, if he allowed another two hours for Browne to return to the Depot from the time he heard the truck at 1:30 a.m., there was a gap of four hours. *What had Browne been doing during this seven and a half hour period? Where had he been?* Drummond drew two conclusions: first, there was at least one previous occasion when Browne appeared to have been in Schoolhouse Lane, and second, as Browne was one of the special twelve, the long number set suggested he was, at that time, undertaking some different form of work. Continuing to explore the limited database for Browne, Drummond found three more journeys on Schoolhouse Lane. He now seriously questioned AWD's contention that Browne was moonlighting at the time of his death.

At 7:00 p.m. Ben Aldrittson rapped on Spencer Johnson's office door.

'Benny. Come in, take a seat. Shut the door.' Johnson waited expectantly.

'You heard Lance Baker died?'

'I did,' Johnson replied, 'it was on the six o'clock news. What happened?'

'Silly bugger topped himself.'

'How come?' Johnson's eyes bored into him.

'Who knows! But I wanted to check with you on that information you got about him. Do you have copies?'

Johnson's response was acid-like. 'You know I don't. That's the deal. You pay well and you pay fast. You look after me so I'm bloody straight with you Benny. You have the *only* copy. Why are you asking?'

Aldrittson paused before answering. 'I'll come to that in a minute. How many sources did you use to put the package together?'

'Several.'

'Are they friends? Are they in contact with one another?'

'As far as I'm aware they don't know each other. Does the credibility of the information concern you?'

'Hell no. I have no doubt about its accuracy. I'm asking for two reasons. It goes without saying that Baker's death will inspire a scrupulous police investigation. That could turn up anything. Additionally, the Premier made it very bloody clear today this suicide is bad news for us. Baker left a note which hinted at problems. Meadows sees Baker's death as an election millstone. I need to be sure your dossier doesn't become another one.'

'Well, so much for love and charity among our splendid politicians.' Johnson laughed harshly. 'The poor bastard is still warm and all you can think of is covering your arse. Charming. You've got the only copy. It will never be connected to you from my enquiries so relax.'

Aldrittson flashed a wolfish grin.

'Never let sentiment get in the way of a good victory Spence. Everything you ever suspected about political backstabbing is utterly correct. Now, how's that diversion scheme coming along?'

'Too early to say. I've got some real good irons in the fire and should be in a better position after the weekend. As soon as I have a firm plan, I'll let you know.'

'Okay Spence, one last thing. You might enjoy this little job. Remember when I first came to you about Santini I told you he had given me a deadline on something.'

'Yeah.'

'His death didn't affect that because the material was for Giuseppe Pescaro. I still had to deliver.'

Johnson interrupted curtly. 'I told you that messing about with the Mafia is dangerous. I hold to that.'

'Pescaro's collector was this absolutely drop-dead gorgeous woman, Teresa Santini. I met her last Friday night at *Ruffles*. I'm seeing her again next Friday, at *The Squid's Legs*. Can you be there?'

'What do you want me to do?'

'I want you to check her out – who she is, where she lives, what she does, what's her background. I want to know everything you can discover about her. Out of ten she's a twelve!'

'You're not telling me you've got the hots for a Mafia sheila?' Johnson's tone conveyed disbelief.

'Only to the extent that I want to get her between the sheets. She's got me intrigued and she's very bloody smart. I want to know all about her.'

'Benny, it's not my place to give you advice, but I will. You're crazy! You just said Meadows warned you about electoral defeat and here you are talking of pumping a Mafia bitch. You know what I think about the Santini caper and the cops aren't buying the "blow-out" theory. For Christ's sake, cool it. Playing with Pescaro is deadly. If he finds out you bumped Santini not only will *nothing* save you, but your death will be lingeringly slow and excruciatingly painful. Now, listen up – keep away from that bird.'

Aldrittson gave Johnson a glacial stare. 'Tell me about the diversion plan. Now.'

Johnson shook his head in wonderment.

'Okay, but understand this – the risk is huge. No, amend that. Put it in the cata-fucking-strophic category. And, my friend, if it goes tits up, *you* wear the consequences.' Aldrittson nodded for him to continue.

'The Russian Mafiya here is restless. They want real money and action but Pescaro's got most things tied down. I'm thinking of putting the two factions at each other's throats. It will be a gamble and could get very bloody. If that happens, it will definitely give the cops a headache but my personal advice is, stay away from it. I'm asking you to think very bloody hard about this before you say: "do it". We'll talk more about it after the weekend.'

Aldrittson remained impassive. 'Find out about the girl. We'll talk about the other next week. I like the concept, it smacks of rough justice. I'll think about it though, there might be an alternative. If there's nothing else from your end, I'll see you Friday at half seven. Be invisible but find out what you can. I'm off to see my Old Man.'

'Righto Benny. One last thing. If we go with this Mafiya caper, it will cost you big bucks, so think about that too.'

Aldrittson opened the front door to his parent's home. Although Jack Aldrittson greeted his son warmly, he seemed subdued. They walked down the hall to the kitchen where Jack turned the TV off.

'You know where everything is – help yourself to a coffee or beer.'

Ben set about building himself a sandwich and coffee.

Jack watched in silence and eventually said, 'I see one of your polly mates topped himself. What was that all about?'

'Don't know really. Came as a shock to all of us. I may have been one of the last to see him alive. Met with him last Wednesday to talk over an alternative power scheme I put up. He agreed to kick in some funding for start-up. He seemed fine then.' The lies slipped out as smoothly as oil across a pond. 'His death is the main reason I'm here.' He brought his coffee and sandwich to the table where his father sipped a beer.

'Baker mentioned he had been working with the New South Wales Environment Protection Authority on illegal dumping. Seems they got quite a scare after that Walwa episode. He told me his crew were working on toxic dumping in Victoria which means we could have difficulties. If New South is on alert it would be foolish to continue dumping there and that also rules out Queensland. You've already mentioned the Browne problem, and your additional workload, so we could be under pressure. And just for extras, Pescaro wants Meadows to accept our waste management scheme ASAP. Are you able to draw back on the dumping rate?'

'No way,' said Jack. 'Pescaro's muscle has made our unlawful activity so bloody good demand is spiralling beyond belief. Today everybody wants more of everything. More of anything means extra waste and demand for toxic disposal is constantly increasing too. As a matter of fact, we had three new enquiries this week. I'm beginning to agree with Pescaro – we *need* to get our scheme legitimised sooner rather than later. Though I am damned if I know the reason behind his pressure, he hasn't explained that.'

This was not the response Ben wanted.

'What about South Australia? We don't seem to be having any ripples there do we?'

'No, I suppose we could up the ante there a bit. But this whole thing is beginning to get me down. We've led a charmed life for so long sooner or later things have to go wrong. If not from some bastard dobbing us in, then from some poisonous bloody shit we dumped years ago being traced back to us. Even worse, there are other pricks doing illegal dumping who could bring us unstuck. Did you see that story about arsenic in the bay the other week? Thank Christ it wasn't ours, but what happened there could happen to us any time and become our nightmare. I appreciate the warning Son because I've heard nothing. New South must be keeping really bloody quiet. We need a long term solution real soon. As I said, demand is up to me fuckin' ears and I have to think twice about knocking people back. Any one of them could get shitty and tip us in. We really do need our scheme approved.'

'Alright Dad, I'll see what I can do with Meadows. Now, what about Martin Judd, what do *you* think?'

'Santini trusted him as much as he trusted anyone – very little – but he trained him well and he commended his work to me more than once. For Santini, that was huge. So, I think he's competent. But Judd doesn't know about the black stuff. Santini kept that to himself and coded the entries. Like I said, I'm having trouble juggling everything else *and* doing Santini's job. Judd hinted a couple of times that he could take the strain, but I don't want him in if he's the sort who'll piss off to the Department of Environment or the cops. That's my dilemma.'

'Is he married?'

'Yes.'

'Got kids?'

'Yes, three young 'uns – all at primary school.'

'Has he got ambition?'

'Don't rightly know. We've never talked about that and I can't say he's done much to show it. He was a truckie before he took this job so I guess he's just your average bloke. I don't think he ever had a crack at starting his own business or anything like that. But,' said Jack slowly and reflectively, 'he has shown a flair for this work. I think he's even surprised himself.'

'Any history, you know, criminal stuff?'

'Don't think so.'

'Okay. I'll get one of my friends to look at Judd. Based on what you've said, I would give him a fly. Can you last another week?'

'Of course I bloody can.' Jack sounded irritable. 'I'm acting now because pressure is building and it's in a month or two that I won't be able to manage.'

Ben changed tack. 'Have the cops been in touch about Santini's death? Browne's too if it comes to that? '

'Not recently, no. And it's been a while since they spoke to me about Danny. Last I heard they were thinking it was accidental. Fluid dripping on a hot brake drum caught fire…something like that. Nothing's changed in regard to Santini. As far as I know, they still think a blow-out caused him to lose control. He was just unfortunate. By the way, his funeral's on Wednesday. Are you going?'

'No. Too busy in the House. Keep me posted on any police enquiries. The minute you hear anything, tell me. I'll give you a call about Judd early next week. Say hello to Mum, tell her sorry I missed her. Maybe you should tell her to slow down on all that charity work, I never seem to see her these days. Anyway, I've got some heavy reading for tomorrow so I better get going. Thanks for the coffee and sanger. Stay well Old Man.'

Jack gave him a wan smile. His double life with Pescaro was taking its toll. Finding out that Santini had been a "plant" for all those years had snuffed out something vital in him.

'Yeah, right son,' he said tonelessly, 'you can see yourself out can't you?'

Chapter
TWENTY-NINE

The impressive neo–Gothic architecture of St Patrick's Cathedral, its 104 metre spire a giant finger pointing towards God, was, Pescaro thought, as much a celebration of vision and stamina as it was reverence for a house of worship. It was an entirely appropriate venue for honouring Nardo Santini's life. Pescaro was pleased that the first little wooden church built on a site bequeathed by Governor La Trobe in 1847 had evolved over ninety years or so to the magnificent structure of today. It had not been easy. Conflict soured the land grant and the gold rush had lured tradesmen away from Melbourne on the prospect of quick riches. In all, three churches were built and demolished before William Wardell's inspirational 1858 design eventually resulted in the present day cathedral.

Pescaro saw parallels between the Cathedral's evolution and Santini's life: humble origins, constant improvement and adherence to a single purpose. Teresa had organised everything perfectly: hymns, flowers, attendants, press notices, obituary, interstate Families, airport limos and superb catering after the service. It would be a fitting celebration and farewell for a loyal and trusted lieutenant.

Pescaro focussed on Teresa. On Saturday morning she had given him Aldrittson's ministerial briefing. She hadn't stayed long and appeared preoccupied. Today he had watched her pinning down last minute details for the funeral – she seemed her usual efficient self. Before going home she mentioned she had matters to discuss with him after the funeral. They agreed nine o'clock Friday morning. Pescaro knew she was ready to talk about the letters.

For him, that matter was not complex. Angelina and Alfredo had disobeyed "the code" and paid the price. Angelina's death had hurt him grievously. Indeed, so deep was the wound he had never contemplated another serious relationship. There had been plenty of women for sex, but nothing else. Feeling so utterly betrayed by Angelina he had deliberately cauterised his emotions. Although time eventually dimmed the pain and softened his anger, his memories of Angelina remained vibrant. At the time, he had also felt deeply for Adriana Marchese. She had had no idea of Alfredo's infidelity and even the presence of her little daughter, Teresa, had not prevented her from taking her own life.

From then on, Giuseppe had committed himself to caring for Teresa. At arm's length he had done so through the Benedettis and believed it worked well. He watched Teresa grow into an intelligent, beautiful and diligent young woman brimming with bright ideas. If she had weaknesses, they were her honesty and insatiable curiosity. And that curiosity was an amazing resource. It caused her to question practices, policies, ideas, systems and techniques so that she constantly sought to refine and improve whatever she was doing.

He knew little about her love life but Family members had reported she was discreet. He had never been aware of any serious liaison – it seemed she had not met the right man.

He fully expected his revelations to shock Teresa. Murder is an ugly subject – messy and awful. His tale would be especially painful because it was about her parents and her loss.

He, of course, had never expected or believed that his Angelina would be unfaithful. They had owned a beach house at Rye where, apart from weekends and holidays together, he occasionally would take Santini fishing. He vividly remembered the warm September weekend in 1975. A meeting planned in Melbourne was unexpectedly cancelled so he decided to take advantage of the good weather and go fishing. He and Santini arrived at the beach house at 4:30 a.m. on the Saturday to start their day on the bay. Angelina had flown to Sydney on Friday afternoon for a weekend with friends.

He and Santini had been surprised to find Alfredo Marchese's car in the driveway. The house was unlocked and when they entered, Pescaro instantly knew his betrayal. He breathed in Angelina's perfume and saw the mix of clothing lying around the lounge room. He had walked quietly to the bedroom and there, asleep in the shadows, the two naked lovers lay entwined, the room redolent with the musky scent of sex. He backed away and summoned Santini. Together they viewed the sleeping pair in silence and slowly, Santini withdrew his gun, a Browning .38 automatic. He had looked enquiringly at Pescaro for what seemed eternity, then stepped into the room. Pescaro had touched his arm, taken the gun, and walked to the bed.

He stood beside Angelina as she breathed softly in her sleep. Tears streaked his face. Suddenly, he raised the gun and fired once into Alfredo's head and, before she fully woke, again into Angelina's head. Death for both was immediate. Pescaro had wept, both for the deception and for the loss of his beloved Angelina and Alfredo, a man he had called a friend.

The shots, it seemed, disturbed no one. He and Santini cleaned up and removed all traces of the lovers presence. Alfredo's car was taken to a Mafia "chop shop." Two days later, Santini removed the heads, hands and feet from the bodies and personally destroyed them in the AWD destructor at Bayswater. Afterwards, the bodies were stuffed into the boot of a stolen car and driven to Sorrento and abandoned on the foreshore. Pescaro circulated a story that Angelina had walked out and disappeared after a fiery row.

When Adriana Marchese called a few days after the murders, worried by Alfredo's absence, Pescaro had faintly implied he might be with Angelina and that she could, if she wished, officially report him missing. He knew Adriana would quickly understand the truth. The Don remained the Don – supreme, powerful and the ultimate dispenser of justice to his world. Even after the bodies were found, the Family remained silent and, within a day or two, Adriana had taken her life.

Later still, Santini received Angelina's letters found in Alfredo's car. Retained by Santini, with several of Alfredo's letters, they were stored in his strong box. Over time, memory of Angelina faded to the point where it seemed that Pescaro had forever been single. Eighteen months after the murders and following extensive renovation, Pescaro sold his beach house. He never went fishing again.

Teresa had to know these facts and deal with the consequences. Pescaro was as fond of Teresa as any father could be of a daughter. He truly believed she would become a first class Family mediator and contribute substantially to the wealth of their enterprise. Above all, he believed she was an excellent replacement for Santini. She was sophisticated and at home with the modern Mafia business world. However, as deep as his feelings were, if Teresa could not conform, she was replaceable. Such was the Code.

Chapter
THIRTY

Drummond was tired. Settled with a cold beer by 7:00 p.m., he was watching the Channel 2 news. Wednesday had been another long, hard day. The previous two had flashed by as he worked to unscramble Santini's codes, yet despite the effort, there had been little progress.

He sucked on his beer. Thinking about the information he had assembled since Browne's death convinced him there was reason enough for police to investigate Aldrittson's firm. The stolen records could certainly help frame an investigation, but their evidentiary value was limited – he was sure they'd be declared inadmissible. Facilitating an enquiry could, therefore, be difficult. Finding a way for Tony to accept the records without revealing how he got them would be tricky – he was a bloody stickler for doing the right thing.

Drummond closed his eyes and lay back in the chair thinking. The name Santini drew him sharply from his reverie. He listened as the news reader continued: '...and St Patrick's Cathedral was filled with mourners today for the funeral of Mr Bernardo Santini who died in a collision on Westgate Bridge earlier this month. People have come from all parts of Australia and include many of his former work colleagues at Aldrittson Waste Disposals. Police were also present as many of those attending are believed to be linked with the criminal underworld including Giuseppe Pescaro, Leonardo Falcone and Giacomo Altierre.' As the story unfolded, the camera panned across scores of men dressed in smart black suits, hand tailored silk shirts and dark glasses. Many wore tough, scowling expressions, designer stubble and excessively short haircuts. Some were slender, others muscled and others, just plain fat. The few women present were stylishly dressed in the latest Italian and German fashions. In the background, the bells of St Patrick's tolled dolefully.

The camera halted momentarily on a slim man of average height in his seventies. His hair was thick and silvery, his face tanned, lined and hawk like. Beside him, standing at the top of the steps, was an attractive woman in her early thirties with short dark hair. Dressed in a simple black frock, she looked composed yet bursting with vitality. The hawkish man and beautiful woman were watching eight sturdy pallbearers struggle down the steps towards a gleaming black hearse. The coffin, an elaborate, bronze coloured affair, seemed crushingly heavy. As it tilted towards its destination, a massive wreath of plain white roses on top defied gravity and remained perfectly positioned.

Behind the hearse, four shining, black, glass-sided Cadillacs formed up to carry flowers. In line behind them, a string of sleek stretch limousines waited to convey mourners to the Fawkner Crematorium.

The camera moved on and picked out a man Drummond recognised as Jack Aldrittson. He was in the midst of a group and Drummond wondered if he was looking at any of the "special" drivers. It struck him that Santini appeared to be much more than a foreman and office administrator.

The news item had alluded to criminal connections: Pescaro, Falcone and Altierre. Here was a new dimension to the puzzle. Given the lustre and solemnity of the occasion, Santini was highly regarded ... *and* he worked at AWD. While Drummond warmed to his line of thought, he realised it was only conjecture. But, a discussion with Tony along these lines might enable his illicit records to be placed squarely on the table.

Ben Aldrittson's day had been equally busy. The pace of the House was frenetic under Meadows' desire to clear the legislative log jam before the election. With huge majorities in both houses, the Premier could afford to gag debate, exercise the guillotine and push matters along. He believed there was little risk to his government because the Opposition was so ineffectual and, by and large, the populace too apathetic to organise resistance. A few meaningless platitudes promising to respect voters and not abuse government power always seemed to cool dissent. Arrogant? Yes! Concerned? No! The Meadows strategy was about putting Liberal ideology in place, an ideology that, under his hand, was intolerant of dissent.

At the end of the session Meadows called a short, sharp, strategy meeting. Cabinet would follow the same procedure tomorrow: new legislation; introductory debate, perfunctory discussion, approval on party lines and move on. It worked well.

Aldrittson lingered after the meeting. The session had been hard slog and everyone was tired. Nerves were still raw over Baker's death and no one was joyful about the gruelling election campaign lurking round the corner. Yet, he had to broach the waste topic.

'Graeme, I have a proposal for you that I think it will be an election winner.'

'Ben, it's a bit late mate and I'm not in the mood right now.' His tone was sharp. 'I told Jeanne if there was any possibility of making it, we would have a late supper with friends tonight for their wedding anniversary. Well, there is time and I'd like to go to that supper.'

'I understand, I'm bushed myself. I'll give you a written outline and five words to think about: waste, litigation, private enterprise and spin. When you have the time, call me. I believe you'll be impressed. Enjoy your supper.'

Aldrittson dropped his proposal on Meadows' desk and walked from the office. He had been brief, to the point and left the ball on Meadows' boot. As far as Pescaro was concerned, he could truthfully say he had hand delivered the proposal to the Premier. And that's what he would tell Teresa. That he didn't have a response was not his fault.

Chapter
THIRTY-ONE

At 7:45 Friday morning Ben Aldrittson's phone rang – the direct line from the Premier's office.

'Morning Ben,' said the Premier crisply. 'Can you meet me? My office, ten minutes. I'd like a briefing on that waste scheme.'

'Be right there.' Aldrittson was surprised and wondered if Meadows had cancelled his supper the previous evening. He pulled a copy of the proposal from his briefcase and quickly scanned it. Not that he needed to. He had written the damn thing and knew it by rote.

He walked down to the Premier's corner and entering the outer office, knocked at Celia's door and waited. Celia Barraclough, the Premier's private secretary, was obnoxiously proper about protocol and pedantically fussy about manners. Minister or not, it was better to avoid endless hassle than cross swords with her. She made life misery for anyone who, in any way, real or imagined, slighted her sensibilities. Nobody entered the Premier's domain without her approval and no one crossed her threshold unbidden. Comics in the Halls of Power whispered that when the word "bitch" was coined, Celia Barraclough had been its inspiration.

'Yes, enter.' The imperious contralto voice resonated through the woodwork. Celia peered at Aldrittson over half moon glasses as though he were some form of insect. 'Yes Mr Aldrittson, why are you here?'

'To see your boss Celia, could you tell him I'm here please.' Aldrittson was disarmingly urbane.

'Is Mr Meadows expecting you?' She sniffed with disapproval.

'Yes Celia, he just phoned me.'

She rose to her full two and a bit metres, adjusted the voluminous floral dress around her impressive girth and moved, bull-dozer like to the Premier's door. She knocked lightly, opened the door and boomed, 'Mr Aldrittson is here to see you Mr Premier.' She nodded Aldrittson inside and closed the door swiftly and silently behind him as though it were a guillotine.

'Jesus Graeme, you've got to get rid of that bloody woman, she's a friggin' dinosaur.'

Meadows chuckled. 'May be so, but Celia is the best damn watch dog one could have. She's efficiency plus and knows stuff about this place that most historians have never even discovered. As long as I'm here, she stays. Now, the waste scheme. Tell me you weren't serious when you said it was an election winner? For Christ's sake Ben! Look at the bloody hoo-hah South Australia kicked up when the feds suggested a nuclear dump in their outback. Think about how hard those bastards in Mildura fought the dump at Nowingi. And what about the noble residents of Geelong? Pissed right off about chemicals on their patch aren't they! And Coode Island. Remember the shit fight after the big fire there? And what about that bloody dump up near Heathcote years back that got vetoed? Waste disposal is a raging bloody headache man! And if that's not enough, the friggin' firm putting this forward belongs to your Old Man. Talk about conflict of interest! You must be on something! Meadows' voice rose with cutting disdain.

'Let's deal with the last first shall we,' said Aldrittson, unfazed by the Premier's bluntness. 'I know it appears like a conflict of interest but don't forget, my Old Man is a voter just like everybody else. And, like anybody else, he's entitled to present ideas for consideration. All I'm doing is providing a sneak preview. If you absolutely damn it to hell then it goes no further. But if you think it could be electorally attractive, then he'll put the concept forward through normal processes and *not* through me. I don't want you to tick this off. All I want is your reaction – whether you think it could work or not. Are you comfortable with that?'

Grudgingly Meadows said, 'Okay, I'll listen. But I warn you –

this is sailing bloody close to the wind.'

Aldrittson was past the first hurdle. 'Before we begin, there are some things you'll be familiar with. If you think they're trivial, stop me, but I want to approach this as though you know nothing about the subject. If that's insulting, tell me.' He paused before continuing. Meadows said nothing.

'I believe this scheme could be a huge money spinner for the government. It'll remove toxic waste efficiently, effectively and safely; it'll cost tax payers nothing to establish and it's a user pays system. It's environmentally sound with a system of quality-control exercised independently by the State Government. I think it'll be one of the smartest things we've ever done. The first question is: what are the alternatives? You can have the most effective recycling programs ever invented, you can pile packaging restrictions on industry, you can invent technology for controlling and cleaning all kinds of emissions, you can have multiple boom-barriers on every major waterway in the State, but … are you going to stop the production of waste? Of course not. The next question is: what do we do with dirty waste, the toxic stuff, the kind most people don't want to talk about? The answer is: basically pretend it's not there. Non-toxic rubbish is a push-over because, comparatively speaking, it's relatively clean and often can be turned into other products. The third question is: how well do we deal with dirty stuff now? The answer is: bloody poorly! And why? Because of all those protests you just reeled off. So what have we done? Taken a disjointed, piecemeal, populist approach that's inefficient and pleases no one. In reality, most hazardous stuff sits around in barrels in company yards. We've never built a high-speed, clean-air incinerator to reduce toxic waste to dust or gas because we'd rather pretend the shit's not there. Think about the hundreds of poisonous chemicals and contaminants left *after* making petroleum, paint, agricultural fertilisers, plastics and other products. Think about hospital waste and residues from a host of industrial plants. *We don't have* a good system for dealing with this stuff. Nor do most other states. And you know it. This scheme puts all development, research, safety and recurrent costs directly onto the people who want this plant. If you've read the proposal, you'll know the consortium already has its land and wants the Government to own and exercise the strictest quality controls. The investment group will fund all start-up costs and pay a substantial annual operating fee to the Government. In return, they want an exclusive licence to operate initially for fifteen years. As the project evolves, the company will solicit toxic waste from other states on the basis of it being another source of revenue for our government and themselves. One of the fascinating aspects about this scheme is reclamation. While the initial goal is modest, the aim is to perfect refinement processes enabling many of the original chemicals and minerals to be extracted from waste. These will be refined to the highest levels of purity and sold on. The benefits include: profits for the waste company, cheaper ingredients for manufacturers, continuing employment and hopefully, some completely new products for the building industry as well as effort to prolong the life of some of our non-renewable materials. During super temperature incineration, the air is washed and cleaned three times to reduce noxious emissions close to zero and the excess heat distils clean from dirty water. There has never been such an integrated waste-disposal system as this.'

'Okay, okay – enough,' said Meadows. 'Your enthusiasm smacks of verbal diahorrea! I grant you the broad concept sounds functional and I understand the points you make. Give me specifics. Last night you mentioned litigation: what did you mean?' Meadows was attentive.

'It is my belief that the US Government is exempt from civil litigation. Their system does not allow prosecution of the *law-makers*. We don't have quite that protection here and we can be sued any time. You can't have missed the epidemic of rampant, ambulance-chasing lawyers wanting to sue the arse off anybody and everybody for every transgression imaginable.'

'Yes, yes, I know all that.' Meadows was impatient.

'Nearly all cases are fought on strictly legal grounds with courts deciding the interpretation and application of points of law. Sources of litigation are constantly refined and extended in ways never before considered or intended. As a result, actions are brought for situations never previously thought possible. For instance, fast food companies in the US have been sued by fat people alleging they manufacture addictive food. In other words, the company is to blame for them being fat.'

'Bullshit,' scoffed Meadows. 'People choose whether to buy and eat the food they see. Food makers don't coerce them to eat. Eating's an issue of personal responsibility.'

'I'm not kidding, Graeme. Laws have been passed to stop people suing restaurants – they're colloquially known as "cheeseburger" laws.'

'Alright,' said Meadows doubtfully. 'I'll take your word for it, but what's this got to do with us? I understand the problem of escalating litigation but we can legislate to prevent such lunacy. We can cap damages or wind back application and appeal times.'

'I'm not so sure we can,' Aldrittson retorted. 'Not only would there be voter backlash, but, as I said before, lawyers are finding new ways to enhance damages claims. They are crossing time, distance, countries, companies and class barriers. They've constructed a new dimension for liability which they call *moral* or *social responsibility*. You do not have to actually break any rule or law to be sued. For instance, if a company *unknowingly* does something that puts others at risk, legal action can be taken against that company. This philosophy takes litigation out of the strictly legal environment into a moralistic one.'

Meadows frowned. 'I'm not sure what you're driving at. What's the connection between "moral responsibility" and say, rules for waste disposal? For instance, if a petrol company illegally discharges toxic waste, we wouldn't be sued, the petrol company would be.'

Aldrittson nodded thoughtfully. 'Normally I would agree. But you have to go the extra step. Our Department of Environment could be sued for not acting appropriately. Either for failing to enforce the laws or, for failing to prevent the discharge in the first place. Just suppose some canoeists fell into the Yarra River and suffered mysterious and harmful skin lesions as a consequence of that petrol company's discharge. In the context of moral responsibility, they could sue DOE for failing to exercise due diligence in their sampling procedures. They might argue that inadequate sampling meant DOE was uninformed and therefore, unable to properly fulfil its responsibilities. In fact, we *know* that DOE has been sampling strictly to schedule. But the moral responsibility approach would argue the whole idea of sampling to a schedule is flawed. Lawyers would claim the petrol company was using those schedules to minimise detection. So, although DOE has not broken any laws, according to the moral responsibility argument its practices have caused others to suffer. DOE therefore becomes liable for *failing* to exercise its social responsibility to the public. If you want an even better example, let me tell you what's presently happening with Dow Chemicals in India and the Bhopal incident from 1984.'

'Don't bother. I've got the drift,' Meadows muttered.

Aldrittson nodded. 'Good, well that's how it works. Today, any business – especially government – that fails to factor social or moral responsibility into its risk management strategy is asking for trouble, particularly as litigation is becoming more expensive. Punters are predicting that over the next ten years, annual US litigation costs will exceed $360 million. And, I tell you now, if lawyers start litigating on global warming issues, costs will be off the radar. My point is this. We need a safer, more reliable and more efficient toxic waste disposal system. Irrespective of anything else, we *need* that. For me, the threat of legal activism and unrestrained exploitation of areas hitherto protected from litigation is a powerful incentive. I have no doubt smart-arse lawyers will exploit this moral responsibility concept and, toxic waste is a plum ripe for picking.'

'Okay,' said Meadows, 'you've raised an issue that needs closer scrutiny. But what about the public? You know how unforgiving they are towards politicians. What's going to make them drop their consistent opposition to toxic dumps? Why would they suddenly want to start trusting us? Everyone says, yeah, we need one, but not in my backyard.'

'In my portfolio Graeme, I spend huge amounts of time with business and international trade as you know. That experience has opened my eyes to a few dirty tricks that surprise even my cynical view of the world.'

Meadows laughed heartily. 'I never thought I'd hear you confess to cynicism Ben, nor to the fact you can still be surprised.'

'I know. What surprised me is the implacable dedication to underhandedness. In some places, dirty tricks are a multi-national enterprise.' Aldrittson marvelled at his own guile. Meadows was beginning to relax.

'Okay, you mentioned spin,' said Meadows flexing his shoulders. 'How does that fit into this scheme?'

'Did you see the comments recently from Exxon and BHP Billiton about emission reduction policies?'

'Yes I did. I think Billiton was claiming that to implement Federal Government emission reduction policies would place overseas investment in Australia at risk. Exxon claimed that investment in renewable energy technology was not economical.'

'Why do you think they made those comments?' Aldrittson asked.

'Quite simple I should think.' Meadows stood, stretched and rolled his shoulders again. 'They're sending the feds a message: don't change the status quo, they like things the way they are. To be effective, however, they need leverage, which in this case, is loss of investment capital. Of course, we don't know the seriousness of the threat so, in a sense, it *is* merely spin, spin to achieve a result that says – *leave me alone*. Another implication is their threat to withhold or re-direct political donations.' Meadows sat down again.

Aldrittson grinned raffishly. 'Precisely. Spin can sell our concept to the public. Even Aristotle recognised the benefit of winning his opponent's endorsement suggesting it outweighed almost anything else you could do to consolidate your own position. So, we recruit activists who would normally work against us and show them that the vision and integrity of our concept is beneficial. Respected environmental activists speaking for our scheme then become a powerful endorsement for change. We embark on a strategy to divide and conquer. We isolate the radicals, cultivate the idealists and convert them to realists. With care and sensitivity we then enlist the realists to agree with our industrial waste disposal policies and programs.'

Meadows threw Aldrittson a deeply sceptical look. 'Bullshit.'

'No Graeme, it's true. Plenty of multi-nationals in the US use this tactic to advantage. In our case, the backers of the scheme would hire several prominent greens to work for them. The rationale is that the best possible environmental advice is wanted – and that's true. In due course, our greenies see the company doing things properly and begin publicly endorsing our concept. *They* seduce the community by shifting from opponent to full time supporter. That brings credibility. But, if green activists can't be recruited the firm moves to enlist help from its biggest clients. A Trust or Foundation is formed and capital is raised to attract greenies with big, fat, juicy fees. Let me give you a classic example. In 1993, Monsanto hired the former Executive Director of the Consumer Foundation of America to support their use of a bovine growth hormone. Through her, Monsanto deflected Congress from imposing a control that would have made them label milk containers with advice that the milk came from cows injected with growth hormones. That extra clout *removed* the push for labelling.'

Meadows raised his eyebrows disbelievingly.

Aldrittson merely nodded and continued. 'We can also infiltrate the local grass-roots opposition with spies of our own. A PR company handles the media, our spies provide updates from the opposition and we keep one jump ahead all the time. We also recruit informers from the project area or people from a place where a similar project has been proposed. They're schooled to know the guts of the scheme inside out, they attend local meetings and ask tough, informed questions to make people see another side to the issue apart from blind emotion. Their role is to create doubt and keep our opposition off balance.'

Meadows merely shook his head. Aldrittson went on, 'What I'm saying Graeme is that by using the right spin and investing money in some or all of the tactics I've outlined, it is not impossible to: (a) get the scheme before voters at *this* election, and (b), make it happen *after* the election. However, the sooner we start, the better.' Aldrittson sat back, pleased with his performance.

After a few moments Meadows said, 'I must say you've stirred my interest. A couple more questions. Are the site drawings, geological readings and soil analyses referred to available? And secondly, is the environmental impact study you mentioned to hand?'

'Yes to all. The only thing not finalised is the media strategy, but that's coming along.'

'Okay give me a copy of everything you've got. I have some people I would like to assess the scheme. They can have a bloody good look at it and brief me independently. After that, I'll decide whether we buy into the idea. I'll take note of the social responsibility issue but, as for tactics, spin or otherwise, I'll reserve judgement until I get the independent assessment.'

'Fair enough. I can almost guarantee no problems but ... these plans are *commercial in confidence*. I don't want to be responsible for any glitches with other people's ideas.'

'I assure you Ben, they will not leave my office, even if I have to tie the assessors to my desk. Thanks for the briefing, very comprehensive. I understand now why you were so positive. See you in the House.'

Chapter
THIRTY-TWO

By three o'clock Friday afternoon, Drummond had been at the State library for two hours. He was trawling the microfiche of local and interstate newspapers for anything about Falcone, Pescaro or Altierre.

He had reached the early eighties without much joy. Obviously, he mused, these characters were gold medallists at the low profile. So far, only Sydney's Leonardo Falcone had surfaced in a short-lived story about extortion. Committed for trial in 1982, the case was dropped when, mysteriously, three key witnesses died in separate road accidents – all in one week. No connection was discovered to Falcone and there was no further attempt at prosecution.

He was beginning to think his idea was futile when he smelt a vaguely familiar perfume. The source was a very attractive dark-haired woman. As he discreetly studied her recognition stirred. She was the woman he had seen on TV at Santini's funeral. Today she was in jeans, a cream top and smart suede leather jacket. On television she had looked a stunner, but in the flesh, she was even better. He watched her walk towards the counter. Then, with a jolt, he suddenly twigged it was not just the perfume that was familiar – he had seen that purposeful walk before. His mind flashed back to the Aldrittson Depot where, crouched by a desk, someone wearing that perfume walked briskly past him to Santini's office. There was no mistaking the build and gait. Drummond was sure she was Aldrittson's second intruder.

He continued watching her. Eventually, she took several microfiche packets to a reader three stations away. Now he was fascinated. He rose, ordered more microfiche and came back to the work-station opposite her.

Teresa's tumultuous feelings had put her off balance: simultaneously she was angry, revulsed and deeply hurt. She had met Pescaro at nine that morning and learned the ghastly story of her parents and Angelina Pescaro. Even though she felt as though her heart was being ripped out she knew she had surprised Pescaro by remaining outwardly stoic. Since discovering the newspaper articles she had lain awake most nights weeping while knowing her bitter and depressing past was unchangeable. Wrongly, Pescaro had construed her reaction as one of strength and conformity to the Family Code.

He stressed that her task now was to master the role of *Consigliere*. She would be the Family's investment manager, banker, realtor, entrepreneur and mediator. In so far as Alfredo and Angelina were concerned, the Code had been honoured. Pescaro had spoken emotionally of his own pain and remorse for Teresa's mother. He had attempted redemption by maintaining a watchful eye over Teresa from then on. And *that* was why she seethed: so much of her life had been a stage-managed fable and she hated it. Hated the deception.

Teresa was industrious and intelligent, proudly so, and she believed she was a good person. She had never harmed anyone, stolen anything or cheated in relationships. She invested and managed Mafia money but that was like monopoly – the money was already there. Through her skills she made it grow.

Yet right now, she didn't know what to do or quite how to behave. She had returned to the library even though she had all the newspaper articles she needed. *Here* was where the truth lay; *here* was where she able to feel close to her parents because of what she had learned; and *here* was where she realised that, in spite of everything, there was an aching void for the mother and father she had not known.

To her consternation, tears began slowly to trickle down her cheeks. *Damn*, she thought, *I don't want to be crying in here*. She took some tissues from her bag, wiped her eyes, gathered the microfiche and returned them to the desk. Still dabbing her eyes, she left.

Drummond hurriedly collected his papers and followed. Her tears intrigued him. She paused under the portico then descended into Swanston Street where she was engulfed by a swirl of students and young people as she walked south.

From behind, Drummond heard the rumble of an approaching skate board. He had seen a group of scruffy youths and their boards at the corner of Swanston and La Trobe streets. Jumping off ledges and onto seats they laughed, clattered, shouted and jostled, deliberately intimidating older members of the public. Glancing round, Drummond saw one of these youths dressed in a bomber jacket and cargo pants weaving in and out among pedestrians, the tails of a red bandana flapping behind his head. He whizzed by Drummond, barely missing a woman walking towards them, wheels whirring on basalt pavers.

When the "skater" reached Teresa, he raised his left arm and drove his elbow into her head. Flying sideways with arms outstretched, her shoulder bag slipped and was whipped off by the board rider who darted into the crowd. Two men immediately gave chase but were no match for the thief's deft and rapid flight.

When Drummond reached her, she was sitting amid a knot of people, visibly upset, a welt already rising under her right eye and across her cheekbone. He watched and listened to the murmurs of sympathy. Face wet with tears, she hugged her knees. Drummond stepped forward and leaned down. 'Are you okay?' he asked.

'He took my bag,' she said, trembling. 'He's got my cards and my money and my keys.' The attack, on top of Pescaro's revelation about her parents had taken her to the edge and, for the moment, she felt bereft.

'Can I call someone for you?' Drummond's gentle voice penetrated her anguish. Can I get you a taxi?'

She looked at Drummond. He seemed vaguely familiar

though she couldn't place him. She raised her hand and gently, he helped her to her feet.

Drummond repeated, 'Can I call someone for you?'

'No, I have a friend in a shop not far from here. I'll be alright. Thank you.'

'Would you like me to walk with you?'

'Thank you, no. I'll be alright. My friend will help me get home. Thank you for your kindness.' She wiped her eyes, adjusted her jacket and continued down Swanston Street.

Drummond was curious. She mixed with people he suspected were Mafia; he was certain she was the breaker at AWD, and, though distressed by the attack, he had seen her strength. Apart from that, she was very attractive. *Well, Miss No-Name*, he thought, *I am going to find out more about you.*

When Teresa turned left into Lonsdale Street he moved. He crossed the street and waited for the traffic lights to change at Lonsdale Street. Opposite, and still some thirty metres away, he was astonished to see the youth in the red bandana coming towards him. *The cheeky bastard*, he thought, *looking for his next victim no doubt.* Drummond decided to wait and confront him. When Bandana arrived at the intersection he sauntered defiantly against the red light clutching his skateboard. A tough and wiry looking twenty year old with attitude, his ill fitting clothes were grubby and worn.

Drummond went after him. Drawing level, he bumped him hard with his shoulder.

'Fuck off shit head,' Bandana snarled.

'Are you talking to me sonny?' Drummond smiled at him.

'Yeah, watch where ya fuckin' goin' dickhead.' Bandana's pock marked face revealed two missing front teeth while dark eyes smouldered with anger. They continued walking side by side. Bandana lengthened his stride but showed no fear of Drummond pacing beside him.

'I 'spose you think you're pretty tough mouthing off,' said

Drummond grinning at him, 'so tough you've got to rob defenceless women. You're as weak as piss.'

Bandana stopped abruptly and swung his skateboard like a scythe. Anticipating the response, Drummond stepped in close, crowded him against a shop wall and belted him hard in the ribs. Bandana yelped, dropped the board and in a trice was kneeling as Drummond pushed his arm up his back to the point of pain.

'Now smart arse,' growled Drummond, 'where's the bag?'

'Dunno what you're talking about,' grunted Bandana.

'Let me help you remember.' Drummond pushed the arm higher and Bandana screeched in agony.

Two by-passers stopped and one said, 'What's going on?'

'This little shit just pinched my wife's bag and I want it back,' said Drummond with vehemence.

'Fair enough mate, push harder.' They laughed and walked on.

'Got the drift shit head? Where's the bag?' Drummond gave his arm another nudge.

Bandana started whimpering. 'I chucked it in a bin down the street.'

'Get up. We're going for a little walk; you can retrieve it.'

'Someone else might have pinched it,' Bandana whined.

'Start praying they haven't,' said Drummond, 'otherwise I'm going to break your arm. On your feet you little prick. We are going to walk together and you are *not* going to cause any trouble. If you do, you'll feel pain like you've never known. Understand?'

Bandana gave a surly nod. He bent to pick up the skateboard.

'Forget it,' barked Drummond.

Resentment flushed Bandana's face. 'It's worth 300 bucks. Get stuffed, I'm takin' it.'

Drummond grabbed Bandana's left wrist, pulled sharply, twisted and held him in an excruciating lock. 'I warned you, on your way. See how it feels to lose something of value.'

They walked down Swanston Street to Turner's Alley. Bandana

said, 'It's up here in a rubbish bin.' They turned into the lane where several large bins stood at one side a few paces off the footpath.

'Go get it.' Drummond released Bandana who rubbed his wrist. He went to the last bin, rummaged in it and brought out a brown leather shoulder bag. 'Open it and put the contents on the lid,' said Drummond.

'There's nuthin' in it,' said Bandana.

'Do it!'

Bandana upended the bag and shook it over the bin lid. 'See, I told ya.'

'Put the bag on the lid and come here.' Reluctantly, Bandana complied. 'Now,' Drummond said calmly, 'there'll be no cops but, I just want you to understand something.' Without warning, Bandana received a brutal blow to his midriff – he gasped and sagged to the ground.

'I want you to understand, my young friend, that I don't like liars and I don't like thieves, and I especially don't like men who pick on women. Where are the contents of the bag?'

Bandana gasped and flapped at his jacket pocket.

'Are we clear about things, sonny?' rasped Drummond.

Bandana nodded again, groaned and drew his knees up to relieve the pain.

Drummond knelt and from the right jacket pocket removed a small silver mobile phone. 'Hers?' he enquired. Bandana nodded. From the left pocket he took a slim, brown, crocodile skin purse. In it was a driver's licence in the name of Teresa Marchese, several plastic cards and $150.

'Is this all that was in the purse?'

Again, Bandana nodded.

'What about her other things in the bag?'

Bandana hesitated. 'There was some newspaper clippings, I ditched 'em down the street. That's all. I swear!'

Drummond took a firm but friendly grasp of Bandana's

shoulder. 'Think before you answer my next question: where are her keys?'

Bandana paled. 'I dunno. I mean, they were in the bag. I chucked 'em into a passing truck after I ratted her stuff. At the time I thought it was funny. Honest, I dunno where they are.'

Drummond stood up. 'Keep your nose clean in future, the next person you deal with may not be as kind as me.' Bandana groaned. Drummond took the bag, purse and phone and left the youth coiled on the ground.

Back in his Balwyn unit Drummond studied Teresa's belongings. He checked the call register of her mobile and found a galaxy of numbers. He downloaded them to his own mobile and from her driving licence noted her address as 16 Rose Street, Burnley – not too far away. He fetched his white pages directory and checked for a land line number – not listed.

Drummond felt he had a conundrum on his hands. He was deeply suspicious of AWD and their practices and he had seen this woman on television at Santini's funeral. Not only that, she was standing next to a man connected to the Mafia. Santini worked at AWD. Jack Aldrittson was at the funeral. With these associations he wondered why on earth she had broken into the AWD depot. *What was going on?* He contemplated taking her belongings to Rose Street but in the end decided to keep his distance and just post them back to her with a note.

Chapter
THIRTY-THREE

Teresa focussed on her meeting with Aldrittson as she deftly applied make-up to her bruised cheek. She was certain he was hungry to add her to his list of conquests and had felt the breath of a predator at their first meeting. Of course, she had egged him on, and by extending the time between their meetings and being difficult to contact she knew she was taunting him. She had been deliberately reticent with her address although she suspected he only had to nod and one of his minions would supply it in a flash.

Walking into *The Squid's Legs* that evening Teresa was impressed by the subdued intimacy – the atmosphere was friendly and welcoming. Aldrittson, who was seated at a round table perusing the menu, scrambled to his feet when she appeared.

'Good evening Ben.' Teresa extended her hand.

Aldrittson shook it warmly. 'Nice to see you again Teresa, come, sit down.' He withdrew her chair and took her elbow as she sat. 'Now, what about a drink?'

'Given the temperature outside and this nautical atmosphere, I think I'll have a rum and coke,' she said cheerfully.

He ordered her drink, another for himself and sat gazing at her. She looked ravishing.

Teresa smiled and relaxed.

The rum and coke arrived promptly.

'Here's to a pleasant evening.' They chinked glasses and Aldrittson smiled happily. With the meals ordered, Teresa took the initiative 'Let's get the business out of the way shall we? Giuseppe is very keen to know how the proposal went.'

'Much better than I'd hoped. I expected Meadows to chuck me out of his office when I first raised it. To his credit, he read it and called me in for a briefing this morning. He's now getting his own independent advice. When he's got that he'll decide whether we go with it. I felt he was at least receptive.'

'That sounds promising. No outright opposition then?' enquired Teresa.

'No, I couldn't claim that. Although, I did have my work cut out convincing him that it is possible to win the hearts and minds of our citizens. I *think* I succeeded.' It was ironical, he mused. He had opposed Santini when he first raised this matter. Old Jack had hung back too and yet, because of the insistence of a wily old Mafia villain, they might just pull something off that would comprehensively benefit the state. Life sometimes took strange twists. As always, he closed his mind to thirty years of illegal dumping. 'Teresa,' he continued, 'I'm really interested to know why Pescaro has been pushing the scheme at this time. The pressure seemed to spring from nowhere and hasn't stopped. Do you know what's behind it?'

'No I don't. Like I said before, he has his reasons. He's a shrewd man and if the strength of his interest in this project is any measure, whatever the motivation, it's powerful. If I were you, I'd simply keep on with it. He's not going to let it drop.'

'Did Santini know why Pescaro wanted the scheme up and running?'

'I don't know, possibly.'

'How did Pescaro react to Santini's death?'

'As you might expect. He was deeply saddened. They had been friends for a very long time.' She volunteered nothing else and did not mention she had stepped into Santini's shoes. Momentarily, there was an awkward pause.

'I saw you on the TV news at St Pat's. You looked wonderful, even though it was a funeral.'

She smiled coyly. 'Thank you.'

Aldrittson laughed. 'Yes, I even remember the black number you wore last Friday at *Ruffles*. In fact, I've thought of you many times this week.'

She smiled again and dipped her head, pleased the fish was nibbling her bait.

Spencer Johnson ate slowly and occasionally sipped his juice. He was on the opposite side of the restaurant in shadow. He could see why Aldrittson was attracted to this woman; she was a stunner who carried herself with poise. Watching them in conversation he sensed something special about her – a depth not to be underestimated.

Dominic Fabrizzi, drove from the underground car park of Lygon Court in Drummond Street, Carlton. He had just dined at *The Pasta House* on Lygon Street and concluded negotiations for his share of cargo stolen from Tullamarine Airport. It was a new scam and running well. He turned left into the narrow divided street and waited for a driver to complete a reverse parking manoeuvre ahead of him. As he watched the the driver's efforts, three men appeared outside his car: two at the driver's side and one at the passenger door. Too late, Dominic saw danger. He was blocked in front by the angled car, hemmed in at the side by the plantation and, when his eyes flicked to the mirror, he saw a large silver Landrover right on his tail. That was to be Dominic Fabrizzi's last view of the world.

A sawn off shotgun roared and a solid slug travelling at a velocity greater than 247 metres per second smashed his window into tiny fragments and blew an enormous hole in Dominic's head. Bone, blood and brain misted the car's interior. Without pause, the second man at the driver's side stepped forward and fired a cartridge of pellets into what was left of Dominic's face.

As the shooting occurred, the parking car pulled smoothly and swiftly into Drummond Street and disappeared into Elgin Street. The big four wheel drive behind Dominic reversed, mounted the plantation, collected the three men and was swallowed up by local traffic.

The execution was over in 50 seconds. It was 8:00 p.m.

At 8:20 p.m. Spencer Johnson's mobile vibrated on his chest. He silently cursed, put down his knife and fork and answered quietly.

'Johnson.'

'Where are you?' Fox asked

'*The Squid's Legs*, watching Aldrittson.'

'Did you deploy assets for his diversionary stunt?'

'No, why?'

'News flash a couple of minutes ago. A well known underworld crim, was shot dead in Drummond Street. Details are scant but there was a veiled hint he was Mafia. The people he was out with found him dead in his car just after eight. It doesn't look good.'

'Meet me tomorrow at St Kilda baths, 9:00 a.m. It's not us.' Johnson looked at the couple in the alcove, they appeared not to have a care in the world. He wondered if Aldrittson had been stupid enough to ignore his advice.

Before their meal arrived, Aldrittson rose and made his way to the toilets. After a few seconds, Johnson followed. The two stood at the urinals. Aldrittson said, 'Can you see everything okay?'

'Yeah. Listen, there's a problem. Did you go against me and initiate your own diversionary campaign?'

'I bloody did not. We were going to discuss it after this weekend.' Aldrittson was irritated. 'Why, what's going on?'

'I think a Mafia bloke just got whacked in Carlton. That's all I know.'

'Well, I promise you, nothing to do with me.' Aldrittson felt an icy finger of fear. The cops were not convinced Santini's death was accidental; Browne's death was still open; Baker had been onto the toxic dumping, and now this. He didn't know anything about this death but he was wary. Instinct told him that somehow Pescaro was in the thick of it.

'So what do you want to do?' Johnson interrupted Aldrittson's thoughts.

'Nothing, it's not connected to me. Continue as planned. I'm going to see if I can get her back to my place. After that, follow her.' He was curt, troubled.

Teresa's phone rang. 'Yes,' she said neutrally.

'Pescaro,' barked a gruff voice, 'Fabrizzi's just been executed in Carlton. Where are you now?'

'Having dinner with Ben Aldrittson. He spoke with the Premier this morning.'

'Good. Stay at my Villa tonight. I've got things to wind up here in Sydney but I'll be back first thing tomorrow. Co-ordinate until I return. Our people will start ringing information through soon. Keep me informed.'

'Sure. I'll let you know if anything further happens. Giuseppe, do you know what's going on?'

'Yes,' he barked, 'I'll tell you when I'm back.' The phone went dead.

Aldrittson returned to find his meal on the table and Teresa standing.

'Is something wrong?' he asked.

'Yes, I've just had a call, one of Giuseppe's friends has been killed. I have to go.'

Not used to being stood up, Aldrittson was annoyed and had to grapple with his temper. 'Do you have to go? I mean, can't Pescaro deal with this? Just because you've been informed surely doesn't mean you have to leave does it?'

'Yes,' she said evenly, 'Giuseppe's in Sydney. I'm really sorry about this I was looking forward to spending a lovely evening with you.' She smiled warmly and collected her purse. 'We can try this again another time.' So saying, she left the restaurant.

Aldrittson was dumbfounded. He wondered what Fabrizzi's death really meant.

Chapter
THIRTY-FOUR

Teresa let herself into Pescaro's villa shortly after nine. Going straight to his office she commenced retrieving messages from the protected phone bank. They were all much the same – Dominic Fabrizzi had been murdered: the job was professional, the killers unknown. The *capos* had responded by immediately committing soldiers to finding out who was responsible and why.

At eleven o'clock, *capo* Emilio Barracusa phoned. He was angry. He told Teresa he believed the Russian Mafiya had executed Fabrizzi and they were planning more. He had learned they were pissed off with Pescaro's vice-like grip on criminal activity and were ready to take him on. They wanted power and wealth. According to his sources, they were not prepared to negotiate.

Teresa rang Pescaro and relayed the news.

He sounded grim. 'It's just as I thought. Bring the *capos* together tomorrow. I'll get a 9:00 a.m. flight home. Organise someone to collect me. Keep me informed.' He hung up.

The phones continued ringing. Three hundred soldiers across Victoria had gone to work within an hour of the event and, by midnight, Teresa had the makes, models and colours of the two stolen cars used for the ambush. By 1:00 a.m. she had eight Russian names, men who possibly were involved in the planning and execution. Their homes were now under Mafia surveillance.

By 2:00 a.m. her information had been converted to a database with names, addresses, vehicles, family members, telephone numbers, frequent haunts, and arrival dates in Australia. Finally, Teresa sent e-mails overseas seeking information about the eight Russians and their backgrounds. She particularly wanted to know their specialist skills and criminal activities. That she could achieve so much in so little time was due to the reach of Pescaro's network, dollar power, which always brought results, and some heavy intimidation by his soldiers.

At 2:30, Teresa dropped into bed, tired, but pleased with her efforts since the murder. She suspected the police were still scratching their heads about the *who* and *why* of the killing, if indeed they were even interested in the death of a Mafiosi.

At 6:30 she rose, washed, and commenced a punishing routine of aerobic and martial arts exercises. Soon after seven Pescaro rang and confirmed his flight at 9:00 a.m. She finished her routine, breakfasted, showered and rallied the *capos* for a meeting at *Luciano's Warehouse* in Faraday Street, Carlton.

After that she checked the e-mails. Valentin Chernamenko was an ex-KGB Colonel and intelligence officer with a double degree in science and economics. Like Teresa, he was a martial arts exponent and had a reputation for brutality. Sergei Vitalev, an outstanding tri-athlete in the old days of Soviet Russia had competed at the 1988 Seoul and 1984 Los Angeles Olympics. He was a trained soldier with special skills in weapons and explosives. Leonid Silverstein was a renowned Vor with many convictions for violence including rape, homicide and serious assault; he was an enforcer, arsonist and extortionist. Anatoly Bilyenko, another ex-soldier, held degrees in mathematics and computer science. He had a formidable reputation for innovative frauds, rip-offs, money laundering schemes, blackmail and tax dodges. The other four Russians, all Vors with many convictions between them, were less illustrious than their colleagues.

Teresa entered the information into her database noting the Russian Government had not recorded any convictions for these men. She supposed it was glad to be rid of them. She printed two copies of the dossiers, including photographs, then e-mailed a file to each of the *capos*. With nothing more than the previous night's information and the overseas e-mails, Teresa made an assumption that Chernamenko was probably their ring leader.

She rang Barracusa and asked that Chernamenko receive special attention. One by one she rang the remaining *capos* to pass on her thoughts about Chernamenko and to request that each of the four principal Russians receive special scrutiny. Every *capo* was asked to bring their latest intelligence to the meeting.

For the moment, there was little more to do. She would collect Pescaro and brief him on the way home. She had no doubt he would be savage about the newspaper headlines she had seen on the net this morning:

Mafia Hit in Carlton
Mob Man Slain
Underworld Assassination

The task now was straight forward. Assembling facts, examining options and devising plans was something she did well. She would be central to all aspects but field action – that would fall to experienced *capos*. While they dealt with that, she would also organise another funeral. At the moment, she was on top of things and perceived satisfaction with her effort from her colleagues.

Current events now put Aldrittson on the back-burner. Even so, she wondered why his previous resistance to accelerating the waste scheme had softened. Nor had she missed his probe about Santini's death. He was not the solicitous type – there would be a reason for asking. Pescaro was suspicious of Santini's death and had heard a whisper among police that the "blow-out" on the bridge was a set-up. If that was true, they were looking at another murder. Idly, she wondered if Ben Aldrittson was somehow connected to Santini's death. It was an interesting thought but one she felt had no legs. She was, however, keen to return to his unit. From her first visit she had been constantly niggled by a feeling that she had missed something, something important.

As for the death of her parents and Angelina, she had pondered many options and all were frightening in their consequences. Of significance was that in the Mafia world, these murders were a mere formality while in the normal world, they were serious unsolved crimes. It was up to her to change the status quo but as the event had occurred so long ago, and in view of current circumstances, there was no urgency.

With that thought she realised she had slipped effortlessly into the role of co-ordinator in Pescaro's absence. Dealing with the dark truth behind the death of her parents and her feelings of ambivalence and uncertainty about her place in the Family would have to wait for a better moment.

They raced, head to head down the length of the pool. Johnson, the big man with arms and legs as thick as posts smashing his way through the water like an exploding chaff cutter. Fox, the bronzed slim man, knifing forward like a circular saw. After ten laps neither was relenting – they were like a pair of giant pistons finely tuned to the same rhythm but with wildly differing styles. The two had agreed fifteen laps, the loser to buy breakfast. Johnson possessed in crude power what he lacked in finesse, yet to onlookers, the older, slender man was toying with him. They turned for the last time, nothing to separate them. Johnson powered away leaving Fox in his turbulence. Fox grinned under water, lifted his rating and cruised in to touch a body length ahead of Johnson.

They received a spontaneous cheer from other swimmers aware that a serious contest had taken place. The two men, grinning like fools, raised their arms and pumped them to their well wishers.

'Your turn mate,' said Fox laconically, scarcely puffing, 'when are you going to learn that, in here, you can't beat me?'

Johnson, still stoked from his final sprint said, with a huge grin on his face, 'That's never going to stop me from having a go you old bastard.'

They scrambled from the pool and towelled off. After dressing, they strolled to *Amarello* restaurant for breakfast and sat outdoors, protected by a glass screen from the cold winds off St. Kilda beach.

'Okay Spence, what do you know?'

'Nothing more than I've heard on the news. I've quizzed my copper mates and, apart from his identity, all they can tell me is it was a professional hit. What about you?'

'A little more than last night. I started thinking about what Holmes and Stanley said last Saturday so rang a friend. Russians. No doubt about it. Moving against Pescaro. My friend says they're frustrated because they can't get their hands on serious money. They're having a go.' Fox looked thoughtful and spoke quietly. 'He doesn't know the size of the contest, but reckons the Russkies believe they're in with a chance. I don't know much about them apart from their brutality as crooks.'

Johnson was quiet for a few moments. 'If a shit fight does start, it will be savage. Aldrittson is getting what he wanted whether he likes it or not. I told him an event like this would be unpredictable and create fear in the community. I'm bloody glad we're not involved.'

Fox nodded sagely. 'I'll second that. I've said before that I think Aldrittson is a dangerous fool. Do you think he might have had a hand in this too?'

'He says not and I believe him. I think he considered my advice and concluded the ride was too wild, even for him. He just hadn't gotten around to telling me.'

'So,' said Fox, a smile twitching on his lips, 'do you think we have a role in this?'

'No way. I'm even thinking of telling my police sources what you heard but, after that, I'd say stand clear and let them get on with it.'

'Any ideas about what'll happen?' asked Fox.

'I've thought of little else since your call last night. I reckon Pescaro will hit back with a wallop. Last night I saw that woman

Aldrittson is moony over. She's a piece of class – and she's Mafia. My impression is she's a lethal cocktail. If she's involved in pay back, I'd say the Russkies could be in for a surprise.'

'What do you mean?" enquired Fox.

'I spoke to Aldrittson last night after the girl left the restaurant. He told me Pescaro had called her after which she pretty much walked out on him. He was livid. I followed her cab straight to Pescaro's. That's why I think she might be involved with their response. She's got a look about her, you know it – smart, sharp, focussed.'

Fox nodded slowly. 'Righto mate. Thanks for breakfast. If I hear anything, I'll call. Similarly, keep me informed. Otherwise, like you, I'm just going to keep my head down.' He rose and left.

Chapter
THIRTY- FIVE

In dribs and drabs Pescaro's team arrived at *Luciano's Warehouse*.
They sat for coffee, then quietly disappeared upstairs. Felipe
Luciano had come from the old country in the fifties. Well versed
in Mafia business, he was now too old to be active. He ran a good
restaurant and maintained a well equipped meeting place. Every
imaginable piece of technology was there including movement
sensitive infra-red cameras and expensive, discreetly placed CCTV
on the restaurant approaches. For meetings as important as this,
Felipe himself monitored the dozen or so screens.

Shortly before eleven, Pescaro and Teresa entered from Dorrit
Lane. Pescaro had been briefed, freshened up and gone directly to
the warehouse. Right now he had no plan other than to hit back
– very hard and very swiftly.

The Don worked his way around the room with a word to his
capos: Emilio Barracusa, Frankie Argolia, Eduardo Masseria, Vito
Franse – Fabrizzi's lieutenant – Alphonse Catena and Salvatore
Moretti. Soon after, they moved to a large oval table where Pescaro
sat with Teresa on his left. The *capos* waited expectantly.

'I regret these circumstances but we are here to decide what
shall be done. Before that, a few details. I have known about
the Russians for some time. In fact Eduardo has been watching
them for me. At the beginning they were not troublesome;
they concentrated on their own kind. In the last few months, I
watched as they subtly expanded and became more predatory. I
thought they would come to me so we could arrive at a sensible
arrangement. After all, around the world our two groups have,
in the main, been able to wash each other's hands. Instead, they
began encroaching and foolishly I watched with curiosity.' There
was a trace of sadness in his deep strong voice. 'I believed that

229

as they ran up against our people and our strength, they would rethink their actions and approach me. I was wrong and I have been complacent. I underestimated their arrogance and hunger. Well, no more. They have made a grave mistake. They will not only be punished for Fabrizzi's death, but learn how unforgiving we are. I have but two objectives: I want to hurt them hard and hurt them swiftly. We are here to discuss the best way to do that. You've all got Teresa's information. These bastards are skilled, clever and unafraid. We have to put them off balance and keep them that way. But,' he paused looking around at them all, 'it's been a long time since we were at war. And that is what it will be. I take counsel from the great warrior Sun Tzu who said victory is the main object of war but if denied too long, soldiers become battle fatigued and morale suffers. I believe that warning demands decisiveness. A word of caution here – a deal is a deal. While our system of governance works well, there are *always* opportunists and manipulators. If another state – let's say Queensland – decides to work with the Russians while we're down, that could be perilous for us all. Remember that. No one benefits from a long war and enemies are everywhere. Speed and effectiveness are vital to our response. A public war is bad for business. We *can* accommodate the Russians as long as they understand *we* take a percentage of everything they do. But we can only do that if they understand they must approach us for a "sit-down" – not the other way around. Okay, Milo, what do you have?'

Barracusa's specialty was the brothel trade. He was tall, curly haired, dark and well manicured. Due to gifted ring craft and extraordinary anticipation, he bore little evidence of his younger years as a successful middleweight boxer. His voice was gravelly and he spoke tersely.

'Some of my men have Russian "grunters". The word from these girls is that Chernamenko wants to be top dog. He wants the Don's empire. Bilyenko, Vitalev and Silverstein, are key players but Chernamenko and Bilyenko seem to be the brains. Vitalev and Silverstein are bruisers. We've been watching them since one this morning and on my last update, they were all still at home.'

Little Frankie Argolia's phone rang. He got up and moved to the end of the room speaking quietly. The others waited.

Argolia returned to the table and said, 'All four are on the move. Probably goin' to Brunswick. They meet in Sydney Road at a joint called *Rasputin's*. I just sent men out there.'

'Good,' said Pescaro, 'back, front and inside Frankie, just observe, no action.'

Argolia walked away again to pass on the message.

'What about you Eduardo? Anything to add?'

'Yes Don Pescaro. Milo's tick-tack on the Russians is right. As you know, the pricks have been leaning on some of our waste customers. Like you asked, I kept quiet. Apart from waste, my sources are the same as Milo's: Russian prossys. They passed on whispers about a takeover. My blokes have been watching Silverstein and reporting to Giacomo Virgona. But before we act, I think we gotta see how they work; what they do, where they go. Teresa's stuff is good, but we want juice right up to the minute.'

Teresa sat quietly and listened carefully. Pescaro's motivation for pushing the Aldrittsons was now clear: he wanted their project legitimised before the Russians destroyed their opportunity through ignorance and brutality.

'Okay, thanks. Anyone with anything else? Something we don't know already?' Pescaro looked around the table, heads shaking silently in the negative. 'Alright, how do we deal with these bastards?'

Salvatore Moretti said, 'Let's fix it the old fashioned way. Invite 'em somewhere for a good feed then knock 'em off on full bellies.'

Al Catena responded, 'Cut it out Sal. Those shits won't come and eat with us, they want to own our bread and butter. An' I ain't goin' to lunch with them for that reason. Don't trust 'em. Don

Pescaro, like Ed said, I think we have to watch, wait, see the patterns then pounce. I know you want swift. Sun Tzu might say swift is good. But swift ain't good if we're in the dark and not ready. Right now, I say we're both. I agree with Ed. We need live information and so far, we ain't got much.'

'Don Pescaro,' Vito Franse spoke haltingly. Although highly competent at his work, he was a young man and, as Fabrizzi's second, unused to stepping up to this level. 'I think we need patience. They will be expecting a swift reaction which means they will be alert and prepared. Time is our friend. Being on alert full time is demanding and draining. I think we should take a co-ordinated approach, wipe out the four top guys in one go, let them think matters have settled and then take out the next four. But let's do it at a time that suits us, not while they think they have the upper hand. If we act now, it means they are pulling our chain, and I don't like that. Let's wait a while.'

'Our people are at *Rasputin's*,' said Argolia as he rejoined them. 'We'll know soon what goes down. I hate to disagree with you Don Pescaro, but I think Vito's assessment is sensible. I say wait three weeks, a month, build up our knowledge about the bastards, even down to their brand of crap paper. Let's act on what we actually know. I don't care how public revenge is, we gotta send a message to the rest. Encroachment ain't tolerated.' Argolia's special interest was any form of unlawful gaming and, as a small man, he had encountered many forms of intimidation. No one had ever scared him. He was as lethal as a snake, excelled with knives and loved fighting dirty. Over time, he had become an effective executioner.

Pescaro welcomed differences of opinion – it led to better plans. As he listened, he heard good sense.

'Right. Emilio, Vito, you will help me. Frankie, you are in charge of intelligence. Everyone is involved. Frankie, co-ordinate and ring through what you have each day. Teresa will organise your information and Emilio, Vito and I will build our plan. Everyone clear?'

Argolia's phone rang again. The group went quiet as Frankie listened.

Felipe appeared. 'Excuse me Don Pescaro, is that your car in Lygon Lane?' He pointed to a CCTV monitor.

Teresa nodded. 'Yes it is,' she said, 'why?'

'Take a look Miss.' Teresa and Salvatore went to the monitor, Felipe adjusted the picture.

'Shit!' she exclaimed, 'that's Yuri Andropov, one of Chernamenko's Vors; he's spray painting the car!'

Salvatore Moretti and Vito Franse were already hurtling down the stairs. Andropov was ambling down Lygon Lane stuffing a mobile phone in his pocket. Teresa could see he would disappear before they reached him.

They stared at the monitors. Argolia scythed through their concentration. 'Tony Florenza is at *Rasputin's*. He's just changed with someone. He says the Russians are drinking coffee and Chernamenko was on the phone to someone then explained something funny to his comrades.'

'Too late,' Teresa cried. Heads swivelled back to the monitor where Moretti and Franse were seen pounding along to Pescaro's car. Andropov was neither in sight nor range of another monitor. Moretti and Franse went to Grattan Street, disappeared for a few minutes then came back to Lygon Lane. They inspected the car and continued on to *Luciano's*.

Pescaro was furious. The Russian's arrogance was insufferable. He waited for Moretti and Franse to return. When they entered the room he barked, 'Well?'

Franse looked at Moretti and then Pescaro. 'He sprayed a message on the bonnet: *We're watching you Pescaro.*

Within the hubbub, anger rose perceptibly. Teresa was torn:

the episode was deadly serious, but the quirky side of her nature saw Andropov's actions as a cheeky schoolboy prank. She could only smile inwardly.

Pescaro's voice cut across her thoughts like acid through limestone. 'They are playing with us. I want the bastards dead by the end of this week. All eight. No more crap about live intelligence. I will not be threatened, insulted or intimidated by Russian arrogance. You are *capos*, you are supposed to be competent. Work with Milo. Milo, take us home then come and see me at 6:00 p.m. with something solid. Frankie, get my car cleaned.'

Giuseppe's mood brooked no demur. While palpably angry, he was also privately annoyed for his public outburst. He had long given up displays of public feeling when Angelina died but public mockery was intolerable and just now, patience was not his strong suit.

Chapter
THIRTY- SIX

While Pescaro met with his clan, Ben Aldrittson brooded at home. He was pissed off that he had been unable to lay Teresa and even more pissed off over his father's early morning phone call and the film he had sent across.

Following their discussion, Martin Judd had become Santini's replacement. His development under Santini had been thorough and in his new role he had been auditing Santini's files. Knowing the man's obsessiveness, Judd expected to find perfection. But he had not. He had found records for two different periods, each of a week, filed in reverse order. The first was the second week of August 1993, the second for the third week of March 2002. This was totally out of character for Santini and there was no logical explanation.

Judd told Jack he had thought deeply before raising the matter but, given Santini's obsessiveness, felt he had no choice. Jack told Ben he had initially been dismissive but as he thought more about it had to acknowledge errors like this were *not* Santini's style. On a hunch, he got Judd to check Santini's computer history. Two entries were found for Sunday 6:06:05 at 1:40 a.m. and 3:45 a.m.

Alarmed, Jack instructed Judd to get the CCTV tapes for Saturday June 5, and Sunday June 6, 2005. They sat in Jack's office watching the film and at 12:32 a.m. on Sunday saw a shadowy figure emerge from the eastern truck shed and move to the Administration Centre. Aldrittson was shocked to see this person enter his own unlocked window. With no surveillance inside the building, they could only guess at what happened next.

Jack told Ben his mind had withered at the thought of potential damage to the company if their information was leaked. They then skipped the film forward and were astonished to see, at 3:05 a.m., another figure clamber over the southern fence and run to the Administration Centre. Like the first, the second person inspected the building then climbed through Aldrittson's window. At 3:14 a.m. a figure left the building and ran to the darkness of the eastern truck shed and vanished.

At 4:58 a.m. the second person was bailed up at Jack's window by the guard dogs. They had staggered into view looking thoroughly drunk. The intruder pointed something at the dogs and they reeled away in distress. That person then jumped from the window, ran to the southern fence, scaled it and disappeared. After viewing the film several times, Jack concluded that despite the enormous coincidence, the intruders appeared to be separate parties. He didn't know what to make of that.

Ben had watched the film dispassionately. Like his father, he too concluded the intruders were unconnected and that security was disgraceful. He had no idea what these people had been after, although Lance Baker's warning reverberated in his head. That *was* a worry because if they were idealistic environmentalists, they could destroy the firm.

He rang his father. 'Dad, what have you actually found missing from the office?'

'Nothing,' said Jack, sounding perplexed. 'Martin found two sets of records stored in reverse order and that was not like Santini. That's what caused the alert. When I asked him to check Santini's computer he told me someone had got into it and looked around.'

Ben groaned. 'Tell me again Dad, just what did Santini have in his computer?'

'All the coded records for our black waste operation – everything.'

'Dad, if they took copies of that, we are in really deep shit.'

'I don't think they did son, they weren't there long enough. It would take hours to print everything Santini had on his computer.'

Ben groaned again. 'Dad, for God's sake get with it! A memory stick could receive the contents of Santini's computer in minutes.'

'Well that changes everything,' Aldrittson said hoarsely, 'especially if they break Santini's code. That stuff will give them all our black waste customers and expose our entire business. Jesus, if that falls into the wrong hands we're fucked.'

Ben heard fear rising in his father's voice and felt his own cold dread. He said, 'In that case, let's hope it was something Pescaro organised as payback for you appointing Judd. At least if it was Pescaro the information will be safe. If it's some environmental nut, we can kiss goodbye to it all … you and me both. I never wanted to think about this but … we need a contingency plan, a country having no extradition treaty with Australia. Some place like Majorca where Skase went.'

Jack groaned. 'I never thought it would come to this. Our enterprise has been so secure for so long, plans like that never entered my head. But it makes sense. I'll look into it. At least we've got the best lawyers in Australia. I'll get it cranked up. You've just ruined my weekend. I feel completely stuffed.'

Chapter
THIRTY- SEVEN

In strained silence Teresa and Pescaro were driven home. Teresa had never seen Pescaro so angry. She suspected his fury burned more from personal humiliation than Fabrizzi's death. Loss of face in public was a serious affront. In this mood any discussion was impossible. Yet, while understanding Pescaro's desire for swift, merciless revenge, Teresa believed it was not the right course of action.

Stone faced and rigid, Pescaro sat sullenly. Chernamenko had killed a good man, had known where his team was meeting and had defaced his car with a blunt warning. Pescaro's complacency was evident to both gangs and Chernamenko was ahead on points. Yet temper would achieve little apart from accelerating his downfall. Mafia history was littered with such examples.

Turning into *Villa del Rosa*, they drove along the white pebbled driveway to the fountain. With a curt nod to Argolia, Pescaro stomped inside. Teresa gazed after him. At seventy-four, if Pescaro could not demonstrate control, there would be a successor – by agreement or otherwise – very soon.

She went to the kitchen and made coffee. Entering the library she almost choked on the thick fug of Pescaro's cigar smoke. He motioned her to sit but remained silent.

After a few minutes he said, 'The situation is not good.'

'I agree,' she said, 'so we have to be practical and innovative with our strategy. Earlier, you referred to Sun Tzu and the need to respond swiftly. It's evident that Chernamenko has sound intelligence and we may find it hard to out-think him. We can learn from another great warrior; Musashi. He would advise that you drop your obvious aim and win by a different method. He says if two forces in conflict appear equal, change tactics; do something unexpected. I think that's good advice.'

Pescaro, sat back in his chair and sipped his coffee. She was full of surprises this one. Then he remembered – she excelled in the physical and philosophical aspects of martial arts. 'Go on.'

'Right now, Chernamenko is on top because of surprise and good intelligence. He'll be ready for rapid payback. But, he could be bluffing. We know little of his capability and we don't know what he knows about us. He might be using "the principle of discovery" as a lure so that our retaliation will reveal our strengths and weaknesses to him. Chernamenko was an intelligence officer and that would be right up his alley.'

Pescaro was thoughtful. 'So, what are you suggesting?'

'Well,' said Teresa slowly, 'I believe our actions should proceed on what we *know* about Chernamenko. I am mindful of innocent victims. We know he wouldn't hesitate in taking revenge publicly nor be concerned by the number of people killed or injured. That's Vor tradition. However, bloody and callous action will terrify the community, arouse intense hostility and bring searing scrutiny from the police. And they *will* put a blow torch to everything! We saw how they responded to the recent gang wars. We have to balance revenge and public wellbeing while preventing the police from interfering with business.'

'Continue,' rumbled Pescaro.

Teresa smiled. 'All war is based on deception. We must never lose sight of that; whether it's us or Chernamenko. Deception and surprise means endless vigilance, ceaseless change, razor like awareness and constant operational refinement. Deception can foster wrong decisions and weaken superiority. In Sun Tzu's eyes, *enemies should be deceived by creating shapes while concealing one's own shape.* Yet deception alone is not enough – morale must also suffer. Reconnaissance, deception and confusion will change our situation while we outflank Chernamenko.'

Pescaro felt more comfortable. A long time admirer of Sun

Tzu, he was receiving a lesson in strategy from a young woman who was not even true Mafia. He smiled at Teresa. 'Alright. No more riddles, what have you got in mind?'

'What does Chernamenko want?' Teresa asked rhetorically. 'He wants a share of the waste business and more of the crime market. We offer him that while *concealing our shape*. We reassure Chernamenko by giving him what he wants while we wait in ambush.'

'The men will think I've lost it if I invite him on board after Fabrizzi and especially after my performance this morning. Why should they think I'm still in control?'

'That's easy, they *want* you to be decisive, they *want* you to lead them. We don't know Chernamenko's capability – we need to dangle a bait, to learn about him then attack his weak points. I believe that would fit the sentiment of our meeting today. But, we take *nothing* for granted. No matter what happens, we don't tell the *capos* the complete strategy. Chernamenko might have a spy among us.'

Pescaro winced and blinked rapidly.

She continued. 'We call for a sit-down and negotiate with Chernamenko. We reach a deal that makes clear a percentage of everything we give him comes back to us. The deal will only be a sticking point if *we* make it so. He wants in at any price. Our aim is to get rid of him and his team but he must take our bait. Anything agreed with him can be re-negotiated after he's gone … if that's necessary.'

Pescaro said ruefully, 'I'm not sure the troops will buy this. I was pretty shitty this morning and they'll be expecting tougher action than this – they'll see this as a sell out.'

'You've just confirmed my point. Chernamenko is likely to think the same. In effect, what you are doing is hiding your intention, and you must keep that to yourself. When the whole plan is in place I'd be surprised if the *capos* were unhappy. After that, to beat the system we use the system.'

'What do you mean?' he asked.

Teresa leaned forward, her manner and tone earnest. 'This idea is intrinsic to Sun Tzu's tactic of deception. We lure Chernamenko close, establish liaison, reassure him as best he will allow because he will be suspicious. We know these thugs came here under false pretences – all of them have sanitised records. With help from overseas, we prove their criminality and reveal *their* deception. Using a respectable conduit, we give Immigration authorities the true dossiers of Chernamenko, Vitalev, Silverstein and Bilyenko. At the same time, we give police the identities and locations of the people who killed Fabrizzi.'

Pescaro nodded. 'That sounds promising, go on.'

'Recent events have shown that Immigration authorities will act swiftly on illegals or people falsely obtaining Australian citizenship. The Russians have breached a fundamental entry requirement – good character. That lie is implicit in their migration application. We don't know yet if they're naturalised, but if they are, their applications will be fraudulent. They will almost certainly fall outside the criteria for favourable consideration because they're not refugees, they are criminals and they're unlikely to have the required skills, family needs or special eligibility status that would allow them to stay. The government demands that immigrants be of good character – these men have deceived the system. Their criminality punctures the government's concept of good conduct and I believe Immigration will kick them out quick smart.'

'Just a minute,' Pescaro interrupted, 'I like the idea but I must ensure it doesn't fail. When we leak Fabrizzi's killers to the coppers, they should find other things with them too – like heroin, amphetamines or handguns. Immigration cannot have any illusions about these bastards or their desire to continue in crime.' The irony of his comment made Pescaro smile.

Teresa grinned. 'Sun Tzu would love it. Once immigration

have them, there's little chance of escape and almost guaranteed deportation. But, we must be ready. Our job is to seduce the Immigration authorities so that all eight Russians are deported.'

Pescaro was silent again. 'Yes. That would humiliate Chernamenko. But I may have a refinement – I'll think about it.'

Teresa was curious but knew Pescaro would not be drawn. 'Now,' she said, 'I've laid this out as though it will all work smoothly, but things go wrong. If you agree to this plan then, no matter what happens, you *must* be prepared for more pain. It will be hard on you and especially the men, but you must *appear* weak; your opponent needs to feel strong, to become arrogant in his confidence. At this point, you have to be your strongest, because only then can you feign weakness. If this works as I envisage, we'll be back on top. Any "left over" Vor problems will be renegotiated on our terms. From then on, they're under scrutiny as junior partners or not at all. With luck, we avoid public bloodshed. At the end, I think the men will be happy. The main difficulty I see,' she cautioned, 'is that this plan can't be rushed – it *will* take time. The troops have to be on a tight leash. They have to know enough, but not all. We can't afford leaks and with some of our people having Russian bedmates, compromise is almost guaranteed. You could say you've reconsidered Franse's suggestion and you want more information about Chernamenko before acting. I think the meeting favoured his idea.'

Pescaro was pleased with the plan. It was subtle yet ruthless, full of deceit but workable. He particularly liked the idea of using government authorities to deal with Chernamenko and his Vors. He would balance the scales for Fabrizzi in his own way. Without comment, he had accepted Teresa's notion of a spy in the camp.

Pescaro phoned Barracusa for an update. '*Pronto* Milo. How are you progressing?' He was silent as Barracusa explained. 'That's good Milo. I've given more thought to Vito's suggestion. I was too hasty this morning. Keep on with what you are doing but temper

NO WITNESS, NO CASE

it on the basis of Vito's idea. We will collect more information and strike when it suits us.' Pescaro listened to Barracusa and said, 'Sure, that's fine. I'll see you at six this evening.' He hung up. 'I think they are relieved. Milo said they were having trouble agreeing in the absence of hard information about Chernamenko.'

'Good ,' said Teresa, 'I think the next phase is yours.'

But the next phase was Chernamenko's. As Barracusa drove to Pescaro's at six o'clock, he was involved in a minor collision in Alexander Avenue just east of Punt Road. Had they noticed, joggers, passers-by or other motorists would have been shocked to see what seemed a perfectly normal exchange of details resulted in the swift and sudden collapse of Milo Barracusa. Pretending to help the stricken man, the Vor driving the other car then rolled Barracusa under his own car and drove away. In the early darkness of winter, it would be some time before Barracusa's body was found and Pescaro's worst fears realised.

Teresa stepped into the shower. Since discovery of Barracusa's body, the last twenty-four hours had been tumultuous. Families had to be consoled, questions asked, funerals arranged and Mafia *capos* called to an emergency meeting. While Pescaro explained his plan to an unreceptive team, Teresa monitored their reactions. Although clearly dissatisfied, nothing she observed among them pointed to a conspirator. After some fiery wrangling, Crown Casino was selected for a meeting with Chernamenko, it was open, public and monitored by CCTV.

As the warm water eased her tension, Teresa began thinking of Andy Drummond. Pescaro wanted him chased down and after the assault in Swanston Street, her hand bag and contents had been returned through the mail – by Andy Drummond. A coincidence? She thought not. She reflected upon the attack – a bit of a blur now. She remembered being whacked by a board-rider and then some considerate bloke offering to help her, a bloke who, at the time, seemed vaguely familiar. Then, a few days later, her things arrived in the mail.

Naturally suspicious, she wondered if there was any connection between the skate-boarder and her helper, the "Andy Drummond" who had returned her goods. How? What? More to the point – why?

On the basis of Pescaro's authority, she decided to take the initiative. Drummond had included his address card with her belongings. She rang him and was about to hang up when a slightly breathless voice said, 'Drummond.'

Teresa chuckled. 'My word, that sounds official. This is Teresa Marchese, you were kind enough to help me in the city recently. I've got my things back and wondered if you might be free for a coffee this evening? I really am most grateful and would like to thank you personally ...' Her voice trailed off. 'Of course if you are doing something ...'

'No, I mean yes.' Drummond thought quickly. His initial notion of events taking care of themselves had not envisaged this development. Wary, but curious he said, 'I've actually just ordered in some curries for dinner this evening, would you like to come and share? Otherwise, we could perhaps meet another time.' He thought his comments would throw her off balance.

'I love curry,' she responded warmly, 'I could be at your place in about thirty minutes. Would that be okay?' Her voice was throaty, engaging.

'Good, I'll see you then.' While he was brusque and business-like, he inferred from her tone of voice she was not going to be put off. Okay, he thought, let's get on with it and see where this goes. He flashed about his tiny unit straightening up. Life in the military had infused him with habits intolerant of mess and untidiness and both he and Susan were fans of harmony and symmetry. At 7:45 p.m. an assortment of steaming, aromatic curries and dips arrived and at 8:00 p.m. his intercom buzzed.

He pressed the button to unlock the front door, went to the top of the stairs and waited. Teresa's familiar perfume wafted upwards. As she reached the landing below his reaction to her easy grace and glossy dark hair surprised him. She was a stunner and his feelings were stirred. She sensed his quiet presence, looked up and flashed a sunny grin.

'This is where you hide, is it?' she said.

'Only sometimes. That is, when I come to Melbourne. Come in.' He smiled warmly, shook her hand and ushered her into the unit.

She took a measured look around. It was a small, neat, scrupulously clean two bedroom unit in soft lemon and cream. While the building was old, the kitchen was tastefully modern and the rest of the place appealingly comfortable. Lamplight throughout gave the unit a cosy, relaxed ambience.

'Nice,' she said, 'Love the paintings, can I take a look around?'

'Help yourself,' said Andy, curious about the real purpose of her visit.

Still and silent, he watched her move about – examining this, looking at that, picking up and touching the other. She was at ease and for some reason he felt good about that.

'Pass, do I?' he enquired lamely.

She turned slowly and nodded. 'Who is this?' She held an elegant pewter framed photograph of an attractive blonde leaning against a large tree.

His eyes narrowed and his face clouded. 'My wife Susan – she died three years ago.'

'Oh, that is so sad. Do you mind telling me what happened?' she asked quietly.

'Cervical cancer with complications. By the time it was diagnosed it had gone too far. Diagnosis to death was only four months.' The husky voice and glistening eyes conveyed deep feelings and Teresa's heart warmed in sympathy.

She carefully replaced the photograph. 'I am really sorry, she must have been a wonderful woman. Want a hand to dish up? The smell of that food is taunting.'

'Sure, it's ready to go.' She watched him retreat from the rawness of his feelings.

'Would you like some wine?' he asked. 'Vinea Marson, a winery up-country near me, makes a bloody good rosé. I know the bloke who makes this and it should go well with the curry.'

'Sounds divine. Let's get into it.'

They served the meal and exchanged mild banter, each adroitly concealing their caution. When it was ready, they sat in the kitchen at a table barely large enough for their curries, rice, naan bread, pickles and dips. Andy poured the chilled wine. A momentary, but poignant silence descended. They looked at each other, two pairs of eyes brimming with questions yet harnessed by wariness. Andy broke the spell by raising his glass: 'Slainte.'

'Slainte,' she replied shyly.

For the moment, Andy thought it best to stick to matters they had in common, especially since the intensity of her presence was causing long dormant feelings to pulse. He had to keep reminding himself – this woman is Mafia. 'Would you like to know how I got your things back?' he ventured.

Mouth full of Rogan Josh, Teresa nodded vigorously.

He launched into the tale of Bandana making her both laugh and wince in describing their encounter.

'I guess a little rough justice is better than court – his punishment is over and done with and I've got my things. Good outcome I'd say.' Teresa's eyes sparkled as she spoke.

He nodded, remaining quiet. After a time he said, 'I have a question for you.'

'I'll do my best,' she said, gazing at him steadily.

'When I first spoke to you after the attack I thought I heard you say you didn't do anything. I personally thought Bandana's attack was a random act of stupidity. I could see you were very upset but your response implied something more. I've been wondering about it ever since.'

Staring intently, she wondered what to tell him. Pescaro was highly suspicious of this man and had made him a target; she needed to be very careful. *I cannot*, she thought, *say something I'll regret*.

Andy observed her thoughtful appraisal. He smiled and said gently, 'You don't have to answer, I was just curious. I'd seen you in the library earlier and noticed you were upset. I simply wondered if there was any connection between that and Bandana's attack.'

His last comment allayed her concern that there might have been a connection between him and Bandana and she came to a decision. 'I won't go into detail because things are still too painful, but I've been doing some research to find out how my parents died. I discovered the truth and was deeply shocked. Then, when Bandana, as you call him, walloped me, I felt as though the world had turned on me and it was all too much. To be honest, I didn't know I had said that.' She took a long drink of wine to mask her expression.

Andy found himself wanting to reach out and comfort her. Instead, he nodded and they ate without speaking, each consumed by their thoughts. For his part, he was busting to know why she had broken into AWD. He figured that if Santini worked there and was part of Pescaro's team, then, as she too was part of that team she could probably get whatever she wanted through Pescaro. The fact that she entered Aldrittsons the way she did implied she was after something separate from her role with Pescaro. Bloody curious.

'I thought I saw you on television the other day – the big funeral at St Pat's. You were standing next to Giuseppe Pescaro.' There, it was done. Without actually saying it he had told her he knew of her underworld links.

Teresa put her wine down slowly and stared at him unflinchingly, daring him to spit it out. Andy said nothing. After few moments silence she said, 'Yes. Bernardo Santini was a friend of Giuseppe's. They had known each other for years.'

'I met Santini you know,' said Drummond, trying to ease the thick and sudden tension, 'just recently. I applied for a job at Aldrittson's – he interviewed me. How do you know Pescaro and Santini?'

'I manage accounts, properties and investments for Giuseppe.' Her face was friendly but masked.

'Oh' he responded, not quite sure what to say next.

'What do you do Andy?' Teresa followed up quickly. 'Why were you applying for a job at Aldrittson's?

'Most of the time I play gentleman farmer on our property at

Heathcote, near Bendigo. Quite recently, one of Aldrittson's trucks caught fire there and, as far as I am concerned, the whole damn thing is suss. The driver was killed – poor buggar. Left a wife and two kids. I thought I would try and become part of Aldrittson's and take a look around but Santini was having none of it. Gave me the flick – politely – but the heave-ho nevertheless.'

Teresa smiled. She liked Drummond's frankness and was in no doubt that had he been hired, he was the type who would eventually have hit upon the scam whether or not he was used as a special driver. She perceived a terrier-like earnestness about him, a never-give-up quality. Giuseppe was probably right to target him. On the other hand, his company was pleasant and she admired his continuing affection for his dead wife. It was evident too from the way he kept the unit they had been a loving pair of home-makers. Idly, she wondered what his farming property was like – might be worth having a look at. And from tonight, she had some good feed-back for Giuseppe. With a start she realised she had not responded to his comment and that Drummond was eyeing her quizzically – intelligent brown eyes in a tanned and handsome face. Her pulse quickened. 'Well, I suppose no one likes missing out on a job application. It kind of dents one's confidence.'

'No, it's not that. I reckon there's something shady going on in that firm.' Teresa's eyes widened and she opened her mouth to speak. Andy raised his hand and silenced her. 'I know, I know. I've read all the market reports and *Financial Times* articles etc. Doesn't change anything for me. I just *know* something is not right there.'

In spite of her briefing from Pescaro, Teresa was warming to this man. He was friendly without being forward, considerate without being smarmy and had refrained from probing her relationship with Giuseppe and Santini. He was very evidently astute. She said, 'Well, if there is something to find I am sure you will be the one to find it but I can't help you. Now, tell me Andy Drummond, what did you do before you became a gentleman farmer?'

Her warm smile and the sparkle in her eyes countered the obvious change in conversation. Mafia or not, intended or otherwise, Teresa Marchese was arousing feelings in Drummond that were making his loins begin to throb. Her flawless complexion, lustrous grey-green eyes, rich, glossy dark hair and lithe, shapely figure made her a compelling and attractive woman. And finally, there was that seductive, delicate perfume, the one he had first become aware of at AWD.

He told her all about his army life, his and Susan's lottery winnings and their plans for life after the army and Susan's teaching. All cut short by cancer.

Teresa was aware of being gently drawn into Drummond's life. In comparison to her own, it had been straight forward, busy, practical, orderly and … logical. Hers, on the other hand, had been filled with secrets, lies, deceit, death and shameful behaviour. Knowing the truth now behind the demise of her parents, her belief system had been shattered. Andy's and Susan's lives had been loving, open and uncomplicated – a breath of fresh air. She wondered what it would be like to experience some of *that* air.

They talked travel, early life, schooling, books and movies – innocuous stuff, nothing compromising or too deep. And yet, even though their conversation was relatively superficial, each had the sense of being stalked by the other. For Andy, Teresa's involvement with the Mafia and connection to Aldrittson's were huge unanswered questions. Yet her softness, humour and the warmth and power of her femininity was like a magnet. He wanted to see more of her.

Teresa too felt compromised. Here was a man who, building upon her encounter with him in Swanston Street had, over the course of the evening, shown himself to be witty, charming, tender and considerate. Perhaps most surprising and quite unconsciously, he had kindled a very deep and sexual desire within her. But, he was a target and having spent the evening with him, understood precisely why Santini had rejected him and why Giuseppe wanted to know more about him. All in all, being in the presence of Andy Drummond was akin to sipping a heady and dangerous cocktail.

'Andy, I must go. I am so glad we met in these circumstances. Bandana may have done us both a good turn. Thanks again for what you did and for returning my things. It was really very kind of you.'

'Not at all. I've had a lovely evening. I have one last question for you: could I see you again?"

Teresa frowned, she knew the correct answer was an instant no. 'I would like that but I have …' she searched for the right words, 'a very demanding and sometimes turbulent life. I'm not saying no but let's just see what happens.'

They walked downstairs and before getting into her car Drummond extended his hand. She took it, pulled him forward and kissed his cheek. 'I really have enjoyed tonight,' she said.

Chapter **THIRTY-NINE**
July

'Why is the slut here?' Chernamenko snarled.

'You know why,' Giuseppe rumbled, unfazed by the Russian's coarseness.

'I want the bitch gone.'

'Mind your manners – where I go, she goes. If you want business with me, keep yourself nice.' Pescaro was continuing his game of brinkmanship.

Almost three weeks had passed since the murders and funerals of Fabrizzi and Barracusa. Throughout that period rancorous negotiations had finally brought Chernamenko and Pescaro together at Crown Casino. Teresa had handled the bulk of discussions and Pescaro was walking a fine line between aggravating the mulish Russian and re-instating face. Chernamenko's misogyny threatened to kill the talks before they had even started.

Arranging them had prevented Teresa from meeting Aldrittson again but she had discerned his guiding hand behind a crusade to smear Victoria Police. The murders of Fabrizzi, Santini and Barracusa were being hailed as beacons of police incompetence. The Force's reputation was being ravaged and the spectre of corruption hung heavy. Only a Royal Commission, the media argued, was powerful, independent and transparent enough to establish the truth. The overt protagonists for this campaign were two silks. One barrister, a well known tippler, did little more than assist in the running of the Bar Council. His repugnance of police was legendary. The other, a slick academic type had, on several occasions, chaired various government enquiries. With several shock-jocks from talk-back radio, the silks and a criminologist had combined to become a strident and articulate force for change. Their collective mantra hammered two points: a Royal Commission and a Crime

Commission. The first to probe police corruption, the second to provide an ongoing forum for corruption investigation among police and public officials. Nothing connected Ben Aldrittson to any of this.

Slowly, however, tiny fragments of information from a variety of sources eventually revealed to Teresa that Aldrittson was at the heart of the campaign. The objective was to keep police off balance, to damage their credibility and divert attention from him and his father. The Mafia murders were a godsend. The public grappled to understand the truth beneath the damaging allegations against their police. The frequency and terseness of public comment were signs of early success.

Intimately knowing Pescaro's activities, however, Teresa also knew the allegations underpinning the campaign were wildly exaggerated.

To her intense frustration, she had managed only two brief calls to Andy, a situation which made her realise just how quickly and deeply her private thoughts about him had invaded her soul. Not that she would tell him so. Instead, she spoke about the discovery of the burglaries at AWD. He had professed keen interest in all she had to say about the event but was otherwise non-committal. Privately though, her news suggested the Aldrittsons were unsettled by what had occurred, and better still, the identities of the villains remained unknown.

And now, she sat at Crown, glaring at a Russian bully of huge girth, bald head, bad breath and serious acne scarring. A bully who was crass, intemperate, fearless, clever and cruel. His thick accent and crude speech seemed only to accentuate his repulsiveness.

Before meeting, Chernamenko had challenged and mauled every aspect of the arrangements: the time, the date, the venue, people numbers, carriage of weapons and of course, topics for discussion. Despite his tactics, Chernamenko had won no meaningful concessions, a remarkable result given the two murders.

Pescaro considered this a revelation about his opponent's power – that he was perhaps not as strong as he portrayed. In the end, Chernamenko came with his seven colleagues who maintained a silent but intimidating presence.

From Pescaro's perspective the meeting plan was uncomplicated: niggle Chernamenko, keep him off balance and slowly build an illusion of his decline. Achieving that outcome was, however, complex. The *capos* –not privy to the strategy – saw Pescaro parrying questions through Teresa, discussing his responses with her, and, to Chernamenko's bitter frustration, frequently allowing her to answer. As the meeting staggered on, Chernamenko's opinion of Pescaro became increasingly negative while correspondingly, he became more confident, more arrogant and more insistent.

He demanded an interest in all Pescaro's main activities: prostitution, drugs, uncut tobacco sales, stolen cars, contraband, credit card and insurance frauds, restaurants, waste management and others. As Pescaro grudgingly gave ground, his *capos* became anxious and sometimes, volubly angry – a reaction confirming Chernamenko's belief that Pescaro was past it. The *capos* saw their empire shrinking at the hands of a tired, fearful old man sheltering behind a petticoat. Without agreement or discussion, they witnessed Teresa's stellar rise in status.

Privately, Pescaro was pleased. His foundation to flush their conspirator into the open was being carefully laid. That person would see him as weak and possibly attempt his removal. And even though the enemy remained concealed, subtle nuances caused him to at least consider one man.

The meeting dragged on. Chernamenko, acrimonious and caustic; Pescaro, deferential yet controlled; Teresa, patiently and persistently bargaining. After two hours, and a bunch of commissions ranging from fifteen to twenty five per cent per activity, Chernamenko took a share of the Mafia crime base. Future disputes would be settled by the two leaders.

Chernamenko professed satisfaction with the deal. Everyone else in the room knew differently; this was only his starting point. It was obvious that he regarded his opponent as a spent force unable to tolerate a duel for supremacy. Chernamenko was confident that he had just taken the first steps towards fully controlling the Victorian underworld.

The *capos* were furious but, for the moment, the deal was done. The more reserved thinkers wondered, however, if the wily old fox had not been playing a game. He was too compliant, just a little too uncertain and not at all the person who had fought and planned and killed to become the Don.

Giuseppe too was satisfied. He saw Chernamenko become puffed with insolence and drop his guard. Chernamenko was not a stupid man but he had been blinded by ego and his own sense of power and self-importance. Seemingly, he had missed the stealth beneath Pescaro's passivity.

As they left, Pescaro saw Masseria head for the toilets – he followed. At the urinals he said to Eduardo, 'I have that bottle of cognac we discussed a while ago. Could you call by on Monday to collect it?' Masseria looked up and nodded. As one of the "thinkers" he smiled to himself. They had never had a discussion about cognac. *The old fox wants to eat some chickens*, he thought.

In the car Pescaro said, 'What do you think Sun Tzu would say of today?'

Teresa looked sideways. 'I think he would have said, "well done". However, I have to say dealing with that brute is truly draining. He is such a vile pig.'

Pescaro merely nodded. He said, 'Did you notice anything between our people and Chernamenko or his men today?'

'Nothing,' she said, 'but then, I was concentrating on containing myself, listening to him, taking your cues and giving the right answers. I didn't have time for much else. Sorry.'

'That's alright. I was merely curious. What did you make of his men?'

'Easter Island statues. I felt that Chernamenko had silenced them beforehand. Our people were much more restless.'

'Yes, well, we learned nothing from their silence except perhaps their obedience to Chernamenko. Now, on Monday, I want you to take another look at Aldrittson's unit. While his campaign is underway he might have forgotten some small detail at home that could throw light on Santini's death. I'll make sure his place is clear.'

Teresa was surprised. With so much happening, she thought Santini's death had receded into the background. Pescaro's tenacity constantly amazed her.

Chapter
FOURTY

Eduardo Masseria buzzed Pescaro's intercom at precisely 11:00 a.m. on Monday, July 4. When his car stopped in front of the Villa, Pescaro was on the steps waiting. They went straight to the kitchen where biscotti and freshly ground coffee had been prepared. Pescaro began loading a tray.

Masseria, taciturn, thoughtful and still wondering why he was here, watched Pescaro in silence. When everything was ready, he followed Pescaro with the tray to the library. After pouring coffees, Pescaro said, 'I know what you are thinking. The answer is, I need your help. We have a problem and I am entrusting the task to you personally.'

Masseria was flattered but remained silent. He was a large man, balding with short greying hair and light brown eyes. Waste management was his special interest and he also ran a string of brothels. Shrewd and cautious, he was thorough and strict. Over time, he had built a reputation for generosity, mainly towards hard workers and needy cases in the community. He likened himself to the first godfather of the American Mafia – Don Giuseppe "Battista" Balsamo. A solid Family member, in his younger days he had been a hard man who had killed, wounded and beaten non-conformers.

'I'll come straight to the point,' said Pescaro, drawing on his cigar, 'I believe someone in our ranks is helping Chernamenko. I want you to confirm or clear my suspicions. In due course, I also want you to remove Chernamenko's team.'

A faint smile cracked the edges of Masseria's generous mouth. 'Ah, so the meeting had more than one layer then, it was not a sell out? I hoped this was the case.'

Pescaro momentarily allowed himself a sly grin and affected

an innocent air. 'You didn't think I'd roll over that easily did you? Eduardo, you disappoint me.'

'No, but you had me wondering. There are others who already are strongly convinced you caved in to the Russian.'

'Well, that's a good thing Eduardo. For what I have in mind, it is essential the *capos* think that way. They will be uncertain and therefore on their toes. I don't want you informing anyone to the contrary either,' he glowered.

'Excuse me interrupting Don Pescaro, but ... Teresa's performance. Was that part of your strategy?'

'Of course, we needed Chernamenko to behave just as he did.'

Masseria sat back and smiled broadly. 'I am much relieved. What can I do?'

'We are gathering intelligence about Chernamenko and I want that to continue. But, I want Chernamenko, Bilyenko, Vitalev and Silverstein under your special scrutiny. It is imperative that operation remain secret. Can you manage that?'

'I won't lie Don Pescaro – it won't be easy. That kind of work needs special skills and with our people already so busy, it will be difficult. I can only say I will confirm as soon as I can. Just as we are watching them, Chernamenko's men are watching us like foxes.'

'I am thinking of arranging some gifts for them, gifts I don't want them to discover. I want to know the best place to leave them and I don't want anyone around who can't be trusted when it happens. I also want their criminal activities accurately tagged. You will have to choose your team wisely.'

'When do you want this Don Pescaro?'

'Yesterday.' Pescaro allowed a grim smile. 'With the Russians nibbling our cake, they will soon want it all. Greed will make that hard to resist. So, when you know your capability, tell me. I am asking a lot, but this is our business we are protecting.'

'Don Pescaro, you didn't ask me here *just* for this – tell me about the snitch.'

'Would you like fresh coffee Eduardo?' Deflecting the question he rose and poured himself another cup. Masseria declined. When he had resettled, Pescaro continued in a matter of fact tone. 'I believe we have a traitor. I cannot rely on our intelligence because that person could either be sending it on to Chernamenko or changing his parts in small important ways before it gets to me. However, I must continue in the same manner rather than draw attention to my concern.'

'Okay, I understand. But what about this traitor? Who is it?'

'This man,' he said coldly, writing the name on a piece of paper for Masseria. Surprise crossed Masseria's face. He looked up to find Pescaro's eyes boring into him.

'I am astonished Don Pescaro. I know he is ambitious, but … that ambitious?'

Pescaro held up his right forefinger, his eyes speared Masseria. 'Think for a moment Eduardo. If Chernamenko has inside help to erode my authority, the outcome will be my replacement – possibly by force. Recall for an instant the reactions of some of your colleagues at the meeting: they hated what I was doing. They think I've become weak, or senile or that I am hiding behind Teresa. It would take very little for someone with ambition to orchestrate my removal. If successful, that person would be elevated and the balance of power will have shifted to Chernamenko.' Then harshly, '*I believe this is what lies behind the deaths of Fabrizzi and Barracusa.*'

Thoughtfully, Masseria nodded, he could see the ramifications of Pescaro's viewpoint. He said, 'What about Santini? The papers are linking him to those deaths as another victim. Is that true?'

Composed again, Pescaro weighed up his response before saying, 'No. I've got Teresa on that now, but I don't believe it is related. Do you have more questions?'

'Only one; what about placing your suspect under surveillance? Hopefully, he won't know you're on to him and I doubt that he'll be dealing openly with Chernamenko. If you are agreeable, I will take care of that.'

'Thank you Eduardo, I would appreciate that. There is always the possibility I am wrong about him. I hope so, he always seems so agreeable. But, I have been around a long time and my instincts on this are strong. I appreciate you taking this task and I will not be speaking to the others, not even Teresa. I say again, your people must be totally trustworthy – the slightest whisper and we have lost.'

'Your trust will be honoured Don Pescaro. I'll be in touch as soon as I can.' Both men rose and shook hands. Soon after, Masseria drove away to begin what Pescaro hoped was another step towards Chernamenko's removal.

Chapter
FOURTY- ONE

Wearing a white uniform, curly auburn wig and dark framed spectacles, Teresa timed her entry to the apartment block perfectly. After waiting patiently in a car near the block, she watched the progress of a middle aged woman in a hot pink track suit being led by a poodle who sensed home. As they entered Aldrittson's units, Teresa slipped in behind them.

The dog lady stood outside the lift, foot tapping impatiently. 'Bloody unreliable lift,' Teresa heard her mutter. When it arrived they stepped inside. The dog lady viciously stabbed the button for eleven. 'Where are you going dear?' she asked brusquely.

'Mrs Ortega,' said Teresa. 'I've got a small parcel from the pharmacy for her.'

'Oh, is the poor thing unwell? She's on ten dear. This bloody, bloody lift. It's so damned slow.' She faced Teresa, ' I have to go to town today for a hair-do and at this rate, I won't make it until next week.'

Keeping her face slightly averted, Teresa smiled her understanding. At the tenth floor she stepped out and the dog lady continued. Entering the stairwell she ran quietly up the stairs pulling on surgical gloves as she went. It felt good having a backstop downstairs. Even with Aldrittson on the campaign trail, his movements were unpredictable: Pescaro had sent two men to watch out for her.

On the twelfth floor, she cracked the door open and peeped into the foyer. A young couple with a baby and stroller waited by the lift – as the dog lady had said, it was slow. Waiting, she heard the lift arrive and its doors close – the foyer was clear.

Inside Aldrittson's unit her senses were tuned to the max. As before, she stood just inside the door assessing. It appeared that

Aldrittson had been working and partying hard. Note pads, pens, papers, glasses and wine bottles littered the dining table, a few dishes were stacked on the sink.

She spotted some lacy black knickers on the arm of a settee and wrinkled her nose. Then she saw a man's sock and pair of bright red silk boxer shorts on the floor by the fireplace. Aldrittson *had* been having a good time. Moving to his bedroom to begin her search she stopped dead: the mirrored wall had a gap at one side running from floor to ceiling. It was a cupboard. She remembered thinking last time there was something odd about this room; it was too austere and didn't match the rest of the unit. This secret cupboard, she now realised, diminished the room while the mirrors created an illusion of space.

She went straight to the gap between the mirror and wall and pushed the door: it didn't budge. After a painstaking search she located a pressure pad beneath the carpet under the left bedside table. After some substantial foot pressure the mirror door opened. Aldrittson's oversight had just become her good fortune.

Inside the cupboard, she found lights and a compact, well organised office containing photocopier, telephones, voice recorders, radio scanner, small TV and computer equipment. Overall, the space was about two metres deep and ran the width of the room – it was a veritable *Aladdin's Cave*.

The shelves were stacked with copy paper, floppy disks, CD, video and DVD blanks as well as a host of day journals. The lode was so rich it was hard to know where to start looking. She pondered, stepped back and, using her phone camera, took a series of snaps of the cupboard, the bedroom and position of the pressure pad. She knew she had to exercise great care in what she did next.

For Pescaro, she was looking for anything that might support Ben's prior knowledge of Santini's death. For herself, she sought a connection between Jack and his son confirming the latter's knowledge of the illegal dumping. She was also looking for information disclosing links to any of the business schemes he had corruptly influenced or pushed through Parliament.

She turned on the sound activated recorder, neutralised the record button, backtracked and heard Aldrittson and presumably the owner of the lacy knickers engaged in lusty, hilarious and breathless sex. She fast forwarded and heard Aldrittson shower and get into bed – alone. At 6:00 a.m. the recorder picked up the sounds of Aldrittson working at his computer. At 8:05, there was a distraught phone call from Aldrittson's mother. Jack was on the way to hospital by ambulance – heart attack. That would be important news for Pescaro but meant she could not be complacent about her search: Aldrittson could return at any time. She rang her watchers and warned them to be vigilant.

Listening to the recorder Teresa carefully flicked through the journals. They were filled with succinct references to conversations involving a multitude of people. One she found referred to a Chuck Taylor of the American computer company, *Phoenix*. Beneath his name was a six figure sum against what Teresa instantly recognised was a coded Swiss bank account. While there was no time for study now, she had a pointer and soon found similar entries. Copying six pages from different journals over a period of ten years, she mentally calculated that a sum exceeding $5 million had gone into this account. Even in this unpolished state, Teresa believed she had just scored strike one.

After replacing the journals she turned to Aldrittson's still active computer. She figured he must have been in quite a state after his mother's call. Connecting a memory stick, she began downloading and smiled to herself: Aldrittson was evidently so confident about his security he didn't bother with a password.

As the memory stick sucked information from the computer, Teresa pored over different journals and found a reference to the Waste Depot and Santini in 2003. Although brief, she could understand enough to see that a series of meetings had occurred between July and August. Something had occurred which involved the Environment Protection Authority and a benzene spill. Prominent by the entry was the name D. Mitchellson and $50,000. Strike two – *gotcha*. Jack and Ben seemed to be working with Mitchellson from the EPA to hide a toxic spillage and most probably, the money was Mitchellson's fee. She copied the page with others containing similar entries for different people and activities in other organisations.

In the current journal, she found the initials S.J. and Santini frequently linked in different contexts – two entries screamed at her. One concerned Santini and S.J. the other, Lance Baker and S.J. The notes about Santini were too cryptic to unravel, but the important thing was the date – ten days before his death. Knowing that Santini had warned Pescaro about Aldrittson she was, once again, astounded by the sensitivity of his antenna. Beneath Baker's entry, a list of names was underscored by the word *paedo's*. On that list she recognised two serving judges, a senior policeman, some government officials and an iconic Melbourne businessman; the others were unknown to her. Was this information in some way, linked to Baker's death? She couldn't tell, but the information was dynamite.

She found herself mentioned with S.J. the night she attended *The Squid's Legs* with Aldrittson. Thinking back to that evening, she could not recall Aldrittson speaking to anyone apart from herself and the waitress. Still, if S.J. was doing his job, he should have been invisible!

Glancing at her watch she realised that more than an hour had passed. Although she had barely scratched the surface she worried about Aldrittson's return. She assumed he was still at the hospital and hoped the soldiers downstairs were alert. She worked quietly probing the journals, every so often copying a page that caught her eye. Flipping through the current journal once more, a letter fell from its pages. At the same time her mobile vibrated.

Hurriedly unplugging the memory stick, she checked the shelves and books and stuck the letter in her pocket. She left the copier on to account for its warmth and hoped Aldrittson would not remember its status. She rewound the recorder to 0815 hours, set the chair back at the computer, checked her phone images, adjusted the chair, then closed the mirror door to within a few centimetres, checks that took worrying minutes.

Peering into the foyer she left the unit and dashed for the stairs. The lift arrived as she skipped into stairwell. Ramming the door shut, she held it a moment, then marginally opened it. Aldrittson and the young couple with the child emerged talking to each other. Silently she closed the door and ran down three flights of stairs before summoning the lift.

Driving back to the Villa, Teresa decided to tell Pescaro everything she had seen except for the pages she had copied and the letter she had yet to read. Recalling her first visit to Ben's unit, she realised she had been incredibly lucky; the sound activated recorder must have been switched off. Had it been otherwise, Aldrittson would, at the very least, have changed the front door lock. *From now on,* she told herself, *I must exercise extreme care – life is fraught and any action I plan against Aldrittson and Pescaro will only make it more so.* She had no idea where her actions would take her but hoped for justice. In a couple of rare moments she had even dared daydream of pleasant times with Andy Drummond.

Chapter
FOURTY- TWO

Aldrittson walked into his unit and was struck by its untidiness. A fastidious man, he liked things in their place. He spied the black panties and laughed aloud remembering his evening with the delectable Paula. He collected the clothes, walked into his kitchen and threw the knickers in the bin. A one night stand, no recriminations. He chuckled at the thought of her bare arse on a cold taxi seat on the way home.

Taking his own stuff to the clothes basket he entered the bedroom and was stricken. The door to his history of intrigue, double dealing, blackmail, influence and corrupt financial transactions was open. He dropped the clothes and immediately checked his secret cupboard. *Bugger!* Both the computer and copier were running. He couldn't remember activating the copier, but then, he had been distracted by his mother's call and he was on the computer at the time. After a cursory check he thought everything seemed okay.

His father. *Shit! What a mess!* Jack had suffered a major heart attack and would be out of action for six to eight weeks. With Santini gone, Judd in Santini's seat for only a month and himself not wanting to be directly connected to the business, he had just stepped on a banana skin. Judd knew neither the history nor nuances of the place and he certainly didn't know about Pescaro. But there was nothing else for it – Judd would have to be placed in charge. And that could be problematic. Others had been there longer and probably, were better managers, but they were ignorant of the black stuff. Judd was not. *What a balls up!* Handled wrongly, his father's bloody firm could bring him down.

His immediate priority was the firm, nothing could be allowed to go wrong. He would visit the staff, tell them about Jack and, for the moment, make it clear that Judd was in charge. They could consult with him if necessary but since he knew little about the actual mechanics of his father's business, Judd was *the* man. He also wanted a cushion between himself and the firm if it went tits up for some reason. Judd would have to hang on until Jack was back.

In thinking about this he realised Pescaro had yet to be told about Jack. He could imagine Pescaro's acid displeasure if something backfired and he hadn't known about Jack's heart attack.

As if all this wasn't enough, Meadow's experts had reported back on the waste scheme saying it was "comprehensive and essential". They were particularly impressed with the safeguards and had told Meadows that, subject to data reliability and a Business Impact Statement, they believed the Victorian system eclipsed anything similar in the world. The fundamental question was: *How quickly could it be implemented*? Good news though it was, it had dramatically escalated the pre-election pressure on Aldrittson. To add to his woes, the experts wanted to conduct their own soil and water tests as a double check on calculations.

Aldrittson knew their logic was sound, especially given the prize at stake, but their suggestion totally screwed his timeframes. He would have only ten days or less to convince the public and his colleagues that the scheme was essential. Even the strategies he had proposed to Meadows could not achieve the impossible.

He was thinking about ways to strengthen the media campaign when his phone rang.

'Yes Spence,' he said after reading the caller ID.

'Yo, Benny. Good news. That little lady you're interested in, I've tracked her down.' Johnson's exuberant voice reverberated in Aldrittson's ear. 'You threw me when you said her name was Santini, it's not, it's Marchese. Turns out she's no relation to Santini at all. Lives at 16 Rose Street, Burnley and drives one of those new Mini Coopers, jet black: TSA 006. It should be easy to spot. Mostly she works out of Pescaro's joint and starts any time between six and eight in the morning and often stays until about ten at night. Her main background is financial management, international investment, the stock market and stuff like that. I suppose you might say she's a market analyst, I'm not sure. Can't tell you much about her early life. Seems she was orphaned at about five. All that's pretty vague and probably doesn't matter anyway. She was an outstanding student at school and brilliant at university. She's had some education in Italy and also worked in some classy financial houses in the UK and Europe. I don't know how she got mixed up with Pescaro. Nothing in her background suggests she's bent, in fact, from everything I've seen I'd say she's straight-up. But, I'm still looking into that. So, there you go. Not only a good looker, but a thinker too.'

'Spence, you astound me. Where did all this come from?'

'Sources old son, sources. Still interested?'

'I'm a bit pissed off to tell the truth. Haven't heard from her since the night Fabrizzi was shot. I suppose she's tied up in Pescaro's affairs. Anyway, good work. Now, on another tack, got any new stuff I can belt the Force with Spence? The smear job's going well. At the current rate, they'll end up with no authority, answerable to a Crime Commission and that bloody Chief Commissioner's "operational independence" nothing but a memory. It shits me that that clown of a Chief can look into things we want to bury.'

'Steady old son, don't forget I was a copper once,' Spencer laughed. 'But, to answer your question, I am working on some material involving a couple of Superintendents and a Commander. Need a day or two to wrap it up. I think you'll be happy with it. The splash should be felt all the way to Brisbane and everywhere in between. It's a matter of drugs and prostitutes; that's all I'll say for now.'

'Is it factual? I mean, will it stick?' asked Aldrittson, his curiosity aroused.

'That wasn't your brief. You only wanted stuff that would damn by innuendo and raise a bad smell. And that's what this is.

These coppers might have been in the wrong place at the wrong time and seen things they should have reported but didn't. Like I said, the blowback could scorch New South Wales and Queensland too. Anyway, there'll be plenty of heat and dust for a few days. That's what you want isn't it?'

'Sure is.'

'I'll send you the stuff when it's ready.'

'One last thing. Did you get a phone number for Ms Marchese?'

'Not so far, she's got a silent line. Won't be long.'

'Can you get it?'

'Of course I can.' Johnson's tone projected wounded pride. 'Money talks. But I do need to be careful. Pescaro has a similar network and this *is* a specialised field of enquiry. If I make too many waves they could lap around his feet and that could be painful for me.'

'Good point, I hadn't thought of that. Well, leave it for the moment. What you've given me is good anyway. Thanks Spence.' He put the phone back in its cradle.

Aldrittson considered this new information: Marchese eh? She was as cool as ice that one. When he thought back to their initial meeting he remembered she had never actually given a surname. He had said Santini and she allowed him to think that. Cunning minx! He wondered about the story behind her being an orphan. He sensed she was even more interesting than he originally thought, a factor which, instead of being a warning, made him only more determined to see the colour of her underwear.

Chapter
FOURTY- THREE

By Friday morning Teresa had the necessary proof to show that Chernamenko and his Vors had entered Australia dishonestly. Although the possibility was slender, she hoped to obtain final confirmation of just how and where their criminal histories had been expunged.

The information had cost Pescaro some big favours overseas and Teresa was apprehensive about compromise in Russia. If word leaked back to Chernamenko their plan was stuffed before it even started. Moreover, it was an absolute certainty that Chernamenko would exact retribution here *and* in Russia.

In the meantime, she was busy analysing details from Ben's computer. Apart from Liberal Party material, Cabinet documents and some personal letters, the most significant item was a set of complex financial trusts, banking and currency arrangements involving millions of dollars – all owned by Ben Aldrittson. While it appeared that Swiss Banks held all this money, nothing indicated which banks. Aldrittson had defied the Australian Securities and Investment Commission and Austrack – the Federal money tracking systems – by using tax havens and colleagues in different companies and countries to carry out his transactions. Unravelling his system of concealment would be difficult.

In short, Ben Aldrittson was obscenely wealthy. Laughably, his pecuniary interest statements, filed in the computer, listed his sole income source as parliamentary salary only. The truth about his financial affairs was explosive. Not only would ASIC and Austrack be intensely interested in his fiscal arrangements, but so too would Premier Meadows.

Annoyingly, Aldrittson's information had to go on the back burner – Teresa's number one priority was collating the daily intelligence about Chernamenko's team. And disappointingly, the

Russians appeared to be doing very little.

At ten o'clock she asked Rosa to make coffee and went to the library. Pescaro, as usual, was wreathed in cigar smoke and ploughing through the morning newspapers while listening to the gentle melody of Debussy's *Claire de Lune*. Outside, soft soaking rain fell steadily.

'Good timing Teresa. I'm getting lazy as I get older. Would you mind lighting the fire please? It's getting chilly in here.' In a moment of tranquillity, they waited for Rosa to bring their coffee and watched the flames begin to dance across the logs. On the spur of the moment, Teresa decided to raise with Pescaro the possibility of visiting Drummond at Heathcote.

Speaking quietly and leaning slightly forward, she said, 'Giuseppe, I have an idea I'd like to explore with you. It could be a little risky, but, I hope you'll hear me out.'

He studied her keenly, it was an unusual opening.

'You'll remember that after Bernardo was killed you gave me several tasks. Since then, more urgent matters have intruded.' Rosa bustled in with fresh coffee and *biscotti* and they fell silent until she left. Teresa poured for them then, in a businesslike manner, continued. 'One of those tasks was to find out all I could about Andy Drummond. It's been difficult because he lives at Heathcote up near Bendigo. However, a couple of weeks ago I was at the State Library checking some international financial journals. Near me, at the counter, a fellow was requesting information about Aldrittson's firm and when his name was called, I found it was Andy Drummond. Later, I spoke with him and as a result, I've had a meal with him. He has a place here in Melbourne which he occasionally uses.' Teresa had finessed the truth.

As he listened, Pescaro became curious, unsure where this was heading.

'I don't think Drummond is connected with Bernardo's death but I am not certain. During our dinner he told me he had been interviewed by police over the smash on Westgate Bridge. I feel he knows more about Bernardo's death than he's letting on, otherwise the police wouldn't have interviewed him. He's a widower and I know he definitely took a shine to me. I think if I spent some time with him I could find out what he knows and how much of a threat he might be.' Teresa smiled at Giuseppe and fluttered her lashes. 'He is not unattractive and I am quite prepared to do what it takes to get our information. We know Drummond's involved somewhere, but not the context. My overall impression is he's not the type to be killing people. In fact, I'm inclined to think your police source gave you wrong information, either by design or mistake. But … I don't know. I hinted that I would like to spend a weekend in the country with him and if I do that, you need to know about it.' It was a bold gamble and Teresa could feel the pulse in her throat beating rapidly.

For his part, Pescaro now thought Drummond almost irrelevant. He was surprised Teresa would go to these lengths. He stared hard at her but saw no guile – what she had said basically agreed with what he already knew. It concerned him though that Drummond might possibly learn too much from Teresa.

She waited, controlling her breathing, appearing calm. Her lies contained indisputable grains of truth, but, was it enough? Was Pescaro even interested in Drummond any more? She was acutely aware that since their meeting with Chernamenko he had become very secretive. Her plan, shallow as it was, embraced two opposing precepts, deception and trust; a trust Pescaro had invested in her over her lifetime. All she could do was hope it worked.

'How do you think he would react to you staying with him for a weekend?'

'As I said, he's a widower. On the basis of our conversation I am almost certain he has not been with another woman since his wife died. What I do know is that he was strongly attracted to me. I believe I could pull it off.'

'Did I tell you Teresa,' he responded softly, his eyes drilling holes through her, 'that recently I had Mario Embone attempt to kill Drummond? The fool bungled the job. Tell me, why do you think Drummond was not responsible for Nardo's death? The police information was pretty damn clear I thought.'

She felt her stomach lurch. Andy had mentioned nothing about an attempt on his life. She knew her feelings about him were probably foolish – one tame evening together and a few phone calls. Yet whenever she had time to think seriously about him she found herself drawn into the type of fantasy that made her belly flutter and her loins buzz with warm, moist desire.

She swallowed. She and Drummond had not discussed Santini's death at all. She had lied about that but knew instinctively Drummond was not involved. The truth, she was certain, lay in those terse, truncated notes between Aldrittson and S.J., the notes discovered in Aldrittson's hidey-hole. She feigned a slight cough before answering.

'He didn't actually say much about the police interview at all, but he did say something else quite interesting – he applied for work at AWD. Bernardo turned him down. While he doesn't know anything about what goes on there, he did go to the truck fire and he's clearly suspicious of Aldrittson's. I really think we should find out what he knows. But, since I've only known him five minutes, he is not going to open up, just like that.' She snapped her fingers sharply. 'A weekend of conversation and honey might do the trick though.' She smiled demurely.

Pescaro remained suspicious however, she *was* a smart operator. If she thought this action would reveal something useful, why not? After all, she was a discreet adult. He appreciated her candour and what she said pointed out a need to recheck his police sources. It was time for an update on that investigation anyway. If she was wrong, he would make damn sure Embone finished the job properly.

He nodded and smiled. 'Be careful Teresa, make sure you are the hunter and not the hunted. What else do you have?'

She ran through her notes discussing the information from overseas then raised her concerns about the quality of their own intelligence. Although he said nothing, Teresa noted Pescaro's frown and the steely glint that crept into his eyes. It was clear he would deal with any deficiencies in that regard in his own way.

Soon after eleven o'clock they were done.

Pescaro said, 'When will you go to see this Andy Drummond?'

She told him truthfully, 'I haven't decided – either late this afternoon or tomorrow. I haven't even rung him but I know there will be no difficulty.' She chuckled and in spite of himself, Pescaro smiled too, colluding in her "deception" of the man.

He said, 'Our lives have been a little chaotic lately and even though this *is* an intelligence gathering exercise, a little space won't hurt you. Take the afternoon off." He smiled benignly. 'If I need you, I'll call your mobile, otherwise, I'll see you next week.'

Chapter
FOURTY- FOUR

Teresa arrived home from the Villa to find a bright yellow Porsche Cayman 'S' across her driveway. Not knowing the car, she was annoyed since the street was virtually empty. As she stepped from her Mini, Ben Aldrittson unfolded from the Porsche looking as though he had just stepped from a fashion shoot.

Teresa was instantly wary. 'Ben! What brings you here?'

'You of course. I feel as though we've lost touch, or that I said something to upset you when we last had dinner.' He shivered. 'How about inviting me in out of the rain?' With a smile he nodded towards her front door. In truth he had arrived only a few minutes earlier to check out her home. Thinking she would be working, he was surprised when she arrived unexpectedly.

Teresa closed the car door after collecting her bag. Smiling, she said, 'I'm sorry Ben, but I'm going away this weekend. I've only called in to pick up my things. Normally I would invite you in, but I'm running to a schedule and I'm in a hurry. So, if you don't mind, that will have to wait for another day.'

Aldrittson had sidled into her personal space. He leered at Teresa saying softly, 'You know Ms Marchese, it's definitely not good for a woman to lead a man on; it usually ends in trouble.'

She was curious about his discovery of her name and address. 'Well I'm pleased you've been doing some homework Ben, but I hope that's not a threat you're making.'

He sneered. 'What, to a woman like you? A Mafia bitch. You're just a bloody tease!'

'I don't know what your problem is Ben, we hardly know each other.' Her tone was even, 'perhaps you're a legend in your own mind, but not to me. Now, excuse me, I have an appointment to keep.' She turned and began walking to the house.

Aldrittson followed then grabbed her roughly from behind; he slid his hands around her slender waist. She stood stock still, turned slowly, a soft smile upon her face, an icy look in her eyes. His blue eyes were wide and dark with anticipation, his breathing ragged as he slid his hand under her skirt and over the silkiness of her inner thigh.

Foolishly, Aldrittson dropped his head to gaze at his plundering hand. In a trice, Teresa delivered a ferocious blow to nose with her knee. He reeled away, roaring in pain, blood flowing freely. Teresa stepped in close, took the offending hand and arm, pulled, twisted, turned, ducked then heaved. Aldrittson flew across her back and landed in the gutter.

Dazed and hurting, he lay on his side moaning, blood and gutter water soaking his fine clothes. She prowled forward and stood over him.

'If you *ever* try anything like that again, or come here again, I personally will break both your arms. And, don't think about complaining – your actions are on film and shortly, that film will be out of here to safe storage. your voters are going to love seeing how you treat women. And know this – I haven't even started with you.' Accumulated resentment from the pain he had caused her school friends and their families was released. She was exhilarated. 'Now leave!'

Lying in the gutter like a drunk, humiliated beyond belief, bested by a short slim woman and now threatened, Aldrittson could think only of one thing – revenge.

Wet through, Teresa marched inside wondering how he would explain his broken nose and black eyes. She would do it again, happily. Aldrittson probably did not appreciate how careful she had been with him – whether he knew it or not, she could easily have killed him.

After a quick shower, she dressed then slipped into the front room to check on Aldrittson – his car was gone. *Good riddance,* she thought. She packed her clothes then studied the directory for the quickest route to Heathcote. She decided on the Romsey-Lancefield Road to Tooborac. At 1:30 p.m. she picked up the phone and dialled Drummond.

In three rings he answered. 'Drummond.'

'Hello Andy Drummond, Teresa. I am just wondering if you would like some company this weekend? It's cold and wet down here and I could really do with some friendly company and cheering up.' She listened to the silence, softly smiling to herself. There had not been a great deal of contact between them but she knew she held his interest.

At the other end of the line, Drummond was gobsmacked. Not only was the call unexpected but her proposition astounding. Today, with all the rain after so many months of dry, he had found himself filled with melancholy and nostalgia at Susan's absence. Yet, ever so subtly, his mind's eye stealthily intruded with images of Teresa. And here she was. Uncanny. With that, caution. *What did she really want? There had to be an angle – she was Mafia for Christ's sake.* He knew as he spoke that his voice was tinged with reserve. 'Um yes. Why not? I've got plenty of room.' Pause. 'Are you sure about this?' Rampant curiosity.

She grinned broadly into the phone. 'I know I sound like a hussy, that I'm forward but yes, I really do want to do this. I have a feeling we share some things in common that we should talk about and since it's quiet down here, I thought it might be nice to see you again … and talk.

'When did you plan on leaving?'

'In a half hour or so.'

'*Jesus!* Do you know how to get here?'

'I looked at a map and thought I would come through Romsey.'

'Good choice, it's pretty that way. When you get to Heathcote turn right at Barrack Street and wait by the footy ground. Call me from there and I'll come and get you. Still in the Mini?'

'Yes.'

'See you in a couple of hours then.'

Chapter
FOURTY- FIVE

By two o'clock Teresa was tunnelling beneath heavy skies, the gloom and rain so dark she needed headlights. At her Richmond bank she deposited the video of Aldrittson and collected copies of the documents she had downloaded at his unit.

She believed she had enough to sink him and today's behaviour was a bonus. While her next step was uncertain, the death of her parents was something she *absolutely* wanted to discuss with Drummond. Yet opening that topic meant exposing Pescaro – a field of reservation and ambivalence. Plagued by doubt, she realised how much and for how long she had been bottling things up. Belonging to the Mafia curtailed normal relationships and Teresa was aware that imperceptibly, her own spontaneous and happy nature had become guarded, tense and watchful. To a large extent her naturalness had closed down. Drummond's recent appearance had thrown a spotlight on her feelings and emotions.

Pescaro's casual disclosure about Embone's attempt on Andy's life had crystallised her feelings for him. Not normally given to flights of fancy, she conceded that somehow, Drummond had penetrated her guard and slipped into her heart. It was frightening and exhiliarating.

Soon she was crossing Bolte Bridge from which the city, lost in a fine grey waterfall, appeared as an opaque water colour where substance was suggested by the merest hint of form. It was beautiful. In no time she was on the Romsey-Lancefield Road, new country to her. Most of her life had been spent either in the city or eastern side of town around the Dandenong Ranges. Out here were broad, flat, grass lands, occasional deep valleys and spacious new housing estates; the city skyline a mere smudge in the distance. As she drove, tension diminished, the wide country seeming to soothe away the need for vigilance.

The little towns of Romsey and Lancefield were captivating with their old buildings and expansive, tree lined streets. They sparkled with a neatness accentuated by clouds of yellow and russet leaves in glistening humps around the trees and fences.

Between Emu Flat and Tooborac, scores of granite shapes thrust from the slopes to compete for attention with ancient weathered spheres improbably balanced on one another. In the misty rain, the old rocks seemed like fearless sentinels kneeling at the ready on a carpet of summer-whitened grasses.

Soon, she was in the long, wide, main street of Heathcote. At the town centre she turned right and stopped at the football ground to ring Drummond. It was just after four o'clock.

'Drummond.' She heard the familiar neutral greeting.

'Hi Drummond, want to come and meet me?' She laughed, feeling light and happy.

'Yep, I'll be there in twelve to fifteen minutes.' He hung up, but not before she caught the happy lilt in his voice. She was enjoying the radio when a Holden Rodeo pulled up in front of her. Drummond got out, wet hair slicked across his forehead and despite his reservations, a big watermelon grin nailed upon his face.

Teresa lowered her window and looked up beaming. 'Can you help me kind sir?' she said, 'I need to get to this country property, but I've lost my way.'

The impossible happened – Drummond's smile grew even larger. 'Yes ma'am,' he said in a fake Texan drawl, 'if you care to follow that ute in front of you, you'll be there in no time at all.'

Even without touching, a current pulsed between them. Drummond nipped back to his ute, made a u-turn then fanged right. Teresa followed. Reaching the western end of town they headed north towards Echuca. Ten minutes later they turned left into Schoolhouse Lane, a slow and muddy road. Two kilometres on, he turned into a gently undulating property through some fine dry-stone walls on either side of a cattle grid. Teresa followed on a rising, curving driveway beneath elegant lemon gums. At the crest stood a homestead with a high tin roof and verandas all round. The house appeared so apposite it seemed to sprout from the hilltop. They drove around a mounded circular lawn and into a double carport.

Free from Pescaro, the heaviness of Chernamenko and the insufferable Aldrittson, Teresa jumped from her car. 'It's so good to see you Drummond,' she said, a wry smile belying the understatement.

Drummond grinned. 'Come on, we'll freeze to death out here, let's get inside. What have you got to bring in?'

'Not much, just a small bag and me.' Teresa took her overnight bag from the boot and gave it to Drummond and carried a plastic supermarket bag of shoes.

'Hmm, matching travel gear, I see,' he mused.

'Of course, I spent ages selecting this shoe bag. Versace would kill for it I'm sure.'

'Who's he? One of your Mafia mates?' He ducked, laughing as she swirled the bag at him.

'I won't even dignify that with a response, save to say that every seriously fashion conscious woman would consider you a philistine for that remark.'

Laughing, they entered a wide tiled hallway through a heavy, glass panelled door. Instantly, Teresa was imbued with a sense of strength and warmth and comfort.

'Right, let's get you sorted,' he said. The entry hall continued ahead to the kitchen and was intersected by a passage leading to the back of the house. Turning right Drummond stopped outside a door. 'The guest room is here or …' His voice trailed off.

'Or?' Teresa teased, eyebrows arched into imperious question marks.

'Or,' he said neutrally, 'if the lady so desires – my room is there.' He inclined his head further along the hall.

'Which is the larger room?' she countered with a cheeky smile.

'Since I'm Lord of this Manor, what do you expect?'

'Then I'll take the larger room and share,' she said. And then, softly, shyly, 'Andy, I'm not quite sure what's happening here,' she paused, gazing into his eyes then shook her head. 'I just had to come and see you … I couldn't keep away.' Her eyes were luminous, her voice mellow as honey.

He dropped her bag, held out his arms and enveloped her, crushing her to his long, lean body. His voice was husky, choked with emotion. 'I know, I feel the same. You seem to be in my thoughts constantly. I never dreamed that anyone could take Susan's place but … but … somehow … you've changed all that. Even though there are problems, I can't stop thinking about you.' They stood and kissed long and tenderly. Gently, Drummond pulled himself away. 'Enough,' he said, kissing her again. 'For now,' he added mischievously, eyes searching her face … 'for now.' They put Teresa's bag in his bedroom.

'Come on, I'll show you around so you don't get lost.' He gave her the guided tour and they returned to the kitchen. 'Now then, tea or coffee? I've got soup and a casserole for dinner. Two of my mates, Mary and Tony Maud, are coming for dinner tomorrow night and I made the soup for them. I can cancel if you like, but, I think you'd like them. They're wonderful people.'

'Andy, friends of yours are fine with me. I don't want to change anything and I'm the intruder here. You didn't have advance warning of my coming. Of course they should come.' She stopped suddenly and smiled, 'come to think of it, I didn't have much advance warning I was coming either.' She laughed. 'And, to answer your question, I'd love a cup of tea. Would you mind if I explore in there?' She nodded towards the lounge room.

'Go for it,' he grinned.

She walked past the bench separating the kitchen from the lounge room and stopped. A sense of space, warmth and peace enfolded her; she felt totally at home. Soft lamps, comfortable chairs, a log fire and languorous music combined with a harvest of rich colours, textures and paintings to create a tranquil sanctuary.

At the stove, Drummond observed her. She was standing perfectly still. 'I think this is just the most beautiful room, it is so … so … serene! How is it the window frames are so deep?'

'It's a straw bale house. The windows sit on the edge of the bales in frames and that makes the wide sills. Most of those windows are also seats. They're a joy to sit in and just look out. My favourite times are rainy days and autumn sunsets.'

Sitting by the fire with a mug of tea, feeling contented and safe, Teresa lapsed into comfortable silence.

Drummond interrupted her reverie with a pointed question. 'Did you say anything to Pescaro about your weekend here? '

'Yes, he knows I'm here with you. Why do you ask?'

He was puzzled. 'Teresa, I'm not really sure why you're here. Yes, we have feelings for each other so don't get me wrong, I'm happy and pleased that you've come. But … you are mixed up with the Mafia, you were at Santini's funeral, Santini worked for Aldrittson's and, well … as I've said before, I think there's something going on between Pescaro and Aldrittson's. So I have to ask the question: what do you *really* want?'

Teresa put her cup on the table and studied Drummond intently. 'I don't blame you for being concerned, I understand that, I do. I'm here because I want to talk about things that deeply disturb me. There really aren't any others I can talk to and I know I can trust you. I know it's not logical but … *I* feel as though I've known you forever. I see you as a man of honour, of depth and integrity. I'm good at reading people and that's what I see. What I have to say has some pretty serious consequences for a lot of people, especially the ones I live and work with. I decided I could talk to you and, well … I like you.' Her voice was calm and steady, her gaze direct and unflinching. She had moved forward to sit on the edge of her chair, hands clasped, manner determined. She sighed. 'Pescaro thinks I am here to spy on you, to gather intelligence. I told him I was prepared to do whatever was necessary to find out what you know about Santini's death. And, having said that, I still would not be in the least surprised if Giuseppe directed Mario Embone to keep an eye on me. However, I'm really here because I am at a personal cross road. I am here because intuitively I know you can help me. And that's all I'm expecting – help.'

'And you're prepared to sleep with me just for that?' Drummond's voice was tinged with a mixture of curiosity and sadness.

Teresa relaxed and wriggled back into the big chair. 'Andy Drummond!' she said in mock exasperation, 'I've just given you a bucket load of compliments and told you I couldn't keep away from you. I genuinely mean that. I don't know what it is, but you've weasled your way under my skin and when I think about you, funny things happen to my insides. I don't know what to expect from this weekend other than discussing a whole bunch of things that bother me.' She paused and grinned wickedly. 'And a loving time. At least if Embone is out there he can report back that I tried hard.'

'Do you mean Embone the woodcutter from Tooborac?'

'Yes, he's one of Giuseppe's men.'

Drummond shook his head, he remained ambivalent. He knew how he felt about her but thought she was pretty full-on for the amount of contact they had had. 'Okay,' he said neutrally, 'one step at a time. So – Pescaro knows you're here.' A flat statement.

'Of course. At the moment, because of what's going on, he is suspicious of everything and everybody and the only way I could do this was to tell him. As I said, he thinks I'm here to spy on you and the reason he thinks that is because he believes *you* are responsible for Santini's death. One of his police informants told him you were seen underneath Santini's car the night before he died. Because of that he wanted me to find out all about you. So that's what he thinks I'm doing.'

Drummond started to laugh. 'He is so wide off the mark. His source is either mistaken or lying.' He told Teresa the full story finishing with his search for the man who vanished.

She was intrigued and said, 'Well at least I can tell Giuseppe most of that. But tell me this: why were you at Santini's in the first place?'

'It was to do with the truck fire. My friend Tony Maud was investigating it. He's not now because its become a murder enquiry. We thought the whole thing was suspicious but had nothing to go on. I went to Santini's house to suss it out for Tony merely because he was part of the Aldrittson team. I didn't know if there would be anything to find or to report on. Depending on how you look at it, I was either lucky or unlucky when that bloke crawled from under the car. Next day, Santini was dead. I don't know who the bloke was, where he went or what he looked like. All I can say is that he was slim and fit.'

Teresa finished her tea and put the mug on the coffee table. She looked troubled. 'What happened next?'

He told her about his trashed ute and the shot into his kitchen. Without elaborating, he implied the latter was way off beam and that he had decided to keep it to himself.

Concern flooded her face. 'I heard about that only this morning. Giuseppe organised it on the basis of that wrong information about you. He told Mario Embone to do it. Do you know Mario?'

'Yeah, just to nod to. Most people around here regard him pretty well. I didn't know he was Pescaro's man. But Tony and I knew nothing about Pescaro. Our sole focus was AWD. I have no idea what happened to Santini's car. I still don't, but I see the press is suggesting his death is connected to some form of gang warfare.'

Teresa frowned and said, '*We* know that's not right – Santini's death is unrelated to the other two. I think this is an orchestrated campaign to discredit the police.' She paused, looking at him with a slight frown, 'Can we treat this Aldrittson thing as work for the moment and just get it done and out of the way? I want to enjoy this weekend and discover more about us.'

'Of course we can. What about a glass of wine to help things along?.'

He rose and went to the kitchen while Teresa drifted around the room. She examined his books, absorbed the paintings, scrutinised the colour, grain and feel of the coffee table and sat in a window seat. She completely devoured the essence of Drummond which so richly permeated the room.

He returned with the wine. 'What are you up to?' he enquired mildly.

She crossed the room, a smile hovering on her lips then kissed him with great tenderness. 'Nothing, merely checking you out. This room speaks volumes about who and what you are. I'm just taking it in.'

He looked embarrassed. 'Well, it's not *all* me. Susan and I did this together – this is how we were. I don't want you getting the wrong impression.'

She sat, her eyes sparkling. 'Oh, believe me, I haven't got the wrong impression – I can see and *feel* that you both created this. And that only strengthens my perception.'

He sat beside her and reached for her hand. Lulled by the whispering rain, a delicate counterpoint to Korngold's wistful music, they quietly watched phantoms in the flames.

With effort, Drummond wrenched himself back to reality. 'Earlier you said you knew Santini's death was unrelated to the other two. How do you know?'

For the next hour Teresa spoke of the Russian Mafiya's plans, the murders of Fabrizzi and Barracusa and Pescaro's intention to emasculate them through immigration laws. She told him about Aldrittson's unit and saw that while he was intensely interested in the secret office, he was dismayed at the danger in which she had placed herself.

Then, excusing herself, Teresa left and returned with copies of Aldrittson's journal pages. Together, they pored over them looking for meaning in the Santini entries linked to S.J. Ultimately, they could only conclude the outcome for Santini was sinister and that Aldrittson was somehow involved. They could take it no further. She spoke of his Swiss accounts, the discovery of Lance Baker's acrimonious letter and finished with an account of Aldrittson's unhappy visit just prior to leaving for Heathcote.

Drummond was furious about the assault but relieved to learn it was on film. He was impressed that Aldrittson's battle scars would be highly visible and probably embarrassing. Nevertheless, he regarded Aldrittson as dangerous.

'All this talking has made me hungry; let's have dinner,' he said, 'we need a break.'

He reached for Teresa who slid from her chair and nestled on his lap, arm around his shoulders, cheek on his forehead. Although their closeness inflamed the chemistry between them, reluctantly, they decided to postpone their more earthy desires. There was still too much to discuss.

Over dinner, they stayed away from serious topics and talked generally about their lives, travel, likes and dislikes, music, food and country life. Afterwards they cleaned up and loaded the dishwasher. Outside, rain fell heavily and the wind moaned and rattled around the house. Inside, their harmony was bliss.

Returning to the big room, Drummond dragged the old couch closer to the fire and left only the standard lamp on. He threw a couple of thick, gnarled ironbark roots on to burn, placed their wine within easy reach and invited Teresa to sit with him. Leaning against one end of the couch with Teresa's back against his chest, heads and faces close, he gently cradled her.

In a voice husky with intimacy, Drummond said, 'You've given some subtle hints before about a darkness in your childhood. That first time we met, you were teary over what you said was family history. Tonight, at dinner, you skirted your early years while dredging some of mine. I can only guess that what ever happened must have been painful so … I'm ready to listen.' He felt Teresa draw a couple of deep breaths and clutch his hand hard.

After a time she said, 'Much of what I want to say is still new to me and … raw. It's not a pretty story. It's ugly, violent and murderous and I feel I must expose a crime and bring people to account. Essentially, that means Giuseppe, and that's difficult. I know who he is, what he is, what he does and what he has done. But paradoxically, he's been nothing but kind and caring to me all my life. My whole existence is contradictory. The work I do is unlawful and breaking into Aldrittson's was wrong. I *know* "noble cause" can never excuse crime yet, I don't *feel* I do anything deliberate to harm people. I know I'm no saint but, as far as Aldrittson is concerned, he's got coming what he deserves. With all these conflicting tensions I've been so knotted up inside and then, out of nowhere, you arrive. A man who supposedly is my enemy.'

Over the next two hours, Teresa told him about her childhood with the Benedettis, her school, university, Italy, Pescaro's entry to her life, living and working overseas, her transition to the Mafia and her recent distress after learning how her parents and Angelina Pescaro died.

Drummond was anguished by her story. His and Susan's young lives had been steady, loving and full of good times while Teresa's had been an illusion underpinned by abandonment, murder and deception. The Benedettis had loved and nurtured her, but they too had been part of a cruel illusion. The crimes Teresa discovered in working for Pescaro were horrific and from his perspective, could not go unpunished. For him the question was: how to do that without placing her in harm's way? The thought of her remaining with Pescaro was intolerable. Yet to leave and give evidence against him would almost certainly result in her death. The only solution he could think of was Tony Maud.

By the end of her story, they were drained. The fire, the wine and the endless lullaby of rain had made them weary. Drummond unwound himself from the couch and, slowly pulling Teresa to her feet said in a voice gentle with tenderness, 'Come on, time for bed.' He had imagined this night very differently but after the power and brutality of Teresa's revelations they lay quietly in each other's arms for a long time before gently making love – fire and passion could wait.

Outside, cold and wet, and mindful of Pescaro's dire warnings about failure, Mario Embone had seen enough to give the Don a comprehensive report. He would telephone in the morning.

Chapter
FOURTY- SIX

'Benny,' Spencer Johnson's voice was harsh. 'I warned you about this sheila. The Mafia is *not* the normal world. Plenty would say serve you right for trying to grope her on the street. For Christ's sake, you're a bloody politician! What the fuck were you thinking? Put your bloody dick in neutral and your brain into gear!'

Johnson was remorseless. Aldrittson had already been a bloody fool and now wanted *him* to arrange Marchese's death. He was nuts! His advice only made the embittered Aldrittson more furious.

'Spencer,' he said bleakly, 'I pay you bloody good money to take risks. Don't lecture me. I want that bitch fixed up! I can take care of any grief that might follow … just get it done. If not, consider this the end of our dealings.'

'Benny, you pay me to take risks *I* assess as manageable. I don't do stupid. Taking out Marchese is bloody ridiculous. You'll have both the cops and Pescaro up your arse and, just in case you'd forgotten: you're not fucking superman. You are a person in the public eye, you are facing an election, you've got good prospects for re-election and you have a bright future in the party. Do you seriously want to piss all this up against the wall because you couldn't get your end in? For fuck's sake, grow up!'

'Just do it.' Aldrittson was implacable. The black eyes and nose plaster gave him a sinister appearance and seemed to bolster his belief in his own invincibility. He simply could not absorb Johnson's practical advice. Revenge was the *only* thing on his mind.

'I'll tell you what I'll do Benny, and this is final. I'll talk to my man. If he says he'll do it, okay. If he refuses, find someone else because I am not interested. And, if that means a parting of the ways, so be it.'

Aldrittson glared at the resolute Johnson. He could always find

NO WITNESS, NO CASE

others for the job but they wouldn't be as careful. And, having too many people knowing his plans was not smart. That's why Johnson was always his first choice. The Santini thing had been unfortunate – if that interfering bloody Drummond hadn't appeared it would have been done and dusted as a spectacular but unfortunate accident. That aside, in all the time he had used Johnson, there had never been the slightest trouble. Grudgingly, he told himself he should listen, but his rage had burned twenty-four hours and still he could not quench it. *He* was Ben Aldrittson, man about town, fixer and shaper of events. He had more power and influence than anyone could shake a stick at. He would *not* be beaten by that Mafia bitch.

Aldrittson rose. 'Alright. Speak to your man and get back to me no later than five this afternoon. I'll wait till then.' He stalked out of Johnson's office.

Fox, as it happened, was exercising in the gym. When Aldrittson left, Johnson called him in. 'Shut the door Foxy. I suppose you noticed our friend leave?'

Fox grinned, 'How could I miss him. Who gave him the shiners?'

Johnson laughed. 'Teresa Marchese no less. And that's the problem – the old red haze has descended. He wants her killed.'

Fox guffawed. 'He's not serious, surely?'

'He is, that's why he was here. He asked me to organise it.'

'What did you tell him?'

'Well initially I told him to go jump, but he wouldn't be put off and said that if I didn't take care of it, we'd be parting company … forever.'

'Bloody good thing I reckon,' said Fox still grinning. 'However, I can feel a "but" coming on. What gives?'

'Well, I said no. But I also said I would ask my man. If he said okay, then I'd arrange it, otherwise, no deal.'

'Since you called me in I assume you mean me. No deal.' There was no hesitation. He then spoke vehemently, 'Marchese may be

Mafia, but she's not a killer and she doesn't do violent crime – she's a glorified book-keeper for Christ's sake! If she were a murderer, a rapist, child abuser or promoter of drugs, then okay – no problem. But she isn't and you know how I think. Secondly, bumping her off would start a vendetta that wouldn't stop until we were all dead and I'm actually quite fond of life. Aldrittson's got rocks in his head to think he can pull on Pescaro and win. This only confirms what I said weeks ago … he's a fool who will bring himself undone. The coppers are already out of the blocks and up on their toes because of Fabrizzi and Barracusa. And they're still uncertain about Santini's death. Why would I risk their attention when right now they're thinking: *underworld warfare*. Marchese's death would be seen as an escalation of that and only make them work harder. No thanks. Tell Mr Bloody Aldrittson that his request poses an unacceptable risk. Triple "A" stupid level. He can find someone else … perhaps. Anyhow, what's the story? How come she did that to him?'

Johnson told him Aldrittson's version of events.

'Jesus Christ! He deserves what he got. I like her style. Bloody pity she didn't break his arms as well. Do you know what his problem is? First, he didn't value her smarts. Second, he didn't listen to all that stuff you gave him about her. Third, he saw her as an easy mark – low grade because she's Mafia and a woman. That he showed no respect for her intellect, status or gender says a lot about this clown. Christ knows how he's fooled people for so long. He can get stuffed. And listen Spence, while I'm giving advice, it's not going to do you any harm to distance yourself from the prick either. If I were you, right now I'd start thinking about some of those overseas body competitions. Aldrittson is losing it and he definitely can't be trusted. If he can get leverage by tipping you in, you'll be in shit up to your teeth before you can smile. Make the most of this – piss him off.'

For the normally taciturn Fox, this was a sermon and confirmed his hostility towards Aldrittson. Without hesitation

Johnson accepted Fox's opinion as reinforcement of his own belief.

'Righto mate, I'll tell him. Your future income won't be as good, but hey, I agree with you. I'll tell him now.' Johnson dialled Aldrittson.

Aldrittson's voice whined through his broken nose: 'Ben Aldrittson speaking. Can I help you?'

'Benny … he says no.' Johnson waited for a response. After a few seconds, the phone quietly clicked. 'He hung up on me. I guess that means he'll look for someone else. Good luck to them.'

Chapter
FOURTY- SEVEN

'He's a dark horse,' said Mary as they pulled up at Drummond's front door. 'He never said a word about getting a new car. That little Mini looks gorgeous. Bit girly though don't you think Tony?' It was the Saturday evening after Teresa's arrival at the farm.

Tony Maud smiled at his wife affectionately. 'Mary, there is nothing girly about Andy. Perhaps a bit more sensitive than most blokes, but nothing girly.'

She had just finished speaking when light spilled onto the drive and Drummond stood in the open doorway, a wide and happy grin upon his face. 'Come on you lot you'll drown out there! Isn't this the best wet for years?'

Both of them put his cheerfulness down to the rain. Mary stepped inside saying, 'You're a sly one. When did you get that great little car?'

Drummond laughed. 'I am indeed a sly one. It's not mine, it belongs to Teresa.' As if by magic, Teresa appeared from behind him, laughter in her eyes, a smile upon her face.

'Don't blame me,' she laughed. 'He wanted to surprise you Mary. He reckons you've been giving him a hard time. Hello, I'm Teresa Marchese. Andy has told me what wonderful friends you are and I'm really pleased to meet you.' Teresa stepped forward, hand outstretched.

Tony was gobsmacked. He recognised Teresa instantly and was struggling to find a response. Drummond saw his dilemma and said comfortably, 'Tony, you know who Teresa is, but don't worry – all will be revealed.'

'Well,' said Mary, looking quizzically between all three, 'I don't know who you are and I don't care. I can see already what you've done for this man. Pleased to meet you, and this big galoot is Tony.' Warmly shaking Teresa's hand Mary gave Drummond an affectionate hug and presented him with the beer.

'Come inside, it's warmer and more comfortable.'

Tony shuffled forward, extending his hand to his friend. 'G'day cobber. Have to say I agree with Mary, you *are* a bloody surprise packet.' He stepped forward again, hand outstretched. 'Hello Teresa. Sorry about my bad manners. Knowing this bloke as well as I do there's bound to be a story. Nice to meet you.'

Teresa's smile broadened, her eyes crinkling with humour. She shook Tony's hand warmly accepting his apology. 'Yes, there is a story and we are hoping you will have a major part in it. I am genuinely happy to meet you.'

'Listen up folks. Seeing it's so bloody cold and damp Teresa and I made mulled wine earlier using some of the new Marson Sangiovese from Mount Camel. Like to try it? We reckon it's a treat.' In a few minutes they were grouped around the fire in the big room sipping the hot, spicy, red wine and enjoying its richness.

After a leisurely dinner full of banter they took their coffee and cognac and regrouped again in the chairs and couch around the fire. An air of expectancy bubbled impatiently in Tony and Mary as they sat in front of the crackling flames. Rain drummed steadily on the roof.

Looking serious and choosing his words carefully, Drummond addressed his friends. 'We are pleased you two are here to listen to a long and painful story. We'll try and keep it brief, but the thing is, we've reached a point where we need help, police help – your help Tony. We need you to tell us what to do next and how to do it.'

Tony nodded, suspecting that what was coming would be well beyond his means at the little bush station.

'First off, although we talked over dinner about how Teresa and I met and how we feel about each other, what you don't know Mary that Tony does is that Teresa has Mafia links.'

Mary glanced at Teresa: concern, bafflement, distress and anger all present at once. She loved Andy as a brother and immediately feared more grief for him.

Self conscious, Teresa was compelled to say, 'I assure you Mary, none of this was planned. As you now know, we met under strange circumstances and our feelings quietly ambushed us. Believe me, I'm very aware that my background makes this friendship complicated. But I couldn't get him out of my head.' She smiled at Drummond. 'It just happened.'

Drummond nodded to her affectionately then settled himself in his chair. 'It's hard to know where to begin,' he said, reflectively, 'it's taken quite a bit of work to put this tale together. For me, the starting point was the truck fire last May, for Teresa it began in 1975.'

Carefully, concisely, Drummond began to relate what he had discovered about the Aldrittsons since the truck fire. He explained the relationship between Pescaro and Jack Aldrittson, the illicit dumping, plans for a treatment centre at Timmering and the political machinations to have the scheme approved through Ben Aldrittson. He detailed Ben's activities concerning the bribes, kickbacks, manipulation, spy network and Swiss accounts.

Teresa followed with what she had learned from Pescaro about the deaths of her father and Angelina Pescaro. Briefly, she explained Pescaro's empire with its *capos* and criminal interests, his police informers and the current tensions involving the Russian Mafiya.

Mary and Tony sat enthralled, expressions of disbelief, anger and dismay moving over their faces like clouds across the sun. When Teresa concluded with an outline of Baker's apparent paedophile ring, Mary leapt to her feet, quivering with indignation. 'This is disgusting! On top of everything you've just confirmed my worst suspicions about politicians – they're all corrupt.'

'Steady on Mary,' said Tony, 'that's not right at all.'

'Tony, you well know my views about politicians. They don't practise what they preach, they lie, they're masters of hypocrisy, they set rules for others but not themselves, they rort perks and allowances, they favour big business over little people and, in this country, the feds especially, prostitute themselves – and us – to that rotten bloody USA. Don't tell me how to think about politicians, they disgust me!' She stormed into the kitchen, her words hanging in the air like a firestorm, a searing condemnation of democratic governance.

Tony looked abashed. 'Sorry mate. I think you stoked her prejudices. Look, just so we all understand what's going on here, there are some things I need to know. For instance, Teresa, what does Pescaro think you are doing this weekend?'

'He knows I'm here Tony, but he thinks I'm having a naughty weekend to dredge information from Andy about Santini's death and the Aldrittsons. He wants me to establish if Andy is a threat to him because, at the moment, he believes it was Andy who was under Santini's car.'

Maud nodded and smiled fleetingly at her comment. 'Were you followed? Do you expect to be watched here?'

'I am sure I wasn't followed but,' she hesitated and looked at Drummond who remained expressionless, 'Mario Embone at Tooborac is one of Giuseppe's men. I couldn't say if he's been asked to do anything.'

Tony was surprised. Embone was well known as a hard worker, not entirely anti-social, but certainly private. 'What do you know about him?'

'Not much I'm afraid. From the little I hear about him I'd say he's a "sleeper". He's occasionally kept an eye on the Timmering development, you know, persuaded people by killing or stealing their stock. But not much otherwise.'

'Is he a violent man?'

Drummond's earlier warning about the shot into his kitchen and not telling Tony about it rang in her ears. She paused before answering. Imperceptibly, Andy shook his head.

Quickly glancing between them Tony said, 'Am I missing something here? What aren't you telling me?' He was frowning.

'He's very low level,' she hedged, 'but the thing is, until you're thrown the ball, you never quite know what will happen.'

Mary entered with fresh tea and coffee. 'I'm sorry about my outburst before,' she said remorsefully, 'I shouldn't get so huffy. I feel I diminished what you were telling us.'

Teresa said, 'No problems Mary. I understand how upsetting all this must sound. You can't begin to imagine how I felt when I learned that much of my life has been a lie.'

Tony said thoughtfully, 'Teresa, it's clear that you are central to everything in this. What are your expectations?'

She considered his question a few moments before responding. 'I have to see things put right for my parents and Angelina Pescaro and I can only do that in court. For me, that is the *only* way I can absolve the lie I have lived so far.'

She looked to Drummond and then Tony before continuing slowly. 'I am also hoping there might be something for Andy and me at the end of this. For instance, if this does get to court I would, in all probability, be a principal witness. Without being melodramatic, that responsibility is a death sentence for me – it's the Mafia way. Not only that, because I know so much about Giuseppe's empire, every effort will be made to ensure my death quickly. I know all the lawyers and accountants and they will make every aspect of any prosecution as difficult and vicious as possible. Just from self interest if nothing else. That means other people will also be threatened with death. Finally, it's a certainty that any convictions will be fought all the way to the High Court. And then there's Ben Aldrittson. I want to see him brought to his knees. My expectation is that this will be ugly, protracted, violent, expensive and possibly end my life, but I want to go on with it.'

There was prolonged silence as her words registered.

Teresa continued quietly. 'Andy and I have discussed witness protection but we know nothing about it. We know none of this will be easy, but there are no short cuts to integrity. We want to face this together and we need support.'

'There's no bloody doubt about that,' said Tony forcefully. 'The important question for me is: how do you propose to get away with this? Sure, we can do witness protection but the danger period is between making the decision and taking the action. Many witnesses equivocate and either end up dead or seriously injured. Either way, the outcome is the same: *no witness, no case!*'

'I understand that Tony, and I'm not planning on becoming one of those statistics. But, I can't walk out on Pescaro right now. I'd be dead before the end of the day. There are things going on with the Russians for which I have to make arrangements. Returning to do that will allay suspicion about my weekend up here. After that, we'll have to play it by ear.'

'What arrangements?' Maud demanded.

'Giuseppe wants to use the migration laws to have the Russians expelled. I've got most of the material together and believe it would be foolish not to let that run, especially when there is a strong probability of success. *And*, it will be lawful.'

'Okay, last question. Is your evidence legitimate? If it's tainted by any illegality, you can kiss much of this case goodbye. And based on what we've heard tonight well … that would be a crying shame. We do need to pull this off because the outcome could be massive. So, please indulge my caution.'

Teresa smiled obliquely. '*I* think all the evidence is okay. When I get to talk to the investigators I guess we'll find out.'

Maud eyed her sceptically but said, 'All I can do from here is facilitate access to the right people. Even so, up here in the sticks, that could still be difficult. I promise to walk you through everything to minimise any glitches. One of my mates in town is connected to the Witness Protection Program, Witsec for short. I can talk to him and get back to you. I've never used it myself and I don't want to mislead anyone. How long will you be here Teresa?'

'I have to go back some time Monday – I can't stay beyond that.'

'In that case, I'll try Rod tomorrow morning. How about Mary and I come out at four tomorrow afternoon?'

'Sure,' said Drummond, 'We were thinking of going to Bendigo tomorrow for a look around, so four would be good. Mary's presence might also help. You know, ease any suspicions if that bloody Embone is poking around. We can't be too careful.'

'Done. That okay by you Mair?'

'In future,' said Mary nodding to Tony, 'don't dare do anything involving these two without me. Teresa, you'll learn I can be pretty blunt and to the point so I'll just say this: I like you and understand why Andy already seems to care so much for you. I hope to God it works out for you both. I really am looking forward to knowing you better because I suspect there's great substance in that little body of yours.'

Drummond laughed. 'How perceptive of you Mary. Teresa, tell them about your encounter with Ben Aldrittson on Friday afternoon.'

By the time Teresa concluded her account, Tony was quietly grinning and Mary was punching the air shouting, 'Yes! Yes! Yes! Go girl!' They all laughed at her pleasure with the outcome.

Chapter
FOURTY- EIGHT

'Yes Don Pescaro, yes.' Masseria responded quietly to the terse query. 'We tracked him to the Russian Employment Service here in Dandenong. Cunning as a shithouse rat he was, but we tracked him. Anatoly Bilyenko was waiting for him and they've just gone inside together. My guess is that Bilyenko is Chernamenko's deputy. I think we can safely say we know how Chernamenko is so well informed. Unfortunately, our man brought one of his team members with him, a young man with good potential. What do you want done?'

Pescaro, at home, was saddened. Eventually he said, 'Nothing hasty Eduardo. We'll arrange a dinner, a remembrance dinner for Dominic Fabrizzi and Emilio Barracusa; it's just on two months since Dominic's death. Set up a banquet at *Luciano's* and tell Felipe to spare no expense. Do it this week, then come and see me. Continue surveillance and discreetly set traps to confirm our suspicions. Do what you think is necessary. When you have the proof, I'll host the dinner – *capos* and their lieutenants will be the invitees. We'll "celebrate" smooth progress with Chernamenko and mourn the passing of Dominic and Emilio. In the meantime, remain silent. Questions?'

'No Don Pescaro. I'll be in touch in a few days. *Ciao.*'

Pescaro, no stranger to treachery, hated this situation. It assaulted his leadership and disturbed his sense of balance and correctness. He had not had to deal with insurrection for a long time and decided that after this, he would not be dealing with it again. Quashing this bastardry would be his last major decision as Don. At seventy four, he felt it was time to let go, time to enjoy his remaining years. Since murder had removed Barracusa, his preferred successor in Santini's absence, his support would go to Masseria. And, while that would help Eduardo, the Family would decide the next Don.

He had reflected often on whether the question of a successor had been a factor in Emilio's death. An innovative and clever strategist, Barracusa was a natural leader. It would be logical, he thought, to remove Barracusa before eliminating himself – that would reduce opposition for the traitor when he came to take his seat at the table, something that might not happen if Barracusa was alive. It intrigued him that others had not seen this possibility, not even Teresa who was alert to such machinations. *Hmmm, Teresa.* He allowed a tiny smile. He hoped she was having a pleasant weekend – it would be her last with this man Drummond. According to Embone's observations, they looked far too close – there must be no chance of a relationship developing between them; it was not the Family way. Drummond had to go. He reached for his phone …

Chapter
FOURTY- NINE

The fire in the big room had burned constantly all week. After removing the bulk of ash, Drummond had flames roaring up the chimney and waves of heat bouncing into the room. Tony and Mary crowded the hearth rubbing their hands and warming their backs and bums after the bone-chilling cold outside. Teresa was preparing a late afternoon tea in the kitchen. It was a pleasant and homely gathering of friends on a wet, wintry afternoon.

After they'd settled Maud said, 'I talked to my mate at Witsec this morning, Rod McDermott. To put your minds at ease, no names no pack drill. We had a hypothetical about some of the crimes involved. After a pretty solid discussion Rod's concern was that without a police investigation having formally commenced, and without protection in place, you would be at grave risk Teresa.'

'I expected as much, but as I told you Tony, I cannot just vanish without completing a few things.'

'I understand that Teresa, and we'll come back to it. However, before going on, do you know any of Pescaro's pet cops?'

'I do. I know who they are and where they are. Most are in the Crime Department. There are some in Ethical Standards and the Force Intelligence Unit and there are a few, here and there, across the state in uniformed areas.'

'We'll need that information up front because apart from anything else, there *will* be a bloody huge ESD investigation. The fact that he's already got plants there confirms his thoroughness. And, you can bet your bottom dollar that once the ESD enquiry starts, your safety is guaranteed to be in jeopardy. Okay, Rod faxed this to me this morning. He says it's one of the best things he's come across to convey the difficulty of living in witness protection. It's part of a statement by a former Federal Drug Agent to a US Senate

Committee during the eighties. I think it has special relevance to you. This bloke said:

> You have say, an extortion victim, a high level executive, an accountant without a criminal past. What do you tell this witness? You have to go to him with a proposition – if you are going to be truthful and honest, you have to say "Mr Witness, we would like you to co-operate with the Government so that we can prosecute those dangerous parasites out there. Now, all you have to do is risk your life, change your family name, sacrifice your career, give up all your friends and accept a much lower standard of living than you have now, and in exchange for that we will let you be of service to your country".

'Rod says this is no exaggeration. Apparently, quite a few people pull out of protection because it is so bleak.'

Teresa and Drummond exchanged troubled glances. Teresa said, 'I didn't expect a picnic but I didn't appreciate it could be quite like that either. Who decides if I'm eligible? The investigating police officer?'

'No, the Chief Commissioner. In practice the decision is made by a Deputy Commissioner. The investigator has no say in the final decision but of course it is up to him to argue the case for the application. Rod says some investigators will make all kinds of promises to a witness that are just crap. For instance, in return for your evidence they might offer big fat fees, stunning accommodation and sometimes, flash cars. But – and read my lips – investigators *can't* promise anything. What these guys do is wrong and the practice is totally discouraged. Any copper who promises automatic protection, a new identity, or overseas relocation is talking through his armpit.'

'Okay, okay, I've got the message. Does that mean I am likely to be refused protection?' Her tone was slightly acid.

'Gut feeling – no. But to be honest, I can't answer that. It depends on a detailed formal assessment and the results of some medical and psych. tests. But I'd say – given your background and evidentiary value, the volume and seriousness of crime involved, and particularly the people you'll be pushing our way – refusal is unlikely.'

'Alright. What do you mean about a new identity? From what I've seen on TV and the movies, I assumed everyone in protection gets a new identity.'

'It's not automatic,' Maud said thoughtfully. 'For many reasons witnesses choose not to change identities, others want a new name because they want a fresh start. Often it's wives or girlfriends fed up with crime who motivate change. Building a new identity takes a long time but once done, it has court protection. No one can track down who you were, who you've become or where you are. Witness protection involves tremendous effort by police and a battery of others – it's a complete system. But – and I stress – Rod says they don't know of any protected Victorian witnesses who have been compromised *if the rules are followed*. They break the rules at their own peril. According to Rod, the coppers who work this program are pretty special. He described his team as cool, analytical and full of understanding and compassion. Equally, they're tough enough to keep their charges on a short leash. And that's important – more than 90 per cent of these buggers are serious crooks. Some of them at times have caused us hellish problems.'

'Charming,' said Teresa with a soft smile, 'what's the worst aspect of this scheme?'

'Ending your present and past life,' said Maud without hesitation. 'Spontaneity and naturalness evaporate. You can't see friends or family or ring them when you feel like it. You can't even write or e-mail them unless it's under supervision. Don't expect your standard of living to be the same either. Favourite places like theatres, restaurants, picnic grounds and sports will all be out of bounds. These are things people don't think of. I'm not suggesting there is *no* contact with family and friends, but, with everything supervised so closely, life can easily become onerous and claustrophobic. For some, it is totally depressing. What most witnesses don't realise is that in protection, you don't have a past, everything has to be re-invented. Let's say you meet someone from your home town. You don't know this person but you are intimately familiar with everything they talk about, you can't join in on a shared knowledge basis. You can't say a thing. One tiny slip could lead to your death. This constant wariness and vigilance takes enormous toll and some protectees have even committed suicide. Naturally, everyone your age has a past. No one can live thirty odd years without leaving some kind of footprint. And how do we function in today's world? Mostly through credit cards. *You* can't get one. Under a new identity, you have no credit rating. You are starting afresh, and at your age, that poses problems. Police won't create credit histories for protected witnesses because most of them are crooks.'

The deep silence signalled anxiety.

'Look,' Maud continued, 'I don't want to make this sound like a total nightmare. The upside is that everyone on the scheme has a contact officer. That person becomes your shadow — they arrange things, explain things, provide company, get you through the blues, talk to you, listen to you, shop with you, organise care if you get sick and, in all ways, look after you. They liaise between you and the investigators and set up all necessary meetings or journeys. Once you're on the program, investigators are always at arms length. Witness protection cops aren't like any you'll ever meet elsewhere, they're literally, guardian angels.' From the pride in his voice there was no doubting Tony's sincerity.

Drummond said, 'We kind of knew it wouldn't be easy, and we are prepared to take it on.' He looked enquiringly at Teresa who nodded. 'What's the next step?'

Tony poured fresh coffee. 'I'll come to that in a minute. A key component will be setting up a meeting between you and the right people for initial discussion. They will want to know all the things you told me, probably in even more detail, so they can develop a plan. You could be interviewed by different specialists for different types of crime, for instance, Homicide Squad for the murders, Fraud people for the financial scams and Sexual Offences Squad for the paedophile ring. Then there'll be joint investigations. The Tax Commissioner, Federal Police and probably Austrack. They'll all want to get into Aldrittson's and Pescaro's local and overseas financial activities and that means talking to you. The Environment Protection Authorities in Victoria, New South Wales, Queensland and South Australia will want to check out things as well. That's just for starters. What you are giving us Teresa is this huge jigsaw; putting all the pieces in place will take considerable effort. I personally reckon a special Joint Taskforce will be needed. As for the next step, I'm seeing my Superintendent tomorrow morning. If he's convinced he's likely to suggest a meeting with the A/C Crime and my Regional A/C.'

'Excuse me Tony,' Teresa interrupted, 'A/C?'

'Sorry Teresa, police speak, Assistant Commissioner. Your matters will have to go to that level for their management, planning, co-ordination and investigation. From the start, security will be paramount. That means finding skilled investigators of integrity and talent, people who will not succumb to bribes or threats. There's an awful lot to think about.'

'Tony,' Teresa sighed, 'In some ways I've lived with this a long time, yet I've only recently discovered my whole life has been a deception. How do you think I feel about all this? Are you implying I should go away and say nothing?'

Leaning forward to clasp her hand, Maud said gently, 'No, of course not Teresa. I don't mean to offend you. But I get bloody angry when I come across this kind of stuff. Most coppers do the right thing most of the time. But the five per cent who don't make 95 per cent of the rest of us smell like sewers. That's when I start believing a firing squad is too good for such bastards.'

Drummond rose and stirred the logs, as much to break the mood as to energise the fire. 'You've given us lots to think about Tony, just as we have given you. For the moment, let's call it quits. Teresa and I will map out our plans, you do your thing. We won't be doing anything that, at least initially, doesn't go through you. Until this whole thing is on track, we'd prefer everything funnelled through you which means that until we're told otherwise, we're not putting our faith in anyone *but* you. I'm sorry if that's a burden mate, but that's what you get for having integrity.'

'Fair enough.' Maud grinned wryly, 'I'll cope. Now, I think we should hit the track again, eh Mair? As soon as I have something concrete, I'll be in touch.'

Chapter
FIFTY

At midday on Monday, Teresa turned into *Villa Rosa*. Leaving Drummond had been a wrench for them both, but there was no going back. They had set the wheels in motion. She was composed and rehearsed. Her story for Pescaro would be mostly truthful. While she would add to and clarify events about Santini's death by throwing suspicion towards Aldrittson, she could not deliver proof of actual complicity.

Thinking about different conversations over the weekend she concluded that Aldrittson's involvement in Santini's demise was, right now, problematic. Pescaro needed him to push their scheme through government and to watch the business while Jack was ill. Yet Santini's death could not go unanswered. Michael Judd was another complication. His appointment had, at least temporarily, removed Pescaro's influence at the firm. He was unlikely to respond to external pressures and was flaky enough to go straight to police if Pescaro began making demands. His loyalty to Jack Aldrittson was beyond question. She guessed Pescaro was tolerating the situation because their grand plan was so close.

After parking the car she walked inside feeling as though she had moved through a lifetime since Friday afternoon. With an effort, she shook off her fears and stepped into her role as *Consigliere*. She knocked at Pescaro's library door and entered.

'Ah Teresa, you are back. How was your weekend?'

'Rewarding Giuseppe, and pleasant. Have you had lunch yet?'

'No. Why don't you make sandwiches for us both and bring them here. You can tell me what you learned.' His silver head was cocked to one side, eyes bright and shrewd, voice calm and mellow.

She smiled and nodded. It was no less than she expected.

Soon they were consuming proscuitto and rocket sandwiches.

Teresa accurately reported all that Drummond had seen the night before Santini's death, his attempt to find the man who'd crawled from under Santini's car and the trashing of his ute. She detailed her suspicions of Aldrittson on the basis of his link to both S.J. and Santini. She did not mention Aldrittson's visit to her home on Friday afternoon – she would deal with that in her own way. If Pescaro asked – because not too much escaped him – she would tell him what happened.

'Do you have any concrete evidence of Aldrittson's involvment in Nardo's death Teresa?'

'No, but you'll remember Bernardo rang to warn you about Aldrittson. Given his intuition and the timing of his death, I feel this link to Aldrittson can't be ignored, especially if considered with Drummond's observations and our discoveries in Aldrittson's home office.'

Pescaro felt she was right. Yet, for the moment, the Vors and his need for Aldrittson prevented him acting the way he wanted.

'For now, Teresa, we'll leave it. The election is critical. When our scheme is on a firm footing with the government, Ben Aldrittson will meet an untimely end. Right now, we need patience. In your absence Teresa, I've asked Ed Masseria to organize a banquet at *Luciano's Warehouse* to celebrate our friends Dominic and Emilio. Please work with him and Felipe to make sure everything is right. I want a sumptuous and traditional Sicilian feast for the *capos* and their lieutenants. In the meantime, give the surveillance boys a roust. Their reports on the Vors are shit. I want good solid information for our Immigration contact and I want it within the next fortnight; two weeks ahead of the banquet.'

'Is there a reason for this timeframe Giuseppe?'

'There is.' He smiled but did not elaborate.

His lack of explanation was not an affront because she understood his way of working.

'Right, I'll check what's come in over the weekend and we'll talk later. I'll also speak to Frankie Argolia. I agree that our field reports are not helpful but the Vors appear ... she searched for the right word, motionless. It's as though they are waiting for something to happen.'

Pescaro nodded. 'Yes, I agree that's how it *seems*. But they must be doing something. In the meantime, I want to read about this new software developed for rooting out insider trading. It could threaten our "laundry" at the Stock Exchange. Ring Aldo Morelli at the Royal Melbourne Institute of Technology and ask him to come and see me. He's that smart alec computer bloke. If anyone knows whether it's as good as claimed, he will.'

After lunch Teresa buried herself in Argolia's weekend intelligence. For a change it looked promising. Chernamenko's gang had committed a series of car thefts, assaults, robberies and drug transactions. Several of the principals had been part of the spree. One report especially caught her attention. Over two days three of Chernamenko's men had met international flights at Tullamarine from four different countries. Four young women from each of the flights were taken to Chernamenko's home. These sixteen women, aged between late teens to early twenties and all speaking Russian, appeared still to be with Chernamenko.

She rang Argolia. 'Frankie, your boys had a busy weekend, what's going on?'

'G'day Teresa. Weird eh? They suddenly got as busy as bastards – it looks to me like Chernamenko flicked a switch. If I didn't know better, I'd say he got some kinda word and cranked things up.'

'Do you think it might be to do with these women from overseas?'

'Dunno. It certainly includes them. The shoplifting was mostly women's stuff and most of the cars they pinched went for a makeover – all that could be linked.'

'What about the women's passports – real or fake?'

'Dunno. I reckon they're sex slaves, and as you know, many of 'em end up dead. I'll get 'em checked out. If they're using fake docs that could take some time. It might have been the docs that stalled action, I dunno. Maybe the Russians are always scatty. Trouble is, we don't know enough about how they operate yet.'

'Any idea when or how Chernamenko was notified?'

'Nah, sorry Teresa, no idea. We can't even bug his bloody house – he's over it twenty-four seven. A very careful operator is our Mr Chernamenko.'

'I noticed some key Vors taking part in activities over the weekend, is that usual? Do they normally go out on ram raids?'

'Yeah, often enough. They like the sport, especially roughin' up people. Those people who got beat up at Brunswick over the weekend were Russians – shop owners. We think they weren't paying their dues and got a lesson in punctuality.'

'What happened?'

'One got his skull fractured with a jack handle, the other got two broken arms. Chernamenko's people walked into their shops on Saturday afternoon and beat the shit out of 'em, broad daylight, heaps of people around. They didn't give a rat's. As far as we could tell, no one called the cops.'

'Let me guess, both assaults by Silverstein?'

'You got it. By the way, they're still hot. They've knocked off another five cars this morning and lifted a bunch of stuff from Camberwell market and that big K-Mart over there. If I was making a comparison with the weather, which I'm not, I'd say the drought has broken. I tell you, their behaviour is weird.'

'Okay. Frankie, I'll make sure The Don knows. Are your people still good? Not being lured away to chase this stuff so you miss something of real importance are you?'

'Good point. Don't think so but I'll check.'

'Thanks. If anything comes up let me know. Don't forget –

Chernamenko is ex-KGB Intelligence. His file says he was good. This might all be a double bluff to unseat The Don somehow, in spite of their agreement.' She hung up, curious about Chernamenko's activities yet knowing the pattern they wanted was beginning to emerge.

With a jolt, she sat upright. *Step back*, she thought. *Am I worried for Pescaro?* How did that fit with her commitment to Tony Maud? She was confused about her feelings and realised she had better deal with this quickly or her plans could be in tatters. Here she was making sure the Russians didn't steal a march on Pescaro while protecting his position as Don and at the same time, wanting him to face justice. Her situation felt surreal. She could scarcely remember her parents and she had never known Angelina. Listening to Pescaro's narration of the executions she had felt his pain, his grief and his deep sense of betrayal. His actions after discovering the lovers were, *he* believed, without choice: he had to honour the Code.

It was this man too who had ensured that from childhood she enjoyed a solid home life, good education and sound employment opportunities. Silently, remotely, benignly, Pescaro had seen that she wanted for nothing. It was his way, she believed, of apologising to the child for the sins of her father and she was grateful for that support. He needn't have done anything. Her decision to make Pescaro pay for the three deaths, juxtaposed with his benevolence, conflicted her deeply. She knew what was right but she could not easily erase the friendship and depth of feeling that had grown between them.

Nor could she deal with this the Mafia way. She felt neither distant nor strong enough to regard her help to the police as merely business. To the contrary, she was intensely passionate about the course she was embarking upon – it was absolutely personal. Yet, as painful as it was, the mental gymnastics were timely, she had to face reality. She was in touch with her strengths and knew she was courageous. Though others might disagree, she considered herself a person of integrity. Conflict or not, she had to stay the journey.

The flame that would sustain was Andy Drummond.

Chapter
FIFTY-ONE

Drummond's mood was as black as the sky. His perfect weekend was over and he was hurting. Having learned most of Teresa's dark secrets, he was particularly fearful of the moment she had to deal directly with the police. Pescaro's crooked cops created a fearful precipice which threatened her very existence, and that deeply concerned him.

Added to this was Teresa's belief that Pescaro had accepted her reasons for wanting to see him. In his opinion, her faith was misplaced. He couldn't fathom why Pescaro would agree to the visit. On Sunday night they had again made love. Passionately, with fire and abandon. And later, slowly and tenderly, exploring each other's bodies, expressing their feelings and commitment for one another. He had lain awake for a long time after that while Teresa slept peacefully. Many times over he dissected every aspect of her visit, each time arriving at the same conclusion – benign as it seemed, it was a set-up. Pescaro could ask innocent questions about the house, its design and the farm layout, all in the context of her weekend "off". When eventually he reached out for sleep, he had committed to becoming proactive.

He had not told Tony Maud about the shooting at his farm and Drummond figured that with Teresa's visit out of the way, Embone would try again. He smiled as he drifted off – all that time in the army had not been for nowt. Mr Embone, if he called, could be in for some unpleasant surprises.

After Teresa's departure, he spent the rest of the day installing a variety of hazards around the house and its approaches. Working on what he *could* control, his mood lifted. He had Teresa, they had a plan and, one day, they might even be together. He needed to be positive and optimistic for them both.

That night, after dinner, Teresa began planning her retaliation against Ben Aldrittson. She had to be patient and needed time but even then, she was uncertain of the outcome. The crucial element was the election; if she could properly mesh with that she believed she had a reasonable chance of success.

From material downloaded at Aldrittson's home she began crafting a document which carefully explained how Aldrittson sponsored companies through the government, received kickbacks and where his bribe money was hidden. Intended for the newspapers, her expectation was *not* that her letter would be published, rather it would become a catalyst for comprehensive investigation by the media. She worked hard not to compromise matters already discussed with Maud and worried that, at some point, she might not be able to keep the different chunks of information separate. Her fervent hope was that Aldrittson would be exposed for the corrupt bastard he was.

By midnight, she had what she regarded as a tight, factual and explosive three page letter set to electrify any decent editor yet still generate sufficient caution to ensure the paper made its own enquiries. The recipient of her document was to be Rosslyn Zimmer, an investigative journalist at the *Herald Sun*.

In all, there would be three such letters. Each would contain new information and build upon its predecessor. Each would be damning. The last would reveal Aldrittson's knowledge of, and inaction about, the paedophile group. By the time Zimmer received this, Teresa hoped to be deep in witness protection.

Mario Embone had already reconnoitred Drummond's farm late Friday evening. It had not been easy – with so much rain the conditions were perilous. Nevertheless, he had been close enough to observe the intimacy between Marchese and Drummond. Pescaro's most recent instructions had been simple: wait for her to leave then kill Drummond. He had driven past the farm a couple of times Monday morning and at 11:30 noticed the black Mini had gone.

Now, at 2:45 a.m. on Tuesday, the rain had ceased and large, inky humps of cloud filled the sky. Every so often, shy, translucent moonlight stippled the ground, light which, to Mario, seemed only to accentuate the bleak July night, though it did ease his way towards Drummond's house. Again, he had walked the gully of the adjacent farm to reach Drummond's copse of winter-naked oaks. He recalled his previous visit: the perfect location, the perfect shot. He was still mystified why, at the precise moment he fired, Drummond bent to the floor. He had been fearful of recriminations from Pescaro yet there had been none. But ... that would not be the case a second time. His intention was to cut Drummond's throat as he slept ... *Bugger!* He kicked free of some thick, dry, dock weed; he hated the clinging burry tops that stuck to his trousers.

In Drummond's bedroom, a bell tinkled – he awoke immediately. Arranging his bed, he pulled on a track suit and slipped into the toilet. Sitting on the lid, door ajar, he waited patiently, his Savage fully loaded with .410 shot and .22 magnum cartridges. Senses razor sharp.

Embone crept closer using logs and shrubs to reduce his presence to a shadow. He was deathly quiet. His reconnaissance had revealed several doors to the house – he would enter the first he found open. It was still unusual here for people to lock up at night, access shouldn't be a problem.

He inched towards the eastern verandah with its doors to the kitchen, lounge and Drummond's bedroom. Crouching by a thick grevillea near the verandah steps, he waited for the moon to disappear. Rising, he moved forward then stifled a gasp as, without warning, he slipped into a deep hole about a metre from the steps.

A sizeable rock at the bottom of the hole caused his ankle to twist. *Jesus Christ!* Tears welled in his eyes; his ankle was on fire. *Shit!* He could have sworn the ground looked solid. He crawled to the steps, sat a few minutes and breathed deeply, massaging his ankle. He stood carefully, testing his weight. It was bloody painful but he could manage. He shuffled quietly to the double doors of the lounge room – locked. He moved on to the kitchen door – locked. He didn't want to chance Drummond's bedroom doors in case it woke him. He checked the sleeping form before passing the room. Slowly, silently, he moved towards the back of the house; his ankle throbbed but was more or less under control.

At the corner of the house, in deep shadow, he became entangled in a hose casually looped across the walkway. He kicked it free then screeched in shock. Something had punctured his leg causing intense pain. He leaned against the wall sucking in air, eyes streaming. Gingerly, he felt his left thigh and calf – he was bleeding. *Christ, what was happening?* He stood still, leg violently throbbing. When moonlight returned, he saw a cord attached to a slender piece of wood clamped to his leg by four needle-like nails. From this, a nylon line tied to the hose ran to a stout piece of bamboo which acted as a spring. *The fucking bastard had set a trap!*

Mario saw red. He steeled himself, removed the spikes, let the blood flow and continued silently forward. He tried the laundry door – open. Given the painful surprises already, he was wary and wondered if the open door was another trap. Remaining outside, he pushed the door gently until it was fully open; nothing happened. He stood quietly for two long minutes before stepping forward. Ahead a closed, glass panelled door sealed the laundry from a hall running into the house. A low voltage night light glowed halfway down the hall. The house was otherwise dark and silent.

Painfully, he limped to the glass door, his leg and ankle screaming. He withdrew a long razor-like blade from a soft leather sheath at his side. *We'll see in a minute Mr Clever Dick just how you like pain,* he thought.

Gently, he opened the door and stepped into the hallway. With his hand still upon the door, one foot in the air, the world collapsed around him. The foot upon the floor commenced to slide and he began to fall but before he hit the floor, a soft clinging mesh enveloped him. Suddenly, there was blaze of light behind which loomed the large dark figure of Andy Drummond, roaring at the top of his lungs and bearing a steadily pointing shot gun. Mario's humiliation was complete when his head cracked upon the tiled floor and robbed him of consciousness.

At 4:00 a.m., Maud and Drummond talked in the kitchen. Embone had been carted off to the Heathcote hospital for a check-up. From the time he regained consciousness until his departure, he had not uttered a word.

Maud was intrigued by Drummond's defence mechanisms. 'You might be sailing close to the wind with that nail device Andy.'

'Why?' enquired Drummond. 'It's my kangaroo scarer. The buggers come right up to the house and eat my plants. It doesn't do them any serious harm but they get the message. If one of them cops it, the mob disappears.'

Maud looked sceptical. 'Yeah, but a court might construe the damn thing as a man trap, and man traps are an offence under the Crimes Act.'

Drummond shrugged. 'It's for kangaroos.'

'Well what about inside the house? You couldn't say that wasn't deliberate.'

'Of course it was deliberate. After our talk on Sunday I considered myself under threat. And I was correct. It was very bloody deliberate. But shit, you'd have to work bloody hard to say that a fish net falling from the ceiling and a patch of grease on the floor was a man trap. Neither are designed to kill, maim or injure – they were merely warnings.'

'Yeah … right. Is that why all those little bells are in your room? Warnings hooked up to trip wires all over your bloody farm. That poor bugger didn't stand a chance.'

Drummond grinned at his friend and said, 'Yeah, well I'm alive and he's stuffed. Apart from his sprained ankle, which I know nothing about, he's only got some small holes in his leg, a headache and a big dose of wounded pride. It could have been quite different. Did you see that bloody long knife he dropped? It's so sharp it'll slice cigarette paper. He wasn't in my house at that hour to talk fishing was he?'

'You're right about that! Army life was handy then?'

'Bloody oath – simple but effective.'

'Okay, come in later today and make a statement. You'd better start thinking about a holiday for safety reasons and, while I think of it, keep Teresa in the loop. Pescaro is probably behind this so she'll need to know. By the way, that meeting with my Super is set for today. This'll add a bit more weight.'

A slow smile cracked Maud's face, 'Bloody good work Cobber.'

After Drummond's 5:00 a.m. call Teresa had risen, completed a workout and meditated. Her lesson for the day was adaptability and flow.

Mid–morning she took coffee to Pescaro. As she entered his library he was replacing the phone, a troubled look on his face.

'What's the matter? You look worried Giuseppe.'

'Tell me truthfully Teresa, what *is* between you and Drummond?' he countered.

'Nothing Giuseppe. As I said before, Drummond is a very personable man, but what I went for, *and* obtained, was information about Bernardo. Why, what's happened?'

Pescaro was inscrutable, his sharp eyes searching her face. Teresa waited, impassive, knowing her opponent was a Grand Master. 'Can I believe what you say?' he rumbled at last.

'If you have doubts then give me a test,' she challenged.

'Would you kill him?'

'You know I would hate to do that.' She shut down her feelings and focussed on every nuance of their conversation – searching for what lay behind his thinking.

He spoke coldly. 'You must be a very good actress Teresa – Embone tells me you two appeared intensely intimate and, I am not talking about mere physicality. I won't allow that. I sent him to kill Drummond last night. The incompetent failed again. I should have cut off his hand the first time. That phone call was from one of our lawyers. Embone fronted the Bendigo Magistrates' Court this morning. Fortunately, he hasn't said anything since his arrest, not even to the court, so he's not on bail. The useless bastard! So Teresa, two attempts on Drummond's life and two failures. What's his secret? More to the point: did you know about Embone's arrest?' Pescaro's eyes pierced her like lasers.

'I didn't know about the arrest,' she lied. 'As for Drummond, he was in the army and I guess he has certain skills. Apart from that he's very fit, he's confident and my impression is that he doesn't scare easily. Are you asking me to kill him?'

'No. I have special people who will not make the same mistake again. Have you spoken to Drummond since your return?'

'No,' she lied again, 'we both knew what my visit was about. I will not be taking matters further. The situation is different now.' She made herself emphatic without, she hoped, sounding false.

'Good. By the end of this week he'll be dead, a matter of principle. Find someone else to dally with.' His manner was curt with no room for argument. 'Has Frankie rung in today?'

'Yes. Chernamenko has brought girls in every day since that first sighting. Gino Duchin in Customs is checking the passports and so far, they seem valid. This is looking very much like sex slavery. Since the weekend, more than fifty girls have arrived from all around the world. Same pattern each time: they arrive in small numbers from various countries, are met by Chernamenko's men, go to his home, then vanish. When we involve the Immigration authorities we'll have some good stuff for them.' She relayed the information automatically, chilled by Pescaro's promise of Drummond's death.

'Okay, I am lunching with Ed Masseria today and might even go on to one of our clubs. I'll see you tomorrow.' She was dismissed.

His attitude was distant and not as she anticipated. With their hunt for a traitor in full flight, she expected to be followed and to have her phone tapped; she also expected a close grilling about Drummond. She had believed her composure would dampen any concern Pescaro might have about him. What she saw however, was suspicion and disbelief in his eyes; what she felt was a vast, cold gulf between them. She had not anticipated the immediate and blunt death sentence for Drummond. *Dead by the end of the week* meant any time from *now*. She was terrified for them both and with Pescaro becoming ever more secretive, needed to watch her own back carefully. From this point on she must always expect the unexpected. Anyone in the Family was expendable and Pescaro's lunch with Masseria was sinister.

At midday Teresa retrieved her film of Aldrittson's assault from the bank, took it to a camera store and explained her requirements. Later, she bought a new mobile phone.

After lunch at the Booktalk Café in Swan Street, she collected her prints. Although she had not specifically detected a "shadow," she was slightly unsettled by a young couple she noticed several times at different places she had visited that day. Given her concerns about Pescaro, she decided to test her suspicion. Going to the first floor of Dimmey's she pretended to browse the materials and spotted the young woman inspecting curtains. Unhurriedly, Teresa worked her way to the escalator. At the bottom, on the ground floor, the woman's partner was absently flicking through some books. He was perfectly placed to watch the escalators and lifts. She no longer doubted she had a tail.

Andy's unlisted mobile rang. 'Drummond,' he answered.

'Hello Drummond. This is what you might call a welfare check. Are you okay?'

'I am, what about you?'

'Better for talking to you. I'm sending a text so we don't have to talk. You'll see why. Bye.'

*

Andy,

Embone seen in Bendigo Court this a.m. by a P lawyer. P asked if I knew about it said no. P highly suss said UR dead by end of week – means any time from NOW!

Will use skilled soldiers. Pls stay Tony and Mary & take a holiday. If anything happened couldn't forgive myself.

This is a new phone & will B on silent. Ring & let buzz twice, cancel, call again. Will know its you. Give number to Tony. No one else has it. Using code I'll know difference.

Was followed today. Never seen them B4. Pretty sure gave the slip.

B careful. I love you.   T

*

Teresa,

Thanks will tell Tony. We're in this together. Pls B gone by end of week. Take own advice B damned careful.

Tonys Super went straight to Regional A/C. He rang A/C Crime who wants all in Melb tomorrow. Tonys credibility! Select things of value & remove from house. Put in storage or give to friend. Departure may be super fast. Need to ask more questions don't know enough.

Ring tomorrow. All my love. Andy

*

Drummond made himself a cup of tea and sat by the fire thinking. The problem, as he saw it, was that if he left now and Giuseppe's men came tonight his absence was likely to increase Pescaro's suspicion of Teresa. That must not happen. It would be logical for Pescaro to assume he had left the farm because of Embone's attack, but with Embone under arrest, there was no ostensible threat. In which case, Pescaro would probably anticipate finding Drummond at home.

He rang Maud's private mobile, relayed the conversation with

Teresa, her new mobile number and outlined his plans. Maud was unhappy but reluctantly conceded Drummond could probably contain anything Pescaro threw at him. There was no question of Teresa's concern being anything other than well founded.

Chapter
FIFTY- THREE

Aldrittson's rage had hardened from white hot fury to cold, implacable hatred. Five days had crawled by since his humiliation at Teresa's hands, five days of embarrassment, public explanation, lying and self justification. Five days in which he saw his standing demeaned. Every time he recalled *that* meeting, bile rose from his gut. But he had not been idle, he had leant on Commander Tommy Duigan from the Crime Department – a member of Baker's paedophile group – for contact with Valentin Chernamenko. Now he waited for the Russian.

'Your guest Mr Aldrittson.' The waiter had arrived so quietly he had been unaware of his presence. He was accompanied by a man of medium height, huge girth and prominent facial scarring.

Aldrittson rose and extended his hand to Chernamenko. 'Ben Aldrittson, pleased to meet you.'

Chernamenko ignored the outstretched hand and growled, 'I know who you are Mr Politician. What you want?' He sat rudely making Aldrittson look foolish, his unaccepted hand stranded mid air.

Aldrittson tried to regain control. 'I have a task I think you might enjoy. But I think we should discuss it in a civilised way over dinner. What do you say?'

'If you are talking to me job,' sneered Chernamenko, 'then better you pay well. What you want?'

Aldrittson stared levelly into the small, bright eyes in front of him; he was repulsed by Chernamenko's foul breath. He said quietly, 'I want a woman killed: Teresa Marchese.'

Chernamenko sat motionless, his interest registered only by the slightest twitch of his eyebrows. Then he smiled cruelly, saying, 'To be pleased. When?'

'As soon as you like, but I leave that to you.' Aldrittson waited expectantly.

Chernamenko reached into his coat pocket and removed a card. 'Ring midday tomorrow. One hundred and fifty thousand dollars you will put at the location told. When job is done, another one hundred and fifty thousand dollars.'

Aldrittson was furious. 'Hang about, I don't operate like that …'

Chernamenko leaned forward and impaled him with a steely glare. 'Mr Politician, you are talking to me already compromised. You think because politician you invincible? You are fool. I know already you turned down by everyone.' Tapping his chest for emphasis he hissed, '*I* am solution to you problem. From now, *you* will arrange when *I* want something.'

Stunned by the sudden reversal of roles Aldrittson found himself saying, 'Listen, I've changed my mind. Don't worry about the job I won't proceed.' His tone was both positive and placatory.

Chernamenko grinned sardonically. 'What you want or not change nothing. Because you request, I not kill Ms Marchese. But price of her life is same as death. Arrangement stands. If money not paid, I personally will get you head. I know where you live, I know you father in hospital and I know where mother lives. You people in this country, weaklings, know nothing of power. *You* now in *my* employ, remember.' Chernamenko rose and without a backward glance, strode from the room.

Aldrittson was numb. *What just happened?* Too much on, that was the problem! Not thinking logically. No, fuck that – he hadn't been thinking at all. More to the point, Johnson's warning reverberated in his head. *Christ!* He stood, put $50 on the table and left, all thoughts of dinner banished by the icy and growing fear of what he had called down upon himself.

A soft footfall in gravel woke Drummond instantly. Since Teresa's warning two days earlier he had maintained his routine and gone to bed at the same time each night. Soon after, dressed in black from head to foot, he slipped outside to bed down on a door he had bolted to the carport rafters years earlier for storage. There, above his ute, he rested on a foam camp mattress beneath a feather sleeping bag. Spartan as it was, it allowed him to see but not be seen; it was the price of surprise. Tonight, the sky was dense with starlight and the temperature sinking to a frost; a half moon sat high in the western sky staring down icily.

The footstep was close to the front door. He moved cautiously, mindful of the rustling bag. Slowly, he raised his head and peered over the edge of his perch. Two dark shadows moved quietly onto the verandah. Banking on his visitor's need to surprise him, he had funnelled their access to the house just as he had for Embone, this time by leaving only the front door unlocked. The plan was to make the intruders obvious and buy time to move while they searched the house.

He slid onto his ute as soon as they entered the house. From under the ute he took a small satchel and sloped off along a shadowy pathway to the ironbarks at the southern end of his house. Scaling the first tree, he sat in the crude hide he had built around a thick branch. From the satchel he removed and fitted night vision goggles then filled his pockets with large steel ball bearings – ammunition for his powerful shanghai. Lastly, he strapped on a belt and looped several articles to it.

Soon after, the men emerged: one from the front door, the other at the laundry door used by Embone. He heard a low whistle. As he watched, another shadow moved to the house from the western side of his driveway. The three met at the front door, and, after a short exchange, two fanned out to look around the grounds while the third searched Drummond's ute then angled off towards the oak copse. They worked in silence.

One of the men moved into open space near the back of the house, pausing mid-step at the call of a nearby owl. The goggles and moonlight gave Drummond a perfect view. He fitted a bearing to his shanghai and fired. With barely a grunt the man fell to the ground, victim to the experience of countless hours spent knocking Corellas out of trees.

Leaving the hide, Drummond ran to the man, checked his pulse, bound his wrists with cable ties then hefted him across to the tree. From his belt he took a length of broad coarse cloth, gagged the man and tied him to a branch using rope he had previously attached to the tree. He checked again; the man's pulse was strong.

A branch snapped behind him. Drummond moved close into the tree and hugged the shadow. Soft footfalls were approaching from the southwest. Crouching low, he moved quickly to the second tree and waited. The intruder continued towards the first tree. Drummond moved again, taking a line that would intersect with the intruder. Three metres from the tree he sank to the ground like a rock. Slowly turning his head, Drummond watched the man creep forward, moving cautiously on his way back to the house. He would pass the tree Drummond was making for. Keeping the tree between him and the intruder, Drummond moved to its trunk and stopped. He eased slightly to one side and coughed quietly. The intruder froze then turned at snail pace. Unable to see either Drummond or the first man, he stared intently into the black pool of shadows. Then, bent low, he moved forwards, his right arm in front of him. Drummond pressed flat against the deep shaggy bark clutching a short thick branch. Two metres from Drummond the man saw the shadowy form of his companion tied to the tree. 'Fuck!' he exclaimed. 'Dom, what happened?' He stepped forward and bent towards his companion as Drummond clubbed him fiercely on the back of the head.

Now, thought Drummond, *let's find the last bastard.* He fastened his second victim to the tree, gagged him, cable tied his wrists then retrieved the man's firearm and stuck it in his jacket pocket. Removing his phone from a leg pocket, he dialled Maud as arranged.

Leaving the two men, Drummond took a wide loop to the eastern side of his house towards the oak copse. About five metres from the trees he removed his goggles and gave the same low whistle he had heard before. From the dark of the oaks, slightly to his right, a hoarse whisper responded, 'Here.' He padded towards it. 'Where is this friggin' prick?'

'Dunno, let's check the tractor shed,' Drummond whispered tersely.

The third man crept towards Drummond who waited, head averted as though listening in the direction of the house. As the man reached his side, Drummond turned, nodded and, without warning, unleashed a mighty kick to the groin followed by a slicing forearm chop to the throat. His victim fell to the ground writhing in pain. Drummond dropped his knee into the man's solar plexus and grinned savagely as air exploded from his lungs. In a trice, he was handcuffed with cable ties and gagged. He hauled the gasping man to his feet and dragged him across to the house where he was tied to a veranda post.

Returning to his previous captives he found one barely conscious, the other still out to it. He took the conscious man to the house, tied him to a post and went back for the last man. He was moaning and Drummond could feel blood seeping through his balaclava. Drummond pulled him roughly to his feet then marched him, unresisting, to the house and cabled him to yet another pole. Throughout his efforts, Drummond remained silent and did not remove his own balaclava. He settled back and waited.

About ten minutes later dimmed headlights turned into the driveway and travelled slowly towards the house. Drummond was relieved to see Tony Maud step from the Heathcote Divisional Van.

'Andy, you've gotta stop this crazy activity. What have we this time?'

'Got these three bastards creeping around the house; couple of them went inside looking for me but I was missing.'

'Have you searched them yet?'

'No, I just caught 'em and tied 'em up until you got here.'

'Righto. Turn the veranda lights on so we can have a dekko.'

'Sure. By the way, have you found a car anywhere near here?'

'Yeah, halfway between your drive and Hunter's Lane up there. Ian Patching and Ken Jones have gone to secure it. We'll know more about that soon.'

Drummond went inside and switched the veranda lights on and returned.

'Shit mate, I'll have to take these buggers to hospital before I lock 'em up. They're all bleeding. What the hell did you belt them with?' asked Maud tersely.

'My steel balls. Silent and deadly.' Drummond grinned wickedly. 'But only one, the other two I just walloped.'

'Yeah, well this geezer doesn't look too flash. I hope it's nothing serious.'

Drummond was not abashed and said with some venom, 'Stuff them! They were after me, not the other way around.'

'Yeah, well … I'm not too sure about that. I just want to make sure they live.'

'The bastards will live alright Tony. The worst they might have is concussion and perhaps a cut scalp. One bloke might have sore nuts too, but I'm more interested in knowing what the pricks are armed with.'

'Well, let's have a look.' Maud removed each man's balaclava. One had a deep gash to a large egg which had risen from his forehead; slowly, it oozed blood. He looked badly concussed. Maud said nothing but began systematically to search all three. Two of the men were in their thirties, the third closer to his fifties. All were pale, shocked and in pain. With the exception of the man whose gun Drummond had already retrieved, they carried hand guns, two had knives and the older man carried a piano wire garrotte.

'Interesting company you keep – how do you manage it?'

Maud gave Drummond a lopsided grin.

'This'll be Patch and Jonesy now.' The station sedan pulled up beside the van. 'They can take the two with the bad head and crook groin. I'll take the other one. I don't want these buggers talking to each other. We'll go to the hospital first and then, perhaps, I'll have a little chat with them. Same deal for you as last time: come and see me later this morning. Oh, one more thing: this is the last time. I mean it! From now on, until this is sorted, *you sleep at our place.*'

Drummond said nothing but went inside and returned with a pair of electrician's pliers. One by one he snipped the cable ties from the veranda posts to leave the wrist ties in place. At 4:35 a.m. Maud and Patching drove away with their cargo.

Chapter
FIFTY- FOUR

Tension from constant vigilance and the action of the night had exhausted Drummond. Even before Maud reached his gate he had drunk a glass of water, locked the doors, stripped off his black suit and jumped into bed. The intruders had destroyed his warning systems but he was too tired to worry about it. As a precaution, he put his nunchukkas on the bedside table next to his mobile phone and turned out the light. In less than two minutes he was asleep. It was 4:40 a.m.

At five that morning, Teresa burst from her bed like a thunderbolt as her home erupted into a fireball. Three muffled explosions seemed to come from the front, the side where she parked her car and the back of her house. Within minutes the weatherboard cottage was ablaze. Smoke and flames swirled through the rooms with choking intensity; searing heat began to blister the paint and, above it all, the thunderous, crackling roar of fire. Pulling a bedspread over herself she crawled to the dining room and retrieved her laptop and mobile phone. In the bathroom she shut the door, pulled a tracksuit over her pyjamas, saturated a towel then opened the window. Flames were gyrating and roaring at either end of the house but, for the moment, she was safe. She climbed onto the basin, draped the wet towel around her head and shoulders, grasped the laptop and jumped to the ground.

Standing between the house and the side fence, she closed the window, clambered over the fence and snuck along the base of the neighbour's house to their sub-floor door. Crawling under the house, she shut the door behind her. Sticky webs clutched her fingers as she felt for a light switch. *Good,* she thought, *there if needed,* as she found one above the door. She called Drummond and waited: his phone rang without answer. She punched in Maud's number and again, got no response. Overhead her excited neighbours were shouting and running through their house; she could hear Anna, the wife, talking to the fire brigade.

The fire had been well planned and Teresa had no illusion of it being anything other than attempted murder. She began to shake, every nerve ending jangling with the knowledge she had just escaped incineration. In that heightened state came unexpected illumination: here was an opportunity for escape. With the house razed, people just might believe she had perished. Her goal now was to remain hidden until she could speak to Drummond or Tony. She hoped no one would think to look for her under the neighbour's house. Apart from a small amount of smoke inhalation, she was in good shape but without money, shoes or clothes – apart from what she wore. She did, however, have the all important laptop with its priceless information.

Once more she dialled Drummond but got no response: it was 5:20 a.m. She hoped he was asleep.

Drummond stirred; was that the phone? Bleary eyed, he reached for it … and froze. A black figure slipped past his bedroom windows as he rolled over. Snapped awake he thought – *there must have been four of the bastards!* He rolled out of bed grabbing his nunchukkas. He might only have a minute, perhaps less. He arranged his pillows and doona to resemble a body in bed and wormed into the hall where he crouched just outside the door. Having locked all doors he would hear anyone breaking into the house.

Suddenly, his bedroom windows exploded under the impact of three silenced shots. Drummond felt the fierce surge of adrenalin followed by a metallic taste in his mouth. He waited. The sliding door was smashed open; someone had entered the room. Silence, then a muffled curse when the bed was found empty. Barely audible footsteps approached the hallway where he waited. They stopped, just inside the bedroom. Silence. Faintly laboured breathing reached Drummond's ears. He gripped the nunchukkas at one end to form a skewer. The hall nightlight glowed dimly. Drummond was a monstrous, misshapen shadow, the bedroom door, a yawning black chasm. He controlled his breathing, quietened his heart rate and focussed on the doorway. The assassin moved forward. His arm and weapon entered the hall as he drew level with the jamb. With the silence of an owl and speed of a striking snake, Drummond burst upwards and drove the nunchukkas deep into his attacker's groin. There was an agonised scream and sound of a shot thudding into the ceiling followed by a deafening hush … and then, the low, whimpering cry of someone in deep pain.

Drummond removed the firearm, fetched some cable ties from the kitchen and bound the intruder hand and foot. Drummond cared little for the man's condition. Collecting his phone to ring Maud he saw two missed calls. To his concern, both were from Teresa – at 5:05 a.m. and 5:20 a.m. He moved away from his prisoner and rang using their code.

'Andy,' Teresa's voice was hoarse and strange.

'Yes, are you alright?'

'No.' Her strangled reply was accompanied by muffled shouts and machinery noises.

'What's going on?' Drummond was gripped with fear. 'What's happened?' He moved back to the kitchen so the intruder could not hear their conversation.

'I think I've been firebombed. Somebody's tried to kill me and my home is going up in flames.' She wept quietly. Over the phone Andy heard the faint sound of sirens and further shouting.

'Teresa, where are you?' His voice was strained and urgent.

'Hiding under my neighbour's house.'

'Are you hurt? Are you okay?'

Hearing his concern, Teresa controlled herself and said, 'Yes, truly I am okay. I am upset about the house. I got out the bathroom window before the fire reached that side. I feel so much better after hearing you. What's that noise?' The intruder had begun to moan pitifully in the background.

'I had an uninvited guest. I was about to ring Tony when I saw your missed calls. I'm sorry I'll tell you about it later. What do you want to do now?'

'Tell Tony what's happened. Now you know where I am I feel quite safe. And look, we can use the fire to our advantage, everyone will think I've burned to death so it's the perfect opportunity to escape Giuseppe. I can stay here without being discovered even though lots of people will be around. I've got the phone on silent, just ring every now and then. We can think of a plan to get me out later. One thing – I've got no clothes other than a track suit and the pyjamas I'm in. Could you get Mary to organise a few things for me? She'll know what I need. I've got the computer and the data is safe. Call me again when you can. I have a feeling we are going to be okay.'

Drummond could sense the anguish beneath her words. 'You might just be right. Now listen, call me when you need to. I'll be there as soon as I can. I've got to go now – this bloke here is hurt and Tony needs to know about him as well as what's happened to you. I'll call when I can. I love you Teresa.'

'I love you too.'

At six o'clock, Drummond rang the police station. Maud answered. 'Andy – everything alright?'

'Not really. After you'd all gone, a fourth bastard came. Very clever. He's all trussed up ready to collect but … I'm sorry mate, he's hurt.'

'*Jesus Christ!* What happened?' Maud sounded both exasperated and concerned.

'Teresa rang – her call saved my life. She said she tried you as well.'

'Bugger! I completely forgot the mobile, it's in the van. Sorry mate. Is there a problem?'

'Her house was firebombed and is probably burnt to the ground by now.'

'*Jesus H Christ!* Is she hurt?'

'No, but let's talk about this when I see you, not on the phone. I want to get down to her as soon as I can.'

'Fair enough. I'll send someone out to you. Come in as soon as my fella arrives. Your joint is a crime scene and we still need to think about court later. Now, go back a step – what about this fourth bloke? I'm afraid to ask: what's wrong with him?'

Drummond drew a deep breath knowing his friend would not be happy with his reply. 'I speared him in the orchestra stalls with my nunchukkas. He's not good.'

'Ouch. Is he conscious?'

'Barely,' grunted Drummond.'

'I'll play safe and send an ambulance' responded Maud. 'It doesn't sound pretty.'

'Tony, I have to get down to Teresa now.'

'Sorry mate, you'll have to wait. These blokes have committed some pretty heavy crimes against you and unfortunately, they've come off second best. You'll have to come in here and at least give me a bloody good outline before you nick off.'

'Fuck that Tony I need to go now.'

'You heard what I said!' Maud's tone was cutting. 'I promise to be as quick as I can, but you've got to give me enough to work with. This is not the bloody movies mate and this is my patch. I understand your hurry but we're going to be doing it right.'

At 7:30, the two men took a break and went to the police residence. Anxious to be on his way, Drummond outlined events to Mary and relayed Teresa's request. In her practical manner she said, 'Leave it with me Lover Boy. When Tony's finished, come back and see me – everything will be ready.' While Maud rang his Superintendent and briefed him on events, including the firebombing, Drummond held a hurried conversation with Teresa. At his suggestion, Maud asked his boss if they could use the fire to immediately slide Teresa into protection while keeping her escape off the radar. The idea would be referred upwards.

By nine o'clock Drummond was free of the paperwork. Tony had taken a detailed statement and painstakingly canvassed his friend's justification for injuring all four men. Although the degree of force seemed appropriate for the circumstances, he well knew that once Drummond was in the witness box, weeks, months or even years after the event, clever lawyers would strive to make those injuries appear anything but justified. And they weren't exactly minor: the fourth man would lose a testicle, the man struck by the steel bearing was badly concussed, the one who'd been clubbed had a head full of stitches and the final victim had cracked a rib. Drummond was unscathed.

When Drummond returned to Mary everything was set to go. 'You're a brick mate,' he whispered, 'thanks.'

'It's okay Andy. If you buggers survive all this, I think we'll love Teresa as much as we loved Susan. So, stay on the ball.'

For Drummond, the compliment was enormous and, after a hug, he scooted out the door. Before driving off, he phoned Teresa again.

'Hi Drummond, are you on your way?' she answered quietly

'Just about to leave now. How are you?'

'Cold, scared, hungry. I heard someone say he was not surprised there was nothing left. The house was old, dry and weatherboard. I know it wasn't grand, but it was mine.'

He heard her pain and said simply 'I understand. Listen, if all goes well I should be there in about two and a half hours. I'll call when I'm close. Okay?'

'Just be careful.'

Chapter
FIFTY- FIVE

The Premier's Secretary, Celia Barraclough, called Aldrittson on his direct line interrupting the wild thoughts somersaulting through his head.

'Mr Aldrittson,' she boomed, 'the Premier would like to see you in five minutes. Please put any other engagements on hold.'

Feeling shitty, Aldrittson said tersely, 'I'll be on a plane to Sydney, Celia, I was just walking out the door when you rang.'

'Then I suggest you catch a later flight,' she snapped and hung up.

Aldrittson put his head in his hands. *What next?* The cause of his angst was an item on the one o'clock ABC News. He had listened with growing astonishment, then dread, to the story of a house fire at 16 Rose Street Burnley. Neighbours had reported hearing explosions and police were treating the blaze as suspicious. The punch line was crushing: the owner, believed to be at home when the fire started, was missing and the house had burned to the ground.

That idiot Chernamenko! He wondered what friggin' part of no Chernamenko had not understood. He had made his change of mind very clear: Teresa was to *live*. He had even paid the outrageous demand so that she would live. He felt ill. He couldn't afford any blowback from this – he had to remove that ugly bastard Chernamenko. He wouldn't use Johnson though, he was suffering an outbreak of scruples. He would have to find a different team.

Too many things on his mind! Even *he* could feel he was losing it. His father wasn't improving and his mother had become a whinging bloody nuisance. Judd at least was doing alright at the Depot and Jack's new security measures had gone well too. *Yeah … good choice Dad*, he thought, *Santini had trained Judd well. Santini.*

Christ, that was a lifetime ago. He rose and stomped down to the Premier's office.

Celia Barraclough ushered him through to the Premier with a haughty sniff.

'Ah Ben, good of you to come,' said Meadows, 'I'd like you to meet Professor Cameron Blake, RMIT, Earth Sciences Unit.'

Blake was dressed casually in jeans, elastic-sided boots, a faded denim shirt and battered sheepskin coat. He had longish fair hair and weathered good looks. Aldrittson guessed he would be in his late forties to early fifties.

Blake extended his hand. 'Pleased to meet you Mr Aldrittson. I've been looking over your waste concept for the Premier. To put it in scholarly parlance, it's shit hot.' His battered face cracked into a grin, Meadows laughed aloud and Aldrittson felt relieved. They shook hands warmly.

'Cameron's kind of stolen my thunder with that erudite comment Ben. I invited him to go over the scheme as an independent arbiter and raise questions about anything of concern. What we discuss today may determine whether the scheme stands or falls. I wanted you to be part of that process.'

'Thanks Graeme,' responded Aldrittson, 'I appreciate that.'

'Over to you Cameron.'

'I'll keep it brief Mr Premier. I know you've already had the plan independently assessed and a double check was suggested for computations on the soil and water tests. That's my forte. I've been to the proposed site and taken samples of the soil and water at various depths. Everything matches the original calculations. To be completely certain, I gave three student groups samples to analyse. Within allowable tolerances, their analyses agreed with mine. This means there is no question about the geologic capacity for handling the waste, provided the methods specified in your plan are rigorously followed.'

'Excuse me for asking Cameron, but the Premier did

promise the second opinion would be confidential. You gave our information to students?'

'No Ben. I read everything here, got acquainted with my brief then conducted my field and lab tests. The students were merely testing my anonymous samples as a lab exercise.'

'Thanks. I misunderstood.'

'No, a fair question.'

'Anything else Cameron?' asked Meadows.

'Only to endorse what's been said. What I found heartening is the innovation and integration of different technologies with nature – it is *so* harmonious. I admire the scope of this plan; it's breath-taking. I also admire the underpinning philosophy, it says everything – *Earth First*. Naturally, your scheme has little impact on consumption, but it should help slow our remorseless assault on the planet. The key benefit of this thinking is that it *comes* from government. Too often, government thinking lags far behind business and the community. In this case, you'll be in the vanguard. This is excellent stuff gentlemen. I am certain there is nothing like it elsewhere in the world. To cap it off, it has a triple bottom line: social, economic *and* environmental benefits. It's brilliant.'

Aldrittson basked in the praise but thought: *you poor misguided bastard. If you only knew what occurred before we got to this point.* Instead, he said modestly, 'Your comments are very generous Cameron, thank you.'

Meadows rose and smiled at Blake. 'If there's nothing else Cameron, I'll let you go. Send your account to Celia and we'll take care of it.' Aldrittson and Blake rose too; all shook hands.

'Ben, would you stay please.'

When Blake left, Meadows said, 'As you can see, Blake doesn't mince words. Had there been flaws he would have said so. Can you deliver a formal submission to cabinet by say, middle of next week, or, at the latest, by next Friday? I know these additional assessments have upset your original plans so let's hire the best and biggest PR guns we can. I'll direct the Cabinet Communications Sub-committee to use our media slush fund to get maximum exposure with optimum spin. While I believe this scheme does stand on its own, you know how twitchy people become at election time. Toxic waste disposal coupled with an election is positively incendiary. One good indicator is that not a single person I've discussed this with has a bad word to say. I've tried to be even handed as well. Many of those I talked to are our greatest detractors – they welcomed it. Looks like a winner for everybody, including Mother Earth.' Meadows beamed at him and waited for a response to his original question.

Outwardly, Aldrittson was calm. Inside, he was as taut as racquet strings. Even under the best conditions with the work he had already done, the deadline was a bastard. But the real snag was Pescaro. He would have to work with him on this and if he discovered he had been talking to Chernamenko, especially after Teresa's house fire, he could probably kiss the world goodbye. He felt ill.

'Well, what do you say?' He became aware that Meadows was peering at him. 'Are you alright Ben? You look pale.'

'Yes. No, it's okay. Bit of a virus. Look, Graeme, I won't pretend – the deadline is difficult. I will give it my best shot, that's all I can say. I'll have a briefing ready by next Wednesday.'

'Congratulations, you've done extremely well. I think even our Labor colleagues will embrace this. In their disjointed, uncertain, fumbling way, they've been demanding something like this for years. Now they've got it, let's see what happens. Okay, that's it. I'll let you know about the PR and media coverage tomorrow.'

'Thanks Graeme, this is really good news.'

Aldrittson was on autopilot. With the confluence of Teresa's fire, approval of the waste scheme, the need to work with Pescaro, Jack's illness and Chernamenko's extortion, he felt as though he had entered that mysterious void that accompanies the onset of anaesthetic. The black abyss pressed downwards, it couldn't be stopped. Yet it was not unpleasant because there was no feeling, just weightless anticipation. If he cocked up, not only would there be intense pain, but the black abyss would be eternal.

And he couldn't stop any of it.

Chapter
FIFTY- SIX

It was mid-afternoon and Pescaro's mood was vile. After learning of Teresa's house fire and being on the phones from early morning, the only concrete thing he had discovered was that neither her mobile nor landline were working. As a consequence he directed Ed Masseria to sniff around. Two soldiers reported that 16 Rose Street was burned to its foundations. Even Teresa's new Mini was a blackened, twisted shell. Pretending to be neighbours, Masseria's men spoke to firemen and learned the blaze was deliberate. They also spoke to street residents who said police were conducting forensic tests and searching for a body. A neighbour opposite Teresa had noticed lights on around eleven o'clock the previous night and presumed she was home when the fire started.

Adding to his woes was news that the men sent to deal with Drummond were now enjoying police hospitality. He was ropable. Four competent men had, somehow, been defeated by one man and not only arrested, but seriously hurt. Drummond had become the focus of Pescaro's cold, implacable fury. While previously he had seemed merely a potential threat, his menace had now become actual and personal.

Pescaro wondered if Teresa's fire and disappearance were connected to Drummond's success. He had no reason for thinking that but he wasn't ruling anything out. What he did know was that the fire had nothing to do with him. Unexpectedly, that caused him to remember Teresa's earlier advice: be prepared for pain in order to *appear* weak. Perhaps this was evidence of the strategy working.

His telephone rang. '*Pronto*,' said Giuseppe.

'Giuseppe, Ben Aldrittson. Good news! The Premier has accepted our waste scheme as part of the election campaign. We need to finalise plans for getting it into government machinery.' Aldrittson was striving to sound upbeat, friendly, but not over the top. He worked harder still to contain his fear.

Pescaro listened. Aldrittson was too effusive, too affable and trying too hard. He decided to play the game.

'Yes Ben, good news indeed. How about meeting me for dinner at *J'taime* in Toorak Village tonight, 7:30 sharp.' He put the phone down without waiting for a response. *A bright spot in an otherwise bleak day*, he thought.

He phoned Masseria. 'Ed, can you tell me if our traitors have recently been in touch with Chernamenko? And do you have anything more on Teresa's disappearance?'

'No evidence of contact with Chernamenko but we can't be certain. I sent in a girl posing as a reporter to speak to the residents of Rose Street – people were happy to talk because Teresa was known and liked by quite a few of them. No one saw anything. The trouble is, it's a bit of a yuppy street, mostly young people who are at work.' Masseria refrained from stating the obvious – Teresa could be dead.

Pescaro was quiet then, in pained tones, 'Okay thanks. In the circumstances ring our Canberra colleague tonight about Chernamenko and his clan. Try to get our information to Immigration authorities by tomorrow.'

'Sure, being from the Embassy he shouldn't find it too hard to arrange a meeting with the Foreign Minister.'

'Good. Make sure he calls back with the Minister's reaction. I want to know as soon as possible. This is very important to us. I now believe that not only was Chernamenko behind the deaths of Fabrizzi and Barracusa, but Bernardo's and maybe Teresa's too. I think that bastard has been stalking us much longer than I suspected.' He heard Masseria's sharp intake of breath. 'Keep me informed Ed.'

Pescaro hung up, pleased to at last be striking back. He had abandoned his initial idea of framing Chernamenko with heroin and firearms. Chernamenko's false immigration information and the sex slavery should be more than sufficient to remove him from the country.

Drummond hired an old van from a rent-a-wreck firm. Next, he bought two green boiler suits, a couple of peaked caps, clipboard and sunglasses. A block away from Rose Street he phoned Teresa and established there was a second sub-frame door opposite her entry point under the house. After arriving at 18 Rose Street he passed a set of clothes through the second sub-frame door. With clipboard in hand and making "notes", he conducted a mock inspection of the fire damaged fence while Teresa dressed then slipped into the van.

As Pescaro was putting the phone down, Drummond and Teresa were walking into the Aspen Street unit. Teresa was cold, trembling and quietly angry. Once inside the unit she had fallen into Drummond's arms and held him tightly.

'Evil bastards,' she hissed, 'evil, evil bastards. They *will* get theirs …'

Drummond held her and asked, 'Do you mean Pescaro?'

'No,' she said fiercely, 'this was not Giuseppe. His means of elimination is face to face. No, this is down to the Russians.'

In the long cold hours under her neighbour's house, Teresa had reflected deeply upon her life and was angry about a number of things, Chernamenko being top of the list. Until she started working for Pescaro she had led a blameless life. Discovering the truth about him had unsettled her and later, made her ashamed for remaining with him. She could neither excuse nor justify her actions, especially since most of her energy had been devoted to converting criminal money into "clean" money. She felt not only damned, but dirty.

Reformation had commenced on learning the truth about her parents; renaissance had come through Andy Drummond.

Through him too the Mauds had opened their hearts and she had rejoiced in the warmth of their friendship and trust. But her sense of being *unclean* juxtaposed with her acceptance by Drummond and the Mauds had stimulated a fear of rejection. This fear profoundly disturbed her.

Acutely aware of both her anger and distress, Drummond smiled and said, "Come on love, a strong brandy is what you need." Gradually, Teresa regained her composure and after a while they were laughing about her escape and blessed her good fortune.

They sat in the kitchen, alive with relief.

'I'd better go and move the ute into Tom's garage over the road' Drummond said, 'I can shut the door there and hide it. We'll keep the blinds shut too – just in case. While I do that, would you ring Tony and tell him we're okay. Oh, and could you ask him what we should be doing next. After that you might like a soak in the bath, to thaw out. I'll be about ten minutes.'

When he returned upstairs to the sound of running bath water, he smiled to himself. It would be good for her to lie in the warm water after all that stress.

'Teresa, have you got everything you need?'

'Yes and Tony has news.'

'Can I come in?'

'Of course.' Drummond entered the bathroom and grinned at Teresa who was lying in aromatic, frothy green water, two pert nipples peeping through the bubbles, hot tap slowly topping up the bath.

'God, you look good enough to eat,' he said, 'I think I'll join you.'

She laughed and flicked froth into his face. 'Enough you precocious man. Tony said his A/C rang just before midday and we are to contact Assistant Commissioner David Tavistock. Tavistock is worried by the fire and your visitors, *plural* – which you didn't tell me about. Tony said he would tell Mary we were ok, and Tavistock's number is on the kitchen table. After that you can join me …' She pouted, half closed her eyes, licked her lips and laughed.

Half an hour later Drummond returned to the bathroom after talking with both Tavistock and Maud. Teresa was asleep in water beginning to lose its heat. She looked beautiful and he knelt and kissed her forehead. Slowly, she opened her eyes, took a second or two to focus and mumbled, 'Must have drifted off.'

'You did and, unfortunately, there's no more time for relaxation. Tavistock wants to see us ASAP, somewhere in East Melbourne.'

'Did he mention witness protection?'

'He did. Without absolutely committing himself he implied emergency entry at the end of the meeting. He told me he's already spoken to the bloke in charge of Witsec so I guess it's taken care of.'

'Andy, we haven't properly discussed if we should go into the program together. We need to agree about that don't you think?'

'I do. I think we should be together but I need about a week to quit the farm. Two reasons: if Pescaro goes to Heathcote again this week I'll be there. It's only a small thing, but it might help strengthen the impression that you died in the fire. I also want to put it about up there that because of these attacks, I'm taking a holiday overseas. Secondly, I have to organise the farm; I can't walk off just like that.' He snapped his fingers. 'I need to cash up – we are in for difficult times. Now, about the farm. I hate the idea of leaving it but since these problems started, I've been thinking of selling to Tony and Mary. Both of them love the place and I can't see them ever wanting to leave Heathcote. If I do that, then I'll always feel close to Sue, the farm and to them. What do you reckon?'

Her eyes grew large and dark with feeling. 'I think it's a wonderful idea. But I'm not sure I can wait a week. Promise me you'll be ultra careful.' She reached up and drew him down for a kiss that was filled with love and tenderness.

Chapter
FIFTY- SEVEN

They walked into the grey government building on the dot of three o'clock. Waiting in the foyer was a tall, slender man in his mid-forties wearing a navy suit. As the heavy glass door closed behind them, he stepped forward.

'Mr Drummond, Ms Marchese?' He shook hands with them both saying, 'Paul Donovan, the boss is waiting upstairs.' He turned, walked to the lifts and stabbed the button. Seconds later, landing bells rang and a door opened, Donovan entered and pressed two.

At the second floor they stepped into a long, wide, carpeted corridor full of numbered doors. They moved to their right and stopped outside number **24**. Donovan knocked, opened the door and stood back to allow Teresa and Drummond to enter.

It was a sizeable room with five comfortable arm chairs loosely circling a low, square wooden table. Two men were standing waiting. One was about fifty, balding, of medium height and nuggetty, the other similar to Donovan but whereas Donovan's hair was black, this man's was fair, short and spiked.

The older man stepped forward and smiled, hand extended. 'Good afternoon, thanks for coming. I'm David Tavistock.' Tavistock's countenance was a burnished nut brown, his smile friendly and open, dark eyes glowed with vitality. Drummond wondered if he played golf – he had that look about him. Tavistock's well modulated voice and clear diction conveyed an English heritage.

'Allow me to introduce Commander Robby Danniellson and you've already met Commander Paul Donovan. These two will be running your case and reporting to me.'

'I understand from your friend Tony Maud that you have much to tell. I'm up to speed with your house fire Teresa and with your intruders Andy.' Tavistock's charm and well mannered style was both disarming and encouraging. He gestured towards the chairs. After everyone was seated he said, 'I thought I'd start by explaining the purpose of this meeting. It's about getting a handle on the scope of the investigation and its various parts. If you don't mind, I'll record our conversation which later will be converted to type – you'll get a copy in due course.' Tavistock's reference to recording was not a request but a statement of fact. He nodded to Donovan who took two small digital recorders from a shelf beneath the table. He activated one.

'For the record,' said Tavistock, 'this is a meeting between Teresa Marchese and Andy Drummond with Assistant Commissioner David Tavistock. Also present are Commanders Paul Donovan and Robby Danniellson. The time is 3:20 p.m. on Thursday, July 14, 2005. The purpose of this meeting is to obtain an understanding of the scope of an investigation prompted by Ms Marchese. Discussion will be general although some parts may become explicit. You need to know from the beginning Teresa that many hours of interviews with various police and other experts lie ahead of you. It will not be easy. Briefly then, we know that Giuseppe Pescaro is head of the Victorian Mafia and that recently, following the death of Bernardo Santini, you Teresa, were promoted to the position of *Consigliere*, or counsellor/mediator within that organisation. As a result, you learned of certain events in 1975 involving Pescaro and your parents. Because of that knowledge, you now wish to tell us about the inside workings of the Pescaro Family. In return, you want us to provide witness protection. Is that a fair summation?'

Teresa's throat felt dry. Reduced to this simple, stark account, the magnitude of her journey jarred painfully. 'Yes,' she said hoarsely. Swallowing, she said again, 'yes, that is correct.' This time, strong and clear.

'Andy, I understand your involvement arises from an interest in a truck fire near your farm. That fire led you to Aldrittson

Waste Disposals and the discovery of criminal behaviour connected to waste disposal. Through AWD, Pescaro forms a common link between you and Teresa. As we understand it, Jack Aldrittson and Giuseppe Pescaro are partners in the unlawful disposal of toxic waste. Have I got that right?'

'Spot on,' said Drummond. He appreciated the way Tavistock dealt with his and Teresa's relationship.

'Let's now run through the main segments of discussion. Firstly, the Pescaro empire. We'll need all the details you know about its various associations and relationships in Victoria, other states and overseas. We'll want to know everything about the money trail: what, who, how and where money is concealed. Then there's the protectors – banks, accountants, lawyers, investment advisors and others, including government officials. Secondly, we want to investigate the murders of Angelina Pescaro and your father Alfredo. Thirdly, there is the long running partnership between Pescaro and Jack Aldrittson and their waste disposal practices. We need to know the clients, how the scam works, who in the firm is involved, the nature of the dumped wastes, dump sites, what kind of money is involved and how it is handled. There are likely to be considerable tax, environmental and health implications flowing out of this part of the investigation. Fourthly, we understand you have information about Mr Ben Aldrittson, MP, and his involvement in bribery and corruption and the concealment of crime. Finally, we believe that you, Teresa, can provide insight to a group of Russian Vors who entered this country under false identities and who may be engaged in murder and other crimes here.'

'And, most recently,' Teresa interposed, 'we have information strongly suggesting the Russian boss, Valentin Chernamenko, is engaged in sex slave trafficking. That's come to light in the last week or so.'

Tavistock scratched his chin. 'Hmmm, the feds will be interested in that, don't you think lads?' He threw an enquiring look at his two Commanders. 'Teresa, do you know if Chernamenko was responsible for the deaths of Dominic Fabrizzi and Emilio Barracusa?'

'I don't know for certain, but Giuseppe and I believe so. Even with *his* resources he's been unable to find actual proof.'

'What about Bernardo Santini? Was Chernamenko responsible for that death too?' Tavistock watched her thoughtfully.

She paused before answering. 'Maybe, but personally, I always believed that somehow, that was down to Ben Aldrittson. Santini warned Giuseppe that he thought Aldrittson was up to something and I know at that time, Santini was pressuring Aldrittson over the waste scheme. I don't know any more than that.'

'Okay, we'll certainly explore that. By the way Andy, I understand we have you to thank for changing our focus on the investigation of Santini's death. Paul tells me that without your information we may never have suspected homicide. The charge which blew the wheel off Santini's car was expertly done and the collision very effectively masked it. Well done.'

Teresa studied Tavistock's face intently.

'Before we leave the Russians, there is something bothering me. As I've said, Giuseppe believes Chernamenko ordered the murders of Dominic and Milo. He also believes Chernamenko is getting his intelligence from someone inside the Family. Recently, he put Ed Masseria to work organising a large banquet and although I can't be certain, I'd be willing to bet he now knows the identity of Chernamenko's inside contact. This banquet signals their impending demise, an event which could happen any time between the night of the feast to twelve months later. Now, I assure you, I know nothing more. Giuseppe has played this card face down the whole time and kept me at a distance. All I can say is, I have a bad feeling about it.'

Drummond saw this news displeased Tavistock. 'Okay, we'll start work on that tonight. Do you have any more little grenades like that Teresa?' His smile softened what otherwise was an acerbic remark. She shook her head determined to say nothing about her letter to the *Herald Sun*.

Throughout their discussion Tavistock was calm and reassuring. Drummond's impression was that little escaped his notice. He was impressive and his manner towards Teresa impartial and non-judgemental, qualities Drummond suspected some coppers could never have brought to a meeting like this given her background. Tavistock was quickly earning his respect and clearly showed integrity.

'Okay, why don't you begin from the start Teresa. Tell us how you got mixed up with Pescaro and the Aldrittsons; flesh out for us some of the events in which these gents have been engaged.'

Relating the tale she first told Drummond and then the Mauds, she added detail after detail, giving examples of where and how monies were invested: banks, countries, trusts, shares, businesses, lawyers, accountants, investment firms, consultancy firms, PR companies, corrupt police and government officials. She explained the overseas money trails, affiliations with Australian and overseas Mafia interests and provided the names of Pescaro's personal contacts in the USA, Europe, England, France, Italy, Colombia, Panama and Pakistan. Additionally, she was able to link these contacts to joint "business" ventures which benefited Pescaro to the detriment of other countries. She also knew the flip side of that process in Australia.

The reach, breadth and diversity of Pescaro's criminal empire was staggering. It comprised a vast and intricate web of legitimate businesses that laundered and grew the bulk of the illegal income through several very helpful banks. As a black economy, Pescaro's total annual turnover rivalled the Victorian Government's annual budget, yet little of it was properly taxed. A veritable army of accountants and lawyers had become sleek and fat defending, extending and ensuring that Pescaro's tax, and other government charges, were minimised to the smallest, legally payable amount. Throughout Teresa's narrative, Tavistock, Donovan and Danniellson, tested, probed and sought clarification.

At seven o'clock meals were delivered. The relief was welcome. Teresa's story, so vividly told, was depressing. The justice system, it seemed, was ill equipped to deal effectively with an empire as large and financially powerful as Pescaro's. An empire whose overarching strength lay in the power to corrupt, subvert, influence and consolidate by cash or intimidation, including murder. As a last resort Pescaro's guardians fell back to endless, labyrinthine legal proceedings fought on technical and theoretical points of law which they were prepared to pursue to the High Court of Australia.

While Drummond thought he had heard most of Teresa's story, he had never fully appreciated the depth of her knowledge. For the first time in his life, he found himself in agreement with Mary Maud's loathing of politicians. As Teresa's endless supply of detail unfolded he concluded that politicians and governments were not fair-dinkum about dealing with crime. Too often it was an election tool used to manipulate fear or create diversion in the pursuit of votes. Years ago he had read Justice Athol Moffitt's book, *A Quarter to Midnight, The Australian Crisis: Organised Crime and the Decline of the Institutions of State.* From Teresa's experience he now drew lamentable confirmation of all that Moffitt had warned against and to which few, seemingly, had listened. Proof lay in the consolidation of a hideous drug trade, unbridled corruption and the growing power of not only the Mafia, but the Russian Mafiya as well.

In a surreal way, Drummond felt he was in a parallel universe and wondered if it was this weird feeling that was responsible for what he felt was a benign approach to law making. The bulk of the community were not grievously injured by Pescaro's activities. In the main, serious violence was confined to other criminals and stayed between criminal elements. On the other hand, few were untouched by the *effects* of Pescaro's criminality: environmental carnage, rising insurance premiums, increased commodity prices, burglaries, delays replacing stolen goods, escalating government charges, laws which perpetuated criminal conduct, corrosion of principle, declining standards and the death of professionalism and acceptance of responsibility in so many small ways. Not to mention the huge cost in human, health, economic and industry terms from the drug trade alone.

Army life had exposed Drummond to graft, corruption and improper influence, but never to the extent he was now hearing. He better understood why Teresa had said she felt dirty and ashamed for remaining with Pescaro. But the irony was that in staying with him, she could now hand these policemen the inside workings of his empire and provide insight to the presence and practices of the Russian Mafiya in a way that would not have happened otherwise.

In this regard, Drummond saw afresh how dignified and courageous she was in co-operating with police. With a start, he realised Tavistock was wrapping up. He looked at his watch, *Christ, it was nine o'clock.*

'Andy, we'll have to deal with you separately I'm afraid,' Tavistock was saying. 'Teresa has an encyclopaedic knowledge and we haven't even come close to reaching you tonight. But I think, given the hour and your experiences today, we should call it quits. It will take a long time to deal with everything Teresa knows and it's fair to say that in my thirty years of policing, I have never encountered anything quite like this. We'll now be setting priorities, choosing the right specialists, working with the Office of Public Prosecutions and looking hard for compromise in our own camp. Our goal is to smash the Pescaro empire, dismantle its infrastructure, run down every conceivable source and repository of cash and appropriate any and every asset we can find. They must have little or no prospect for regeneration. If we are to achieve that, I want as few people as possible knowing we are talking to you. I propose to put you in a very safe place tonight and enter you into protection tomorrow under the emergency provisions. The formalities of a full application will take a little longer.

'One thing David,' queried Drummond. 'I've got a farm to deal with, a unit here in Melbourne and numerous things to organise and close off. Could I join Teresa in say, a week or ten days?'

Tavistock looked unhappily at his two Commanders but said, 'Let me give that some thought. We'll meet here at ten tomorrow morning and talk it through. Rob will pick you up and Paul will take you to your destination tonight. You'll find everything you need where you are going,' he smiled at them both, 'we had a little inside help. This interview is now concluded at 9:10 p.m.'

Chapter

FIFTY- EIGHT

Fox and Johnson sat in the sheltered forecourt of *Amarello Restaurant* at St Kilda beach. They had been for their usual contest at the pool nearby which resulted in the usual outcome. The morning light was soft, the air crisp and the sea hushed: it was one of Melbourne's wonderful July mornings where the union between temperature, sunlight and sea air creates magic.

'What did you think of the article in *The Age* this morning Spence?' Fox asked thoughtfully.

'Curious. You told me the other day you saw Chernamenko and Aldrittson together at *Ruffles* and now, Chernamenko's incarcerated, courtesy of the Immigration Department. I wonder how that happened?' Johnson's tone was flat, the look on his face cynical.

'Don't know but I wouldn't be in the least surprised if Aldrittson engineered it to protect himself. He was obviously intimidated by Chernamenko. The real question is: why was he meeting him in the first place? But you're right, it's odd. We know things are going on, like Aldrittson wanting Marchese dead. Then, hey presto! Her house disappears in flames and she's missing, presumed dead. We also know about the friction between Pescaro and Chernamenko, and wham – Chernamenko is detained.' He lapsed into silence.

Johnson sipped his coffee.

'You know,' resumed Fox, 'on reflection, Pescaro could have arranged this to rid himself of Chernamenko. It all seems just a bit too convenient.'

Johnson began to laugh. 'There's another theory Foxy. Don't you give any credit to Federal authorities having done this by themselves?'

Fox joined Spencer's laughter. 'What? After *our* Government threw one of *our Australians* – Vivian Alvarez – out of *her* country claiming she was a foreigner? And in another case using a detention centre to hold Christina Rau, a mentally ill *Australian* woman in the belief she was a refugee? Who do you reckon carried out *those* investigations? You've got to be kidding!'

They were discussing the front page story of The Age which proclaimed: **Forged Identities Threaten Australia.** The story alleged that four Russian criminals with long, violent histories had destroyed their Russian police records and lied about their character to enter Australia. According to the article, all four men were criminally active in Victoria. Allegations included intimidating and extorting Russian émigrés, murder, drug dealing, prostitution and sex-slave trafficking. Department of Immigration officials and Federal Police had swooped on the men in simultaneous raids on Sunday morning. They had been arrested and taken to the Maribyrnong Detention Centre pending the outcome of a deportation application by the Department. The story implied that deportation was likely since the prime qualification for entry, good character, had been breached, continuing criminality was alleged and none of the Russians were minors. All had lived in Victoria for periods of two to six years. A spokesman for the Department reportedly said that if the application was successful, the detainees would be back on their own home soil within two weeks of their arrest.

In his library, Pescaro sat with *The Age* across his knees. He had just hung up from Ed Masseria after organising a gift to the Italian Embassy official and to thank Masseria for his prompt action. He was pleased. His phone rang again.

'*Pronto.*'

'You think you can do me this Pescaro? You are dead man, just like the woman. Watch you sleep from now on!' Chernamenko's thick accent hissed venomously. Pescaro had expected a response, but not from Chernamenko personally.

'So, it *was* you who killed Teresa. Filth! Enjoy your plane ride. I am about to eradicate the rest of your clan.' Giuseppe heard the phone at the other end gently replaced. Threats were nothing – he had lived with them all his life. They were an occupational hazard and needed to be managed. He started on this one straight away.

'Argolia.'

'Frankie … Giuseppe. Put surveillance on the other four Vors *now*. I want matters finalised by the end of this week in the way we discussed. Use only your most trusted on this. Anyone who talks will personally answer to me. Questions?'

'No Don Pescaro, I know what to do.'

'One more thing. You know about my itch in the country?'

'Yeah, I'm right up to speed.'

'I want you to scratch it … permanently.' Pescaro's tone was steely and unequivocal.

At 1:30 that same afternoon, Aldrittson's phone rang.

'Ben, Graeme Meadows. Drop everything and come and see me. Now!' From the tone of voice Aldrittson knew immediately that Meadows was seriously pissed off. He hoped it was nothing to do with the waste submission, he had worked his arse off to get the bloody thing ready.

He rose from his desk, slipped into his coat, combed his hair and checked his tie. He looked good. When he arrived at Barraclough's sanctum, unusually, Celia was waiting by the Premier's door to usher him straight through. Her face was as dark and irritated as a Darwin storm. *Not a good sign.* He walked into Meadows' office, piqued with curiosity.

Meadows, standing in front of his desk, looked haunted. He was quivering with anger. He said with icy calm, 'I've just had the *Herald Sun's* Rosslyn Zimmer on the phone. She's working up a story about you and wondered what I had to say about a few things. To be frank, I had nothing to say because I was gobsmacked by her allegations. I rather hope you might be more enlightening. Unfortunately, we both know that two things are absolute with Zimmer: there is *always* powerful substance behind what she's investigating, and, with incredibly rare exceptions, *no one* survives her razor.'

'Yeah, so what is she alleging?' Nothing passed through Aldrittson's radar that caused him concern. His problems outside Parliament were rapidly taking care of themselves: Teresa was dead, Chernamenko had been snaffled by Immigration, Pescaro was on side with the submission and the firm would soon be in steady hands again because Old Jack was at last recovering. His reversal of fortune had all occurred since standing in this office only last Thursday, a mere four days ago.

As Meadows continued in the same controlled manner, Aldrittson realised that he was not *just* angry, he was seething.

'Zimmer is alleging that for much of your parliamentary career, and all your time as Minister, you have been on the take.' He spat the words like darts. 'That you dispensed favours, received and solicited huge commissions, bankrupted local companies, blackmailed people, bribed and cajoled a multitude of officials and, to cap it off, she claims you own a series of secret accounts in Switzerland. She even had the names of the banks. As I said before, Zimmer's research is impeccable and none of the attacks she's launched on us, none of them, have been without foundation.' Meadows' voice was laced with contempt.

After some moments Aldrittson corralled his rampant thoughts and said weakly, 'Newspaper talk Graeme. Where's her evidence? I'll sue the bitch,' he said as an afterthought. In the Premier's eyes, he was guilty. With the clarity of a man before a firing squad, Aldrittson saw he was doomed. Nothing would convince Meadows that Zimmer was wrong. Vividly, he suddenly recalled the Premier lashing them all about jeopardising the government's chances for a third term in office.

Meadows pointed to the door. 'Dictate your resignation to Celia, out there, then get out of my sight. Be out of your office by close of business today. And, if you know what's good for you, you'll resign; not just your position as Minister, but from government and from the Party. Now get out!' All colour had drained from Meadows' face. He didn't need a Royal Commission or police enquiry to know the truth. Zimmer's reputation was flawless and Aldrittson's immediate physical and verbal responses were all the confirmation he needed. Meadows was gutted, betrayed and, as for victory in the election, sabotaged. As a politician, he could wheel and deal with the best, he claimed no self righteous purity, but corruption and duplicity of this magnitude was utterly unacceptable.

Aldrittson slouched into Barraclough's office. He mumbled in a barely audible voice, 'Type out my resignation Celia.' In less than three minutes it was done: Aldrittson's years of machinations, manoeuvrings and manipulation to become Premier of Victoria were destroyed in the blink of an eye. He could scarcely comprehend the enormity of his fate. How had Zimmer tapped his secrets? Sick with loss and embarrassment, punctured by Meadows swift, merciless action, he could not even begin to imagine how this had occurred or how he might retaliate. Nor did he have the wit, at this point, to realise things would only get worse.

The Great Barraclough, on the other hand, had seen it all before. She had no need to speak – Aldrittson was beneath contempt. Instead, she speared him with a poisonous glare and flourished the resignation. Aldrittson looked at her through glazed eyes, her haughtiness stirring his juices back to life. Mentally, he shook himself, signed with flare and said, 'Well Bitch, this is where we part company.' He stalked to the door. She merely sniffed, disdain being superior to insult – *he was nothing*. Now she could freely tell her cronies how she had never liked him, had always known he was a cocky false pretender and, knowingly or not, fissured with self-destruction. *Oh yes,* she thought, *the Great Barraclough, is an excellent reader of men's characters.*

Chapter
FIFTY-NINE

At their Friday meeting, Tavistock reluctantly agreed that Drummond could enter Witsec two weeks behind Teresa. He was blunt in pointing out that Drummond was at risk and made it clear he thought deferral a poor decision. He had smiled disarmingly at Teresa when he said, 'Did you know this man was so stubborn when you met him? He's the kind that gets people killed.'

After a long day of questioning, Drummond drove back to Heathcote. His concession to Teresa's and Tavistock's concern was staying with the Mauds each night. Over the next three days he worked fiendishly to pack, sell his cattle, chooks and geese. He had not mentioned to Tony or Mary his plan for disposing of the farm, or the legal instrument he already had prepared to facilitate that.

During these busy days he had seen numerous cars and trucks travel Schoolhouse Lane but none attracted suspicion. Until today. Mid afternoon. A navy blue Nissan Pulsar had driven at slow speed along Schoolhouse and into Hunter's Lane. Half an hour later, the same car repeated the journey. Watchful, but not afraid, Drummond kept his Savage .22 magnum under and over handy. On its second journey he examined the car through binoculars and saw that it carried two dark-haired occupants – he was unable to read the number plate.

As he promised Tavistock, he rang the police station and reported his sighting. Now, on his evening drive to Maud's, he kept a sharp lookout for the navy car.

He drove off High Street and parked behind the station residence, locked the ute and walked in through the back door. Mary was labouring over the stove amid delicious smells of curry.

'Hey, Andy love. Thought I would make one of your favourites – curry on a cold night will go down really well.'

'You bloody ripper Mary. I've got some bottles of Marson Rosé in the ute. My first dinner with Teresa was curry and chilled rosé. I'll nip out and get it.' He placed a fat, buff coloured envelope on the kitchen table saying, 'We'll talk about this after dinner.'

He removed the wine from a cooler bag behind his seat and was locking the ute door when simultaneously he heard a pop and harsh whisper accompanied immediately by enormous tearing pain in his right shoulder. He fell to the ground unconscious, oblivious of bottles smashing around him and screeching tyres roaring towards Chauncey Street.

Vaguely, Mary heard the spinning wheels but was concentrating on the coconut sauce. A few minutes later she realised Drummond had not returned. She walked to the sink and looked over to his ute. The pale light from her kitchen window stuck to a lumpy shadow by the ute. Fearful, she ran to the kitchen phone and buzzed the police station. When Ken Jones answered she blurted, 'Jonesy, I think something's happened to Andy. I just heard a car squeal off and I think Andy's lying beside his ute. I'm going out to check.'

'No Mary, don't,' he barked. 'Raise the ambulance instead, we'll be there in a second. If I wave, it'll be an emergency, otherwise, don't worry.' The phone went dead.

Mary was explaining to John Pridmore the ambulance driver when Tony and Jonesy ran into the yard and began waving furiously. A controlled calm settled as she said, 'John, it's an emergency – back of the police residence. Hurry!'

'On the way Mary. Ring the hospital and alert casualty.'

Maud stayed with Drummond while Jones scouted Heriot and Wright Streets. Mary, inside, was still unaware of what had occurred.

Drummond lay on his left side, legs twisted. Unconscious, his breath sawed in ragged gasps; globs of blood bubbled from his mouth. Tony worked hard to staunch the blood spurting from his friend's shoulder. Mary appeared briefly then shot inside for clean towels. As she came out again, the ambulance pulled into the yard, headlights blazing on the deathly tableau.

'Mary,' Tony yelled, 'go with Andy and John. Jonesy and I will go and look around. Haven't got a bloody clue what we're looking for but we've gotta start. Get a message to Teresa as soon as you can.'

At the hospital, casualty staff were ready and smoothly removed Drummond to theatre. Pridmore told Mary that Drummond would probably go either to Bendigo or Melbourne after he had been assessed.

As the magnitude of the shooting settled on her, Mary was conflicted about whether to be angry with Teresa for drawing this "grief" to Drummond, or with Drummond, for not immediately going into Witsec. She bit her lip, teary at the thought of Teresa dealing with this alone, in witness protection. While she and Tony would weep for their friend, they at least could console each other.

Forty minutes later, John Pridmore returned from casualty. 'It's not good Mary. He's going to Melbourne. The doc says the bullet smashed its way through his shoulder and has gone into the thorax between the second and third ribs. At this stage, they're not quite sure where it has lodged. There's a hell of a lot of damage and his condition has been classified as critical. The air ambulance is on the way and will take him to the Alfred at Prahran. It should be here in about twenty-five minutes.' Pridmore reached forward, took her hand and gave it a squeeze. 'Would you like me to call Tony and tell him?'

Speechless, Mary nodded, eyes stung by tears. *One minute curry and wine, the next, near death. How tenuous life could be.* Pridmore went to the reception desk and returned a few minutes later. 'I've just spoken to Patch. He's given what he can to Bendigo, Axedale, Kilmore, Craigieburn and Seymour. Tony and Ken are out looking for the blue Pulsar Andy rang in earlier. But it's a needle and haystack situation. Tony's going to call here soon. I'm sorry Mary, but I'll have to go.'

Ten minutes later, Maud and Jones entered the reception area. Tony was ashen but steely and determined. Jones was similarly focussed.

'Hello Mair,' said Tony softly, 'bastard of a situation. The air ambulance is nearly here. We've had a quick burst around town looking for stray Pulsars. Nothing yet. I contacted A/C Tavistock personally and he's going to set up road blocks. I understand why, but I think it's a waste. We've got buggar all to go on and with Andy unconscious, it's going to stay that way. Tavistock is arranging for Teresa to be told.'

'Tony, sit a minute.' Mary patted the seat beside her, eyes full of tears. 'He's not good – he could die. John Pridmore said he's critical and has terrible injuries. I feel ashamed to say this but I am so angry about him getting shot; angry that he exposed us all to risk and angry that he was so bloody pig-headed about sorting out his farm. We could have done that for him. He should have stayed with Teresa. I'm torn because I feel like this, but if you'd been out there … you could be lying there with him.' Tears coursed down her cheeks.

Tony slumped, his eyes moist. He said hoarsely, 'I know how you feel, he's a good friend to us both, but we all knew the risks. Defending himself at the farm must have really stirred the hornet's nest. Will you go with him Mair? Stay at his unit until we know what's going on. I truly understand everything you say but …Teresa can't do anything, even if she wanted to. She'll be gutted by this.'

The receptionist called Maud to the phone. As he sprinted towards her, Jones followed. Maud took the phone. 'Yes Patch, go ahead.' Slowly, he turned to look at Jones. 'Okay mate, thanks, we'll go there and have a look at it. Pass this straight on to the A/C's Staff Officer, his number's on my desk by the phone.' He handed the phone to the receptionist and said to Jones, 'Claire Farrelly just walked into the station. She told Patch she passed an abandoned navy blue car tucked into the scrub in Ironbark Lane near Andy's joint. She didn't know the make but said it looked like a recent model. If it's what I think it is, we've got no bloody idea what the bastards are driving now or where they might be.'

The staccato beat of a helicopter throbbed from the south – it would land at the hospital helipad and take Drummond. Soon after, prickling with tubes, bags and monitors, Drummond appeared on a hospital trolley accompanied by medics. Mary and Tony followed. They hugged then went their separate ways.

Chapter
SIXTY

Aldrittson lay on his lounge before the gas log fire becoming gently pissed. The city lights tinged his darkened room with a phosphorescent glow and burnished the spattering rain as it dribbled slowly down the windows. The gloom suited his mood.

After his spray from Meadows he had gone from Parliament House to the Epworth Hospital and told Jack he was quitting. He said he had finished with Parliament and the waste scheme and was moving to Europe. He hadn't directly said, *You're on your own*, but his manner and tone was unmistakable.

His attitude had wounded his father, he knew that. *Too bad*. He had to think of himself. He had called in favours and obtained a first class flight to London from Tullamarine at eleven the next morning. Everything was paid up front, including a $10,000 commission. He didn't care about that – it guaranteed escape. He would take minimal luggage, replenish in London and disappear. Supported by huge funds secreted around the world, with a new identity and modest plastic surgery, he would re-invent himself. He would be unstoppable.

In the meantime, he thought hard to discover how that bitch Zimmer had discovered his secret, a secret that had enraged Meadows. All of *that* information was stored in his hidden office. Nowhere else. Scores of people had visited over the years and Mrs Mandrell cleaned every week – no one had even come close to suspecting the den's existence. Zimmer's breakthrough was a sickening mystery.

He finished his whiskey. Time to stop. He wanted to be clear-headed, not hung-over. He flicked the telly on and listened half-heartedly to a Channel 9 news bulletin. A man had been shot in the backyard of the Heathcote Police Station in Central Victoria.

When he heard it was Andy Drummond he laughed aloud. *He was the shit who had told police about Santini's prang on the bridge. Someone had good sense. He was a bloody pest and a permanent holiday was perfect for him.*

At 9:45 p.m. his phone rang. Irritably, he looked at the caller ID and saw it was his mother. *Shit*! He sighed and reluctantly answered, 'Yes Mum, how are you?'

She was babbling hysterically, unable to speak.

'Mum, what's the matter? Take hold of yourself. What's going on?'

Between sobs she managed to say, 'It's your father. He's ... he's ... dead ... a massive heart attack.'

Jesus Christ! What an inconsiderate bastard! Well, that alters nothing, he thought, *I'm not hanging around.* 'I'll get over to Epworth and fix things up, in the meantime, get your friend Gladys to come over. I'll drop in and see you later.' *What a fucking nightmare.*

Unexpectedly he thought of Lance Baker. *Christ,* he lamented, *I hope Zimmer hasn't got all that too.* With Jack dead and Zimmer in pursuit, Pescaro would hunt him to the ends of the earth. Nowhere on the globe would be safe.

He shook his head, locked up and caught a taxi to the hospital. Five minutes later, his father's doctor, Teddy Drake, stepped from the lift and ambled across to him. Drake was a tall, thin man with wispy straw coloured hair and a melancholy expression. His skin was so pale Aldrittson wondered if he ever saw daylight.

'Ah, Mr Aldrittson.' Drake's light voice seemed suited to his physical appearance. 'So sorry about your father. Come up to my office and we'll get the details sorted.' Drake's manner imparted genuine warmth and concern.

Aldrittson nodded and followed Drake to the lifts. They stopped at four and walked along a brightly lit corridor pungent with cleaning agent. Drake's office was small and basic – a desk with wooden shelves at one end, his chair and two visitors chairs.

'We'll be issuing a death certificate of course, but I do need to ask a couple of questions. Can you tell me what you talked about while you were here?'

'I told him I thought he was looking better, gave him a run down on the election campaign and let him know about recent events at his firm. You know, the usual stuff,' he lied.

'Hmmm,' exclaimed Drake. 'It's just that one of our nurses said after you left he seemed very distressed. He tried getting out of bed and was attempting to pull out the tubes he was connected to. She said she couldn't quite understand what he was muttering but it was to do with you.'

'No. Our conversation was mundane.'

Drake shot an enquiring look at Aldrittson but said nothing. He opened a drawer in his desk saying, 'These things belonged to your father.' He handed Ben a white plastic bag of personal effects.

Shit, thought Aldrittson, *all that wealth and power and it comes down to a cold body and a plastic-bloody-bag of toiletries and underwear. How pathetic.*

'Do you want to see your father Mr Aldrittson?'

He equivocated. *His dad was probably in the best place he could be. No bastard could hurt him now. He wasn't really a bad old prick.* 'Yes, I will see him, where is he?'

'In our mortuary downstairs.'

'Can I ring the undertakers from here before we go down?'

'Sure, I'll be back in a few minutes.' Ben Aldrittson's reaction to his father's death surprised Drake. Aldrittson seemed … distracted or … greatly inconvenienced. Still, Drake had dealt with these situations so often he knew there was no set pattern when a loved one died.

Aldrittson studied his father lying under a sheet on a trolley while Drake stood at the door. A hundred things ran through Ben's mind. Their relationship, although friendly, had been a contest, especially in later life. Jack's work had been all consuming and Ben had drowned himself in his quest for political power. But now, in the hospital mortuary, he remembered warmer feelings for his father long since forgotten. As a boy, when he became annoyed or frustrated with schoolwork, Jack would say, 'Listen Son, lean into the wind and you'll rise above it.' And that was how Ben, through persistence, discovered the value of money.

He worked hard to please his father. At nine he was considered very bright. Bigger kids in his grade thought he was a spoilt, rich, smart arse and hassled him outside school. Being smaller and skinnier than most, he always came off second best. One day three boys had him bailed him up on the way home from school. Fortunately for Ben, an older boy came by and kicked their arses. Ben gave him a dollar in appreciation. The boy had seized the opportunity and suggested that for a dollar a day, he would see the aggravation ceased. For Aldrittson the lesson was important, he learned that for a price he could entice other people to do, or not do things – just for him. He never told his parents and when he got older, the problem disappeared. Through sport and sheer hard work, he excelled to become a hero among his peers.

Years later he told his father the story. Jack had grinned and tapped the side of his nose. 'My boy, that skill, developed wisely, will take you anywhere and get you anything.'

Ben put a hand on his father's forehead and murmured quietly, 'Good bye Old Man, I know you'd understand.' He looked at Dr Drake, 'Thanks Doc, I appreciate your time. I'd better get over to see Mum now.'

At midnight, Aldrittson returned home, exhausted by the day's events. He had placated his mother, explained the arrangements, given her the names of the undertakers and convinced Gladys to stay the night. Her presence would take the edge off his mother's pain. Walking into his own place, he felt relief, relief underscored by the two packed bags ready in his hallway. He had wiped the computer hard drives, scrubbed his phone tapes and trashed his journals and records. Copies of crucial details were in a safety deposit box and other vital information was in his luggage on disks. Everything was taken care of. He had one more whiskey, asked his father's forgiveness, went to bed and dived into sleep.

At eight the following morning he stowed his bags in a taxi. So far, things were ticking over smoothly. He had listened to the news and heard nothing about Zimmer's story. Not that that meant anything; she was obviously still digging.

The airport was calm and orderly and he proceeded through formalities without a hitch. At 10:15 he was called, with other first class passengers, to board the aircraft. As he rose from his seat he was tapped on the shoulder by a tall man with short, cropped, fair hair.

'Excuse me sir, Commander Daniellson, Victoria Police. Would you mind accompanying me to the office please?' Danniellson nodded towards the Airport Security Office.

Aldrittson immediately protested but read something in Danniellson's eyes that chilled his nerve. He desisted.

In the Security Office the presence of his neatly paired bags hit him like a punch in the guts. He was completely unaware that for thirty minutes prior to boarding, Robby Danniellson had been studying him closely. Tavistock's passport alert to all Australian exit points had paid dividends sooner than anticipated.

Danniellson was the iconic iron fist sheathed in velvet. Possessing a deceptively gentle style, he was also blessed with a healthy dose of mongrel, which is why Aldrittson thought he was leaving the country. For Danniellson, jousting with sacred cows – among whom politicians were most sacred – was a sport to be enjoyed. He had waited patiently and at the last minute, struck like a viper.

Inside the office Danniellson said politely, 'As I said, I am Commander Robby Danniellson, Victoria Police. I believe, Mr Aldrittson, you can help us with an investigation we are conducting involving bribery, suborning government officials, receiving secret commissions, concealing criminal offences and unlawful waste disposal.'

Aldrittson was astonished. He had never personally done anything nasty, money had always been his muscle; others did the dirty work. His financial power had always been sufficient to insulate him and intimidate others. Yet, in tough situations with only himself to rely on, he folded quickly. He understood his position perfectly: somewhere, someone was leaking very accurate and very harmful information. The only thing he could do was keep his mouth shut.

Chapter
SIXTY-ONE

As Teresa's Witsec handler, Senior Constable Aleisha Campbell was a godsend. After receiving news of Drummond's shooting, Teresa felt she would go insane. Yet Aleisha's constant reassurance and calm strength had carried her through. Daily hospital bulletins kept Teresa informed of Drummond's progress, and, in every way possible, Aleisha showed she cared.

Because Mary Maud's contact with Teresa was restricted to the secure Witsec phone, she visited the hospital each day and was able to provide a little more information than the official bulletins. Today, ten days after the shooting, Mary had good news. Although still serious, Drummond was being moved from intensive care – his condition was no longer life threatening.

Shot by a .357 calibre hollow-point bullet, it had ploughed into his body at greater than 300 metres per second destroying the top of his right humerus and much of the shoulder blade socket joint. Bone and bullet had savagely torn through the lungs and bored into his body until the bullet stopped near his heart. Initially, its position was considered too dangerous to conduct a safe operation. But with Drummond's chances of survival being less than 50/50, surgeons finally decided there was everything to gain and little to lose by operating. After four hours, the bullet was successfully removed and the lungs repaired. The shoulder was patched to await further repair while the more serious wounds began healing.

The next stage involved a total shoulder replacement. The top of the humerus would be removed, a metal rod and ball joint inserted into the bone and the shoulder blade reshaped to receive a new plastic socket. With physiotherapy and exercise, and a little luck, Drummond might regain as much as 80 per cent of normal movement.

As for the shooters, they had vanished. Teresa learned from Tony that milk crates had been stacked behind the fence for a view of the police yard. Eventually, the forensic team concluded the crate platform had collapsed in use, an event which most probably interfered with the shooter's aim and saved Drummond's life. It was also the most likely cause of the shell casing being left behind as they departed in haste.

The Nissan Pulsar found in Iron Bark Lane turned out to have been stolen from Moonee Ponds a week prior to the shooting. Four days after the shooting, the Manager of the Bendigo Colonial Motor Inn reported a white, four wheel drive Range Rover abandoned outside unit 23. It had been stolen from Wallan six days before the shooting.

Tavistock and his team learned that two young men were seen in the Pulsar in Heathcote the afternoon Drummond returned from Melbourne. They had bought three pizzas from *Heathcote Kebab and Fast Food* in High Street. Two similarly described men were staying in unit 23 at the *Colonial Motor Inn* under the names Adam Smith and Henry Browning. They were quiet, polite and paid in cash for a week. They claimed to be on holidays and interested in the old goldfields around Bendigo.

As can happen with investigations, chance intervened. The woman delivering breakfasts to unit 23 told police that on Tuesday morning after the shooting, a man from 23 put a bag into the boot of a green BMW outside unit 26. Unit 26 was occupied by a Mark Kennedy of Blackburn who checked out alone shortly after nine on the Tuesday morning. Later, the BMW was found to have been stolen from Brighton six days before the shooting.

The conclusion was that a team of three using stolen cars had stalked Drummond and struck at their most opportune moment. Descriptions of the men were inconclusive – all in their thirties, short dark hair, Australian accents, discreetly dressed. Except for the observation of the bag put into the BMW, the occupants of units 23 and 26 appeared unknown to each other. It seemed reasonable to think that "Smith," "Browning" and "Kennedy" had met in Bendigo on Tuesday morning and left the stolen Range Rover outside unit 23.

Subsequently it was established that all three men had used false names and addresses and, according to the forensics team, had been ultra careful about leaving trace evidence behind. A further complicating factor was the daily room cleaning – it was of high standard. In the odd spots where finger prints might have been expected, only unidentifiable smears were found. The recovered cars too had been scrupulously cleaned.

Intuitively, Teresa knew Pescaro was behind the attack and advised Commander Donovan. After learning the method of attack, she nominated Argolia's team. Donovan told her that for the moment, there was nothing directly linking Pescaro to either the shooting or to Argolia. As an added complication, they could not exclude Ben Aldrittson either.

But today was significant for Teresa. Not only for the news about Drummond, but because Rosslyn Zimmer had shone a spotlight on Ben Aldrittson under the banner headline: **Politician Under Investigation.** The story contained the bones of Teresa's information thoroughly fleshed out by Zimmer's own research. True satisfaction lay near the end of the story: Premier Graeme Meadows had requested Aldrittson's resignation from his Ministry and next morning, police intercepted him attempting to leave the country. The article concluded by stating that Mr Ben Aldrittson was now "helping police with their enquiries".

The two events caused Teresa to feel that at last the sun was beginning to shine. It was 9:30 a.m. and at 10:00, Aleisha was coming. She was visiting regularly and explaining the difficulties of living under witness protection, particularly the psychological pressures.

Deep fears were known to arise from being a target. Aleisha

gave many examples of the problems of living under a false life history. She had spoken too about the difficulties of entering a new community, the need to develop new habits and new behaviour patterns while exercising ceaseless vigilance. And not only was there risk of danger to friends and family, but the deep pain and loneliness of having those ties severed. There was a possibility of depression, feelings of anxiety, isolation, anger and even a range of physical ailments from these stressors. Constantly concealing the past, Aleisha had said, was exceptionally wearing and responsible for many people leaving the program. Some protectees had even committed suicide.

On the other hand, there were witnesses who experienced none of these problems. For them, the program was a way out, a new beginning with a clean slate. The dumping of sadness, misery and sometimes, evil.

At ten sharp there was a rap on the door. Squinting through the peephole Teresa saw Aleisha. When she opened the door the two women smiled at each other. Aleisha observed a subtle but important change even before Teresa spoke.

'Alright, out with it. What's going on?'

Teresa smiled broadly, her grey-green eyes shining. 'The very best news: Andy's out of intensive care and though not out of the woods, I just know he's going to be fine. The second best news is that rotten hound Ben Aldrittson is getting his come-uppance.'

Aleisha chuckled at Teresa's pleasure. 'Sounds to me like you want to throw on the glad-rags and celebrate.'

'Oh I do! Could we go out for a coffee somewhere? I feel so cooped up in this unit and it seems a lifetime since anything nice happened.'

'Yes of course we can. I'll just let the boss know.' In the short time she had been managing Teresa, Aleisha had grown to like her. Unlike many women she had met on the program, Teresa was classy, polite, sensitive, interesting and thoughtful. She did not fit the stereotype of a Mafia moll. Although there had been little opportunity to see it, Aleisha also suspected that lurking within this woman was a quick wit and sparkling sense of fun. Teresa's resolute dignity and focus on the task before her was impressive and it was pleasant working with her.

They went to a quiet strip shopping centre and entered a small classy restaurant. Inside Teresa said, 'Oh this is nice, I'm buying. What about staying for lunch?'

Aleisha said, 'We can do that, but I must be gone by two o'clock. As you know, in this early phase just being with you is important. You need to feel okay about the system, understand everything and have your questions answered. This is as good a way of doing that as being shut up in the unit. Even if your man walked in right now, he wouldn't recognise you in that long blonde wig.'

Teresa laughed, noting Aleisha's avoidance of Drummond's name. 'Yes, well I told him once I was good at dressing up.' They both laughed and ordered extra hot coffees. Teresa asked, 'How did you get to be doing what you do?'

'A couple of things really,' Aleisha replied. 'I'd had enough of general duties policing and some time ago the Force reviewed the witness protection scheme. Some changes after the review opened it up for me. They realised the need for more women in the Unit as more women and children were entering the Program. Secondly, they changed Witsec recruiting methods and it became more accessible than it had been. When I read the selection criteria, I thought, "this is for me". After interviews and an integrity check, here I am. I've only been here a few of months. You might remember that politician who suicided – Lance Baker. My application for this job had gone in a couple of weeks before his death.'

Teresa nodded and said thoughtfully, 'Lance Baker; did you know him?'

'Heavens no. I delivered the death message to his wife Marnie,'

Aleisha spoke slowly, seriously. 'We've since become friends. She and her little girls are lovely people and his death was a terrible shock to them. They had no idea it was coming. To make matters worse, that last day he went to work they'd had a row and she feels guilty. It's all still out there, unresolved. As a matter of fact, I'm having dinner with her and some others on Saturday night. She's shifting house down to Kongwak to be near her sister. As part of the clean out she gave me a box of videos from Baker's boat. She didn't know what they were and didn't want them. Because I love film, I took them. I think they're golden oldies, but I haven't had a chance to watch any of them yet.' She glanced at her watch. 'Ever noticed how so few restaurants have clocks around? I can't believe it's almost midday. Want to order lunch?'

Teresa nodded. 'Yes. The events of today have made me hungry.' Privately she was wondering if the videos from Baker's boat would hold any evidence helpful to Tavistock. Much as she would like to discuss that possibility with Aleisha, she realised it might also compromise Tavistock and his team.

Chapter
SIXTY- TWO

Pescaro's crooked cops were feeding him unpalatable advice. Most of it about Ben Aldrittson. They warned of a secret high powered task force investigating Aldrittson and other matters. Anything linked to Ben Aldrittson, thought Pescaro, was a worry, but just as worrying was the news that David Tavistock headed the task force. Tavistock was not only incorruptible, but clever, thorough and strategic. They had crossed swords over a series of bank robberies and large scale fencing rackets when both were much younger. Pescaro escaped prosecution by the skin of his teeth but his then lieutenant, Franco Zirconi, was gaoled for fifteen years and died there.

Tavistock's task force, he was told, was handpicking members on the basis of incorruptibility, investigative experience, track record, motivation and initiative. Bridges had been established with the Office of Public Prosecutions, Federal Police, Customs and, at this stage, New South Wales and Queensland Police as well as the Office of Police Integrity. Other similar liaisons were likely to follow. Beyond that, everything was secret.

The news spoiled an otherwise good week. The banquet at Luciano's was finalised and three of Chernamenko's second tier had been removed. The fourth member, Pyotr Asimovich, had escaped Argolia's roundup and vanished. Pescaro was confident they would get him later.

Argolia said the Russians had been tough and unafraid, hurling abuse at his men until the last moment. Not that it made any difference: they had all been shot dead. Even the mock raid at Aldrittson's Bayswater Depot attracted minimum publicity. Nothing appeared in The Age and only a small story ran on page 7 of the Herald Sun: **Armed Men Rob Nightshift Staff.** Not unexpectedly, passing comment was made to the investigation of Ben Aldrittson by police but it was a bland regurgitation of past news. The article reported that three masked and armed men had robbed the small night shift crew at Aldrittson's Waste Disposals in Bayswater. Money, watches and mobile phones were taken from the victims. After the office safe was ransacked for a measly $55 the robbers left the nightshift crew gagged and bound. The robbery camouflaged the true purpose of the visit – disposal of the dead Russians. While the robbery was occurring, three of Argolia's men were grinding the Vor's bodies to a pulp in the huge destructor. With an eye for detail, they had left little to no evidence.

But there was another matter which had tarnished Pescaro's week – Drummond. He continued to survive. Despite that, he congratulated Frankie for his team's Heathcote performance. The coppers had not got a clue where the shooters had come from or gone to. He smiled to himself. He might let Drummond recover enough to think himself in the clear, then snuff him out.

His thoughts returned to the troubled Ben Aldrittson. Now unmasked for long standing corruption on a scale which surprised him, Pescaro was uncertain of what to do next with the firm. With Jack conveniently dead and Ben snared by the cops, the firm seemingly was leaderless. To the contrary, it was not. A deal struck between Aldrittson and Pescaro years before had swung into operation: Pescaro now had full control of the firm. But when lawyers had conceived their contingency plan, they had not foreseen the kind of investigation now being conducted by Tavistock. For Pescaro to assume control of the business at this time was both delicate and dangerous, even though the takeover would be managed through a blind company.

He would need legal advice. If Aldrittson started blabbing about their illegal waste dumps, he, as owner would be implicated, notwithstanding the firewalls constructed by his lawyers. More than ever, he wanted their waste scheme implemented. Not only was it sound, but would make millions of dollars. Ben Aldrittson had become a dark unsettling spectre.

Pescaro reflected deeply on Teresa's house fire, Jack's death and Ben's very public political demise. He did not believe in coincidence and with these events coalescing, it was too much to be synchronicity.

Thinking about Teresa raised another issue; her remains. Nothing had been found and he knew forensics investigators were very capable and could easily differentiate various types of ash. The absence of Teresa's remains was alarming. While he could not quite put a finger on the origin of his foreboding, it was there. Another menacing shadow.

His unease caused him to wonder too about the sudden press scrutiny of Aldrittson. Where did Zimmer get the story? Someone had to have tipped her off. Who would do it? Feeling as anxious as he did, he could not ignore the possibility of another traitor in their midst, one who now threatened his entire empire. Worse still, there was potential fallout for the interstate Families. He wondered if this was the reason behind Tavistock's operation and shivered. The implications were bad.

In the meantime, he would severely pressure *all* of his police sources to sniff out more about Tavistock's investigation. They were on generous retainers and many were virtual sleepers. Time to wake them up; the dirt he had on them would be greedily accepted by the Ethical Standards Department and OPI. Not only that, it was dirt that didn't involve him, they had done it all by themselves years ago. Everyone needed insurance – now it was time to collect.

Clearly he needed a meeting with his principal legal team, Wyvern and Sprite. His businesses, investments, accounts, partnerships and other "arrangements" had to be scrutinised for vulnerability. There had not been a need to test the legal firewalls and loopholes in this way before but Tavistock made him nervous.

He sighed, it was a blessing that the law could, at times, be so technical. With adroit manipulation, investigations had been known to be kept at bay for years. Which reminded him, he needed to top up the retirement fund of his most secret snout: $500,000 should be enough. No one suspected the Attorney General was in his pocket. He was a good source to be used sparingly.

Pescaro smiled grimly. Funny, he thought, living a life of crime can involve so much treachery and betrayal among people who supposedly were straight: coppers, politicians, government officials and a host of others including, unfortunately, his own men. Well, tomorrow would sort them out.

Chapter
SIXTY- THREE

Luciano's Warehouse was closed to the general public and packed to the rafters with Mafiosi. It was Wednesday, August 10, 2005. Outside, a cold blustery wind heralded rain and the pungent smell of ozone laced the air. Inside, Pescaro, his *capos* and their favourites were in attendance – 150 respectful men respectably dressed to honour Dominic Fabrizzi, Emilio Barracusa and Bernardo Santini.

Many of the younger men had never been to such a banquet and the older ones were trying to remember the last. It could have been after the Market Murders of the sixties. Some ancient hands secretly worried the feast foretold death among them.

Pescaro was relaxed and full of *bonhomie* as he mixed and talked with various members of the Family. After a positive day with his legal team, he was confident of withstanding the closest scrutiny. The requested audit would take about ten days and was already at full pace. Casually, he sought out Ed Masseria. 'Everything in place Ed?' he asked quietly.

'Yes Don Pescaro. I don't anticipate any problems.'

'Okay. Last chance reprieve. Has anything happened that should change my mind?'

'No.' Masseria mentally reviewed the hours of effort put into confirming the identities of the traitors. 'No, they've been quiet since the feds hit Chernamenko but we know the bastards are still in touch with Asimovich. They have to go.'

'You know what to do. Plenty of pain first.' Pescaro smiled warmly at Masseria and they drifted apart.

At eight o'clock they sat at fifteen large round tables set with starched, embroidered cloths from the Isle of Murano. Every setting harboured a forest of gleaming silver and brilliant cut crystal glasses. Fine English bone china graced the settings with matching linen napkins. At the centre of each table, a tall graceful, silver candelabra glistened; each burned ten deep gold candles.

As Pescaro rose, the lights dimmed, the evening would be lit by 150 candles. 'Friends and brothers,' his sonorous voice caressed the gathering, his manner courtly. 'Tonight is a special occasion to mark the deaths of three members of our Honoured Society. Each of them different in their own way, but all good, trusted men who gave much to our Family.' He spoke slowly without notes, choosing his words carefully, his solemnity underscoring the importance of the occasion. 'I welcome you to this commemorative banquet and trust you will find much to reward and remind you of who we are and what we stand for. I am not going to talk for long but I will address the qualities of my dear friend, Nardo Santini and touch briefly on our missing *Consigliere*, Teresa Marchese. Vito Franse will later talk about Dominic Fabrizzi, and Vincenzo Mendico about Emilio Barracusa. Since I am an old man and do not need as much food as you younger ones, eat while I speak. Firstly, my congratulations to you Felipe.' The old man, dressed immaculately in a dinner suit, stood near the kitchen entrance bursting with pride. 'You have surpassed all expectations. Everything looks magnificent and feels perfect. I am sure the food too will be superb. Thank you my dear Felipe.'

Pescaro paused, drowned out by noisy acclamation. As the applause dipped, he continued. 'My friend The Wraith came here as a ten-year-old boy. His family were among thousands who helped themselves and this country after the war – in their case, on the Snowy Mountains scheme. Nardo was known as The Wraith for good reason – he could move among people and not be noticed. He went in and out of situations like a hand in water, making no difference, leaving no trace, yet observing everything. Wonderful skills, yet not his best qualities. No one was more courageous or more poised than Nardo. He was a true *capo* and did what he had to do properly and with appropriate hardness. Some said he was a fussy, fastidious man, yet he rarely made mistakes. But even these traits were not his best qualities. He loved his garden and, like a true Sicilian, could grow anything. Few knew of this hobby yet the irony was he publicly disavowed his Sicilian roots. Over time, however, he turned his backyard into a beautiful Mediterranean haven of vines and vegetables, terrace and tables. Yet these too were not his best qualities. Nardo was resourceful, thorough and surprisingly sensitive. He was as tough and dangerous as an old bridge spike but astonishingly perceptive and intuitive – clairvoyant almost. Surprisingly, these were not his best qualities either. Bernardo Santini, my friend of decades, was a man of loyalty. And *that* was his best quality. He served me faithfully, supported me totally, disagreed with me respectfully and always advanced the cause of our Family. He lived for his work and his work was for us – the Family. He even chose the Family over marriage. His loyalty to me personally and to the Family generally was a beacon in the blackest of nights. I miss his counsel, I miss his friendship and I miss that loyalty – his best quality. My friends, please raise your glasses to Nardo Santini, a loyal and trusted Family friend.'

Quietly they stood, raised their glasses and said in one voice: '*Nardo Santini – a loyal friend.*'

Throughout Pescaro's speech, Masseria discreetly watched the men for whom it had partly been crafted. When Pescaro spoke of loyalty, they had exchanged subtle glances, one man's lip curling in disrespect.

Pescaro remained standing and motioned the men to sit. 'Finally, I would like to briefly mention Teresa Marchese. In appointing her as Nardo's replacement, I know many of you disagreed; firstly because she was a woman and secondly because her journey was not traditional. But … times are changing. We are doing, and have to do, things differently. It is hard enough for me to keep up with the evolution of mobile phones let alone contemplate computers. In this regard, Teresa was gifted. Her acumen for finance, international business, banking and technology was comprehensive and her skills have grown and consolidated our businesses substantially. Many of you would know how easy she was to deal with, yet she had a quiet toughness most of you would not have seen. She was an incisive analyst always looking for intelligent pathways into the future. Indeed, it was her idea to use Immigration authorities to remove the Russians. Regrettably, the Russians removed her too – Chernamenko personally boasted of this to me recently. Like Teresa, I also believe the Russians removed Nardo, so I am pleased they will no longer bother us. Gentlemen,' Pescaro raised his glass, 'in memory of Teresa.' Once again, they all stood and said quietly: '*Teresa.*'

Pescaro sat, slowly sipping mineral water, waiting for his meal and acknowledging individual salutes to Nardo from various members in the room. He was satisfied his message had been delivered to the traitors.

Conversation ebbed and flowed as dinner came and went and, at 9:15 p.m., Vito Franse rose to his feet. The room quietened.

'Don Pescaro, friends and brothers,' he began, 'sadly I stand before you as the replacement for a good man killed after a social outing. We all know, of course, that the Russians were responsible for the death of my former *capo*, Dominic Fabrizzi. Dominic was a man who bubbled with energy, he had a huge sense of humour and an eye for a deal. He sensed deals where others couldn't even sniff potential; he could close a deal with more speed than a rat trap, yet with more style than Versace. He was a thoughtful instructive *capo* who, in building friendship and trust, inspired others. Yet he was hard when he needed to be. The night he died marked completion of a new deal at Tullamarine airport. From my numerous conversations with him I know that like Bernardo Santini, he too lived for the Family. But, he was grounded in the old ways. He couldn't see the value of new technology, he was unable to imagine the potential of internet fraud and he wasn't receptive to modern management practices. In these things, he was captive to older, long gone traditions. Dominic was a good man, a loving father and husband and immensely kind to his friends. He was a solid, dependable and consistent *capo*. As a friend and mentor, I miss him dearly. Gents, please raise your glasses to Dominic Fabrizzi – a Family man.' They did not stand but raised their glasses and chorused: '*Dominic Fabrizzi – a Family man.*'

At 10:00 p.m., Vincenzo Mendico stood and rapped a fork against a glass for attention: he would pay tribute to Emilio Barracusa.

At 10:20 Pescaro rose and began farewelling friends. He stopped at Mendico and said, 'Your words were fitting and I agree with your sentiment. What neither of you knew was that in Nardo's absence, I intended recommending Emilio as *my* replacement.' He shook Vincenzo's hand and moved on, eventually seeking out Vito Franse. He smiled kindly. 'Your tribute to Dominic was a fine one Vito, the affair was such a waste of talent and so regrettable.' The ambiguity of his words hung in the air, disarmed by his gentle smile.

Vito accepted Pescaro's words as a compliment, saying, 'Yes Don Pescaro, the deal he stitched up that night for Tullamarine was a good one. As I said earlier, he was a man of talent. And by the way Don, this was a fine evening and a great concept. Thank you for the invitation.'

'Not at all Vito. I'll be seeing you at our next meeting. Good night.' After saying his goodbyes he paused to shake Masseria's hand.

'Everything is in place,' Masseria said quietly. 'Good night Don Pescaro.' He nodded his head and stepped back as Pescaro left the room.

At 11:30 p.m., Roberto Gibaldi left Luciano's and made his way through light, cold rain to his car in Cardigan Street. He was just a little the worse for wear after a generous intake of wine. Turning from Faraday Street into Cardigan Street he bumped into two men walking towards him, heads down against the rain. He stumbled and apologised as one of the men put out a hand to assist him and, in the next second, gasped as he felt a sharp sting in his side. He stumbled again and slowly began to collapse. The men stepped in close, draped his arms over their shoulders and assisted him to his car where they placed him inside.

At 12:45 a.m., Vito Franse doused the headlights after turning into his driveway at Templestowe – he didn't want to wake his wife or small children. Waiting for the roller door to open, he remembered his wife's car was away for servicing and drove into the centre of the double garage. With nothing but a dim glow from the automatic door lamp illuminating the garage, he missed the two shadows sliding into the space barely above floor level. He opened his door, stuck one foot on the floor and turned to collect his rain coat and umbrella from the passenger seat. Suddenly, he felt a stinging pain in his right calf and swore, then mumbled stupidly at the man in a ski mask rising from the floor beside him. He toppled slowly into the passenger seat.

The two men lifted the unconscious Franse from his car, took the door zapper from the centre console, placed the house and car keys on the dashboard and quietly closed the car door. After carrying Franse to the bottom of his driveway and placing him in their vehicle, one man zapped the garage door shut and put the device in the letter box. The exercise had taken less than five minutes.

Ten days later The Age proclaimed: **Gruesome Discovery in Charnwood Grove,** while the Herald Sun bannered: **Sickening Find in St Kilda.** Both stories related the discovery of two naked, bound and mutilated bodies in a car boot in Charnwood Grove, St. Kilda.

When the report reached Tavistock's desk it was accompanied by post mortem results. The two men, identified as Vito Franse and Roberto Gibaldi, known Mafiosi, had, after extensive torture, been jammed into the boot of Gibaldi's car; their ears and eyes had been removed. The post mortem disclosed that each man's stomach contained remains of one of his own ears while the other ear, along with their eyes, had been rammed into their mouths which had been stitched shut.

The message was unequivocal: *hear no evil, see no evil, speak no evil*. Mulling this over, Tavistock reflected on Teresa's warning that Pescaro suspected he had a traitor and the banquet possibly heralded death. On this basis, he had put Luciano's Warehouse under surveillance. All banquet attendees had been identified – including Franse and Gibaldi – entering and leaving the restaurant under their own steam. Tavistock's men had noticed nothing unusual about the departure of either man. On the other hand, they had not known who Pescaro was targetting. Neither had Teresa.

As yet, no direct link had been established between Pescaro and the deaths. No one saw Gibaldi or Franse abducted and while Franse had at least arrived home, there was no indication of Gibaldi's place of abduction. Both men, the post mortem revealed, had been injected with a powerful, fast acting anaesthetic.

Tavistock decided they should start by interviewing Eduardo Masseria, the man Teresa thought the most likely appointee for uncovering Pescaro's traitors. At the same time he was thinking that if this was how Pescaro dealt with his own for disloyalty, he was bound to take an even more ruthless approach towards Ben Aldrittson.

In his own interest, Aldrittson would have to receive more immediate attention. He sighed. Teresa Marchese was undoubtedly a nightingale of the finest voice but her melody was brutally jarring.

Chapter
SIXTY- FOUR

After receiving the anonymous letters about Ben Aldrittson, Rosslyn Zimmer had worked tirelessly. She was pleased with the piece that would appear in the *Sunday Herald Sun*. A curious trail of events had substantially shaped the story she considered explosive. Zimmer's mother and two old friends had shared a gossipy afternoon tea. One of those friends, Celia Barraclough, had dropped a juicy titbit about Ben Aldrittson's sacking. Mrs Zimmer had said to her daughter, 'Of course dear, everything was mentioned in strictest confidence' as she rushed, headlong, into repeating what she had heard. At the time, one element of her tale had seemed inconsequential – a meeting between the Premier, Professor Cameron Blake of RMIT and Aldrittson. The meeting had occurred shortly before Aldrittson's sacking.

Initially, Zimmer ignored the morsel. Premiers regularly hold meetings with all kinds of people, especially their Ministers. It lay quietly at the back of her mind, unobtrusively gestating. Then she remembered it was Cameron Blake who had won a major science prize in 2004 for discovering an enzyme from algae which neutralised harmful petroleum wastes and converted them into a useful product for the building industry. With that recollection came a new train of thought: waste plus Aldrittsons plus Blake. Why would the Premier be discussing waste treatment with Blake and a Minister whose father owned the largest and most reputable waste disposal company in the state? Waste was always a topic of political controversy. With the material she already had on Ben Aldrittson plus his sacking, it might be a story. Or it might be nothing.

On gut feeling, she somersaulted her thinking and began discreetly enquiring about black waste disposal methods. She went to Brooklyn and Bayswater and watched Aldrittson's in action. She checked the company through the Australian Securities and Investments Commission then posed as a company director wanting industrial waste removed. She hit pay dirt when she got an appointment at AWD with Martin Judd.

Using a false name, she implied to Judd she was part of a new company at Dandenong making plastic extrusions and other products. Their waste would require at least monthly collection and AWD had been privately recommended as a reliable company. Almost as a throw away, she said there would be some highly toxic liquid by-products. Could Judd advise how best to deal with this?

Rosslyn Zimmer, a short, slender and pugnacious red head with a clear mind and unnerving tenacity was skilled at reading body language. Knowing people and unpacking the truth was her business. She had seen a reaction in Judd at the mention of toxic liquids, an uneasiness, a knowingness, and then – the veil. Immediately she knew *he* knew something he didn't want others to know. Judd fobbed her off. 'We don't do toxic waste Ms Black. As for your contract, I can't send anyone to assess your job for at least a month – we are pretty full on right now.'

As she left Aldrittson's, she remembered a fire that not so long ago involved one of their trucks – somewhere near Bendigo. Because there was a death in suspicious circumstances, the story belonged to police roundsman, Gavan O'Connor.

She rang O'Connor to find out what he knew about that fire. Succinctly he filled her in and said the case was still open. His police sources had suggested arson caused by a deliberate explosion. Highly toxic chemical traces were found on parts of the truck as a result of which they were investigating a murder. O'Connor said his research had found Aldrittson's to be squeaky clean. Nobody could think of a reason for the company to be involved in his death. Although it had been suggested the dead driver was moonlighting, it was hardly sufficient reason to kill him. His death remained a mystery. O'Connor's private view was that someone was applying pressure to acquire Aldrittsons'. So far, however, he had nothing to support that theory.

Zimmer settled back in her chair, closed her eyes, and allowed the different pieces of information to mill around in her mind. In a detached way she watched the pieces moving, bumping, forming and reforming until an altogether different picture of Aldrittsons' began to emerge, a picture at remarkable variance to their public face.

The following day she returned to Brooklyn, made a huge fuss and found herself back in Judd's office. This time, she was Rosslyn Zimmer reporter, not a pseudo company director from a make-believe plastics factory. What followed was one of the most remarkable interviews of her career. Wracked by guilt and remorse, Judd said he had been unable to sleep properly and was haunted by the constant fear of discovery. With Jack Aldrittson dead and Ben in deep shit with the cops, it was time to come clean.

Over three hours, Judd explained in minute detail every aspect of the family's dual waste disposal business. He gave Zimmer information concerning their largest black waste clients, how long they had been using AWD, the types of waste offloaded, dumping sites and the astonishing profits from these activities.

Initially, Zimmer was sceptical, but after sighting various documents and long held files, she knew her story was dynamite. During the interview, Judd fluctuated between tears and anger, balance and tirade. He hated what he had fallen into and what he had become. The money was fantastic but no substitute, he realised, for peace of mind or, with his marriage now in fracture, family life. Conscience was burning a hole in his gut and the environmental damage caused by Aldrittson's was unforgivable.

After probing the Premier's Office and Professor Blake to discover what knowledge they possessed, she had written her story. She had no illusions about the wounds it would cause to respected personal and public reputations. She anticipated wide scale litigation at a criminal and civil level. Her unshakable belief, however, was that truth and transparency were not negotiable – particularly when it came to government. Given the extent of this evil, and its duration, the public not only had a right, but *had to know* what Aldrittson's had been doing. The story could not be concealed. After extensive checking and rechecking and considerable soul searching, the editor and the newspaper's lawyers agreed to its publication.

Thus, the *Sunday Herald Sun* carried a remarkable expose of dirty business and dirty politics, greed, corruption and callous disregard for the environment, the law and the community. The story raised questions about the nature of democracy and who really made the rules: business or government? The article concluded with a comprehensive profile of a man once considered a brilliant government Minister with potential to be Premier. A manipulative man driven by power, ruthlessness and an insatiable appetite for wealth – no matter the cost to others. A man utterly devoid of principle.

Chapter
SIXTY- FIVE

Lying on the lounge, Teresa Marchese read the lead story in the *Sunday Herald Sun*. With growing amazement, she found that everything she hoped would emerge to engineer Aldrittson's downfall now stood revealed. He was publicly shamed and humiliated. For a man who cherished his urbane, sophisticated image of power, he had truly been dropped in the duck pond to emerge reeking of slime. *Rosslyn Zimmer, you absolute legend*, she thought. As she read on, an occasional soft chuckle erupted as she found snippets of her own information interspersed with new material from Zimmer's ample research.

As comprehensive as the story was however, two key factors were missing: the brilliant new waste-disposal concept and Aldrittson's partnership with Pescaro. Zimmer apparently had not discovered these aspects. Not surprising – Aldrittson, Pescaro and Santini had worked diligently to bury them. Soon though, even they would emerge. She fervently hoped the new toxic waste scheme would surface unscathed and be seen in a positive light – it did not deserve to become a casualty of either politics or evil men.

After a month in protection, Teresa had changed significantly. At first, traumatised by Drummond's shooting and prevented from seeing him, she felt scarred, guilty and vulnerable. It was *her* lifestyle and *her* connections that had brought death so close. No amount of counter argument by Mary and Tony or even Aleisha Campbell, could convince her otherwise. Direct contact with Drummond was prohibited because the medical staff wanted a strong recovery before his shoulder reconstruction and they had embargoed any social intercourse. Thus Teresa's progress reports were mostly second hand, a situation which slyly fed her festering guilt.

Just as she had been warned, the monotony and restriction of witness protection was gruelling. She missed choice, spontaneity, stimulation and freedom. Even Aleisha, who was magnificent in her support, could not lessen the grey, exhausting repetition of police interviews, endless television, reading and confinement, a confinement punctuated only by the spark of an occasional small, safe, outing.

Adding to this cage of horrors was growing uncertainty about her own future. From her many discussions and interviews with Commander Donovan it was plain that her role in Pescaro's empire was seriously criminal. She had always known the money she moved, managed and invested had unlawful origins. Somewhat naively, she once had said to Donovan that it seemed like monopoly money.

'That's the very point,' he had responded with a crooked smile, 'it comes from a highly structured, efficient and well organised *criminal* monopoly. What you were doing Teresa was wrong. It's called money laundering and it's a serious bloody crime.'

Donovan explained they would be seeking a transactional indemnity against prosecution in return for her evidence against Pescaro and others. Negotiating this process however was a matter of intense frustration. Co-operation was the very heartstone of Teresa's actions yet Donovan still could not say whether indemnity was certain. Glumly he told her that a couple of powerbrokers in the Office of Public Prosecutions were unhappy about the request for immunity – they preferred she got some form of sentence. Their argument was that evidence from criminal informers was always tainted and raised questions about the propriety of the prosecution. The balance, they said, lay in a lenient penalty which acknowledged the quality of the evidence and results obtained.

Donovan's news was not cheering and Teresa feared the OPP's resistance might be driven by one of Pescaro's many "plants". Safe under police protection, her deepest fear was that Pescaro would exploit this impasse to find and eliminate Drummond, and then herself.

Self-doubt, uncertainty about the future and the tedium of "protection" combined to drag her into the dark and claustrophobic vortex of depression. She became withdrawn, moody and encrusted with lethargy. She felt old, saw new shadows and lines crease her face and experienced numbing exhaustion. Not even Aleisha's bright company could banish the phantoms.

But today – today was different. Zimmer's expose was uplifting. Teresa's faith in a higher authority being able to correct all manner of wrongs had, for the moment, returned.

Nearing the end of the article she heard a soft knock at the door. Checking the spy hole, she opened up to Aleisha Campbell who was beaming and bearing a large bunch of flowers.

'Hi girl. Felt I just had to come and say g'day. I see you've got the good news bulletin,' she nodded towards the paper on the couch. 'I got mine early this morning, read Zimmer's story and thought, this calls for a celebration. What a show stopper. And, what an absolute prick is that bloody Aldrittson. How could people elect such a rotten bastard to government? All I can say is, he must have been deft at hiding his double life.'

Aleisha's good humour was infectious and Teresa laughed with her. 'I know! I told you he was a shit. Now the world knows it too.' Inwardly, she glowed with satisfaction at being Zimmer's secret source.

'Okay girl, get your glad rags on. We are going to kick our heels up today. Where would you like to go? Somewhere you like that we haven't yet been.' Aleisha's eyes sparkled, her mood was irresitible. 'And while you get yourself ready, I'll drown these flowers in something. Is there a vase?'

Teresa laughed, 'You should know. This place has, at least for me, redefined the term *minimalism*. The best I can suggest is that you retrieve a plastic fruit jar I pitched with the rubbish this morning. That'll have to do. Tell me, have you ever been to Maling Road?'

'No, where is it? What is it?' Aleisha busied herself rinsing the plastic jar and trimming the flowers.

'It's a small street off Canterbury Road tucked in behind the Canterbury railway station,' replied Teresa. 'It's charming and reeks of the 1920s and 30s. I love going there. Old fashioned tea rooms, interesting shops, beautiful artwork and a curious antique place in what used to originally be a theatre. It's a good place for a celebration.'

'Good. I have another little surprise for you too, but not until we get underway. Are you a long or short and curly blonde today?'

Teresa laughed. 'Well, I think Maling Road is a classy place so I'll attempt to be the sophisticate – I'll have long hair today.'

Half an hour later they drove away from the Witsec unit in an unremarkable blue Holden Astra belonging to the police fleet.

'Alright Ms Campbell, we're underway, what's the surprise?' Teresa was curious and though her eyes shone with the prospect of a day in Maling Road, a small pucker of uncertainty creased her forehead.

Aleisha looked sideways and grinned at her. 'Two things actually. First, I can share a small secret about those videos from Baker's boat and second, we are going to see Andy … Hey! It's okay. That's meant to be good news.' Aleisha pulled gently to the kerb.

Her *news* had brought instantaneous and total shock. Teresa thought she would burst; tears flooded her cheeks. It would be the first time she had seen Drummond since their goodbyes in mid-July. She wanted to laugh with joy but could only weep; her throat was constricted and her heart thumped. Even breathing was difficult. Gradually, she regained her composure. She turned to Aleisha and smiled, a mixture of fear and gratitude on her tear stained face. 'Aleisha Campbell,' she said softly, 'you are a bitch. Why didn't you tell me this back at the unit? At least I could have repaired all this damage before we left.' She gestured to her face.

Aleisha reached across and clasped her hand. 'Andy Drummond will find you beautiful make-up or no make-up. I didn't tell you because I really did want to surprise you and secondly, Andy's shoulder reconstruction is tomorrow. It's almost five weeks since the shooting and he's made excellent progress. My boss knows everything going on and he suggested this visit. His opinion was that you not only needed, but deserved it.'

Teresa leaned across and kissed Aleisha's cheek. 'Thank you, thank you. I know that's inadequate, but I thank you from the bottom of my heart. And please thank him too.'

'Good. Are we right to go?' Aleisha was touched by Teresa's sincerity and understood the importance of this meeting. Her decline had been discussed at Witsec and they favoured direct contact in the hope it would lift Teresa's "blues". Continuing in comfortable silence, Aleisha allowed space for Teresa to think. Teresa, on the other hand, could scarcely contain herself. Head spinning with anticipation, reigning in tumultuous feelings and picturing Drummond's reaction, she was ready to explode with happiness.

Eventually Aleisha said, 'We have to take precautions. As far as the nursing staff are concerned, we are both detectives. Every step we take will be monitored. When you are with Andy, apart from medical staff, no one else can enter the room. Unfortunately, you can only have ten minutes because this visit is very risky. So, minimal exposure. Clear on all that?'

'Yes – crystal.' Teresa, still overcome by her feelings, spoke in a low husky voice. 'Ten minutes?'

'Yep. Absolutely no more. Normally, we don't do this but sometimes, unique circumstances demand unique actions.' Aleisha's gentle smile softened her unequivocal tone.

'Oh, I forgot,' Teresa exclaimed, 'you mentioned something about Baker's videos?'

'Yes, I sensed your curiosity about them even though you

didn't say much. I had about thirty to get through and all but three were genuine – it took quite a while I can tell you. The three non-genuine ones were all porno stuff involving kids – boys and girls – between the ages of about five and twelve. They were homemade and apparently put together by members of Baker's group. Baker's in them by the way. I'm not going into detail because it's disgustingly horrible. As soon as I realised what I had I asked for an appointment with A/C Tavistock. I told him everything and he brought Commander Danniellson in. I went through it again, gave him the videos and left it at that. Now we'll wait and see. Anyway, last Friday afternoon Danniellson's Staff Officer rang me. He was oblique and a bit crass but told me to watch the news on Sunday night. I would recognise some amateur actors he said. His message was about the videos. Maybe we'll know tonight.'

'What about Marnie Baker and her girls? Are they in the know?'

Aleisha frowned. 'Look, the truth is, I don't know. I did raise my concerns about them with the A/C and he understood. Being the man he is, I would imagine he's dealt with all that tactfully. Naturally I can't discuss it with Marnie while the investigation is proceeding. In a sense, Baker is irrelevant because he's dead, but all the others are still around. A word out of place by me could jeopardise the enquiry before it is completed. I can't take the risk of talking to Marnie about it.'

Teresa nodded and remained silent as they drove into the hospital carpark. She was tense and watchful. Stepping into the lift, Aleisha punched six: "Surgical".

They stepped from the lift into a wide corridor smelling of antiseptic and followed floor arrows to the Nurses Station. Aleisha pressed the buzzer on a small counter outside the station. A petite Asian nurse stepped from the glassed room. 'I've been told to meet Sister Hibbert here. Is she available? I'm Aleisha Campbell.'

The nurse vanished. Moments later a tall angular woman in

her mid forties appeared. 'I'm Louise Hibbert, I've been expecting you. Follow me.'

Hibbert stopped and pointed ahead. 'Third door on the right from here. Aleisha, you are to keep time from the moment your colleague enters the room. When you are done, come back and check in with me on your way out. Clear?' They both nodded. Hibbert turned and swished away, rubber soles squeaking on the polished floor. Aleisha and Teresa moved on to Drummond's room.

Outside his door they stopped. Teresa apprehensive. Aleisha read her uncertainty and said, 'Go on, you'll be right. Tell the copper inside I'm waiting out here to speak with him.' She gently pushed Teresa towards the door.

Although only a little after eleven o'clock, the room was darkened. Drummond was in bed next to a window at the far end of the room watching TV and listening through a set of headphones. He glanced briefly at Teresa then turned his attention back to the screen. As Teresa spoke quietly to the police guard, her eyes remained fixed on Drummond. The upper half of his body was encased in bandages, his arm strapped across his chest. He was attached to an electronic monitor – drips and drainage tubes hung from him. Slowly, silently, she walked forward, eyes glowing.

Conscious of her presence, he turned to face her. He removed his head phones and looked at her closely, eyes beginning to widen. 'Teresa,' he whispered incredulously.

'I told you I was good at dressing up,' she said, her voice low and husky as she flicked her long blonde hair,

Drummond's eyes glistened. 'Teresa.' His voice, although barely a croak, was still Drummond's voice. He raised his left arm and drew her down and they kissed. In that instant, all Teresa's doubts, fears and guilt about how he might feel towards her evaporated in a wave of tenderness. It was a kiss of both joyous reunion and complete absolution.

'What are you doing here? You look so … so thin! God I've

NO WITNESS, NO CASE

missed you. Dreamt of this for weeks. How are you sweetheart?'

'Enough, enough. Too many questions,' she said, pressing her finger across his lips. She smiled lovingly. 'Andy, I've only got ten minutes, probably eight now. The Witsec people arranged this and thought you were well enough for us to talk. I'm okay but I have been so worried about you and feel so guilty about all this.' She pointed to his bandages.

'No,' he wheezed, 'Tavistock warned me, remember? Home not a good idea. Not your fault. Own pig-headedness. What other news?' His speech was laboured and breathy.

'Well you probably know all about Ben Aldrittson and that Jack died.' Drummond nodded. 'Two of Giuseppe's men – Franse and Gibaldi – were executed and I suspect that was organised by Ed Masseria. Giuseppe believed he was being sold out to the Russians. Those two went missing after a big banquet he sponsored. I know the method is crude and old fashioned, but it's the way they do things. Tavistock and his team are working hard. I've had so many interviews my head hurts and my evidence is looking like *War and Peace*. Donovan suspects I leaked information to Zimmer and has given me hell over it. I'm not admitting to it though and I'm sure there'll be more grief tomorrow about today's article. I know I shouldn't have done it but, by God I feel good.' She grinned broadly. 'Tavistock is still having trouble getting me indemnified against prosecution but thinks it will work out in the end.'

'Whoa, whoa; back up. What do you mean – prosecution? What are you talking about?'

'All that work I did for Pescaro – money laundering. As you know, I want to testify about that and everything else. The police want me indemnified against prosecution in return for my evidence. Someone at the Office of Public Prosecutions is objecting and it's taking a while to sort out. Tavistock is pretty confident it will be okay.'

They kissed again. 'Enough of that. What about you? Will

your voice and lungs return to normal? And the arm and shoulder – what's happening there?'

'Voice okay,' he rasped, 'just not used much. Lungs healing well – matter of time. Can't say much about the shoulder. Surgeons say my fitness helped. Mobility might be seventy five – eighty per cent – don't know. Means lifestyle change though.'

'Yes,' whispered Teresa, eyes searching his face. 'Andy, I've missed you so much, when you get out of here I'm determined not to let you out of my sight again. Andy Drummond, after this is over, would you consider marrying me?'

'Thought you'd never ask. In fact, I demand it.' Andy smiled, overwhelmed.

She touched him gently on the cheek and kissed him tenderly. 'I love you,' she said. 'I've only got a minute left. They are rigid about the time because of the risk and they don't want you too excited before tomorrow. Donovan said we have to think about another country to live in. He says my face is too well known among Mafia families here. Australia would be too dangerous. So, while you're lying there getting soft and fat, think about where we could live.'

She looked up as the door opened and Aleisha entered. 'Got to go,' she said softly. 'I love you Andy – never doubt it. Good luck tomorrow, I know you'll be fine. They'll tell me as soon as they can.' They kissed again. 'Be sure to watch the news tonight; something is breaking.'

'Be very careful my darling,' said Andy hoarsely, 'I love you too.'

She walked towards Aleisha and vanished through the door.

Chapter
SIXTY- SIX

On Sunday evening, in their various locations Drummond, Teresa, Aleisha and Pescaro, watched the seven o'clock news on ABC television. Introducing the lead story, anchorman James Richardson said, *'In a remarkable day that has shaken the government and many highly respected Melbourne companies, there is mounting evidence of huge environmental damage caused by the dumping of toxic materials. It has been alleged that Aldrittson Waste Disposals dumped poisonous chemicals and fluids in at least four states for more than twenty-five years as part of an illegal multi-million dollar black industry. It is also alleged these activities were concealed inside their legitimate waste business. They have even been accused of trying to legalise their scam. Managing Director, Jack Aldrittson, recently died of a heart attack. His son, disgraced former politician Ben Aldrittson, presented Premier Meadows with an elaborate proposal for handling toxic waste just three months ago. Had the scheme been approved, it is alleged that Aldrittson's would not only have continued their previous illicit activities under government sanction but also gained huge profits. This afternoon Premier Meadows refused to comment on the matter and Mr Aldrittson could not be located. In an exclusive interview to the ABC this evening, Professor Cameron Blake of RMIT said that in mid-July Premier Meadows asked him to examine a proposal for the destruction of toxic waste. Professor Blake said he wanted to set the record straight because he was concerned that people would misconstrue his, and RMIT's, involvement in the Aldrittson scandal. He said he attended a meeting with the Premier and then Minister for Trade and Industry, Ben Aldrittson, on July 14. The Premier was seeking a second opinion on a waste destruction scheme. Professor Blake said that in his opinion it was a brilliant and important innovation and he did not know then that Aldrittson's had allegedly been dumping black waste. 'It would be a great pity,' he said, 'if the waste concept I examined was scuttled for legal or political reasons. What I saw was innovative, comprehensive, well regulated and intended to be very legal.'*

It is believed that Victoria Police are investigating these allegations in conjunction with police and Environmental and Health authorities from New South Wales, Queensland and South Australia.

In other breaking news, Victoria Police announced it has smashed a highly organised paedophile ring involving at least a dozen men. It is alleged that members of the group filmed themselves in pornographic acts with children as young as four and no older than twelve years. Investigations also uncovered a substantial and highly active internet sales and distribution network run by the group within Australia and several overseas countries. It is believed that members of the group were confirmed from several home videos found among the personal effects of deceased politician, Lance Baker. In a clockwork operation across Melbourne suburbs today, twelve men were arrested on charges of pornography and sexual misconduct with minors. All have since been bailed after suppression orders were placed on their identities. The ABC has lodged an application with the Supreme Court of Victoria to contest the order which is listed for hearing on Friday, August 26. Even though the men cannot be named, the ABC has learned that among them is a Judge of the County Court, two senior police, several prominent public servants and executives from some of Melbourne's most prestigious companies. The investigation was commenced several months ago after a cache of pornographic images showing children at different locations around Melbourne was found in a Collins Street office building. The ABC understands that nothing among those images identified members of the group. While police kept their investigation low key, matters accelerated when the Baker videos came to light.

Neither the Premier nor Attorney General was available for comment about these events.

Mr Baker's widow could not be contacted and members of her family said she is overseas with her children.

In a separate matter today, the Assistant Commissioner for Crime, Mr David Tavistock, and the Assistant Commissioner for Ethical Standards, Mr Si Nguyen, announced that fifteen police were suspended from duty over serious corruption allegations. Two of the fifteen are believed to be attached to the Ethical Standards Department. Five of the fifteen were, late this afternoon, charged at a special sittings of the Magistrates' Court at Melbourne and remanded in custody after bail was refused. Offences alleging bribery, theft, assault, the manufacture and distribution of illicit drugs, possession of unregistered firearms and conspiracy were brought against the men. The remaining ten officers have been suspended from duty and their passports seized. The Assistant Commissioners said while their investigations remained ongoing, they were satisfied that for the moment, they had intercepted and interrupted a deeply embedded group of corrupt police engaged in broad scale criminal activity.

Unlike the paedophile story, we can bring you the names and locations of the fifteen police officers who include …'

Pescaro's aged malt whiskey suddenly tasted like vinegar. Every one of the fifteen names was a key source. None had been missed. When earlier he had considered the possibility of a major leak in the Family he had been somewhat sceptical – he was wrong. That all fifteen snouts were identified at the same time suggested a highly placed informer. This, on top of Franse and Gibaldi, was incredibly bad news.

He turned the television off to think. After mentally reviewing the qualities of his *capos* he was as certain as he could be that the informer was none of them. The deaths of Franse and Gibaldi had had an electrifying effect on the Family, particularly his *capos*. None would be so foolish to attack him now. Apart from that, he had spoken to Ed Masseria about a formal handover. He wouldn't be Don for much longer.

He sat reflecting quietly. Gradually, there came a triangulation. At first he thought it preposterous, but the more he reflected, the less it became so.

He knew of Tavistock's secret enquiry but not the extent to which Ethical Standards was involved. They had kept that really tight. Over the past few days he had picked up murmurs from the OPP. These too had involved Tavistock and centred upon a dispute in that office involving a high powered informant. His last piece of information had come from a police source only yesterday – no human remains had been found in Teresa's ruined house.

These discrete pieces of information together with Zimmer's story today led him to the impossible conclusion that Teresa was the informer. *She* had turned and dobbed him in. Ice cold rage swept through him. After everything he had done for her. The loss of his police spies was catastrophic and there was no time to cultivate new ones. He would have to confirm his suspicion by other means. He picked up the telephone, totally pissed off that he had to ring the State Attorney General at home. For all the Judas coin that bastard had received HE should have called HIM days, if not weeks ago.

Chapter
SIXTY- SEVEN

By 6:20 the following morning, David Tavistock had been at work an hour. Not that he was a workaholic, he firmly believed in balancing life between work, family and leisure. Rather, the Marchese case with its poisonous mix of politics and organised crime required his closest scrutiny. That several of Melbourne's most influential names were embroiled in the waste scam was added pressure. Additionally, the Chief Commissioner had asked him to personally guide matters to their proper conclusion. Tavistock appreciated the Chief's confidence as the previous Chief Commissioner – a controversial political appointment – had eroded much of the independence required between government and police. The new Chief was working hard, and against the odds, to restore that independence. An intelligent man, he picked his battles wisely and was fearless in his public confrontations with government. Ever a prudent man however, he demanded, and received, dry ammunition. While the Marchese case had, so far, failed to reveal the full depth of government complicity in the Baker – Aldrittson – Pescaro imbroglio, the Chief was taking no chances. That meant very long days for Tavistock.

He stood, stretched, eased the tension in his neck and walked to his window. From the sixth floor of Crime Department Headquarters he gazed down on the broad tree lined carriageway of St Kilda Road. Spring was imminent. Evidence of bud-burst and the promise of fresh growth peeped from the elm and plane trees. Varied hues of green blushed from the grounds of Melbourne Grammar School and the gardens surrounding the Shrine of Remembrance. A cheeky, but thin film of sunlight gnawed at the night shadows. On the footpath, Tavistock saw pinched pale faces set against the cold. Cold that was accentuated by a blustery wind teasing debris and grit into flurries of nuisance. Two trams lumbered by. Cars and trucks constantly expanded into the space, most with headlights burning. Bicycles, mounted by frantic and colourful riders, darted boldly along the stately boulevard, in and out of traffic like weft in the warp of some giant loom.

At 6:30 his two Commanders, Danniellson and Donovan, entered. He ushered them to the round table. These meetings shaped not only the day but often the week and kept them all in the loop. Tavistock's careful and cryptic session notes were recorded in a day book, open on the table. They were an organic history of clarification, task verification, resource allocation, progress, problems, solutions, personnel matters and incidents throughout the day. The gathering was a familiar ritual.

'Morning lads. Hot fresh coffee on the hob if you want it.' He inclined his head towards the credenza at one side of his office. 'How did our friend Aldrittson react to the story in yesterday's paper Rob?'

'Not to put too fine a point on it Boss, he's shittin' tacks.' Speaking over his shoulder with a lop-sided grin, Danniellson's tone was wry as he moved on the coffee. 'I think he expects Pescaro around every corner. When he rang Saturday morning to see if he could do a deal in exchange for protection, he was terrified. He'd received two death threats that morning, which we have on tape, and when I picked him up,' Danniellson wrinkled his nose at the recall, 'he was a mess. He's safe now though and happy to talk about his shonky deals.'

'Any trouble with prison authorities about getting in to see him Rob?'

Danniellson shook his head. 'No, none, they've been great.' They joined Tavistock at the table with their coffee.

'What about you Paul; everything right with Teresa?'

'Yes Boss, although she's very concerned about the OPP's opposition to the indemnity.' He frowned. 'Do you really think they'll push it to the wire and *insist* on her prosecution?'

'No.' Tavistock was quietly thoughtful for a few moments. 'No. Look, I fully appreciate that Pescaro runs his empire like a multi-national corporation and uses a business model to launder his cash, but when the OPP learns the full scope of what she's given us, and sees the detail, they'll roll over. Remember, so far they've only had some briefing notes and a couple of information sessions. We've barely scratched the surface. There's a hell of a long way to go before we reach prosecution. Anything else?'

'Yeah,' said Donovan nodding. 'Had a call from Witsec yesterday. They took Marchese to see Drummond for the first time since he was shot. They allowed her ten minutes – his shoulder reconstruction is today.'

'Any problems?'

'No Boss, it all went well.' He grinned, 'I understand that her minder – Campbell – said afterwards Marchese was overdosed on happiness.'

'Good,' Tavistock allowed himself a wry smile, 'she deserves a bit of that. Changing direction slightly, have you lads given any thought to the implications of the *Sunday Herald - Sun* article or the ABC news last night?'

Both Commanders nodded.

Danniellson said, 'Yes, I watched the Channel Nine news and thought the story would be a big kick in the teeth to Pescaro. He'll be angry and want to retaliate. He may or may not know about Marchese, but, if he does, he'll be doing everything he can to find her. We still have to be vigilant inside our own camp – I think we should ratchet up security on Marchese and Drummond.'

'Paul?'

'Couldn't agree more Boss. Had exactly the same thought. Another thing too. I chased up Zimmer. She had a lot of precise detail that worried me. Turns out Martin Judd, one of our suspects from Aldrittson's, spilled the beans. She was quite co-operative.

I let her know there's more to come so she's promised to check with us about anything that might potentially compromise the investigation. The deal is that when we can, we give her some early leads. She's pretty good.'

'Don't disagree, but put it through the Media Office first. I have to say I was concerned about all that detail too. Did Zimmer say how she got it?'

'Unusually, she did. She was laughing about it and I have no reason to doubt her – a gossipy afternoon tea between old ladies at her mother's home. Beyond that she wouldn't say more but evidently, one of the attendees was in the know.'

'Okay, back to security. Paul would you see to Marchese and Drummond please? A couple of things, make sure the OIC at Communications is up to speed. If we have to mobilise troops suddenly, I want everything oiled and ready and, if you put extra people at the hospital, make sure they are experienced.'

'Sure.'

'Where are you at with that list of Pescaro's companies you got from Teresa?'

'Well, there's more than fifty of the buggers. Some are incorporated in other states and the others are off-shore. The whole web is extraordinarily complex and as we anticipated, Wyvern and Sprite is the common thread. Main thing is, we are slowly building a paper trail and have a solid beginning. We've enlisted aid from interstate forces and the feds are examining the overseas stuff. Feedback from them is that progress is either snail pace or zilch in places like Nauru, Mexico, Cayman, Lebanon, Colombia and Pakistan. I guess that's why Pescaro chose them. I'm anticipating losses there. Speaking of the feds boy, have they copped a migraine.'

Danniellson, consuming a mouthful of coffee looked concerned. 'Why, what's going on?' he asked.

'Well, they're liaising with ASIC and the ASX over Pescaro's insider trading scam ... You know Boss, if Pescaro had taken another life path, he could still have been hugely wealthy, but honestly so.' Donovan's voice was tinged with a mixture of wonderment and disgust.

Tavistock's eyes gleamed, the corners of his mouth twitching as he suppressed a smile. 'How so Paul? You're not going soft on me are you?'

'Hell no, far from it. It's just that his patience and willingness to study the lessons of history for making money is, to say the least, unusual. His insider trading rort for instance is a classic case of stealth, patience and long term vision.'

'Come on,' said Danniellson laughing, 'don't keep it a secret, maybe we can all get rich.'

Donovan grinned, 'We don't have enough time Sunshine, it's taken Pescaro years. I was talking to an ASIC investigator last Friday. They learned from Marchese that Pescaro was impressed by the amount of private money pumped into Australian development and infrastructure between 1945 and 1960. About two thirds of it came from private enterprise and Pescaro regarded it as his to milk. By the late sixties the mining boom was on, insider trading was rife and there was very little regulatory control. Pescaro was on his way up and saw opportunity. He encouraged soldiers with bright children to put them into universities. By doing that he acquired a suite of skills in law, finance, banking, management and so forth. As these kids qualified they were inserted into big law firms, accountancy practices, stockbroking companies, banks and investment houses.' Donnovan had settled into his chair comfortably and was recounting the tale with a touch of awe, almost as though he were speaking of a friend. 'These kids were then mentored, guided and moved around and up. They matured, acquired influence in their various fields, became directors and were head-hunted for cross directorships in multiple companies, a practice akin to holding the biscuit barrel. They got to choose precisely which piece of "inside information" they wanted to make use of.

Throughout all this the Family team constantly, but not greedily, traded securities and shares using agents to purchase and conceal transactions. Systematically they rorted the system and amassed big money. It was hard to discover and harder to prove. The whole scam was assisted by laws that were pretty much toothless and by regulators who virtually ignored this kind of stuff. The ASIC guy told me that between the sixties and eighties, insider trading scarcely got a look in. The main concern then was market rigging, share price ramping, hoarding and company directors who abused their powers. Pescaro saw this blind spot and siphoned it to the hilt. The profits must have been stupendous because he was virtually unhindered by law or enforcement. The result is that he's been able to weave scores of influential people and companies into his empire, compromise them by quick, illicit wealth and consolidate his own executives in a raft of prominent companies and positions. It's almost impossible to determine who's genuine, who isn't, who's tainted and who isn't. It's been a hard nut to crack. I'm just glad this is a federal headache and not ours. It's been a right bastard,' finished Donovan.

Tavistock said quietly, 'The lesson for us is to be doubly careful with every facet of our investigation. Double, triple check, take nothing for granted and never underestimate our opponents.'

Donovan nodded and continued. 'Bloody oath Boss, I agree with that. And that leads me to the tax trail – polished, complex, tortuous. That's the good news. The downside is that as long as the ATO gets its whack, it's not particularly interested in helping us with other crime. In two of Pescaro's matters it looks as though his minders came to *an arrangement* with the ATO to pay a fat chunk of tax irrespective of income legitimacy. So Boss, the money trail is hard grind for everyone and it's taking time. This week, we're concentrating on the interstate companies. As you might expect, Wyvern and Sprite are obstructive bastards and their firewalls are bloody good.'

Tavistock grinned at Donovan. 'I did warn you – Pescaro is no fool. But, the bonus is that by the time we finish, not only will we have enough to "pot" Pescaro we'll also have enough to shut down Wyvern and Sprite and a few other shady bastards too. I know it's a slog, but keep up the good work and please pass my compliments on to your teams – both of you. I hope to get out soon to tell them personally they're doing a great job. Let me know if you need more resources. The Chief is prepared to take Meadows on in a public shit fight if necessary – he's rabid about all this public corruption.'

'Rob, what's on your plate this week?'

'We're still working the paedophile thing. Chasing down victims and offenders and trying to locate Australian porno sellers and buyers on the internet. The Sexual Offences Squad has successfully uncovered a clutch of internet stalkers who've been pursuing kids through chat rooms. Some contacts have actually resulted in physical meetings and in one case, a sixteen year old girl went home terrified after meeting her cyber "pal." Fortunately, she had the good sense to tell her parents who then told us. From that we've established another tentacle of Baker's group. We are also concentrating on fall-out from the twelve we arrested yesterday. We've started hauling in various company directors named by Aldrittson too. These guys have been paying or receiving kickbacks and are linked to his money trail. We know he's still keeping stuff to himself and we haven't told him about the documents Marchese gave us. That's interesting too because quite a few of her papers don't match what he's provided. We think he's trying to preserve a nest egg somewhere. Optimistic bastard isn't he? Anyway, he can play his game, we'll just keep working through it all. By and large though, he's been pretty co-operative. He's a very frightened man. The two blokes I sent to Ethical Standards will be there for weeks, maybe months. We need to keep that under review because they'll want more bodies – it's a can of worms that just keeps expanding.

Corrupt cops, Mafia links to Telstra, the Courts, OPP and, we believe but haven't been able to confirm yet, the ATO. It's like Pescaro's had this great invisible lasso around us for years which has enabled him to keep five steps ahead all the time. Finally, I sent two young colts to help the EPA, a couple of Divisional detectives. Brought them in for a briefing, gave them everything we had and cut 'em loose. They check in every few days with Johnny Morton, my Super. The EPA is grateful and these young fellas have got their teeth into something different and important. Using Marchese's information, they went straight for the jugular and nailed a bloke called David Mitchellson. He's right up there in the EPA food chain but not quite at the top. He rolled over quicksmart and they've got him for receiving bribes and falsifying EPA records regarding toxic spills. It appears as though Jack Aldrittson paid him around a million dollars over the last five years. That sent some hairy old ripples through the place let me tell you.' Daniellson was serious as he briefed Tavistock and referred to various comments in his notebook throughout his delivery.

Tavistock nodded and smiled at his men. 'Thanks lads. Seems everything so far is on track. This is a big task, but so far, so good. Well done. I've been keeping tabs on the '75 Marchese and Pescaro murders. Teresa's DNA has been matched to a sample retained at the Coroner's Court and we can now categorically state that the headless corpse in the car boot at Sorrento was Alfredo Marchese. The Homicide Squad has tracked down siblings of Angelina Pescaro, nee Petrosino, in Italy. They are not, nor ever have been, Mafia. They did ask questions after Angelina's death but ran into a Mafia fear squad. Since then they've remained silent. Arrangements are being made to obtain DNA samples from a brother and sister of Angelina. We'll compare them with our mortuary sample and once we have results, we'll probably start moving on Pescaro for those murders. After all this time it's not going to be easy to prove, especially as the only witness, Santini, is dead. But, Homicide is up for the challenge. Paul, it just occurred to me, would you have an encouraging word to the people at the Alfred Hospital? Make sure their CCTV is top notch at every point – no weak spots. Let them know we think there's a heightened risk of trouble and if anything does occur, to go along with what's happening. We don't want dead or damaged heroes – there's been enough of that already. Tell them we'll be upgrading Andy's security. Also, double check that all our electronic surveillance of Pescaro is up to scratch. I don't want any stuff ups.'

'Okay Boss, will do.'

'Right lads, thanks for your time. Keep me posted.'

Chapter
SIXTY- EIGHT

By 8:45 a.m., Pescaro's *capos* were solemnly assembled around the antique French table in his dining room at *Villa Rosa*. He had turned on his white noise and anti-bugging equipment and instructed his men to turn off their mobile phones.

His mien was dark, foreboding and tinged with a trace of regret. He was not looking forward to this meeting but quickly went straight to the heart of the matter. 'My friends, we are under serious threat. We must unite more strongly than ever to deal with this threat. That is vital now. At the time Franse and Gibaldi left us I was concerned by the amount of information the press was publishing on matters close to us. Specifically, the Aldrittson plant and our waste business. Mixed up in that were also stories of Ben Aldrittson and his foolish behaviour. I thought someone wanted to hurt us. At first I was uncertain. However, with Tavistock leading something special and after the arrest of my police sources, then the swoop on Baker's paedophile ring, my uncertainty disappeared. I rang a very important source last night. He told me they have Teresa in Witness Protection – she's singing like a canary.'

Growls and mutters of disbelief and anger rippled around the table.

'I apologise my brothers. I know some of you objected to her becoming *Consigliere* and thought she was getting an armchair ride upwards. But, that was never the case. Teresa *is* a woman of remarkable talent and intelligence and I believed she would be good for us. So did Nardo. However, that does us, and me, no credit now. I thought long about her motivation and concluded it relates to personal matters involving her father back in 1975. The sad part is that as a result of those events, Teresa's mother took her own life because *she* couldn't live *without* Alfredo, despite what he had done. My opinion was confirmed last night when I learned Tavistock is controlling Teresa. That relationship explains why all my snouts got pinched at once and means this investigation could inflict huge fucking damage to us. We must act on several fronts simultaneously. We have to penetrate the Witness Protection system, find out where she is and get rid of her. Drummond has to go too. I don't know what that prick's role is in all this but somehow he and Teresa hooked up and he's been a thorn in my side ever since. All of you need to fireproof your activities. I've put systems in place and had word from Magnus Wyvern that Tavistock is pressing hard in unusual places and soon, if he keeps going, he *will* get results. He never gives up. I detest the man but I have great respect for his ability. All of you will have to assist me with information from your own copper sources. Be extremely discreet – I don't want your blokes going the same way as my bastards. Be prepared to cut them loose at the slightest hint of trouble. Aldrittson can hurt us too. I don't know where he is; he seems to have disappeared.' Pescaro gave a tiny smile. 'Mind you, that was after I threatened him for arranging Nardo's death. In a way, dealing with the Russians was easier than this: at least you knew what to expect. Dealing with Tavistock is like dealing with a Chameleon – he constantly changes his tactics and style to camouflage his attack. Finally, talk to your soldiers. Make sure they all know that, for the moment, we tread softly. We've got to get Tavistock off balance while we hunt Teresa and Aldrittson. Never forget: no witness, no case. Your snitches are going to have to work hard. Pressure them any way at all if they resist. Suggestions anyone?'

'Don Pescaro, I've got someone near the witness protection mob,' said Alphonse Catena. 'I'll see what he can do. Mind you, the bastard will try to rob me blind, but he'll probably come up with the goods and not be suspected by his copper mates.'

Pescaro nodded. 'Good Al, see what you can get.'

Sal Moretti spoke, his voice and manner thoughtful. 'I was

wondering about Aldrittson, Don Pescaro. We should check the prison system. If he's not in police protection, and you scared the shit out of him, my bet is the high security wing. He can't do a runner because the cops have his passport and we could find him in five minutes in any other state. All that tells me he's done a deal with the cops and is probably hiding in prison.'

'Good thought Sal. I'll bring that up with my contact. Ed's been looking for him over the last few hours and it's like he's gone up in smoke. Now, one last piece of news. I decided some months back to step down and recent events have confirmed my decision. My successor was originally to have been Nardo Santini then, after his death, Milo Barracusa.' He noted the surprised looks at his disclosure and idly wondered if they thought he would remain Don until death. 'I wanted to deal with Franse's treachery and then step down. Now we have Teresa. Obviously there is no right time to appoint a successor but, I put you on notice – I have spoken to Ed Masseria.' He was interrupted by a short burst of well wishing, confirmation that his choice was popular.

'I feel it only right,' he resumed, 'to see this mess through. But the way is clear for a smooth transition to my successor. I want to show Ed a few things and all of you have my blessing to work with and confide in him as you do with me. Review your operations; draw back; speak to your people; warn them. Think about methods for upsetting Tavistock and put your ideas into practice. But – make sure I know. One good way is allegations. If any soldiers get pinched, especially by detectives, they are to make allegations as standard practice – assaults, verballing, theft, fabricated evidence – doesn't matter. Anything. Complaints clog the police system internally and often work their way into the courts. They can stop court cases, damage a cop's reputation and get the public offside. You might even want to sacrifice a few soldiers as part of that strategy, however, make sure you look after their families. One last thing – I don't know how we'll fare but our organisation has survived for centuries. No amount of police or government action can remove us because wherever there are opportunities to make money outside the law, our lives and our way are guaranteed by the weakness of human behaviour.'

Chapter
SIXTY- NINE

The regimentation, sounds and smells of prison were getting to Aldrittson. Like the invisible pain of a migraine, they lacerated him. Yet he felt safe and had time to think.

A crucial snippet gleaned from Danniellson was that police were still unaware of his role in Santini's death. They had asked many questions about Santini but only in the context of work for his father. They had also asked about the initials, S.J. and he had referred them to his gym. He explained his use of the owner, Spencer Johnson, as a fact finder for his political life. Johnson had been a federal cop with a huge informant network. It was Johnson, he said, who unearthed Baker's paedophilia. When questioned over the link between himself, Santini and Johnson, he told a part truth and said he suspected, but wasn't sure, that Santini was a Mafia plant. He told Danniellson his father was linked to Pescaro from years gone by. Neither of them knew Santini was Pescaro's man until Johnson found out. Soon after, Santini died. The death, he told Danniellson, was due to differences between Pescaro and the Russian Mafiya – at least, that's what he believed.

Danniellson had pressed hard about the last time he had seen Johnson. He could only say weeks ago. Johnson, as far as he knew, was in the UK and Europe for body sculpting competitions. In the end, he decided that as long as police were unaware of his part in Santini's death, there was no reason to rat on Johnson. He could still be useful to him in the future.

It was now September 15, two days before the election. From gaol, with television and newspapers his only guide to Meadows' fate, he thought the result could be close. Daily he watched Government popularity slide as both Opposition and media landed savage blows to an exposed underbelly – ethics, transparency and

Ministerial accountability. Public confidence was maimed by examples of negligence, corruption, malaise and incompetence. The Government was living its worst dream – the public had stopped listening and turned it's back upon Meadows.

Aldrittson knew he had probably triggered this slide but felt no remorse – politics worked like this. His pain, when he analysed it, stemmed from the discovery of his own misconduct and, in his mind, Meadows unworthy treatment of him.

His reverie was interrupted by the hissing, electronic clunk of the cell door. He rolled to his side, head propped on his hand. A tall, thin warder stood in the doorway but did not enter the cell. He was new to Aldrittson and said nothing. The silence extended languidly and became taut and menacing. Disconcerted, Aldrittson barked, 'Who are you? What do you want?'

The warder nodded slowly, imperceptibly and said, so softly Aldrittson had to strain to hear, 'I came to check on your wellbeing. Giuseppe said I would find you here.'

Aldrittson's reaction was instantaneous: colour drained from his face and his gut lurched. He sat up terror-struck, breathing hard, body quivering. The warder coldly observed and, nodding slowly said softly, 'I'll be back.' He closed the door gently and left Aldrittson on the edge of hysteria.

Fox, in Johnson's absence, was running the Sunset Fitness Club. They were in regular contact and careful about their conversations. They had agreed not to obstruct police but neither would they help. Their role would be benign. When the police came looking for Johnson, Fox had not been of much help. He provided Spencer's mobile number knowing that Tanya had already given it to them. He could only say that Spencer was overseas competing and, as usual, he had stepped in to manage. Tanya could confirm this was a normal pattern over the last three or four years. Nor was it unusual, he told them, for Johnson to be away on these competitions for anywhere between two and six months. Club and tax records would confirm that too.

At 5:30 p.m. Fox hung a sign on the door advising patrons that due to a personal emergency, the Club would be closed until 7:30. He showered, changed and drove to the Alfred Hospital to see an old SAS mate admitted for rampant prostate cancer.

After finding a vacant spot against the basement wall, Fox parked, smiling at the antics of two men in a dark car two rows forward. Struggling to be discreet, they awkwardly donned white coats before getting out of their car. Suddenly, the spell broke and Fox's sixth sense went into overdrive. Their behaviour was most unusual.

He opened his door quietly, took the phone from its console, eased himself into the space between the car and the wall, crouched and watched.

Stepping from their car they casually, but carefully, examined the basement and cars cruising for spaces. They missed Fox. Sauntering towards the lifts, they looked every inch young professional doctors, particularly when one took a stethoscope from his pocket and hung it around his neck. Fox didn't believe the charade – they were men with a dark purpose. Real doctors parked in the reserved medical area, didn't dress in their car or scan faces and passing cars so keenly.

Discreetly, Fox followed. At the lift, with half a dozen others, he nonchalantly, joined them, inwardly acknowledging their brazen confidence. Short hair, clean shaven, neat shirts and ties, sharp creases, average height and build. At level six they stepped out, nodded to each other and walked in different directions. Fox alighted too but stayed in the foyer to read the directory. Slowly he followed the man he had labelled "Stethoscope" who was striding towards the Nurses Station. When he turned the corner to the Station, Fox accelerated swiftly and quietly after him.

Stethoscope continued past the Station. Fox watched from the corner and saw a uniformed policeman sitting on a chair half way along the corridor. As Stethoscope approached, the policeman stood to face him. The second "doctor" entered the corridor from its opposite end and began to glide down behind the policeman. Stethoscope moderated his pace while the second man closed silently. Stethoscope picked up pace again, waving to attract attention. It was a simple plan for ambush.

The man from behind removed a cord from his pocket. The policeman moved towards Stethoscope who engaged him in conversation. Too far away to help and not knowing if they were armed, Fox pulled back behind the corner, punched 000 into his mobile and asked for police. When the operator responded Fox said tersely, 'Listen up. I'm on level six, Surgical, Alfred Hospital. A copper on guard duty here is being attacked by two men dressed like doctors. I'm going to help. Send back up.' He clicked off and peered around the corner to see the second man loop the cord around the policeman's throat while Stethoscope delivered a vicious blow to his belly. Winded, unable to draw breath, the policeman was quickly subdued. Stethoscope took a syringe from his pocket and jabbed the policeman who sagged to the floor unconscious. The two "doctors" quickly removed him to the staff toilets and shoved him inside.

The whole incident had taken a little over a minute and incredibly, nobody else had appeared on the floor. The two men returned to the previously guarded door, paused, then confidently strode inside.

Fox had no idea who was in there but knew that someone was about to receive unorthodox treatment. He bolted down the corridor skidding to a halt before the door. Gently, he cracked it open. Another policeman lay prone just inside. He opened the door to see the men advancing upon a form in bed at the far end of the room, a form heavily wrapped in bandages and struggling to rise.

Fox emitted an ear-splitting yell and charged into the room

at full tilt. The two men whirled, bracing for attack. Frantically one tried to get something from his pocket. Fox, bent double, covered the distance at lightning speed. Two metres from them he threw himself to the floor and slid on his side, one leg drawn back. His foremost foot slammed into Stethoscope's shoes at which instant Fox unleashed his bent leg to deliver a powerful kick to the kneecap. There was a sharp crack and Stethoscope fell to the floor, deathly pale, writhing in agony and screeching.

Fox twisted, rolled and still on his back, delivered a mighty double footed kick upwards to the gut of the second man whose gun had snagged on his coat pocket. Bouncing to his feet, Fox grabbed the convulsing man's gun arm and broke it across his knee at the elbow as though it were a piece of kindling. The gun fell to the floor, the man screamed and fainted.

Taking a handkerchief from his pocket, Fox lifted the weapon from the floor and took it to the bandaged man whose nameplate proclaimed: *Andy Drummond*. Fox's dusky features broke into a wry grin as he realised the irony of the situation.

He said, 'You'll be needing this. You should be okay, I've called reinforcements.'

Drummond's eyes had not left Fox's face since observing the amazing spectacle. A frown creased his brow, questions blazed in his eyes. 'Are you a copper?' he croaked hoarsely.

'No.'

'Have we met before? You seem familiar.'

Fox's grin widened. He said laconically, 'Not formally, no. Take better care of yourself. I've got to be off.' He walked from the room. Watching him leave, Drummond's mind flew to a rain soaked June night in Collingwood when he saw a man roll from beneath a car and walk into the night. There was something about him reminiscent of that man. Only after the door had closed did Drummond ring the emergency bell for help.

Within minutes, two nurses arrived. One stopped to assess the policeman on the floor, the other came to Drummond, eyes wide, stepping around the groaning men on the floor near his bed.

'What happened here?' cried Nurse Siu Lee.

'These two blokes,' rasped Drummond nodding to the men on the floor, 'came in here, belted the policeman and came for me. One had this gun.' He nodded to the revolver nestled in his lap. 'Look around, you'll find a syringe on the floor.' He pointed to *Stethoscope,* 'That fella had it ready to stick into me. A third man ran in, knocked 'em rotten and left. What happened to the policeman outside?'

Siu Lee shrugged. 'I don't know.'

With that, two detectives and a huge uniformed Sergeant rushed into the room. The Sergeant appraised the scene as he came up to Drummond. 'Sergeant Gunter Schmidt from Prahran. What the hell has been going on here?' Drummond repeated his story then handed Schmidt the weapon.

Schmidt said, 'Did you know this bloke who helped you?'

'Never seen him before in my life,' lied Drummond.

'I thought there was a copper outside this room,' said Schmidt.

'There was,' whispered Drummond, 'he seems to be missing.'

Schmidt turned to the detectives. 'Check out the rooms off the corridor would you Sam. Start with the toilets, they're closest. Derek, find the Administration Centre and see what's on their CCTV.'

The door pushed open and Paul Donovan walked in. Drummond watched him assess the scene as he walked towards them. 'G'day Andy, Schmiddy. I've had a full briefing on the way and extra troops aren't far behind. We'll get these two characters off to be repaired ...'

Stethoscope snarled from the floor, 'You fuckin' bastards are going to cop every fuckin' writ known to man for the pain and fuckin' suffering you've given us, wait and see. Your miserable fuckin' lives and shitful treatment will be all over TV tonight and headlines tomorrow. You're nothin' but fuckin' scum.'

' … and then we'll have a crack at finding out who they are, why they were here and who they're working for,' continued Donovan. 'But, from the sound of those remarks, perhaps they don't need any treatment. Do *you* know who they are Schmiddy? Andy?'

As Drummond shook his head a doctor arrived with aides, trolleys and four uniformed police. The villains were lifted onto the trolleys, handcuffed to the side rails and wheeled out leaving a trail of poisonous invective behind them.

'To be truthful Boss,' said Schmidt to Donovan, 'I'm only just ahead of you and I wanted Mr Drummond's story before hearing what they had to say.'

Donovan said grimly, 'I think we've just been dealing with Pescaro, though we'll be scratching for evidence to prove it. What's on the CCTV?'

'I don't know yet. I sent Derek Connelly off to find out,' said Schmidt.

Sam Bowden and Derek Connelly returned together, the latter holding a tape cassette.

'Do you two know Commander Donovan?' asked Schmidt. They nodded. 'What can you tell us then?' Schmidt enquired.

Connelly said, 'The tape says it all. Footage starts at basement three with our assailants getting into the lift. Mr Drummond's rescuer joined them there with several others. It's possible this bloke saw something in the car park. It looks pretty clear from the tape he was tracking that foul mouthed prick with the broken leg, the one with the stethoscope. Sam says our police guard in the toilets was injected with a sedative. He's also got a nasty ligature burn around his neck. The copper in this room has a fractured jaw. What did they clobber him with?'

Drummond spoke up. 'I thought I saw something on the hand of the bloke with the gun – knuckle dusters or something.

They might be on the floor. I didn't see it again after my "helper" attacked them.'

'Anything more Derek?' asked Schmidt.

'Only that our good Samaritan has already disappeared. Seems he didn't hang around so we don't know who he is or why he was here.'

Donovan took the tape and said, 'We'll know more when we look at this. I think we'd better get the scenes-of-crimes blokes in and formalise guards for those two villains. So let's wind it up. Andy, do you want me to let your friend know what's happened?'

'Yes, I'd appreciate that. Thanks Paul.'

'Right. Schmiddy – stay here with Andy until we get replacement guards and take a statement about this evening's events. Organise a blood sample from that drugged guard too. It might turn up something useful. The A/C and I will discuss security arrangements and we'll keep you informed. Are you cool with that Andy?'

'Yep. They never touched me, I'm fine.'

Chapter
SEVENTY

Tavistock was jaded, it had been a long day. He rose from his desk and walked to the credenza. 'Don't know about you blokes, but after all these goings on today, I need something a bit stronger than coffee. What will it be, scotch or beer?'

'A cold beer for me Boss,' said Donovan.

'I'll join you in a whiskey thanks, Boss,' replied Danniellson.

Tavistock opened a door in his credenza to reveal a small refrigerator and removed an ice cold *Boag*. From the cupboard next to it he took two squat crystal glasses and a bottle of *Johnny Walker Black*.

He returned to his desk with the drinks and set them down on one corner. 'Help yourselves.' He raised his glass: 'To the incarceration of bastards,' he said with a weary grin.

Danniellson and Donovan smiled and raised their drinks with him.

'Okay Rob, a brief recap so I've got it clear. The Chief wants an update at 2030 and I want it right.' They could hear fatigue in his voice and saw the shadows under his eyes had deepened. Even so, his dogged personality would never yield to a villain like Pescaro and despite his weariness, his briefing to the Chief would be crisp and accurate.

'In brief Boss,' commenced Danniellson, 'Aldrittson was visited in gaol today by one of Pescaro's hit men. Tony Rosario is inside for a series of stabbings. A woman came to see Rosario on visitor's day and soon after he arranged for a warder named Levine to be paid $45,000. Rosario borrowed Levine's uniform and got the codes and keys to visit Aldrittson. I don't know what they were thinking, or why they even thought they could get away with it. Come to that, since Rosario got to Aldrittson, I'm buggered if I know why he didn't kill him there and then. Anyway, we've got most of the action on the gaol's CCTV, we've got Levine, who's already rolled over, Rosario's in solitary and Aldrittson is now gibbering in the New South Wales high security bin. He seems a broken man.'

Tavistock had settled into his chair and closed his eyes, both hands across his stomach holding the tumbler. 'Thanks Rob, good result. Paul?'

'I see today as a high point for us Boss. I think pressure forced our opponent into error. I mean, really – that stunt in the gaol was bloody stupid. So was the attack on Drummond. Although, it did lead to the arrest of two of Argolia's men – Silvio Iacocca and Francis Rivera. Apart from complaining, they've said nothing since we reeled them in. We even had to apply to the court to get their prints because of their behaviour. Made no difference of course, we got an Order, took prints and DNA and confirmed their identities. Their bloody complaints are astounding. Allegations against Gunter Schmidt and me for assault, fabricating evidence, planting a firearm, theft of personal monies, destruction of a mobile phone and on it goes. The firearm is at Forensics and I had a call just before coming here. Early indications suggest it is the weapon used on Drummond at Heathcote – a fifteen centimetre .357 Smith and Wesson magnum revolver. We'll probably clean up that shooting too. As we speak, Argolia is being interviewed downstairs. We don't expect much, especially with that supercilious Lorton – bloody – Sprite present. But, bringing him in was more about sending a message to Pescaro than anything else. We've decided to leave Drummond where he is with extra security. At most, the hospital want him only another two or three days. After that, he can join Marchese and we'll arrange outpatient care. He's comfortable with that. Lastly, we've re-interviewed Colin Fox. He was the bloke who came to Drummond's aid. When we checked the hospital CCTV footage we connected him with Spencer Johnson. Interesting fellow – cool as ice. Ex-SAS, bit unusual for an Aboriginal I think. Claims he went to the Alfred to visit a mate recovering from surgery. We checked and it's true. Says he saw Rivera and Iacocca and reckoned they were up to no good. He rang 000, called for back-up, saw what they did to our guards then went in and demolished them. We've checked it out and everything tallies. There's no link we can find between Drummond and Fox and the military will confirm tomorrow if their paths ever crossed in the Army. But … my gut tells me Fox is somehow involved. He works either for or with Johnson who's poncing around in some bloody body sculpting competition overseas. Christ, the prick's over fifty and still reckons he's got it.'

Tavistock opened one eye which twinkled with mischief. 'Wait till you reach my age Paul – you'll find chronology has little to do with how old you *feel*'.

They all laughed. 'Sorry Boss, forgot you're in the zone. Anyway, Johnson has worked for Aldrittson and with Fox linked to Johnson and Aldrittson to Pescaro, I am very suspicious. Unfortunately it's only instinct. Fox was not unhelpful, very much in control but … I felt he was laughing at us. Like he knows a bloody sight more than we do. He's likeable enough, nothing hostile or unpleasant about him. That's it.'

'Good, thanks Paul. Homicide had a break today too. A blood sample found in the car with the bodies of Franse and Gibaldi was different to theirs. DNA testing matches it to a very nasty piece of work called Angelo Tomasetti. He's one of Masseria's soldiers and Masseria is one of Pescaro's *capos*. Homicide have got a couple more things to clarify but they're ready to drag Tomasetti tomorrow morning. So, good news all round. Certainly enough to keep the Chief happy. Anyone for another drink?'

Chapter **SEVENTY- ONE**
October, 2006

Monday, October 30, 2006. Thirteen months had passed since the failed attempt on Drummond's life at the Alfred Hospital. Much had happened.

The State election of September 17, 2005 had brought a tortured victory to Labor's Clive Crystal. Exit polls disclosed a level of hostility towards the Meadows government not shown since the dumping of Premier Kennett in 1999. Animosity towards Meadows was fuelled by perceptions of corruption, sexual misconduct, maladministration and self-interest. Although a distorted belief, it was widely held. Thus, while Crystal had a slender majority, he was compelled to negotiate with a large number of prickly Independents holding the balance of power. A good result for democracy, a blow to the Party system.

For months after the election, sullenness had lain like a dark stain across the community. Countless letters, editorial pieces, radio talk back, current affairs programs and various political analysts teased out four elements of governance shouting for reform: responsible leadership, ethical behaviour among politicians, transparency and accountability, and demonstrable representative democracy. The populace was fed-up with the sleazy, behind-scenes machinations occurring between big business and government, practices starkly exposed *after* the election.

When Premier Crystal examined the Aldrittson waste scheme and understood its breathtaking scope and application, he conceded its brilliance. As a novice Premier under pressure however, he also knew that to endorse it would be political suicide. For the life of the present government at least, it would be shelved. Jakob Kindler's solar energy program on the other hand, was overwhelmingly supported.

Aldrittson avoided the humiliating public stocks of court by pleading guilty to all charges and foreclosing on a trial. His barrister, James Sylke, QC, dismissed himself and left Aldrittson to his fate. That fate was eighteen years gaol with a minimum of fifteen. Life in custody compelled a name change and for reasons of protection, interstate imprisonment. He remained unconnected to Santini's death and, for his own reasons, Pescaro too remained silent.

Spencer Johnson remained overseas allowing Fox to run the Sunset Fitness Club. At the same time Fox gently nurtured a mutually satisfying relationship with Johnson's receptionist, Tanya Taylor. Every so often, when time allowed, Danniellson dropped in to chat with Fox. His suspicion of Fox's connection to Aldrittson's dirty games never disappeared, but Fox's laconic manner, dry wit and good nature were beginning to wear Danniellson down – they were in danger of becoming friends.

And on this day, Monday October 30, 2006, committal proceedings against Giuseppe Antonio Pescaro commenced. The charges were legion and other protagonists such as ASIC, the Federal Police, Australian Customs Service and the Australian Taxation Office were all circling for chunks of Pescaro's wiry old frame.

Wyvern and Sprite had done a masterful job building a bulwark of legal entanglements around the mighty Pescaro Empire. Yet despite their formidable efforts, that Empire had become too big and too convoluted even for them to effectively manage. Through dogged application and remorseless persistence, small chinks in the labyrinthine defence were exposed by Tavistock's multi-disciplinary team of lawyers, forensic accountants, business analysts, computer gurus, health and environmental experts and police investigators. The chinks had become cracks, and the cracks valleys. As a result, Wyvern and Sprite found themselves on the back foot defending their own existence before the Bar Council on multiple allegations of unethical and unlawful practice. On this day however, they were still tenuously operational and still shielding their valued, and of course, well paying client.

At the top of the list were four charges of murder against Pescaro for the deaths of his twenty-two year old wife, Angelina, Alfredo Marchese, Vito Franse and Roberto Gibaldi. Next were three charges of conspiracy to kill Andy Drummond followed by a host of accessory charges among which were money laundering, conspiracy, receiving, deception, prostitution, drug dealing, gun-running, bribery, *and* unlawful waste disposal. The Vors' deaths and their disposal via the Bayswater destructor had, so far, remained off the police radar.

Wyvern and Sprite, optimistically aiming for victory, opposed everything the Prosecution suggested which might have shortened proceedings. The Crown case had upwards of 500 witnesses – Wyvern and Sprite intended to mercilessly test each and every one. Their approach was pedantic, comprehensive and powerfully argued. Concession and loss were foreign to their philosophy.

Tavistock gritted his teeth, addressed his troops and told them to be patient, to stay focussed, to de-personalise matters, and above all, to stick to the truth. This case would be an ultra-marathon. It would also, he said, be a trial that besmirched the Force's reputation and diminished police standing in public eyes because of the depth of corruption unearthed among its members. They had to be mentally and emotionally prepared to withstand that.

The safety of witnesses caused Tavistock serious concern. If eliminated, their case would be substantially, if not irrevocably weakened. Prominent among these witnesses were Marchese, Drummond, Judd, Aldrittson, Mitchellson and several others.

During the thirteen months it had taken to assemble Pescaro's prosecution, Andy and Teresa were together in witness protection and, like Aldrittson, were interstate. They saw Aleisha Campbell regularly and had developed great affection for her. She and the Witsec team were fully aware of Pescaro's treacherous tentacles inside and outside the Force. For them it was a matter of professional pride that no one would ever suspect, let alone know, Drummond's and Teresa's location.

With the committal about to start, the pair returned to Melbourne. Their evidence would be presented by video link from protected sites that could change daily. Knowledge and selection of these sites was vested solely in court officials. If a personal appearance was required at the hearing court, it was easily arranged. The threat to witness security was extreme and everybody fully understood the gravity of the simple dictum: *no witness, no case.*

Pescaro's committal attracted national media interest. It was a case that had vacuumed up politicians, members of the judiciary, highly respected Melbourne families, government and local government officials, police, lawyers, accountants and many ordinary people too. The clean-up had filled a dirt bag with malfeasance, depravity, corruption, greed, politics and power. The promise of explosive headlines, stories of inside deals, intrigue and falls from grace was straining at the leash of fulfilment.

Yet, for a day so auspicious in Victoria's criminal history, it began with the mundane process of determining legal proprieties. Counsel representing the army of maligned and interested introduced themselves, named their clients, listed their interests then paid attention to the charges levelled against Pescaro. The remainder of the day was consumed by legal argument over whether he would remain on bail or suffer its revocation. Bail had not been a problem to date: Pescaro was a model defendant and reported graciously every two days to Prahran police station.

On the weekend prior to committal hearings however, federal police presented Tavistock with evidence of three confirmed accounts in overseas banks which, painstakingly, had been traced back to Pescaro. They totalled $130 million. The Prosecution argued that as this information was previously unknown, and certainly not disclosed, the probability of Pescaro's flight had significantly increased. An embarrassing precedent for this lay in the form of drug lord, Tony Mokbel. Unresolved by day's end, Pescaro found himself whisked off to the Remand Centre for a night in custody. Strike one against his legal team, thought Tavistock who had come to sit quietly at the back of the court for the session that afternoon. He watched Pescaro, stony-faced and flint-eyed, marched off between two prison guards.

The following morning Chief Magistrate, Julia Deschamps, ruled in favour of continuing Pescaro's bail.

And so the case proceeded with lengthy opening addresses from both prosecution and defence, an infrequent practice for a committal. Over the next days, weeks and months, the case against Pescaro was meticulously constructed. Yet for every 'i' dotted and 't' crossed, either Magnus Wyvern or Lorton Sprite shone in their efforts to eviscerate the proof and offer counter explanations. Gifted destroyers in cross examination, they appeared to win many of the technical arguments. Their strategy was simple and effective – clever tactics to trip witnesses and tarnish credibility combined with reasoned argument to exclude damaging evidence on the grounds of it being highly prejudicial.

As Donovan and Danniellson watched the sham day after day, concern grew and they wondered if the defence and prosecution were talking of the same defendant so different was the picture presented by each side. While Tavistock grimly reported progress to the Chief Commissioner and Force Command, he still believed that justice would prevail. Nothing could shake his faith that their prosecution would do anything other than succeed.

Eventually, four months after proceedings had commenced, Teresa took the witness stand. Lorton Sprite was ferocious in his demand that she be brought to court to face the man who had nurtured, guided, employed and loved her; the man she now falsely accused of murder. Magistrate Deschamps dismissed his application and informed the court that witness Marchese's evidence would, like several others, be delivered by video from a remote and secure court site.

Sprite staged a livid and blustering attack upon her decision and threatened to obtain a ruling from a higher court. He subsided, however, when Deschamps made plain she had given deep consideration to Lord Hutton's opinion that video evidence was required to be of such relevance and importance to the Crown that *to proceed without it would be unfair, especially if the process itself did not prejudice the defendant's interests.* In reaching her decision Deschamps said she would be balancing protection of the witness against any unfairness to the defendant from video evidence. She remarked that if Counsel had bothered to read the case of R – v – Lynne from the Victorian Supreme Court of 2003 it was there noted that *mere use of technology need not (and must not) be to the detriment of the highest standards of justice.* Icily, Deschamps said since she was satisfied that those elements had been properly met, Marchese would *not* be brought into court. She would, as arranged, provide evidence from a remote site.

Over the next three days, through a television screen, Teresa's evidence-in-chief was delivered to a curious court in a calm, clear and impartial manner. Her presentation was detailed, logical and damning. And then came the surgical probing from an implacable, silver-tongued warrior at law, Lorton Sprite. Sprite, a short puffy little man with a shaved head and cherubic face dressed with such perfection that he gleamed like a freshly minted coin. His voice, like his appearance, was silky and mellow and disguised the sharpness of his interrogation.

He began by asking questions about the work she undertook for Pescaro, by drawing her into the maw of Mafia life, by painting her as a willing, complicit member of the criminal underworld. He queried her about the money she managed for Pescaro, the investments and the profits from those investments. Sprite confirmed with Teresa that Pescaro trusted her financial and business skills to

the extent that she had *carte blanche* to invest where she saw fit.
She agreed that she knew and used secret banking accounts and
systems in other countries, that monies in those accounts were the
proceeds of crime and that, in truth, she was in charge of money
laundering. She admitted under cross examination that twice she
had broken into Aldrittson's flat. Slowly and systematically, Sprite
built a moat of admissions around Teresa for acts that were either
outright offences or would make her an accessory, before or after
the fact.

'And tell me Ms Marchese, what charges have the police laid
against you?'

'None sir.'

'None, yet you readily admit to these crimes in this court. Is
that correct?'

'Yes sir.'

'Why is that Ms Marchese? Why have the police *not* charged
you with all these offences?'

'I have been indemnified against prosecution.'

'So, you've made a cheap deal to avoid prosecution. What have
the police paid you to give this evidence?'

'Objection.' Prosecutor Dougal McIntosh leapt to his feet
and interjected vehemently. 'Your Worship, my learned colleague
is accusing the witness of accepting bribes from the police. This is
patently untrue. We explained to this court in our opening address
that she is under protection; in that context she is receiving police
care and support. That is not a bribe.'

'Your Worship,' said Sprite patiently, 'my point is that this witness
is nothing more than a common informer receiving a gratuity from
police to give evidence. It is my contention that evidence presented
by police in this manner is tainted and therefore, fully open to
question. In my view, questions of the kind I am putting go to the
very heart of this witness's credit.'

'I understand your argument Mr Sprite,' said Deschamps coolly, 'but unfortunately for you, Parliament has seen fit to legislate a Witness Protection Scheme into being, and this witness is part of that scheme. As such, she must receive protection and that will take the form, at minimum, of shelter and sustenance. Are you suggesting more than that Mr Sprite?'

'Your Worship, what I am suggesting is that *anything* of value given to a witness in return for testimony is a bribe. It matters not whether that "valuable" is provided by some private person or the state, it is purchase of testimony. I say that is tainted and I say the state, through its Witness Protection Scheme is party to perverting the course of justice.'

'Answer me this Mr Sprite: what is your alternative? Do you consider witness protection unnecessary? You already know from the Prosecutor's opening address that one witness in this case has been attacked three times and sustained horrific injuries. In your view, does state provided protection counter the validity of evidence from such witnesses?'

'Your Worship I must agree, in light of what you say, there are times when protection *is* necessary. However, I am arguing that the very principle of providing protection is an inducement. Because it is an inducement I am entitled to fully explore this witness's credit. That is all.'

'Mr Sprite, you may test the witness's credit but you will *not* do it through the medium of the Witness Protection Program. That is a legislated Program and I take judicial notice of its intent and functionality. You will desist in this line of questioning.'

'Very well your Worship.' Sprite was not in the least rebuffed. 'Ms Marchese, would you outline for us please the agreements you have made with the police for compensation to appear here?'

'Objection. That matter is confidential between the Chief Commissioner of Police and the witness; it is a matter protected by law. My colleague knows that your Worship. I submit that in spite of your instruction, he is clutching at straws in trying to discredit a very credible witness.'

'Sustained Mr McIntosh, but save me your speeches. Get on with it Mr Sprite. Stick to the instruction I just gave you. If you continue in this manner I shall be forced to take action against you.'

'As your Worship pleases. I put it to you witness that you are a woman of the Mafia, you are motivated by revenge and you were fully aware of the criminality of the acts in which you participated. Is that not correct Ms Marchese?'

'No. I am not strictly of the Mafia and I am neither lying nor motivated by revenge. I was given information about the death of my father which I believed was a crime. I told the police about that crime. That is the responsibility of every person.'

'Tell me witness, why should any credence be placed on your evidence when you have knowingly committed criminal acts?'

'It's quite simple Mr Sprite, I am telling the truth. And we in this Court all know that you too have done things for Pescaro that are not lawful.'

'Enough Ms Marchese!' Deschamps' tone lashed Teresa. 'Stick to the facts, answer the questions and keep your private opinions to yourself.'

And so it continued. Sprite with his probing, McIntosh with his objections and Teresa unruffled, predominantly respectful and always believable.

Chapter **SEVENTY- TWO**
February, 2007

On Thursday, February 22, 2007 the remote video site for that day was in the eastern suburbs. It was an old Court House of red brick with thick chunky bluestone steps leading to a foyer from the street; entry was through two huge, heavily panelled wooden doors. When Teresa and her Special Operations Group escorts entered the foyer, a tall uniformed Constable was waiting for them. From previous sites, Teresa knew the Constable's presence was unusual and sensed instant wariness among her escorts. The Constable walked towards them holding a slim document satchel and said, in a firm voice, 'I've got some papers here from the Prosecutor that you will need to refer to in evidence today.'

After that, all hell broke loose.

Much later, Teresa would recall events in slow motion. The Constable had seemed relaxed and held the satchel in front of his right hand. When he was about nine paces from her two things happened. First, the SOG man on her right yelled, 'You! Stop right there!' Second, the Constable fired through the satchel and shot her twice in the upper body. In the same instant, he dropped the satchel, fell to one knee and kept shooting. The SOG men on Teresa's left and right were felled. The third SOG officer behind her fired three shots at the Constable who jerked, spun to the right and fell to the floor, blood darkening his uniform.

Stunned, shocked and bruised, Teresa and the two SOG officers lay breathless, praising the inventor of Kevlar and bullet proof vests.

A frightened, pale-faced video operator stuck his head timidly into the foyer. Dazed by what he saw, he slowly became aware of an SOG member bellowing: 'Get off your arse and ring for ambulances; at least three. And tell the Magistrate what's happened.

Tell her that Marchese is okay and so are the SOG men. Don't come out here again – it's a crime scene.'

When the video operator relayed his brief account of events to Julia Deschamps in the Hearing Court, she ordered the video screen turned off in response to consternation from the press and public gallery. Without success she tried to regain order. Suddenly, the court room was bristling with police and the hubbub subsided.

Deschamps, pale and upset, addressed the Prosecutor. 'Mr McIntosh, you will see that an enquiry into this incident commences immediately. Please inform the Chief Commissioner. Mr Sprite, I advise you that as of now, bail for Mr Pescaro is revoked. For the rest of this hearing, however long it takes, he is remanded in custody. If you disagree with my order, take it to a higher court. This court stands adjourned to one week from today when it will resume at 10:00 a.m.'

There had not been such a brazen attack upon a witness since the murder of Raymond "Chuck" Bennett at the old Melbourne Magistrates' Court on November 12, 1979. Bennett, involved in committal proceedings for charges of armed robbery, was being transferred from one court to another when he was assassinated inside the court building.

'All rise!' The Clerk of Courts commanded those in attendance to pay attention while announcing the appearance of Chief Magistrate, Julia Deschamps. She entered the court, arranged herself and without further ceremony asked, 'Mr McIntosh, what do you have to report?'

Prosecutor Dougal McIntosh rose and said gravely, 'Your Worship, police have the investigation of this shooting well in hand. Firstly, I can report no injuries other than heavy bruising to the three people shot by the deceased. Secondly, I can report the deceased was *not* a police officer but a man in the employ of one of the co-defendants before this court, Mr Eduardo Masseria, a man associated with Mr Pescaro. The man masquerading as a police officer has been identified as Nino Costello. Thirdly, I can advise that police are very close to discovering just how it was that Costello: A, identified the remote court site; B, obtained a police uniform and firearm; and C, penetrated the security perimeter established at the remote site.

Finally, I can report, without going into detail, that stringent security has been arranged for protected witnesses throughout the remainder of this committal. If anything further comes to light, I shall keep both your Worship and my learned colleagues informed.'

'Thank you Mr McIntosh. Mr Sprite, do you wish to add anything to what has been said?'

'Only this your Worship. My client, Mr Pescaro, had no prior, or subsequent knowledge of that event and is deeply distressed by its occurrence. It was a shocking tragedy and most awful slur upon the sanctity of this court. In spite of the fact that this committal has at times been heated, I have to say we are all diminished by events of this kind. Thank you your Worship.' Sprite resumed his seat. He appeared contrite and seemingly, had spoken with sincerity.

'Very well Mr Sprite. If I am not mistaken, before the adjournment you were cross examining Ms Marchese were you not?'

Sprite rose again. 'I was your Worship but, under the circumstances, I believe no further cross examination is necessary.'

Magnus Wyvern and Lorton Sprite resumed their double act of cross examining alternate witnesses and once again, the committal slipped into a regular pattern well known to the courts and media. The sting, previously so abundant in their spirited defence, seemed blunted. Tavistock, who attended court at least twice weekly, believed that for all their bravado, for all the shonky activities in which they participated, concocted or concealed, the shooting was probably the first time they had seriously dirtied their hands or been close to the truth of their client's business. They didn't like it.

Well, so much the better for us, he thought.

Drummond, Judd, Aldrittson and the remaining protected witnesses came and went without a hitch as did Christmas, New Year and the 2007 summer break. On February 26, 2007, Julia Deschamps committed Pescaro for trial on all main charges and a host of lesser ones. She said there had been considerable replication among lesser charges and ordered a significant number struck out. The Tavistock team was jubilant and relaxed for the first time in months. Base camp had been established and now the true ascent could begin.

First, however, important actions regarding Drummond and Marchese had to be completed. Immediately after events at the remote court site, Chief Commissioner Jim Scott, Assistant Commissioner Tavistock, Director of Public Prosecutions, Mitchell Blomberg and the new Attorney General, Andrew Chalkley met. It was agreed that before the trial the two witnesses should be moved overseas, change their names and complete the necessary enabling formalities as quickly as possible. Chalkley, mindful of a previous messy and protracted overseas witness resettlement – an example of federal insularity – undertook management of the federal-state aspects personally.

Tavistock, privy to the preferred country of resettlement, pushed the group to serve notice for trial evidence to be given through an overseas video link rather than risk returning the pair to Australia. His motivation was powerful – Masseria had infiltrated the Justice Department and bribed an official having knowledge of the remote video sites. And, while investigators could not directly tie the attack upon Teresa to Pescaro, Tavistock and senior Justice Department officials nevertheless suspected Masseria had acted on his instruction.

On Sunday, May 6, 2007, Sinead and Finnbar O'Donnell, formerly Teresa Marchese and Andy Drummond, quietly departed from

Sydney airport en route to Dublin. Tavistock had learned Dublin Airport was expecting up to fifteen million people through its gates between April and October that year. As he saw it, those numbers would help camouflage the arrival of their protected witnesses.

The only person to see them off was Aleisha Campbell and all three were awash with tears – strong friendships had been forged. With promises to meet again and aching with emotion, Teresa and Andy walked through the Departures Gate. Their Qantas flight would take them to Heathrow from where they would fly to Dublin and begin a new life.

Behind them lay their close and dear friends the Mauds, Andy's farm and Teresa's grey and grainy past. For both it was a past that wrenched at the core of their being, yet for each, the reasons were different. Now they had each other and believed a bright future was ahead.

Four months later, on a warm, Saturday afternoon in mid-September, Pescaro was enjoying the sunshine and strolling the exercise yard among a group of prisoners. Men on remand changed constantly as some were bailed, some went to trial, some moved on after sentencing and and still others exited on Community Service Orders. Few were acquitted outright. Peter Simons was there for aggravated assaults and burglaries – he had entered remand on Friday afternoon. A surly, ominous man exuding attitude, he had been watching Pescaro as he lounged against the wall. The strollers ignored Simons having picked him as a loner. As the group passed, he suddenly lurched from the wall and cannoned into Pescaro. The men rippled apart.

'I don't think you should have done that friend,' rumbled Pescaro. 'Do you know who I am?'

'I know exactly who you are old man,' Simons hissed, his voice thickly accented, 'more to the point, do you know who I am?'

'A nobody, that's who you are. Nobody,' barked Giuseppe.

Simons smiled lazily, his eyes flashing dangerously. 'Not a nobody. I am somebody with a message and I have waited patiently to deliver it. I am Pyotr Asimovich – I am the one you missed at Bayswater. My message is from Valentin Chernamenko. He wanted you to know he *always* keeps his word.' Asimovich watched Pescaro intently. Pescaro's eyes widened fractionally in recognition. Then, without warning, Asimovich stepped forward and struck Pescaro twice.

Warders, who had seen trouble brewing, swooped too late. Pescaro lay on the ground, his life blood seeping from a ruined eye socket and punctured brain, a sharpened toothbrush embedded deeply in his neck. When the warders arrived, Pescaro was dead, his carotid artery pierced by the fatal blow. A lifetime of villainy had ended in a cold and grimy concrete remand yard.

EPILOGUE
Autumn, 2012

'Patrick! Come on, stop dawdling, we'll be late,' Sinaid scolded. 'Hurry up, your Dad's already out front with Thomas. We've got a big day ahead and everyone has to pull their weight. Including you Sunshine.' She smiled at the dark haired boy with rosy cheeks who was kneeling and fussing over his shoe laces. Her eyes in Finn's face. What a treasure. Indeed, what three fine treasures her menfolk were. Thinking back to the dark days in Australia so long ago, she blessed herself a hundred times over.

Before leaving for Ireland, she and Finn had secretly married in the Assistant Commissioner's office. Throughout the long investigation they had become significantly more than mere witnesses to Tavistock and his team.

Tavistock had invited the Mauds to Melbourne ostensibly for Tony to receive a Certificate of Commendation for his role in the Pescaro enquiry, but in truth, to attend the wedding. Like everybody else, the Maud's knowledge of Drummond and Teresa as protected witnesses was strictly limited. They were unaware they would be seeing their friends, let alone witnessing their marriage. Apart from the Police Chaplain, the only other guests were Paul Donovan, Robby Danniellson and Aleisha Campbell. No one could remember such an event in an A/C's office before and though discreet, it was joyous and emotional.

Too soon, it was over. Finn, Sinaid and Aleisha returned to New South Wales in preparation for the journey to Dublin. Then, suddenly, they were gone. Off to Heathrow, the world's busiest airport, and after that, County Wicklow.

Six years had vanished. Sinaid's financial skills had grown Finn's Australian lottery winnings and they had settled comfortably on ninety-five beautiful acres south of Wicklow overlooking the Irish Sea. Heavily into organic farming, the moist climate and rich soil was perfect. Finn's interest in trees was building a sizeable plantation of Irish birches and he had become immersed in a local study to improve the genes of birch stock.

Sinaid, on the other hand, was besotted with goats. Having scoured the net, she could find only two places in Ireland making goat's milk products: one at Corleggy near County Cavan, the other at Glenisk between Portlaoise and Tullamore, close to Wicklow. After several training courses, a lot of hard work and a good deal of money, the O'Donnell organic cheeses, yoghurt and milk were steadily building a fine reputation.

In those six years, wee Patrick and later, Thomas had arrived. Over that period too, the trials of Pescaro's *capos* were finalised with Drummond and Teresa giving evidence from Australia House in London. By March 2009, the whole sordid affair was over with every *capo* behind bars for years. Donovan's men eventually were able to prove that Andy's attackers in the Alfred Hospital had also been his shooters at Heathcote. The third member of that team, Nino Costello, was the man who had shot Teresa at the courthouse. Only Santini's death remained unsolved.

Aleisha Campbell remained in touch and had written advising that federal authorities – ASIC, ATO and the police – were still dismantling large chunks of Pescaro's Empire. Along the way, Wyvern and Sprite had become victims of that scrutiny and were out of business and under investigation for perverting the course of justice.

For the O'Donnell clan, stability prevailed to the extent that they had recently taken the huge step of abandoning their protected witness status. From that point on, the Mauds and O'Donnell's were in regular contact and today, at 1:00 p.m., the Mauds would arrive in Dublin. The envelope, so long ago left on the kitchen table the night of Drummond's shooting, contained documents deeding the farm to Tony and Mary for a peppercorn fee of $5,000. Intensely reluctant to accept, but afraid not to because of their love for the property, they had agreed to the offer and now lived there. Tony was enjoying long service leave and on completion, would retire from the Force after twenty-nine proud years of service.

Watching Patrick tie his laces, this cavalcade of dark events had flashed through her mind. Today that past no longer intimidated and the arrival of their friends promised to be a great reunion.

Five minutes from touch-down, Anton Gromyko relaxed four rows behind the Mauds. He sighed hoping this flight was the end of a long and tedious wait. Truth to tell, he could not stomach living in Australia and pined for Mother Russia.

Gromyko, known in Bendigo as Tony Gromwich, a mechanical engineer, was one of Chernamenko's long term sleepers. A slim, nondescript sixty year old with a bald pate and cropped red hair, he had spent the last six or so years maintaining a low profile, working hard and keeping tabs on Tony Maud. Chernamenko had reasoned that Marchese's and Drummond's complete disappearance meant they were somewhere in witness protection. Whether it was Australia or overseas he didn't know. Between them, Pescaro and the Police had dealt his infant Australian crime empire a mortal blow and information was hard to come by. Nevertheless, having discovered that Mauds were living on Drummond's property he thought it probable the parties had a continuing connection. He inserted Gromyko, a non-threatening individual with remarkable skills, to observe what he believed might potentially be a weak link.

When Gromyko reported that Maud was about to leave the police, Chernamenko ramped up surveillance. He instructed Gromyko that no matter what the Mauds did or where they went, they were to be followed. He had gloated to Gromyko that

Australians were a complacent lot, not used to the hard ball of Russia's Mafiya and would never comprehend the Great Bear's limitless patience. That complacency, he laughed, would be their undoing. And that undoing would deliver him Teresa Marchese, architect of his downfall.

Gromyko had no idea why the Mauds were travelling to Ireland but what he could see and understand was some fairly unrestrained body language sparkling with happiness and anticipation. That, he thought, was a very positive sign.

Acknowledgement

As a first time story teller, finding inspiration and reaching the end of this tale which started in 2005 were new experiences for me. My mother-in-law, Molly (now deceased), would frequently say: *Agatha Christie always said her stories came from just around the corner.* Believing that to be sound advice, I liberally plundered the newspapers for ideas, information and themes relevant to my story. To *The Age*, *The Australian* and *Herald Sun*, I express my heartfelt appreciation.

Information about the Mafia came from many sources, including the internet. Particularly helpful were Paul Elliot's, *Brotherhoods of Fear* and the work of William Balsamo and George Carpozi Jr, *The Mafia: The First 100 Years.* For an understanding of the Russian Mafiya, I am indebted to Robert I. Friedman's stark account of their activities in his book, *Red Mafiya.* The hostilities which occur between these two criminal elements in this story is my fiction, although it is not difficult to imagine that, from time to time, it could happen.

Helpful Australian texts included: Frank G. Clarke's *Australia in a Nutshell – A Narrative History,* the *Herald Sun's One Hundred and Fifty Years of News From The Herald,* Gordon Greenwood's *Australia: A Social and Political History,* W.H. Newnham's *Melbourne Sketchbook* and John Ritchie's *Evidence To The Bigge Reports.* From the last, the fictional politician, Lance Baker, claims Major George Druitt as a forbear. Druitt was Chief Engineer of the Colonial Establishment in 1817. Baker's claim is myth but the slim account of Druitt's life in my story is fact and may be found in Ritchie's work.

Teresa Marchese's interest in the martial arts is drawn from three sources: *The Book of Five Rings* by Miyamoto Mushashi, as translated by Bradford J. Brown, Yuko Kashiwagi, William H. Barrett and Eisuke Sasagawa; Samuel B. Griffith's *Sun Tzu: The Art of War* and of course, an old favourite, Machiavelli's *The Prince,* translated by George Bull.

Other helpful references have been James Morton's *Gangland: The Lawyers,* J.P. Chaplin's *Dictionary of Psychology,* Dr. Cyril H. Wecht's *Crime Scene Investigation, Death's Acre: Inside The Legendary Body Farm* by Bill Bass and Jon Jefferson, Helena Kennedy's *Just Law,* Robert Payne's *The Corrupt Society,* Athol Moffitt's *A Quarter to Midnight* and the amazing book of political dirty tricks by John Stauber and Sheldon Rampton, *Toxic Sludge Is Good For You.*

To the authors of these books I express my gratitude for creative guidance and insight. Any failure to optimise their ideas and information is due to my own inadequacy.

To the men and women of the Victoria Police Witness Protection Unit I am deeply grateful. Their amazing work, quite properly unsung and unheralded, is performed with commitment, compassion, infinite patience and steely resolve. The ideals portrayed by the fictional Aleisha Campbell reflect the work of not only Victoria Police, but similar units in each of Australia's States and Territories.

The difficulties experienced by witnesses in protection are substantial. The quotation in Chapter 49 which alludes to these comes from a former USA Federal Drug Agent appearing before a Senate Committee on Governmental affairs. It is also recorded in a Report to the Commonwealth Parliament of Australia prepared by a Parliamentary Joint Committee on the National Crime Authority in 1988 titled simply: *Witness Protection.*

I am indebted to Professor David Wells of the Coroners Court, Victoria, for his practical and helpful discussion of DNA and retention of body parts.

Many places referred to in this story are factual: Gaffney's Bakery at Heathcote, The Rose Café at Kilmore, Di Mattina's in Carlton, Connoisseurs, Andrew's Bookshop (now departed), The Booktalk Café in Richmond, Dimmeys, Borders (now departed), The Queen Victoria Market and others. And, while the Alfred Hospital is probably known to most Melbournians, the layout of the carpark and Surgical Wing described herein is fiction.

Apart from Major George Druitt and a handful of contemporary people who attract passing reference such as Lord Hutton, former Premier, Jeffrey Kennett, Vivian Alvarez, Christina Rau, John T Cusack, "Chuck" Bennett and Tony Mokbel, all my characters are wholly fictional.

Profound thanks goes to my litmus readers for wading through the original manuscript and making constructive suggestions to improve presentation, style and story: Sabina Robertson, Kevin Gaitskell, Glenn Zimmer, Alex McAllister and my good friend Graham Sinclair who, since completion of this tale, has passed on. The value of their contribution has been inestimable. Particular thanks for help with final polishing are also due to long time friends Bob Haldane, Chris Fyffe, Jeff McCubbery and my great mentor, S. I. "Mick" Miller.

To the editors, Julie Capaldo and Paul Bujiea whose brilliant work honed my story to its final form, my gratitude is boundless. To my publisher, Mark Zocchi of Brolga Publishing Pty Ltd, without whose support this book would not have seen the light of day, my sincere thanks.

Finally, to my wife Jennifer, for her endurance and patience, her debate on so many aspects of the story, her probing questions, eternal support and constant exhortation to 'simply enjoy the experience,' my endless thanks and love.

W.H.G.R.
November, 2012

NO WITNESS, NO CASE

Bill Robertson

		Qty
ISBN 9781922175243		
RRP	AU$26.99	.....
Postage within Australia	AU$5.00	.....
	TOTAL★ $_____	
	★ All prices include GST	

Name:...

Address: ....

....

Phone:..

Email: ....

Payment: ❏ Money Order ❏ Cheque ❏ MasterCard ❏ Visa

Cardholders Name:...

Credit Card Number: ....

Signature:...

Expiry Date: ....

Allow 7 days for delivery.

Payment to: Marzocco Consultancy (ABN 14 067 257 390)
PO Box 12544
A'Beckett Street, Melbourne, 8006
Victoria, Australia
admin@brolgapublishing.com.au

BE PUBLISHED

Publish through a successful publisher.
Brolga Publishing is represented through:
• **National** book trade distribution, including sales,
marketing & distribution through **Macmillan Australia.**
• **International** book trade distribution to
    • The United Kingdom
    • North America
    • Sales representation in South East Asia
• **Worldwide e-Book distribution**

For details and inquiries, contact:
Brolga Publishing Pty Ltd
PO Box 12544
A'Beckett St VIC 8006

Phone: 0414 608 494
admin@brolgapublishing.com.au
markzocchi@brolgapublishing.com.a
ABN: 46 063 962 443
(Email for a catalogue request)